SAGER WAS STRUCK BY HER SPIRIT

Few white men—or women—ever heard the winds speak as she had. For someone so aware of the world around her, the strangest things upset her. Frightened her, even. And despite her fear, she was here on this trail today, away from the wagons, alone with him. She was tenacious and brave, like a desert violet blooming in the winter sun. He had an unsettling urge to pull her into his arms and promise her nothing would ever again harm her.

But that wasn't true. *He* would harm her.

He went to retrieve some jerky and his canteen. She wasn't what he'd expected in Old Jack's daughter. Dammit all to hell. A kinder man, one less bent on revenge, would change his plans.

Too bad he wasn't that man.

RACHEL
and the
HIRED GUN

ELAINE LEVINE

ZEBRA BOOKS
Kensington Publishing Corp.

www.kensingtonbooks.com

ZEBRA BOOKS are published by

Kensington Publishing Corp.
850 Third Avenue
New York, NY 10022

All Kensington titles, imprints, and distributed lines are
available at special quantity discounts for bulk purchases
for sales promotion, premiums, fund-raising, educational, or
institutional use.

Special book excerpts or customized printings can also be
created to fit specific needs. For details, write or phone the
office of the Kensington Special Sales Manager: Attn. Special
Sales Department. Kensington Publishing Corp., 850 Third
Avenue, New York, NY 10022. Phone: 1-800-221-2647.

Zebra and the Z logo Reg. U.S. Pat. & TM Off.

ISBN-13: 978-1-4201-0551-3
ISBN-10: 1-4201-0551-5

First Zebra Printing: January 2009

10 9 8 7 6 5 4 3 2 1

Printed in the United States of America

*This book is dedicated to my husband,
who took my dreams and made them his own.
He is the hero of my life.*

*It's also dedicated to my kids,
Aaron and Ryan,
for never losing patience with
their perpetually daydreaming mother.*

Acknowledgments

I'd like to give special thanks to a few people:

To my critical readers: Michelle (my wonderful daughter-in-law), Darla, Carol, Arlene, Sandi, and Channah. Their eagle eyes, consistent belief in me, and unfailing cheer helped in more ways than they could know.

To my friends at my Romance Writers of America local chapter, Colorado Romance Writers. I've never known a writing organization more supportive of it's members. Together we can!

To my mother-in-law, Evelyn Levine, and all her wonderful friends, for greeting this book with excitement and enthusiasm.

And finally, to Kate Duffy, editor extraordinaire! She saw the magic in this story and gave me my start. It's an incredible honor to get to work with a master in this field—I'm soaking up all the craft and industry knowledge she so generously shares!

Chapter One

The Oregon Trail, Eastern Dakota Territory
April 1867

Rachel Douglas shivered beneath the brittle cottonwood. The light was failing, but she could see the wolf's spiky fur. He watched her, head lowered, shoulder blades making peaks in his back. Though he was a dozen paces from her, she smelled his hot, fetid breath. She squeezed the stick she held until the bark pricked her palms.

"Ellie, I'm sorry. I'm so sorry," she whispered to the little girl in the tree above her. Whimpers were her answer. "You're going to have to get yourself back to the wagon train." More whimpers. "Do you hear me, Ellie?"

"Mmm-hmm."

"Do you know which way is west?"

"No. Miss Rachel, please don't stay down there." Rachel heard the catch in Ellie's voice. "He's gonna eat you. Please, ma'am, please come up here."

"You'll have the sun on your back in the morning

and on your face in the afternoon," Rachel continued, ignoring the child's plea. "Stay close to the river. Are you listening to me, Ellie?"

"I can't do it." She was crying now, in full-belly sobs that excited the wolf. He growled, his lips wrinkled into a snarl, baring white fangs. Rachel steeled herself to the heart-wrenching sound of Ellie's fear as she considered the animal before her.

Wolves had often followed the wagon train, but Rachel had only seen them from a distance. Captain Norbeck said they wouldn't attack people. What was wrong with this one? White foam dribbled from his long jaw, and his steps were unsteady, his strong legs wobbly. He coughed and shook his head, sending spittle everywhere before settling into a growl again.

"Don't come out of that tree until morning," Rachel warned Ellie. "If you can find my horse"—*if he's still alive,* she thought to herself—"you can ride him back to the company. You'll be fine. You're no more than two days away from camp, if you follow the river and ride hard."

Rachel heard riders coming in fast, horse hooves pounding. The end was near. Ellie felt it, too. She screamed at the same time the wolf crouched, his muscles bunching to power his leap. He jumped forward, his massive, foamy mouth open, his fangs arching toward her.

Rachel extended the stick, pushing upward, eyes squeezed shut. The wolf fell short of his target—her throat—ripping a length of her skirt from waist to hem instead. It was then she heard the dying echoes of a gunshot. The wolf lay unmoving at her feet, the faded wool of her skirt snagged in his fangs. A bullet hole in his side seeped blood and an arrow protruded from his neck.

An arrow.

Dear God—Indians! A new fear filled her, deeper and colder than ever before. Her head jerked up as she looked for the source of that arrow. The horses she'd heard a moment ago pulled up in front of her, their riders an Indian and a white man. At least, she assumed one was a white man—he wore cowboy clothes.

Maybe they hadn't seen Ellie yet. Maybe they weren't here for trouble. They had killed the wolf, after all.

The cowboy dismounted and let his reins hang loose in front of his horse. He was tall and broad-shouldered. His long coat was unbuttoned and spread about him like dark wings as he came toward her. His black hair was cut unevenly and hung in jagged wisps about his tanned face. A few days' growth of beard shadowed a hard jaw. His eyes were a pale color, indistinct in the failing evening light.

He looked her over, his gaze missing nothing, his face angry. She wished she wore her coat, but she'd given it to Ellie. The man looked at the dead wolf and said something over his shoulder to the Indian in a language Rachel didn't know.

"Don't move," he ordered her, holding up a hand. He looked up in the tree, where Ellie was crouching, whimpering. "You hurt?" he asked her. Ellie shook her head. "Then c'mon down." He reached up and plucked her from the branch.

"Miss Rachel!" Ellie cried, reaching out to her.

"No, mister! Leave her alone." Rachel grabbed for the little girl. "Give her to me! Ellie!"

The cowboy pinned Rachel against the tree, his hand on her collarbone, his face full of dark intent as he turned sideways, keeping Ellie away from her. "I said don't move." He held the crying Ellie face down on his hip like a sack of flour. Rachel could only watch helplessly as he handed Ellie off to the Indian, who picked up the reins of the cowboy's horse and his own, then led both horses up the hill to the small campfire Rachel had left burning.

"Miss Rachel!" Ellie called again, reaching her arms out over the Indian's shoulder.

"Please—don't let him hurt her. She's only a little girl," Rachel pleaded.

The cowboy's stone-cold eyes turned on her. "He'll take care of her. He's gonna get some food going. She doesn't need to be here." He pulled the stick out of Rachel's hand and tossed it over by the wolf. Giving her a warning look, he shrugged out of his coat and hung it over a low branch, a little ways away. His vest soon followed. He lowered his suspenders and pulled his shirt free of his pants, unbuttoned the cuffs, then yanked it over his head.

Rachel glanced around, trying to find a way to run—a place to run to. He was big, and he was close. She wouldn't get far. And even if she did, what about the Indian by her campfire—how long could she elude the two of them?

A sick feeling boiled up in her belly as she looked at the man's smooth, naked chest, a wall of dark skin, full of muscles and rippling sinew. He was going to rape her. There was nothing she could do about it. She couldn't run. She couldn't fight—if she did, he might kill her. She had to stay alive for Ellie, had to get her back to the wagon train.

The man gave her a dark look as he leaned over to untie the thongs that held his holsters to his thighs. Rachel watched him, the evening air cold on her tear-streaked cheeks. He straightened and unbuckled his gun belt, laying it over his clothes on the branch. He took his boots and socks off and set them near the riverbank.

The Indian brought a blanket down, some clothes, and a leather pouch of something. He looked at Rachel and spoke in a low voice to the cowboy, then left.

The cowboy gathered up kindling of small sticks and dried grass and as much old wood from the riverbank as he could find. He laid it out in a large circle, then took a match from his coat and lit the pile. Flames spread hungrily over the dried wood and thin sticks and grass. Soon the fire roared. He added still more wood to it.

She watched him pick up the dead wolf and gingerly set it on the bonfire. The flames hissed as the fire consumed the wolf's fur. The sweet scent of wood smoke was soon fouled by the eye-watering smell of charred fur. He went to the river and rinsed his hands, rubbing at them with the soap he'd taken from the pouch. He walked back toward her, his gaze taking in every detail of her person.

"Now, we can do this the hard way or the easy way. But either way, you're gonna strip and get in that river."

She stared at the dark cowboy as panic fused her muscles. He wasn't some random man who happened upon her and Ellie; he'd been sent by her uncle. How else would he know to taunt her with the river? "No," she said, her voice a puny whisper.

"You are. That wolf was rabid. And you have its foam all over you. I've seen a man die of rabies—it's a hard death. It doesn't come on real fast after an encounter. You think you're gonna be okay. Then the fever comes. A week of agony as it chews up your mind, and you're dead. Were you bit?"

She looked at the wolf in the fire, his blackened face still contorted in a snarl. A shiver rippled down her spine. It made sense now, all the saliva, the wolf's weakness. She sighed with relief. This stranger intended neither rape nor to carry out her uncle's mischief. She swiped at the tears on her cheeks. He was right. She had to bathe. "Please, turn around."

"No. I'm not takin' chances—I'm not letting that spit out of my sight. Hand me your clothes, I'll burn 'em."

"You can't! What will I wear?"

"You don't have a change of clothes with you?"

"No." She'd left in a rush to go with the Hansons to find their daughter. She'd barely packed any supplies. The rest of what she owned was back at the wagon train with her mule.

"Then I guess you'll wear a goddamned blanket. Strip."

She glared at him, now grateful she wasn't wearing her coat—at least it wouldn't be burned. Her hands shook as she reached behind her to unfasten her tunic's bow. She lowered her gaze, unable to look at him. She folded the apron front of her tunic over the skirt, then unfastened the skirt.

"Careful—" he coached. She knew her face turned fiery red as he watched her slip the skirt down over her petticoat. She handed it to him. He dropped it on the fire on top of the burning wolf. Light flared as the flames roared over the fabric. Her gaze flew to his face. He met her look, his expression dark, unreadable.

She turned her back on him and began unfastening the buttons down the front of her shirt. She undid the cuffs, then pulled it off her shoulders, holding it out behind her. He took it, and again she heard the fire hiss when he dropped it on the flames. Then she felt him tug at the laces of her petticoat.

"No!" She whirled to face him.

"You're taking too long."

"I don't need your help," she ground out as she pulled the petticoat over her hips and handed it to him. The fire hissed. She untied the drawstring at the neckline of her chemise and drew the garment up over her drawers and camisole. She handed it to him. The fire hissed. Except for the thin cotton material of her camisole, drawers, stockings and boots, she was now naked. She'd abandoned corsets early in this trek—they were far too constraining for life on the trail. She regretted that decision now, preferring as many layers as possible between her skin and this man's cool gaze.

"That's good enough." He crouched down and undid the laces of her boots. No traces of saliva on the dusty leather, she noticed. They looked clean enough—surely he wouldn't burn them? When he took hold of her calf, she stifled a gasp at the unfamiliar contact of a man's hand on her leg. Worse, she had to touch his bare shoulder for balance as he freed first one foot, then the other. His skin was warm beneath her cold hand. The muscles of his back bunched and worked as he pulled her stockings down from her knees and set them with her boots off to the side. She watched him warily as he moved the blanket to a branch near the river, took up the soap bar, and waved her on to the water.

"Let me do this myself." She hated the catch in her voice.

He shook his head. "That water's barely above freezing. Once you're in there, you'll have about one minute before you go into shock. It'll take that long for you just to breathe when the water hits you. There's no way in hell you can do this yourself."

"You'll freeze, too. What's the difference?"

"I'm bigger than you are—takes longer for the water to chill me. Let's go. We're gonna do this quick. I'll dunk you, lather you up, dunk you again and get you outta there." He held his hand out to her. "You gotta remember to breathe."

Rachel ignored his hand and took a couple of steps into the water, trying to hide her fear. The water was deeper than she thought. And bitter cold. He knocked her legs out from under her, pushing her to her knees in the water. The fast-moving current washed over her, her panic rising with it. He set his hand at her neck and forced her down under the water, then pulled her up quickly. It was cold, so cold. Her body locked up on her. She couldn't inhale.

"Breathe, damn it, breathe!" he growled in her ear, crouching behind her. He dipped the soap in the water and rubbed it roughly over her stomach. Rachel sucked in a chest-full of air, clinging to his thighs for there was nothing else to hold on to, nothing to keep her from being washed away except the man behind her. He rubbed the soap over her breasts and chest, her neck and arms, scrubbing at her hands. Lifting her with an arm around her ribs he scrubbed at her thighs and knees. Then he lathered her hair, rubbed her face, and dunked her again, quickly swishing the soap off her body and hair.

"Done!" He straightened and dragged her out of the water. Pulling the blanket from the branch, he wrapped her in it, covering everything but her eyes, then scooped up her stiff body. At last she sucked in a breath with a deep gasp. He looked down at her, his eyes pale in the dark shadow of his face.

"Rachel Douglas, I think you're gonna live."

She shut her eyes, too horrified to look at him. God, he was her uncle's man. How else could he know her? She'd come so far. She'd almost escaped them.

The cold air froze the exposed skin of her face and feet. Violent shivers racked her body. He carried her up the hill, depositing her on her bedroll in front of the fire. Anxious to find Ellie, she drew the blanket down, away from her head, unable to see much the way he'd wrapped her up.

"Hi, Miss Rachel." Ellie waved to Rachel from her seat on the Indian's knee. "This here's Blue Thunder," she said, pointing a thumb behind her.

Relieved that Ellie was unharmed, Rachel tried to give her a reassuring smile. The way her teeth were chattering, it was probably more a grimace. She studied the Indian, taking his measure. He wore a necklace of several strands of white beads, a peach calico shirt, and leather jacket and leggings. His face was clean-shaven, and a thin braid bordered both sides of his head. He'd taken more care with his appearance than the cowboy had. Was he one of the hostiles Captain Norbeck was always on the lookout for? He didn't seem very fierce. Ellie certainly appeared at ease around him. And he had prepared food for them. Ellie was scooping something out of a tin cup, eating with gusto. Stew. Rachel caught a whiff of it cooking over the campfire. And coffee. Her stomach growled.

"Was you taking a bath, Miss Rachel?" Ellie asked.

Rachel could only nod; her jaw wasn't working. She hadn't had a chance to talk to Ellie since finding her moments before the wolf caught up with them. The little four-year-old had wandered off from the wagon train nearly three days earlier, delirious with fever. She seemed much recovered, though shadows darkened her eyes, and her small face appeared drawn. There were a few scratches on her neck and cheek, and new tears in her dress, but nothing too terrible considering the adventure she'd been through.

"Blue Thunder said you stunk," Ellie said with a grin, holding her nose. Rachel looked at the Indian. *So, he must speak English,* she realized. He returned her look with a steady, expressionless regard.

"My ma can wash herself," Ellie said, her mouth full of stew.

Rachel groaned, thinking how this was going to spread like wildfire when they got back to the company.

The cowboy rejoined them then. Rachel was relieved to see he'd put his clothes back on, including a dry pair of trousers. He set his wet pants on a nearby boulder, then started rustling through her saddlebags.

"Wh-what ar-re . . ." Her teeth were chattering so that it was hard to form words.

"I'm looking for something dry for you to put on. I can't believe you came out here without any change of clothes. A shirt, somethin'. Here we go!" He held up her cotton nightgown. The wind caught the material, making it billow like a sail. Rachel felt hot blood flood her face. As cold as she was, it burned her skin. She cast a quick glance at Blue Thunder, horrified to see him looking at her nightgown.

"Damn. There's enough fabric here to cover a wagon," the cowboy commented. "If that don't fix your sensibilities, well, I reckon I don't know what will."

"Th-that's a n-nightgown."

"So it is. And it just happens to be night, so I'm guessing it's the right thing to wear. Get over here and put it on."

Rachel shook her head. This was unbearable. Surely he wouldn't make her change in front of everyone? The cowboy gave a long sigh, then went to his pack and took out a blanket from his bedroll. "Look, I'll hold this blanket up. You'll have all the privacy you need. Little Ellie, there, can holler if I peek."

Rachel was still not moving. She was so cold, even if she wanted to she couldn't have gotten her limbs to cooperate. She just wanted to lie down and sleep. The stubborn man came over and picked her up, taking her a little ways off from the fire. Rachel cast a nervous glance back at Blue Thunder as her bare feet hit the ground.

The cowboy followed her gaze. "You don't have anything he hasn't seen before." Rachel's gaze flew to his face. His hair was damp and hung heavily about his face and shoulders. This close to him, she could see thin wrinkles at the corners of his eyes.

"'Cept maybe he hasn't seen anything quite so white—" he frowned.

"E-nough!" Rachel took the nightgown from his hands. He pulled up his blanket, blocking her from curious eyes, his own included as he turned his back to her. Rachel dropped her damp blanket, gasping as cold air enveloped her. Blast it all. She would have been fine in her underclothes. The blanket had absorbed most of the moisture. She peeled off her drawers and camisole, then jerked her nightgown over her head, instantly feeling less cold. Maybe this wasn't such a bad suggestion.

"Finished?"

"No!" Rachel shot a look over her shoulder to be sure she still had cover. Her fingers were stiff. She couldn't button the front of her gown. It hung open well below her breasts.

"What's takin' so long?"

"I c-can't b-b-button this-s—" Before she knew what was happening, the dry blanket descended on her shoulders, and the cowboy came around in front of her. His fingers made short work of the tiny buttons. His large body blocked her vision, so she stared at his chest, defeated. He buttoned every last button, right up to her chin. Rachel was shivering so much her jaw rattled. A cold draft came up her legs from her bare feet.

She drew the blanket tightly about herself, refusing to blush as the cowboy picked up the damp blanket and her undergarments to lay them out next to his pants. She turned toward the fire, her feet burning from the cold ground. She took a step. And another. Her body was so stiff, so heavy, it was hard to move. The fire wasn't more than twenty feet away. Not far at all, but she wasn't going to make it. Her knees started to give out. Suddenly, she was lifted against the cowboy's strong chest.

"Wh-what's wrong with m-me?" she whispered, all resistance gone out of her.

"You're freezing." He carried her to the campfire, setting her down on her bedroll.

"My ma can dress herself," Ellie announced, coming

over to kneel by Rachel. "I can dress myself, too, 'cep-t'n' I can't tie my boots."

Rachel folded her knees up in front of her, cover-ing her feet and legs with the cowboy's blanket and burying her face in her knees. This was not going to go over well back at camp. Not at all. The cowboy returned, carrying a white linen towel and a bottle of whiskey. He sat behind Rachel, spreading his legs out on either side of her. He rubbed her head with the towel until tears came to her eyes, then milked the long wavy tendrils of her hair with slow, squeez-ing strokes.

"My daddy never dries my ma's hair," Ellie com-mented, watching the proceedings with avid interest.

Rachel stifled a groan. The company would expel her. Good Lord, what would she do then? She had to get to her father's ranch. Surely they wouldn't just leave her out here in this wilderness? Perhaps she could convince this man that her father would pay more to get her to the Crippled Horse than her uncle had paid to return her to Virginia.

His ministrations had eased into light touches against her hair and scalp. She held herself in a tight ball, refusing to lean back against him, refusing to touch any more of him than was necessary in this compromising position. Blue Thunder handed him a bowl of stew and a cup of coffee. The cowboy leaned forward, his arms coming around in front of her as he poured a measure of whiskey into the coffee.

Rachel watched the flames through the bottle of amber liquid. That was the color of the cowboy's eyes, she realized. Amber.

"Who ar-re y-you?" she asked the man sitting behind her. "H-how d-do you kn-know me?"

"The name's Sager. Your pa sent me for you."

"My f-father! M-my father hi-hired you?" She twisted around to look at him. Not her uncle?

"Yep. Take a sip of this." He held the steaming coffee to her lips.

She let the steam warm her face, then she took a sip. It was hot and burned all the way down her throat, but nothing had ever felt so divine.

"Lean back. We gotta get you warmed up."

Rachel took the coffee, holding it close to her face as she leaned stiffly against his chest. Blue Thunder brought another blanket and spread it over the two of them. The comment he made in that strange language was met with stony silence from the man behind her.

"What did he say?"

"Nothing worth repeating. Eat some of this stew," he ordered, shoving a spoonful in her mouth. He ate a spoonful, then fed her another. She realized she was starving. She had eaten very little for the last few days in the interest of conserving her supplies. She sipped her doctored coffee between spoonfuls of stew, beginning to feel warmed through and through. She relaxed a little, nestling into the warmth he offered. The blanket smelled like horse and dust, but she didn't mind. Her jaw had stopped rattling; she thought she could finally speak without stuttering.

"Better?" he asked, his mouth close to her ear. His voice, rough and velvety, touched her like a living thing. She nodded; her shiver this time had nothing to do with cold. "Good. Then suppose you tell me what the hell you're doing out here alone? No gun, no supplies. What the devil were you thinkin'?"

Not fair, Rachel thought. He'd lulled her into

complacency, nestling her in the warm cocoon of the blanket and his body. She knew there was no answer that would satisfy him. There simply was no good answer. She had foolishly exposed herself to danger, but she wouldn't apologize; she'd saved Ellie's life—that had to be worth something.

"I went with the Hansons to find Ellie. She'd just wandered off that afternoon. She hadn't been gone more than a couple of hours. I didn't think I was going to be away long—I wasn't planning on being out almost three days."

"And what happened to the Hansons? They go back to the company?"

Rachel knew without looking that Ellie was still listening with rapt attention. She didn't want to talk about this in front of the little girl. Frightened of the hostiles Captain Norbeck said were in the area, her parents had quit searching. What choice did they really have? Captain Norbeck said he would hold the company back for no more than two days. At dawn this morning, they turned back. They left their own child alone in the wilderness, abandoning her to the elements and a rabid wolf while they returned to the safety of the wagon train.

Rachel would never let Ellie know that. "They went back for supplies," she fibbed.

"And what of the woman your father had your uncle hire to chaperone you? Did she just let you go off with the Hansons?"

"I don't have a chaperone. I paid a fee to the Hansons to let me travel with them." Her uncle hadn't made her travel arrangements. In fact, she hoped he didn't know where she was.

"Are you riding in their wagon?"

Rachel shook her head. "I have my horse and a mule with my supplies. I was lucky to find a family willing to chaperone me. It's not acceptable for a woman to be in the company alone. There are . . . problems that causes."

"I'll just bet there are," he growled. Silence. She felt the muscles in his arms and thighs tighten around her. She sipped her coffee. "So anyone been giving you trouble? There anyone I need to deal with when we catch up to the train?"

"No." This trek had not been easy, but it was by no means the hardest thing she'd ever done. There was no need to tell the truth; no good would come of it. No good at all.

Sager eased the coffee cup from Rachel's hand, glad sleep shielded her from him. He pulled the blanket higher about her shoulders, breathing in the soft scent of her hair. He'd expected Old Jack's daughter to be the spitting image of her pa. Short, squat, and mean. The only feature she shared with him was her sky blue eyes. She had long, palomino blond hair with just a hint of a curl to it. She was average in height with curves that would make a madam rich.

Every time he shut his eyes, he saw her stripping out of her clothes, her slim fingers working the buttons, bows and ties, piece by piece. He remembered the way her hands had gripped his thighs in the river, her back arching against him.

If dry clothes, food and blankets don't warm her, you'll have to make love to her, Blue Thunder had helpfully suggested, as if Sager hadn't already been thinking the same thing.

Except it wasn't love he intended to make.

He eased himself away from Rachel's warm body, settling her next to Ellie's sleeping form and adjusting the blankets over them. Blue Thunder was awake, watching him. Sager met his brother's look, trying to shutter his expression. He wasn't successful.

He shoved his hands into his coat pockets and walked away, heading down to the bonfire. Tossing more wood on the flames, he stared at the enormous, blackened carcass. If he and Blue Thunder had arrived just a few seconds later, Rachel would have been dead for sure.

Norbeck was going to pay for this. His irresponsibility had almost cost Sager his revenge.

"She is brave, for a white woman," Blue Thunder said as he came to stand at the rim of the fire. "She will be a good wife to you. I am pleased. I am glad I came to meet her with you."

Sager glanced over at his brother. "She's nothing to me."

"Not yet, perhaps."

"Not ever."

Blue Thunder briefly put his hand on Sager's shoulder. "The mind cannot override the soul's intent, Brother."

Sager looked away, ignoring the cold ache that crept into his gut. Blue Thunder's predictions were never wrong. He was the last in a long line of shaman. He had known, way back, when his parents adopted Sager, what the cost would be. He had known, and he had been a brother to Sager anyway.

Chapter Two

Rachel turned stiffly on the hard ground. Her feet were cold, and her ears were cold, but her midsection was warm. Ellie had snuggled next to her during the night, and Rachel curled into that warmth.

Ellie. Rachel's eyes flew open as she remembered everything from last night. Finding Ellie. The wolf. Blue Thunder. The river.

The cowboy.

She half rose, supporting herself on her elbows as she looked about. Her breath clouded the air. Sager crouched near the fire, cooking something. Steam rose from the coffee pot to blend with the tantalizing aroma of bacon and biscuits. Rachel's stomach twisted with hunger and anxiety at his reaction to her tardy rising.

"I'm sorry. I didn't realize how late it was!" She scrambled to assemble herself so that she could leave the protection of her covers with some modesty, dressed as she was in only her nightgown.

"Rachel, there's no hurry. It's early yet."

Sager's calmness gave her pause. He wasn't angry

at her laziness. She looked at him and he at her. In the morning light, she could see him much more clearly, see how the dark fringe of his eyelashes contrasted with his pale amber eyes.

"Mornin'." He grinned at her, aware of her perusal.

"Good morning," she belatedly greeted him, feeling a blush warm her skin. "Where's Blue Thunder?"

"Gone. Are you hungry?"

"Yes." The eastern sky was a faint lavender glow. Dawn was near. Not only had she gotten to sleep in a bit, but he had breakfast cooking—both luxuries that made her uncomfortable. "I think I'll just wash up first."

Rachel eased her coat off Ellie and tucked the blankets in around her small body. She pulled her coat on and buttoned most of it before lifting the blankets away from her lap. Someone had brought her boots and stockings up from the river and set them next to her bedroll. She turned her back to Sager and pulled on her stockings, then stuffed her feet into the boots and laced them. After retrieving her underclothes from the boulder, she headed down to the river where the wolf's pyre was a shocking reminder of last night's adventures.

She stared at the charred remains, remembering how close to death she had come. Forcing herself from that gruesome site, she found privacy in the shrubs and took care of her morning needs, then washed her hands and face. She removed her nightgown and donned her underclothes, then dressed again in her nightgown and coat and returned to the campfire.

As Sager handed her a cup of coffee, strong and hot, she asked, "Sager—how did you find us?"

"Old Jack sent me out as soon as he made arrangements with Norbeck. Norbeck always uses the trail he's on—I just followed it east. When I met up with him yesterday mornin', he told me you'd gone off with the Hansons looking for Ellie."

She looked at her guide, waiting for the tongue-lashing she knew she'd earned. It didn't come. "I'm grateful to you for finding us—and for coming just when you did. I've never seen rabies before. I've never seen a wolf that close, either. I wouldn't have done the right thing, assuming I survived its attack."

He met her gaze. "I'm paid to do it."

Disturbed, she looked away. Ellie was stirring, at last. After getting her washed up, they both came back and shared a plate of bacon and biscuits. "When do you think we will catch up to the company?" Rachel asked.

"Depends on how hard you two can ride. Norbeck's holding the company back until we return. We could be there tonight."

Rachel looked at the little girl sitting next to her, eating another biscuit. She wondered what Ellie's parents were going through right now. It sickened her that they had walked away from Ellie, left her to die. Did they even mourn the loss of their daughter?

"Are you up to a hard ride today?" Rachel asked. The little girl nodded. "Why did you wander off from your family like that?"

"I don't really 'member." Ellie shrugged. "I was hot and thirsty. I went lookin' for water. And then I got lost. And I kept lookin' for the wagons, but I didn't know where they were. And I was gettin' hungry, too. Then you found me."

"Your mama is going to be so happy to see you again."

"I know." Ellie smiled. "She'll cry, huh?"

Rachel smiled. "That's a safe bet."

They kept to a brisk pace that day, breaking only for lunch and to rest the horses. Sager drew to a stop on a slight rise that evening, waiting for her and Ellie to come even with him. Down below, pulled into a circle formation, was Captain Norbeck's wagon train. Dozens of campfires glittered and smoked, casting an orange haze over the wagon circle. People and dogs and children milled about. Livestock were penned for the night in the temporary corral in the center of the wagons.

Looking down at the company, Rachel was overcome with relief. She had lived in close association with these people in the last couple of months. Though her situation caused tension among the women and interest among the men, she knew how dependent she was on them for her survival. She was a long way from her father's ranch. Too far, she hoped, to be turned back to her aunt and uncle's home in Virginia.

Rachel looked at the hard profile of her guide. He, and his paint alike, stood still, assessing the wagons below. The wind tossed his jagged bangs, adding to his agitated look.

"It's them! Mama! And Papa! And everyone!" Ellie shouted. "You did it, Sager! You found them. You are the smartest man in the world. Smarter even than Mr. Norbeck, and I'll tell Papa you are, too."

Sager did not respond, his attention riveted on the camp in front of them, a muscle working in his jaw.

"Ready to see your family?" Rachel asked the little girl seated before her.

"I am. Let's go fast!"

Rachel touched her heels to her mount's sides, pushing him to one more short exertion. As if he sensed food and rest awaited at the camp below, her horse flew down the incline, leaving Ellie's giggles hanging in the air behind them. Hearing Ellie's glee, Rachel laughed and looked toward the wagon train. The members of the company had spotted them at last, but their reception was not what she had imagined.

The Indian alert went up.

Even over the thundering of her horse's hooves, Rachel heard their shouted alarm echo through several voices. "Indians!"

She looked over her shoulder, wondering if Blue Thunder had returned. She could only see Sager, astride his brown and white Indian pony. His hat had come off and, with the wind tearing at his hair, he looked every bit the crazed warrior. She urged her horse forward, bringing him galloping into the jarring sound of rifles being cocked. Sager was only one man—surely he couldn't frighten a whole company of men! Did they think he chased her?

Her eyes watered from the stinging lash of the wind across her face. Sager had pulled to a stop a few feet behind her. Several men gathered around him, rifles leveled at his chest. Ellie squirmed free of her restraining hold.

Rachel's gaze lifted from the circle of rifles to Sager's face. By the light of the fires, she could see there was no fear in his eyes, just something hard and cold in the way he faced the men. He sat atop his paint, one man challenging ten. The men gave Rachel a cursory glance. Her disheveled appearance must not have helped their anxiety, for they kept their rifles trained on Sager.

"Ellie! Dear God! It's my baby!" Mrs. Hanson shouted. She pushed her way into the semicircle of men, Mr. Hanson close on her heels. "Stop this tom-foolery!" she ordered. "He's brought my Ellie back. And Miss Douglas, too. He doesn't mean us any harm." She lifted Ellie away.

"Hi, Mama. I'm home." Ellie announced as her mother hugged her.

Fear paralyzed Rachel. She knew how easily tensions could degenerate into violence. Her uncle often worked himself into a frenzy over some small issue, and when he did, she'd made herself scarce. But she could not back away from this confrontation; there was nowhere to hide. Couldn't they see Sager had helped the two of them?

Mr. Hanson pulled Ellie from his wife's arms. He squeezed his eyes shut as he pressed his cheek against her temple. When he met Rachel's glance, she saw a blend of gratitude and guilt in his eyes. "Dan, Hector, Schmitty, it's enough!" he ordered. "He brought them back. They're safe."

"It's okay, men!" Captain Norbeck's voice joined Mr. Hanson's as he elbowed through the crowd. "He's a hired gun for Miss Douglas's pa out by the Medicine Bow Mountains. I sent him after Rachel. Sager, you son of a bitch—you did find them."

A gunfighter. Rachel studied Sager's harsh profile. What had she thought he was? A rancher? A farmer? He was a hired gun, and he'd seen her nearly naked. She looked at his gloved hands. A gunman's hands. Hands that had killed. Hands that had scrubbed her body clean of infected saliva.

"Are you meaning to ride with us, mister?" Hector Ramon asked, spitting a stream of black tobacco juice at the hooves of Sager's horse.

"I'm meaning to get Rachel to her pa's spread, whatever that involves." Sager's hard gaze moved to Norbeck. "We've got some talking to do."

Captain Norbeck cleared his throat. "Right. Well, that's my tent over there. Come see me when you're settled. You are gonna ride with us, aren't you? Heard the Sioux were hitting the trail kinda hard."

White teeth flashed in Sager's tanned face. "Norbeck, the Sioux ain't gonna give a rat's ass that I'm traveling with you," he scoffed.

"Maybe so, Sager." Norbeck leaned forward and lowered his voice. "Maybe so, but it sure will make the womenfolk feel better, having a scout with your reputation along. 'Sides, your Shoshone blood could come in real handy if we do run into Indian trouble."

Sager frowned and sent Rachel a quick glance. "We'll ride with you till you hit the Sweetwater," he accepted. "Then we head south." Captain Norbeck nodded. With his urging, the crowd began dispersing, heading back to their campfires.

"I'm obliged to you, Mr. Sager, for finding my daughter," Mr. Hanson said. He held out his hand for a shake.

Sager gave him a hard look, ignoring the gesture as he dismounted. "The name's just 'Sager,' and I didn't find her—Rachel did."

"And then he killed the wolf that was gonna eat us," Ellie cut loose in the start of what promised to be a long and troubling monologue, "and Miss Rachel had to take a bath 'cause she stunk, and Blue Thunder made me stew, and—"

"Blue Thunder?" Mr. Hanson interrupted, looking from his daughter to Sager and then to Rachel. "An Indian?"

"A friendly Indian," Rachel explained. "The wolf was rabid. Sager and Blue Thunder got to us just in time."

"That's quite a story," Mrs. Hanson said. "Come to the fire with us, Miss Douglas. I want to hear all the details. We still have some supper in the pot. I'm sure you're hungry. You and Ellie can tell us what happened while you eat. Seth, call Pat to tend Miss Douglas's horse."

"I'll tend her horse," Sager interjected. "And she'll be along shortly—I need to have a few words with her."

Rachel dismounted. She was still wrestling with the knowledge her guide was such a rough cut of a man. He took the reins of her horse. Nervous, she folded her arms in front of her and looked up at him. He was an Indian, and a gunfighter.

And the most handsome man she'd ever seen.

Sager sent a cursory glance around the camp before looking back down at her. "What are your arrangements with the Hansons?"

She looked down, away from his disturbing eyes. "I help with the chores and the children. I provide my portion of the meals from my own supplies."

Sager frowned. "And what do they do in exchange?"

"They give me their protection and act as my chaperones."

He scoffed at that comment. "Where do you sleep?"

"Usually, beneath their wagon with their children. Though when it rains, the kids and I pile into my tent."

"Sounds like they made a helluva bargain. How are your supplies holding out?"

"Well enough, I guess. My stock of cured meat is lower than I would like. I left most of my supplies here when I went to fetch Ellie—hopefully Captain Norbeck didn't redistribute them yet."

He studied her face. "Rachel, we can stay with the company for a while as Norbeck wanted, or we can strike out on our own. It'll be slow going if we stay. We could get to the Crippled Horse sooner if we go it alone."

She stared up into his pale eyes, bracing herself for his reaction. "I don't want to travel alone with you. I thought my father would come for me himself."

Sager frowned as he looked at her. She was a strange, skittish little thing, but he didn't try to soothe her nerves by telling her she was safe with him.

He didn't like to lie.

"I'm cleared with your pa. You're gonna have to make do with me."

He watched her chin lift as her mind raced to form more arguments. "Never mind," he bit out. "Let's get you settled. If you decide later you wanna light outta here, I'm in." He started walking toward the Hansons' campfire, leading the two horses.

Rachel hurried after him. "Where will you be? How will I reach you?"

"Riding shotgun. Scouting. Norbeck'll know how to get me if you need me during the day." He unloaded Rachel's saddle and saddlebags, then started to lead their horses away.

"Sager, won't you eat before you go?" Rachel asked, stopping him.

He glanced back. He didn't need to look at Mrs.

Hanson to know what she thought of Rachel's invitation; he'd heard her gasp. "I'll see to my own meals, Rachel. Good night."

At the temporary corral, Sager tended Rachel's horse and found food and water for him. Then, taking up the reins of his horse, he made his way to Norbeck's fire. The company captain sat with a couple of the men who had given Sager such a friendly greeting earlier.

"Norbeck." Sager faced the captain.

"Sager." Norbeck nodded at him. "You want some grub?"

"Nope. I came to talk to you 'bout the protection fee you charged Rachel's father. Since you let her go off on her own, with no gun, no guide, no protection, no goddamned supplies, I'm thinkin' you broke that contract."

"Whoa . . . now, don't be jumpin' to conclusions," Norbeck said as he stood up and slowly came around the campfire, hitching up his pants.

"You gonna refund that money, or do I take it outta your hide?"

"I told her not to go. I told her it was dangerous. It ain't my fault her pa sent her without a gun. And it ain't my fault she don't listen worth a damn."

Sager shook his head and let loose a right hook that connected with Norbeck's chin, knocking him flat on his back. The two men by the fire jumped up, charging Sager. He decked the first one and was rammed in the stomach by the second one, slamming the both of them to the ground.

"Sager, Hector—enough!" Norbeck hollered as he got to his feet. "This discussion's between me and Sager. Enough!" He shouted at the two men rolling in the dirt. Sager had just landed a decisive blow to Hector's face when they heard the trail captain's gunfire.

Mrs. Hanson handed Rachel a cup of stew. Rachel was hungry. She was always hungry and always thirsty and always tired. And always dirty, too. She chewed the thick stew, listening while Ellie recounted her tale.

The little girl repeated several parts, each time with more embellishments. Rachel was thankful the role she and Sager played in Ellie's adventure seemed inconsequential to the little girl, and after her tale was told, no one was the wiser for the liberties Sager had taken. Soon the children wandered back to bed. Mrs. Hanson gave Ellie a quick washing in their wagon and put her into a fresh nightgown.

Despite being bone tired, Rachel gathered their dishes and washed them in a bucket of water set aside for that purpose. When Mrs. Hanson returned to the fire, she eyed Rachel warily. Rachel knew that look—it usually accompanied a lecture of some sort—and was glad they were alone by the fire now. She hated having these discussions in front of Mr. Hanson. When she wandered too far afield during their dung gathering sessions, she got the lecture. When Hector Ramon or his brother, Schmitty, paid too much attention to her, she got the lecture. What had she done now?

And whatever it was, please God, don't let it be so bad they would revoke their patronage.

"Miss Douglas, as the closest thing you have to an older relative on this journey, I feel compelled to have a discussion with you about your gunfighter."

Sager! Of course. Had Ellie said something after all?

"I am extremely grateful to him for rescuing you and Ellie. But he's a gunfighter, dear, a man who lives in violence. I would prefer if you didn't invite him to join meals at our fire."

Rachel thought about that, wondered if what a man was and what a man did could be different things. Sager hadn't pressed his advantage last night. He certainly could have—there would have been little she could have done to defend herself. "Mrs. Hanson, he rescued us—"

The older woman held up a hand, stopping her defense. "He's a killer. And he has mixed blood— he's part Indian. What more need I explain to you? Consider this, Miss Douglas: is he the type of man your aunt would invite into her home?"

Rachel almost laughed. Even she had not been welcome in her aunt's home. "We aren't in my aunt's house now," she quietly answered. "We're in this strange and harsh territory. And I have a feeling we should accept any help sent our way."

Mrs. Hanson considered her comment. "Perhaps you are right, dear. It's hard to know what's right and wrong out here. I'm just thinking of the children. Heaven knows it's a rough enough environment we're bringing them to—I don't want them idolizing a killer. I suppose we'll know by his actions what his character is." She sipped her coffee.

"Miss Douglas," she continued after a pensive moment, "you must promise me, if you have any concerns at all about traveling north with him, you will continue on with us to South Pass City. I'm sure your father could send someone else up to escort you. And you would be safe there while you waited—"

A gunshot interrupted their conversation. The two women jumped to their feet. There was a commotion over by Captain Norbeck's campfire.

"What is it? Can you see anything?" Mrs. Hanson asked.

"No." There were too many people milling about. Moments later, she saw Mr. Hanson walking toward them with an arm around Hector Ramon, steadying the big man.

"Good heavens! Was he shot?" Mrs. Hanson hurried forward. She helped her husband settle him by their fire. Blood was running from his nose, down his chin, all over his clothes. "Miss Douglas, go get some cloths and water. Hurry!"

Rachel gathered the items and brought them to Mrs. Hanson. "What happened? Was someone shot?" she asked.

Hector Ramon pulled his hands away from his face, showing Rachel the gory river coming from his nose. "Your breed did this. He slugged Norbeck, and when I tried to stop him, he broke my goddamned nose."

"Where is he? Hector, who was shot?" Rachel boldly persisted, hoping the frightening man her father sent out to help her hadn't gotten himself shot his first night in the company. "We heard gunfire."

"No one was shot. Norbeck fired into the air, trying to scare the breed off me, like the dog that he is."

Rachel turned toward Captain Norbeck's campfire. If this big brute of a man looked this bad, Sager had to be in bad shape, too.

Hector Ramon grabbed her arm to stop her, smearing blood on the sleeve of her coat, his grip painfully tight. "You brought trouble to us when you came back with that breed," he commented bitterly. "I just hope he don't kill us all in our sleep."

Rachel looked from him to the Hansons. They regarded her with suspicion and blame. *We'll know by his actions what his character is,* Mrs. Hanson had said. Rachel felt fear settle into the pit of her stomach, the same fear she'd lived with all her life. She didn't want to go back. She had to get to the Crippled Horse.

"Miss Douglas, go sit with the children," Mrs. Hanson suggested. "I'm sure the commotion scared them. Mr. Hanson and I will handle this."

Rachel turned toward the wagon, the knot tightening in her stomach. She had learned how dependent she was on the Hansons, learned that lesson too thoroughly to alienate them now. She pushed her way between the blankets with the younger Hanson children and lay still, trying futilely to catch the hushed conversation going on between the Hansons and Hector.

She stared up at the wagon floor above her, exhausted but unable to sleep. If her father's guide was not dependable enough to get her safely to his ranch, she would find another way. She had to, because she was never going back.

Chapter Three

Rachel felt the hot sun heat through her cotton shirt as she bent over to pick up another dried buffalo patty to put in her burlap sack. Strange how cold one day could be and how hot the next was. The spring weather was so fickle here on the High Plains that she never knew what to expect. She lifted her face to the breeze, cooling her damp forehead.

Several days had passed since she, Ellie and Sager had returned to the company. Tensions had eased somewhat, due largely to the fact that Sager was never around. Each morning he brought her mule and horse over, saddled her horse up, packed her mule, and left them tied to the Hansons' wagon. She rarely had occasion to exchange words with him— Mrs. Hanson saw to that.

Given the commotion that followed their homecoming, she'd been relieved to find out how well Sager fared the next morning when he brought her horse and mule over. He bore no outward signs of the altercation, unlike Captain Norbeck, Hector and Schmitty, all of whom sported bruises on their faces.

Rachel looked back at the ridge she had come from, knowing she was moving a little too far from the company. She couldn't see the other women. She picked up a flat buffalo patty and tossed it into her sack. She had found a gold mine of fuel; her sack would be filled in no time. Despite the relentless sunshine, she heard the rumble of distant thunder. The cotton of her dress stuck to her armpits. Rain would be a welcome change—it would cool things down. She could only see a few thunderheads building in the brilliant blue sky toward the east, though a dust storm was blowing in; a big, brown cloud was rising from the south. Pulling the strings of the burlap bag, she started back toward the camp.

"Rachel!" Hearing her name, she looked up. Sager was galloping toward her, shouting something at her. She couldn't quite hear what he said. The thunder behind her was getting louder.

"R-u-n!" Sager stood in his stirrups, pointing behind her. "R-u-n!" Looking back toward the dust storm, she saw that it wasn't a storm at all, but a heaving black mass of stampeding buffalo. She dropped her sack and began running at a right angle to the herd, heading for the closest hill, lifting her skirts for greater speed. The ridge was too far, and the herd was coming fast. She wasn't going to make it. The thunder was now a deafening roar, the dust enveloping her, choking her.

A band of steel closed around her waist as Sager yanked her off her feet, knocking the breath out of her as she landed on her stomach across his lap. Her mouth opened, but her lungs didn't work—she couldn't breathe. Her chest was paralyzed. She couldn't move her arms or her hands, couldn't hold on, couldn't do anything to save herself from slipping off Sager's pony.

Sager grabbed a fist full of fabric at her waist and re-settled her across his lap. At last, she gulped in a breath of air, getting a mouthful of grit along with it. Coughing, she buried her face in Sager's calf, wrapping both hands around his leg. The thundering roar of the stampede seemed all around them now, but they were climbing the ridge she'd been running toward. The paint labored with the incline of the slope and the speed Sager kept him at. They drew to a stop at the top of the hill, above the herd. Dismounting, he lifted Rachel down to stand with him.

"You okay?" he shouted, his hands like steel vices on her shoulders.

She nodded, then grabbed his shirt. "Sager—the company!"

"They're a ridge over, to the east. They're not in danger," he yelled, drawing her into the warmth and safety of his arms.

Feeling as if her legs had gone boneless, Rachel accepted his embrace, though she didn't return it. Again, he'd saved her, at considerable risk to himself. Mrs. Hanson's words ran through her mind again. *We'll know by his actions what his character is.*

Rachel watched the stampede below them. The running herd was the most fearsome thing she'd ever seen, much like watching a huge forest fire might be, she thought—something vast and devastating and far beyond human control. The run went on, endlessly, quickly stretching to both horizons.

She listened to the thundering hooves and the snorts and grunts of the herd, gradually becoming aware that Sager rubbed her back. After a few minutes, she looked up at him. His hands stilled on her back as he looked down at her, his amber eyes darkening.

"Thirsty?" he asked, shouting to be heard above the running animals. The dried parchment of Rachel's throat was far beyond thirst. She nodded.

"Follow me." He turned toward the rocky bluff behind them, leading his pony. The thundering quieted a bit as they moved away from the draw. A thin, clear stream appeared from the middle of the bluff and spilled down a narrow ravine, rolling slowly toward the draw.

"How did you know this was here?"

"I've been on this trail a time or two."

Rachel sat on a rock at the edge of the bank. Rinsing her hands, she cupped them and scooped up the cold water, drinking until her hands were dry. The water tasted like melted snow and washed away the grit she had sucked into her throat. She greedily consumed all that she could, wondering if she made as much slurping noise as Sager's pony a little ways downstream.

When at last she was sated, she untied the kerchief from around her neck and dipped it in the water. She rinsed her forearms and face and neck. She unbuttoned the top few buttons at her collar and dipped the cool, damp kerchief between her breasts. She was about to repeat that process when she remembered Sager.

He was crouching on the bank across from her, watching her, watching her hands. His face was taut with some emotion she didn't understand. She grew still, like a wild animal sensing danger. He wiped the water from his lips with the back of his hand and stood up, turning away. Rachel dabbed the cold kerchief against the base of her throat, then wrung it out and retied it about her neck. She refastened her buttons, thankful Sager had turned away.

Hesitating a moment, Rachel drew a fortifying breath and stepped across the stream. She went to stand next to him, at the crest of the rise, watching the river of buffalo pass below them, a mottled brown and black stripe against the pale green prairie hills.

"How long do you think they will be running?"

Sager shrugged. "I've waited as long as two hours for a stampede to pass, but that was well east of here. The grass is thinner and shorter here—the herds are usually smaller. Shouldn't be long now."

"Sager, why were you fighting with Captain Norbeck the night we returned?"

He looked at her. The wind blew his black hair forward over his shoulders, framing the harsh planes of his face. "He cheated you."

Rachel frowned, shaking her head. "When?"

"Your father paid him an extra fee to protect you. When he let you leave the wagon train, to my way of thinking, he broke that contract."

"He told me not to go," Rachel defended Captain Norbeck. "He told me there were dangers out there I wouldn't be able to deal with."

"He let you go. No gun. No man to protect you. He didn't even make sure you had enough supplies."

"I went with the Hansons, Sager. I wasn't alone."

Sager cursed. "What the hell good did he think they were gonna be to you? That faithless pack of cowards abandoned their own kid—and you—to save themselves. Norbeck knew they were greenhorns.

He shoulda done better by you. He was paid to do better."

Rachel studied Sager's face as he frowned down at her. She focused on the Hansons to distract herself from the shocking revelation her father had paid a protection fee for her.

For her.

"The Hansons have four other children to think of besides Ellie. They were off the trail, riding around in unfamiliar territory. If they got lost, if they broke a wagon wheel, they would have been undone. What would become of their family then? Besides, Captain Norbeck said there were hostiles in the area. If the Sioux found them, the Hansons would have been slaughtered."

"You stayed. You didn't run off with your tail between your legs."

"I had to find Ellie, or find her body. I had to know what became of her."

Sager stared down at her. The buffalo had passed at last, and silence stretched into the moment. "You shouldn't have been in that position, Rachel, but it was brave and honorable of you. Old Jack'll be proud."

Watching her, Sager was unprepared for the blinding smile she unleashed on him. It lit her face and put color in her cheeks. He tore his gaze away, freeing himself from the seductive grip of her big blue eyes.

"Time to go." He whistled for his horse, who leisurely strolled over and stopped in front of him. Sager swung up into the saddle, then emptied the stirrup for Rachel to use as he gave her an arm up to sit behind him. He turned toward the draw, now a brown mess of dirt and torn up grass.

Squeezing his pony into a lope, he rode the mile separating them from the camp, ignoring the feel of her slim arms wrapped around his waist, ignoring the movement of her breasts against his back as she moved with the pony's stride.

Chapter Four

Sid Taggert glanced up from the papers on his desk as the door to his library slammed open. His wife entered, her face white with rage, her dark blond hair tucked into a chignon—neat, controlled. Perfect. She wore a morning gown of fine rose silk. It hissed with each step of her angry stride toward him. He let her come to a stop in front of his desk before he dragged himself to his feet, a small insubordination that added a degree of tension to her features.

"Good morning, Cassandra."

"Your breed of a son has gone after Jack Douglas's daughter."

Sid's smile was cold. It was hard to believe he'd ever fancied himself in love with his wife. Eighteen years ago, she'd seemed his salvation, a woman alone with her young son. So like Isabel. Yet now he realized she and Isabel were as different as gravel and pearls.

"I'll explain it one more time, Cassandra. Please tell me if I'm not perfectly clear. Sager is not a breed. He was a Sioux and then Shoshone captive, as was my wife."

"He was raised an Indian, Sid. After all he has done to you, how can you persist in calling him your son?"

"I persist because he is my son. And yes, he has gone to fetch Rachel Douglas. Jack and I discussed the possibility of a union between Rachel and Logan. It seemed the easiest way to end the rustling. Sending Sager for Rachel ensures she'll arrive here safely."

"Safe. You think your heathen spawn will leave her untouched?" Cassandra's fists balled at her sides. "Your plans will ruin my son's future. Do you know that?"

"Our son," Sid interjected.

"He's my son, Sid. Mine." She thumped her chest. "And if you won't give him the future he deserves, then I'll see to it myself."

"Cassandra, sit down," he said, gesturing toward a chair. "Let's discuss this rationally."

"I won't sit down. I can't rest—I can't calmly watch you destroy Logan."

Sid's face hardened. He took his seat though his wife remained standing. "Exactly what is it that you're objecting to? Sager or Rachel or the possibility of Logan's marriage?"

"All of it!" She whirled about to begin pacing the room. "I don't like the Douglases. They're uncivilized. Jack allows his cowhands to eat in the house, for God's sake. His house is a hovel. He's made no improvements on his property. I can't imagine his daughter is any better. I won't have you chain my son to this barbaric Territory you've stranded us in. He deserves better. *I* deserved better."

Sid leaned back in his seat, adopting a relaxed posture despite his screaming nerves. When had he begun hating Cassandra? She'd been his hope—his bandage, the healing he craved after first losing Isabel and his son to the Sioux, then learning of her death. He and Cassandra had met and married in a whirlwind he'd welcomed. He had brought Cassandra and young Logan home to the Circle Bar right away. A scant few months had passed in relative peace before her bitterness began to surface. Perhaps it had been there all along, and he'd just been blind to it. God, he'd been blind to so very much in his life.

"Are you listening to me?" his wife interrupted his musings.

Sid leaned forward, rubbing the bridge of his nose as he focused on her tirade. "Of course, dear," he answered. "You're screaming. How could I not hear you?"

Cassandra leaned on Sid's desk and spoke through clenched teeth. "I don't want Jack Douglas's daughter for my Logan. I want a political connection for him."

"So, the issue is Miss Douglas, I gather? Her maternal aunt and uncle raised her. Her uncle is a prominent government lawyer. From what I understand, she's only recently left school back East. She should be quite the proper young miss. I think we owe it to both her and her father to give her a chance."

"I want more for my son."

"Do you?" A coolness entered his dark brown eyes as he met her angry gaze. "Jack Douglas has fifteen thousand acres of prime rangeland—half again what we have. Logan could do far worse for himself. And you might want to remember that Sager, as my eldest son, will be inheriting the Circle Bar. So I'd be damned pleased to see Logan set up so well and so close by."

"Sager!" Cassandra's lips twisted with the name. "He's been no son to you—not like Logan has. He doesn't even bear your name!"

Sid came to his feet, his face carefully bland. "You are quite right, my dear. You saw to it that he could be no son to me, didn't you? But I will, nevertheless, persist with my foolishness, for it gives me pleasure. I have two sons, madam. Two. I love them both. Logan will have a financial settlement that is quite generous—if I can stop the rustling. But if it continues, I'll have nothing to give either of the boys. It is to Logan's enormous benefit to court Rachel.

"Now, if we've nothing else to discuss this morning, I'd best return to my accounts." He watched Cassandra pivot and stride from the room before he sank tiredly to his chair. It was his fault. All of it. Cassandra. Sager. Even Isabel. He wasn't going to mess things up with Logan. Giving the boy a chance for peace, for a life of his own, was the best thing he could do for him. Cassandra would have Logan return to her family's land back East. Perhaps he would do that one day, but marrying into the Crippled Horse spread gave him an alternative.

And what of Sager? Would he ever accept the Circle Bar?

Chapter Five

Rachel waited anxiously for Sager to bring her horse and mule over the morning after the buffalo stampede. Her guide still made her nervous, but she wasn't entirely sure it was a bad feeling. Though he looked hard-edged, he was kind and gentle— so unlike her mother's family.

Twice he'd saved her life. If anyone could get her to the Crippled Horse, she was certain he could. For the first time since she'd run away from her aunt and uncle's home, hope took root in her soul.

Rachel hurried through her chores, determined there would be no reason Mrs. Hanson could use to keep her from her plans for the day. The children had finished eating and were dressing. Mr. Hanson and the older boys were yoking the oxen. The dishes were done, the fire banked, the wagon packed.

Rachel didn't have long to wait. Sager walked through the dusty, busy camp, leading their horses and her mule. Rachel's heartbeat quickened.

He nodded toward her, his expression a little quizzical as she stood near the end of the Hansons' wagon, clearly waiting for him. "Mornin'," he greeted her.

"Good morning."

He tied her animals to the back of the wagon. She summoned her courage. "Sager, I'd like to ride with you today."

He didn't immediately answer her. Instead, he busied himself loading her pack on her mule. He looked forbidding, unwelcoming, even. She thought he would deny her request. "Please." Rachel touched his coat sleeve.

Before he could answer her, Mrs. Hanson noticed the two of them. "Miss Douglas, come help me with the children."

Rachel didn't move. She knew her eyes were pleading with his, but she had little pride left. "I'm riding with Sager today," she answered her chaperone, though her guide had not yet accepted her request.

Mrs. Hanson gasped. "Miss Douglas, I don't think that is a good idea."

Sager turned his amber gaze on her chaperone. "She'll be fine with me, Mrs. Hanson." He looked back at Rachel. "You ready to ride?"

She nodded, excitement swirling in her belly.

"Then let's go."

"Rachel Douglas, this is not a wise course of action!" Mrs. Hanson hissed, her hands on her hips.

Rachel sent Sager a look, begging his patience, then went over to Mrs. Hanson. "I need to do this, Mrs. Hanson. Please understand," she said quietly. "Soon I will have to travel a great distance alone with him. I need to know if I can trust him, now, while I have options, while I still have the protection of your family and the company. It's just for the day. I will be back to help with supper."

Mrs. Hanson pursed her lips and looked away. Taking that as acquiescence, Rachel quickly led her mount over to the wagon steps and scrambled up to his back before she could change her mind. She caught up to Sager, grinning at him with foolish glee. He studied her as if he'd never seen a happy person before, which made her wonder when she had last been joyful like this.

Never, maybe.

She lifted her face and watched the dawn's pink sky harden to bright blue. "Where are we going?"

"Where do you want to go?"

She looked at him. "Anywhere. Anywhere at all, Sager." It was the truth, she realized.

He swallowed and looked away, squeezing his mount into a lope. They rode to a rise and walked parallel with the wagon trail in the valley below. A little frisson tightened her nerves when she looked back and saw how far they'd gone from the company, which only now was beginning to roll out.

"So, where are we going?" she asked again, more serious this time. She began noting landscape details so that she could find her way back if she needed to—without Sager.

"Norbeck wanted me to find a likely spot for a laundry stop. We'll ride ahead and see what we can find."

At noon, they drew to a stop atop a limestone bluff overlooking an endless valley of short grass and sagebrush. Other low bluffs broke the raw horizon here and there. The sky was a bright, unrelenting blue, which no clouds softened. Not a human nor animal could be seen in the wide expanse, though Rachel knew the land was alive with snakes and rodents, rabbits and birds. She dismounted and walked closer to the bluff's edge, listening to the stiff breeze.

Sager took the reins of her horse from her and ground-tethered him near a wide patch of grass where his own mount was already grazing.

She closed her eyes and let the sun and warmed air blow around her, filling her with a strange languor. Sager came to stand next to her, but she didn't open her eyes, and he didn't speak. A moment passed, luxurious in its peace. Rachel felt connected to the land, a part of the sky and the earth, whole in a way she'd never been aware of before. She turned to Sager and slowly opened her eyes. His hat hung by its thong around his neck. His jagged hair, tossed by the breeze, lay restlessly against his face. He watched her, his eyes and tanned skin blending in to the world around them. He was connected to it, too, she realized.

"It's almost as if the wind talks," she whispered, afraid to break the moment.

"It does, to some."

She looked at their grazing horses and realized, idiot that she was, that this was their lunch stop, and of course she had not packed for it. Fear blew away her tranquility as she hurried over to her saddlebags to see what she could assemble for them to eat, quickly before he became angry at her foolishness.

"Rach, what is it?" Sager asked as he came up behind her.

"I—I know I have something here for us to eat. Please, just let me—"

He took hold of her hand, halting her frantic search as he turned her around. "Come away. You're spooking your horse," he quietly ordered as he drew her a short distance away. "What were you looking for?"

He had to know she had nothing edible in her packs. "I, uh, I was looking for something we could eat. I know I should have learned, after what happened with Ellie, not to leave the company without packing properly." Warily, she looked up at him, waiting for him to cuff her as her uncle would have done. "I haven't any food."

Sager's brows lowered. He crossed his arms and looked puzzled. "I have food for us. And water." She studied his eyes, searching for the lie in the softness of his voice. "Did you think I would let you starve?" he asked, humor whispering across his features.

She glanced away, ashamed at her ignorance.

"Rachel, has anyone ever shown you what you should carry in packs? Captain Norbeck? Mr. Hanson?"

She shook her head and heard him sigh.

"Tomorrow, before I load up your mule, I'll show you what to pack. Then, with or without me, with or without the Hansons, you can begin to rely on yourself."

She nodded, wishing she weren't so utterly inept.

Looking at her bowed head, Sager was struck by her spirit. Few white men—or women—ever heard the winds speak as she had. For someone so aware of the world around her, the strangest things upset her. Frightened her, even. And despite her fear, she was here on this trail today, away from the wagons, alone with him. She was tenacious and brave, like a desert violet blooming in the winter sun. He had an unsettling urge to pull her into his arms and promise her nothing would ever again harm her.

But that wasn't true. *He* would harm her.

He went to retrieve some jerky and his canteen. She wasn't what he'd expected in Old Jack's daughter. Dammit all to hell. A kinder man, one less bent on revenge, would change his plans.

Too bad he wasn't that man.

Chapter Six

It took the wagon train two days to reach the stop Rachel and Sager had scouted. Captain Norbeck announced the camp would be staying where it was for an extra day to do laundry and make repairs to the wagons. The reprieve was a welcome one, and the company made an impromptu celebration of the event.

Someone started playing a fiddle. As families finished supper, they gathered around the music. The Hanson children were anxious to join the fun, so Rachel shooed the family off. After doing the supper cleanup, she sat alone at the campfire, listening to the music and watching the revelers.

Something drew her attention to the horizon, a movement, a sound—she wasn't quite sure what. Scanning the hills, she saw the silhouette of a man and a horse standing next to each other, the moon rising behind them.

Sager.

He had avoided her since their day together. He tended her horse and mule in the evenings and mornings. Otherwise, she saw little of him and rarely spoke to him. Looking at his dark form, she felt he watched her.

She turned her attention to the revelers, forcing herself to concentrate on something other than Sager. It didn't help. She still felt the weight of his gaze. Making a pretense of stoking the fire, she walked around it to sit with her back to the hill. That, of course, only made it worse, as she felt his gaze burn into her back.

Why didn't he join those gathering around the fiddler? Perhaps he felt as alone as she did, with the company but not of them. That thought spurred her to motion. She moved away from the circle of wagons and started up the hill. Instead of being alone apart, they could be alone together. The incline was fairly steep. Every time she looked up to get her bearings, she saw him watching her climb the hill.

"Hello," she said, stopping a few feet away from him.

He looked at her for a long moment before greeting her. "Rachel." The music and sounds of people singing and laughing drifted up to them. She felt suddenly awkward and far, far away from the safety of the company.

"What are you doing up here? You don't dance?"

She shook her head.

He frowned. "Why?"

"I don't know how."

"It's easy. I'll show you." He held a hand out to her.

Rachel's eyes widened as she looked at his outstretched hand. She'd never danced before. It was the one social grace her cousins' tutor, Master Tidwell, couldn't teach her. She'd gone once, with her aunt, uncle and her two cousins, to a weekend house party where there had been dancing. But she had been there as attendant to her aunt and cousin, not as a participant. She'd sneaked a look from the servants' door into the ballroom, pretending she was part of the gala affair.

Until Uncle Henry had caught her watching them.

She put her hand in Sager's, letting him lead her up to the flat ground at the top of the hill. The fiddle settled into a slower tempo that filtered up to them. Sager took hold of her waist and lifted her hand. His grip, warm and sure, made her feel stiff and clumsy, like a puppet with its joints glued together. "What do I do?"

He smiled at her. "Nothing. Just go where I go." He took a step, and then another, his movements slow, metered. She followed, concentrating on not moving faster than he did, worried she would trip over her own feet.

"Rachel, your feet don't need to be watched. Look at me instead."

She lifted her worried eyes to his.

"How is it that a gently reared young lady doesn't know how to dance? Don't they teach that in finishing school?"

Nothing about her childhood had been gentle. "I didn't go to school." Master Tidwell had worked with her at night, after her chores were finished. His attic room was near hers. Their sessions were secret. He would have been dismissed had her aunt or uncle known he taught her. He was the only kind person she'd ever known.

Until now.

Sager increased the speed of their steps, moving

in sync with the music. "I think you're getting the hang of this. Not hard, is it?"

She shook her head. "Who taught you how to dance?"

"A wh-woman I knew in California."

The terrain was rough and uneven, but his arms were masterful, and he whisked her about as though they danced on the polished oak floors of the ballroom she had secretly watched. She forgot she was in the middle of the prairie, forgot she danced her first waltz—alone and unchaperoned with a gunfighter. She was barely aware of the ground beneath her. She laughed, delighted and enthralled, consumed by the dance.

After a while, the fiddler changed tunes, switching to a haunting folk song not meant for dancing. Sager led her into a dance that was slow and unfamiliar to her. It wasn't quite the waltz they had just been doing, nor was it similar to the country dances the others had been dancing earlier. Rather, it was a gentle swaying, a graceful motion that was intimate, though he kept a proper distance between their bodies.

She hoped the darkness hid the heat in her cheeks. She avoided his gaze, for it was warm and steady and wholly unnerving. The collar of his faded blue cotton shirt was open at his throat, his skin dark next to the material. Her gaze moved up the cording of his neck to the hard line of his jaw, lingering over his mouth, following along the lower curve of his bottom lip before drifting across his cheek to his hair, which was intensely blue-black in the bright moonlight.

Time ceased to tick away in her mind as the music

continued. He slowly closed the distance between them, easing their bodies closer. She'd never known dancing could be so magical. The moonlight and the music and Sager's warmth all combined to overrule her better judgment. She moved her hand across his shoulder to the back of his collar, settling it beneath his hair, letting the silky strands brush against her knuckles. Her fingers opened to let his hair spill over them, between them. She felt the weight of his gaze pull at her.

They were so close that she had to arch her neck to see into his face. His gaze was mesmerizing, hypnotic. His arm tightened about her, pulling her to him until the buckle of his gun belt pressed into her ribs. She could feel the whole, heated length of him. Every time he swayed, his leg pushed against her skirts—first one thigh, then the other. Rhythmically. Pushing and receding. Breathing became difficult for her.

His hand on her back lowered to her hip, molding her to his swaying body. The touch would have been a shocking intrusion, but Rachel's mind felt drugged. She moved her other hand up to his neck and let both hands touch his hair. It occurred to her that they were no longer following the beat of the music, but were moving to a far more private tune. She met his eyes again, and saw that he, too, knew they were outside the music, distanced from everything but their touching bodies. His eyes were hooded. Hungry. Predatory.

His head bent toward her. She was shocked to realize she wanted him to kiss her. She, who had dodged the unwanted attention of men and boys since she was fourteen, wondered what it would be like to be kissed by a man such as Sager. She felt her blood pause, then surge through her body. She arched toward him.

Sager brushed his lips against the slim column of Rachel's neck, glad she hadn't pulled away yet. Her body was lithe and supple and moved in every way he led her. His skin tingled where she played with his hair. Did she know how difficult she was making this for him? His breathing was ragged, his nostrils flaring as he drew in the scent of her with each pull of air. He looked at her flushed face, her passion-darkened eyes, and swallowed an oath.

He lifted his hands to her face, touching her with the backs of his fingers, pretending for a moment that she was his, not Logan's. Pretending that when he seduced her, it would be for love and not revenge. He ran his fingers over her cheekbones and down her cheeks, letting one hand ripple over her lips and chin. He drew the back of his fingers down her neck and up again to her chin, slowly, watching her eyes all the while. He ran his fingers lower, over her collarbone, down along the outsides of her breasts. He felt the breath she drew as her chest expanded to press against his fingers. He led his fingers down her ribs, to her waist, and down to her hips before slowly running them back up to her neck. He wanted to kiss her, wanted to taste her lips, craved it as badly as a man dying of thirst gulps at the water that would kill him. He wanted to dig his hands into her hair and shove his tongue into her mouth. He knew that she would let him, too.

His lips touched hers, tentatively, softly. The best he could do for her would be to raise her passion.

If she desired him as he did her, it wouldn't be rape. Would it?

The kiss stayed chaste. He stopped dancing, stopped his racing thoughts. The wind blew her blond hair toward him. He breathed in the smell of wood smoke, the soap she used, the tantalizing scent that was hers alone. She was like a dry prairie in fire season, ready to burst into flames and scorch everything around her. He'd best remember she was just a means to an end.

"I think we better call it a night, Rachel," he rasped, pulling himself away from her.

Rachel stared at him, her eyes lit with confusion. She crossed her arms around her waist as she drew a long breath. She turned away, heading gingerly down the hill to the wagons.

He watched her go.

The women in the company were up before first light the next morning. No sooner was breakfast eaten and the dishes cleared, than they were lugging tubs of dirty laundry, soap, and washboards down to the river. Several men and children had stripped down to their long underwear, wearing only their coats or blankets for warmth and decency.

Hector came to visit the Hansons. Rachel continued gathering her laundry, trying to ignore the way his gaze crawled all over her. He pulled Mr. Hanson aside, speaking in a hushed voice. The two men looked at her. Rachel turned her back to them as she fetched her washboard out of her mule's pack. After Hector left, Mr. Hanson called his wife over. They, too, exchanged hushed, agitated words. Rachel groaned inwardly, knowing she was going to get a lecture about her behavior last night. Hector must have seen her with Sager. Mr. Hanson took the children off, leaving her alone with his wife.

Rachel looked at Mrs. Hanson. Her face was pale, her expression stricken. "Is it true?" she asked.

"Is what true, Mrs. Hanson?"

"Were you alone with Mr. Sager last night?"

Rachel felt a hot blush warm her cheeks. "I shared a dance with him, yes."

"Mr. Ramon saw you. It was more than a dance, wasn't it?"

Rachel thought of the way Sager had held her, how they moved together, how she'd wanted him to kiss her. "Yes," she answered reluctantly.

"Then I'm afraid, Miss Douglas, Mr. Hanson and I find we are no longer willing to sponsor you. I have to ask you to make your own campfire from now on. I'm sorry, Miss Douglas, but I won't have a woman of your character around my children." Mrs. Hanson gathered her laundry and left, heading for the river.

Rachel stood where she was, frozen. She was well and truly alone. Mr. Hanson returned and pulled her tent out of the wagon, setting it next to her supplies, away from their camp. She was too ashamed to look at him. She heard the sounds of the camp all around her, as if she were outside herself. Random sounds. The wind. A hammer on metal. Men's voices. Children's voices. A robin.

She forced herself to pick up her bucket and laundry, washboard and soap. She forced herself to go to the river. She had to get through this day. She had no sponsor now. But she had Sager. She wouldn't be abandoned here, in this godforsaken, barren land. And she wasn't going back.

At the river, the women eyed her, growing quiet as she neared them. So, the news had spread already. She shifted her bundle, ignoring their assessing looks. She was not a stranger to them, nor they to her. She had helped with their children, given her medical supplies to some, dined with others. Yet now, they would refuse her access to the river to do her wash? Even little Ellie, who had been playing with a couple of girls on the bank, stopped to stare at her. Her expression, at least, more bewildered than angry.

Rachel turned, her back as stiff as a statue, and moved further upstream where the river still ran clear. It was one thing to be barely tolerated by the women, and something else, something dangerous, to be excluded from their company altogether.

She had just begun sorting through her laundry when a set of long underwear, a flannel shirt, and a pair of denim pants landed on top of her clothes. Her head shot up. Sager stood above her.

"Mind doing a few extra pieces?" he asked, his tone cheery and nonchalant. She sent a surreptitious glance toward the women to see if they had noticed Sager. Of course they had.

Rachel gritted her teeth. "I don't mind."

"And this." Sager pulled his shirttails from his pants, unfastened a couple of the top buttons and, arching his back, drew it over his head. Rachel stared at his bared chest, her face heating. There wasn't a hair on his torso. His nipples were small and dark and puckered from the cool breeze. His muscles rippled from his ribs toward his waistline like the ridges in her washboard. His shoulders were broad, nearly twice the width of her own. He handed his shirt to her. She wondered, as her eyes strayed to his hips, that if she had his long underwear, what was he wearing beneath his jeans?

"Want these, too?" he asked, unfastening the top of his pants.

Rachel squeezed her eyes shut. "No!" He stood in front of her, half-naked, where all the women could see him, could see her reaction to him, giving proof of her intimacy with him. There would be no talking her way back into the Hansons' good graces now. "Please go."

He shoved his hands in the front pockets of his denims and leaned back against the rough bark of a cottonwood, ignoring her request. "So are you the only one with sense enough to find clear water for your washing, or is there another reason you're dangerously far from the other women?"

Rachel gave a quick shrug. "They weren't too welcoming this morning—they must have seen us last night."

"We did nothing but dance, Rachel."

She looked at him. She knew her fear and desperation were in her face. She was never good at camouflaging her emotions, even after a lifetime of practice. Sager's eyes darkened. For a moment, he did not speak. "Do you want me to stay with you?"

Yes! Rachel almost shouted. But she couldn't break another of the women's rules. Washing was done exclusively by the women so that they could bathe when the work was finished. "No. I'll be fine."

Sager pushed off the tree he'd been leaning on. "Then I'll head back to camp."

When he was out of sight, Rachel removed her stockings and boots, then hiked up her skirts. Looping her hem into the waistband of her apron, she waded as deep as she dared into the frigid river to fill her small washtub, then lugged it back to the bank and started to work. She washed her blouses and skirts and various undergarments in short order, rinsing them in the river, then picked up Sager's things. They were large—far larger than her uncle's or Cousin Jeremy's. She felt odd handling Sager's clothes; it was too domestic, too intimate a chore. She thought about last night, remembered the feel of his arms about her as she and Sager danced, remembered how she wanted him to kiss her.

She shoved his shirt into the water and vigorously scrubbed it against her washboard, pushing those thoughts aside. She repeated the process with the rest of his clothes, rinsing them and laying his few items out next to her clothes on various branches and bushes. Arching her back, she stretched her sore muscles. Though some of the women downstream were still washing, several were already bathing themselves. There was no reason she couldn't take a quick dip herself.

She quickly peeled off her clothes, stripping down to her drawers and camisole top, then hurried back into the river with her soap bar. The water was so cold that it stole her breath. At least it was a warm day. She wouldn't catch a chill as she had the night Sager found her. Not of a mind, though, to linger in the water's icy depths, she lathered and rinsed her hair quickly, scrubbed and rinsed her body, then left the water in short order.

Only a few women were left now. If she didn't

hurry, she would be alone, she worried as she stepped behind some bushes to dress. She donned her dry clothes over her wet underclothes, pulled her stockings and boots back on, then left the cover of the bushes, fastening the last few buttons of her bodice.

Standing there, waiting for her, was Hector Ramon.

"Mr. Ramon!" she gasped, clutching the open top of her bodice together.

"I looked for you last night. I wanted to dance with you."

Rachel stepped around him and started toward camp. "I don't like to dance, Mr. Ramon. You know that." Her calm demeanor was a farce. She gauged the distance before she would be free of him. If she could make it past the ridge ahead, she would be within view of the camp. Surely they would not ignore her if she screamed for help. Her wet undergarments made her dress cling to her body. She pulled the damp material away from her chest, but as soon as she released it, it molded itself to her curves again. Hector stepped in front of her path, moving backward as she walked so that he faced her. He'd cornered her before, but never in so isolated a spot, never wearing the look of raw determination as he did now.

"It took me a long time to find you last night," he said, grabbing her shoulders, halting her flight. "When I did, you know what you were doing? You were dancing with that breed of yours. Like this." He bumped his hips against hers, his hands moving down to cup her buttocks.

"Let-me-go!" Rachel choked, trying to push away from him, panic making her numb. She heard a man clear his voice a short distance away. Hector's head shot up.

Sager smiled at them, his posture casual—one leg bent, the other straight. He wore his denims and a flannel shirt that he hadn't buttoned. His thumbs were hooked in the waistband of his pants, spreading his open shirt and emphasizing the guns strapped to his thighs. He looked at Ramon, challenging him as he came toward them.

"What the hell are you doing here, breed?" Ramon growled.

"Rachel, c'mon over here," Sager calmly suggested. She did as he asked, moving next to him and suppressing a shiver at the look he was giving Hector.

"You know what the Shoshone do to a white-eyes rapist like you?" Sager asked in a deceptively quiet voice, ignoring Hector's question. "No? Well, let me tell you. They strip him naked and spread his arms and legs apart, then stake him to the ground. They let the bastard bake in the sun until his white flesh blisters, then they skin him—alive." He shrugged for effect. "It's worth seein'. They know how to make the strips of skin exactly one inch wide. Quite a science." He smiled at Ramon. "Touch Rachel again, and I'll peel every inch of your skin off your ugly hide."

"You're sick, breed. Norbeck wouldn't let you get away with that Indian shit."

Sager's smile deepened. "You think he'll see me? Hell, you'll just disappear one night."

Hector Ramon's eyes bulged. Rachel could tell he weighed his options; did he fight now or choose a more opportune time? Apparently the latter won, for he turned and stormed back to camp.

Sager turned to Rachel, looking her over critically. His expression was unreadable, but tension showed itself in the knot at his jaw, in the darkness of his pale eyes. "Next time, Rachel, try fighting," he suggested.

Rachel gasped at his sarcastic comment. "He had my arms pinned down—I was about to scream when you came along."

Sager advanced on her, his movements threatening, his voice low. "You know nothing of the Territory we're in. In case you hadn't noticed, women ain't in plentiful supply hereabouts. I guess a few lucky men find female companionship a couple times a year." His amber gaze made a slow pass over her damp torso. "I can almost guarantee none of them have ever had a lady like you."

Feeling the chill beneath his fiery eyes, Rachel moved backward, stepping down the gradual incline of the riverbank, backing into a clutch of trees. Why was he so angry?

"Hold candy in a kid's face and, right or wrong, he'll bite it," Sager continued ruthlessly, baiting her. "Know why? Because *ladies* are rare and untouchable. They smell good. If you ask me though, they ain't worth the perfume they're made of. They can't take the heat or the wind or the dirt that's a way of life out here. And at the littlest sign of rough goin', they pack up and run east."

"I'm no lady, Sager, so your poor opinion of them doesn't apply to me." Rachel stopped retreating and returned glare for glare. "I will make it out here. You're wrong about that." *I have no choice.*

"Am I? Let the wrong man near you, sweetheart, and he'll run roughshod over you. It only takes one bad one." Sager took hold of her arms, pinning her as Hector had done.

Rachel realized she'd been backed into a sheltered spot all but invisible to any onlookers there might have been. "What are you doing?" she asked in a voice breathy with fear.

"I'm the wrong man, Rachel." He pulled her toward him.

Chapter Seven

Rachel's heart raced. Reacting instinctively, she banged her forehead against Sager's. The instant he pulled back, she brought her arms up between their bodies and tore free of his grip. His body blocked her only escape route. She shoved at him, but he stood like a stone wall and wouldn't move. Her mind shut down and hysteria took over. She was trapped. Again.

"Use your nails," Sager whispered.

She dug her nails into the naked flesh of his stomach. Strips of blood traced her marks, but still he didn't budge.

"Your knee—shove it into my groin."

In a fever to be free, she complied. But his hand blocked the blow. Leaning over as he was, his cheek and throat were near her face. "Use your teeth—bite me," he ordered, pointing to his jugular vein.

Rachel frowned, hesitating. Why was he telling her how to hurt him? At her hesitation, air seeped into her lungs, calming her hysteria. He had been coaching her all along. "No. I won't."

Sager studied her eyes, seeing the madness ease away. "Don't ever let a man—or anyone—back you into a corner like this. You can fight for yourself."

Sager's face wavered as Rachel looked at him through a sheen of tears. She didn't want to cry. It was just a relief to realize he hadn't meant her harm. He was her last hope for getting to her father's ranch. Gratitude and embarrassment surged through her. She opened his shirt and touched the skin near the marks she'd made below his ribs. His belly contracted reflexively at the gentle arc her fingers made.

"Look what I've done to you."

Sager shrugged, closing his shirt. "Forget it."

"No, let me wash this—I have some salve back at the camp."

He took hold of her wrists, lifting her fingers away from his stomach. His hands were warm and rough, and she could feel the abrasion of his calluses. Her gaze traveled the long path up his chest and neck, to his face. His eyes had lost that look of unholy anger, but not the heat that went with it.

"Go back to the camp, Rachel."

Rachel built her own campfire that night. She made a small stew and a small pot of coffee. She'd put her tent up earlier and now sat between it and her fire. It was night; it was cold, and she was alone, but she refused to panic. She had supplies. The company hadn't thrown her out completely. Though all now viewed her as a pariah, her camp was still within the ring of wagons. She bent her legs in front of her and leaned forward, resting her forehead on her knees.

There was a good side to this too, she reminded herself.

She didn't have to cook and clean for a family of seven. She didn't have to tend an endless stream of children. She could eat when she wanted and clean up when she wanted and sleep when she wanted. And no more lectures.

"What's this?" Sager's voice cut into her thoughts. She looked up to see him frowning as his gaze took in her tent and fire.

"It's my campfire."

"What happened?" He looked at her.

Rachel couldn't help the catch in her voice. "I'm a loose woman, not fit for the likes of the Hanson family, nor anyone in this company, it seems."

Sager crouched next to her. "Rach, you're not makin' sense. What happened?"

"Hector Ramon told the Hansons that I was alone with you last night, that we weren't just dancing. The Hansons have withdrawn their sponsorship of me. They don't want a woman like me around their children. I've been asked to make my own camp from now on."

Sager swallowed a curse, bothered that he felt her pain. "It was just a dance, Rach. You didn't do anything wrong." A tear spilled down her cheek. He wanted to wipe it away, but didn't trust himself to touch her just a little, so he kept his hands still as he watched the path it made to her chin.

"It didn't feel like just a dance, Sager," she whispered.

He sucked in a breath. It wasn't just a dance. He'd been learning her body, the way she felt in his arms, the way she moved. He'd been gaining knowledge he would use against her later.

He stood up and began settling in for the night.

He put his saddle next to her tent, then unfurled his bedroll.

Rachel watched him warily. "What are you doing?"

"You can't sleep alone, Rachel. There's a reason Ramon had you cut out of the herd. Tomorrow we head out on our own."

Rachel jumped to her feet. "No. Not yet. Please."

He stepped toward her, towering over her, large and dark and male. "What are you afraid of?"

Her answer was a single word that slipped past her lips. "You."

He didn't immediately respond. "Good."

Rachel woke early the next morning, exhausted. Her mind had churned the night through, searching for ways to delay their departure from the wagon train. She bent her legs and rested her forehead against the blanket covering them, wishing she could slow the morning down. Her mind turned to the subject that had tortured her the night through—Sager. She thought of the dance they'd shared, the way his hair felt in her hands. The butterfly-light touch of his lips when he did kiss her.

She was not ready for this day, but she was very ready to reach the Crippled Horse. In all of their interactions, not once had Sager harmed her. She had no choice but to trust him and see this last leg of their journey to its conclusion.

She dressed, then tied up her bedroll and went outside, coat in hand. The camp was coming alive. Dogs barked, fires glittered, and the heady scent of coffee floated through the air. Sager already had their horses saddled and her mule packed. As soon as she was out of the tent, he was there to take it down. She dragged her eyes up the dark brown leather of his duster to meet his gaze.

"Mornin'," he greeted her, his expression unreadable. She nodded at him.

"I thought we'd get right out. We can stop in a while for an early lunch."

Again she nodded. "How long to my father's ranch?" *How long will we be alone?*

He shrugged. "A week. Ten days." He moved around her and set about dismantling her tent.

She drew her coat on and went to the river's edge to tend to her needs. When she returned, their camp-site was gone; the only indication they'd been there was the small black circle where their fire had been.

He stood next to her horse. Rachel retrieved her bonnet and tied it under her chin, stalling. She usually used the Hansons' wagon steps as a mounting stool. How was she to get on her horse? Yesterday, she had used boulders or tree stumps. Seeing her hesitation, Sager grinned at her.

"I can lift you up, or you can use my thigh. Which is it?"

Either choice meant more contact with him than was smart. "Thigh."

Sager knelt and offered her his thigh. He took hold of her hand, helping her onto his leg. Rachel closed her mind to his proximity, the strength in his hand, the power beneath her booted feet. She stepped into the stirrup, then swung her leg over her horse and settled her skirts over her legs. Sager handed her reins to her, then mounted his own horse. She looked around at the waking camp, wondering if she should say farewell to anyone—Captain Norbeck at least.

"Sager—"

"Norbeck knows," he said, correctly anticipating her question. "I spoke to him this morning. Ready?"

No. She nodded. He turned his horse south. With a last look back at the camp, she followed him away from the protective ring of the wagons.

The afternoon was well-advanced when he selected a spot for their camp at the high point of a grassy knoll near the base of a steep, evergreen-covered line of mountains.

Dinner was a satisfying meal of boiled potatoes and roasted jackrabbit. After cleaning up, Rachel had a hard time keeping her eyes open as she sipped her coffee. It would have taken the wagon train three days to cover the miles she and Sager traveled today. Too tired to make polite conversation with Sager, she gave no argument when he took her coffee cup and told her to turn in for the night.

Sometime during the night, Rachel woke up. She lay still, listening. The wind was blissfully calm. She tried to make out the soft sounds of Sager sleeping. All was quiet. Fear began a staccato beat in her heart. What if something had happened to him? What if he had left her? What if she was alone?

She donned her coat and stepped outside. Sager was not lying near the fire. She sent a wild look around the perimeter of their camp, calming only slightly when she saw his horse dozing next to hers. Moving away from her tent, she saw Sager standing at the crest of a low hill. She took a few calming breaths. Realizing she was now too awake to go back to sleep, she made her way toward him, amazed at how little sleep he needed.

"Hi," she said as she came up next to him.

He looked at her for a long second, then turned back to the prairie he was watching. "Hi, yourself."

"Aren't you tired?"

"No."

Since he seemed disinclined to talk, she stood silently near him as she, too, looked at the prairie. The moonlight was as bright as midday. It spread a silvery brown light over the endless expanse of the range, illuminating the low hills that rose and fell like waves before disappearing into the far horizon. The breeze rolled over the short grass in its path, bending and lifting it by turns. The wind on the prairie, with only the grass to catch it, sounded different than it did where she came from. She liked that difference.

A coyote sent up a cry that was quickly answered by another, and another, until several yapping wails joined the first. Wild dogs surrounded them. She stepped closer to Sager.

"They're more afraid of you than you are of them," he reassured her.

Rachel folded her arms around herself, trying to reassure herself. "That can't be possible."

Sager wrapped an arm around her, pulling her to his side. The shudder she fought rippled through her as his heat enveloped her. She looked up at him, seeing his face clearly in the bright moonlight. Her eyes lowered to his full, curving lips. She shivered again, thinking of their dance, their one, tender kiss. Sager turned her to face him, rubbing her arms.

"I—I think I better go back."

He pulled his hands away. "G'night."

She'd taken only a step when a fresh chorus of wails froze her in place. "Sager, would you walk me back?"

He nodded and started with her toward their camp. Rachel had to hurry to keep up with his long stride. Intent on staying near him, she didn't see the prairie dog hole until it snagged her foot. She cried out as she lost her balance, afraid once she was down the coyotes would get her. Sager whirled around just in time to grab her before she hit the ground.

Rachel found herself caught up against his body, her hands fisted in the lapels of his duster, her feet barely touching the ground. She drew his scent into her lungs, the smell of fresh air and leather, and tensed, sensing what was to come—hoping for it even as she feared it.

He bent his head toward her, his black hair falling over his shoulders as his lips met hers. The contact was gentle, the touch completely at odds with the emotions burning in his amber eyes. The kiss was an easy thing; it relaxed her fears and fired her curiosity. She didn't know a man could be so gentle, especially a man like Sager, who lived on the far edge of civilized society.

Rachel tightened the pressure of their lips and felt the stubble of his beard prick her skin. His head twisted slightly. His lips parted and hers followed suit. His tongue entered her mouth, its heated length shooting flames into her belly. He explored her mouth, his lips crushed to hers. Her fingers curled into his raven hair, clutching for a grip on reality as her world narrowed to his arms, his body. His lips.

He broke the kiss, his mouth dipping to the arc of

her neck. He ran his tongue up the soft center of her throat. His lips curved around the apex of her jaw. When his mouth came back to hers, he paused, lips parted, barely touching her lips. She breathed his breath, his essence, and moaned as a deep, keening need to be nearer to him consumed her.

Her eyes flew to his—had he heard her? A one-sided grin slowly lifted his lips, answering her question. He set her from him, but her body rebelled at the break in contact with his.

"We better get you back," he rasped.

Rachel stared at him a long moment. The feel of his arms around her, his kiss, had been unlike anything she had ever experienced. She folded her arms in front of herself, trying to stop her shaking as she forced her feet to move toward her tent. Being oddly reluctant to leave him, she didn't immediately duck inside. He drew her to him again, holding his hands just below her shoulder blades. He lifted her against his body and pressed his forehead to hers, his nose next to hers, his mouth to one side of hers, open, catching her breath, giving her his.

He looked into her eyes, his expression lost in the shadowy light. "Don't seek me out, Rachel." His voice was raw, like her nerves. "You will not survive me."

And then he was gone.

Rachel struggled to catch her breath. Cold air touched where his heat had been. She entered her tent and sat stiffly on her bedroll as her ears strained for any sound, any hint of danger.

The coyotes now seemed the least of her fears.

Chapter Eight

Two afternoons later, they stopped by a fast-moving stream. Sager set up camp, then went in search of game for their supper.

Rachel decided to do a bit of laundry and take a quick bath. Hurrying so she would be finished before he returned, she stripped down to her underclothes and waded gingerly into the stream's swirling depths. It was shallow and not very wide. Nothing to be afraid of, she told herself. She quickly removed her underclothes and scrubbed herself, then lathered her hair. When she had rinsed all the soap away, she washed her camisole and drawers, then donned them again. The water was too cold to linger, so she went to sit on a large boulder on the bank, drying herself with Sager's linen towel. The rock surface was warm, radiating heat through her. Feeling decadent, she laid back, letting the hot sun dry her undergarments with her in them.

A mild breeze blew, just enough to keep the day from being too hot. Shutting her eyes, she listened to the rustle of wind in the nearby trees and grasses, grasshoppers snapping about in the warm sun. When she opened her eyes a couple of minutes later, she noticed a dark branch next to her shoulder. Funny, she hadn't seen it before. She turned her head to get a better look at it and saw it move. A snake!

It was as thick around as her wrist. She stayed still, paralyzed with fear, until it started to move closer to her face. She reacted instinctively, grabbing its neck as she lurched to her feet. She held it as far away from herself as she could, screaming hysterically. The touch of it in her hand, the feel of its scales was unlike anything she'd ever known or ever wanted to know. But as soon as she stood, it began struggling with her, whipping the rest of its body about in great horrid, thrashing jerks.

She hurried away from the boulder, lest more of its kind were nearby, and called Sager's name over and over in a hysterical litany, forgetting that he'd gone hunting, forgetting she was utterly alone.

Sager dismounted near Rachel's tent and untied a pouch of quail from his saddle. He called for Rachel, but got no answer. He was preparing to clean the birds when he heard Rachel's first scream. Her terror sliced through his mind, and his blood went cold. He ran toward the stream, withdrawing his knife as he leapt over the edge of the stream's bank. He landed in a crouch, ready for battle.

Rachel stood ten feet away holding an angry blacksnake in her fist and screaming at it for all she was worth. Her arm jerked with the force of the snake's struggle, and each time it moved, her screams began anew. Sager straightened and sheathed his knife, laughing at the ridiculous sight she made screaming at her captive. Though she held it parallel to her shoulder, it didn't clear the ground. It was over five feet long—a good catch. Too bad he'd already found supper.

"Sager! *Do* something!" she railed at him.

He strode toward her and took the snake, laughter still rumbling through his chest. "You know, in this Territory, it's a crime to scream at a snake," he teased.

Rachel's face folded with disgust as she looked at the snake he held. She wiped her hand repeatedly across her stomach and shivered, unable to take her eyes from the reptile. "Do something with it! Get rid of it!"

He grinned at her. "Are you finished bathing?"

"Yes!"

He set the snake onto the sandy bank, watching it move rapidly into the rocks and undergrowth. Rachel made another face and rubbed her hands on her thighs, wishing she could wipe away the feel of its wet scaly skin, its thrashing body.

Sager's gaze followed the movements of her hands, his humor fading. She stood before him in her thin cotton undergarments. They were only partially dry and clung to every inch of her delectable body. Her breasts were high and full, her dark nipples raised against the material. The liquid fabric was plastered to her slim ribcage and narrow waist. His gaze traveled down her hips to a darker area between her legs, down further along the length of her thighs. Jaysus, she was perfect.

When he finally lifted his eyes to hers, she was watching him warily. She'd stopped rubbing her thighs—for that he was immensely grateful. He didn't move—he couldn't. His hunger for her was hot and savage, and the pain of it immobilized him. His gaze lowered to her lips. They were soft and rounded, and he remembered the taste of them. He could kiss her. He could pull her against his burning body and make love to her.

Sager forced his lungs to take in fresh air. He shut his eyes. He didn't look at her again, just pivoted and headed back to camp.

They spoke little that night. Through the flaps of her tent, Rachel could see past the fading orange flames to where Sager slept. Watching him, she drifted off into a light sleep until the sound of his voice woke her. He was talking to someone in Shoshone—she couldn't make any sense out of it. Had Blue Thunder returned? Sager's voice grew stronger and louder. She peeked through the opening of her tent.

No one was there. A chill scraped her spine as she realized that Sager was talking in his sleep. She went outside, standing hesitantly by the entrance to her tent. Should she wake him or wait for his dream to pass? His words became a shout, a feverish dirge, and the torment in his voice clawed through her reserve. Hurrying over to him, she tried to shake him awake.

"Sager! It's just a dream. Wake up." When he didn't respond, she touched his face, her fingers caressing his unshaven cheek. He grabbed her hand, his eyes open and on her, but unseeingly. He rolled her over, shoving her back into the dirt, pressing his knife to her throat. The steel of his blade nicked her skin, and she saw her death in his sightless eyes. He held one of her arms stretched above her head, the other was pinned between their bodies. His legs across hers kept her immobilized. She was afraid to struggle—it would be nothing for him to draw the blade across her throat.

Sager heard his name called. The voice was drawing him away from his mother and sister. He wanted to run to them. He screamed their names. They needed him.

"Sager!" the voice came again.

The dream was different this time. He wasn't just a stupid boy. He was a man. He could stop the butchery. He lunged at the white-eyes whose Colt revolver had blown his sister's hand off. He had him down, had the bastard pleading for his life. But another gun went off. Sager turned in time to see crimson blossom across his mother's chest, to see her legs crumple beneath her.

"Run, my son!"

"Sager!"

"I'm not Sager!" he shouted in English, his own voice waking him from the old nightmare.

"Oh, God," Rachel whispered, seeing him return to her at last. Sweat dampened his face. His breathing was ragged. The firelight showed the stark terror in his eyes, his beautiful amber eyes. His knife fell from his grip to lie useless beside her. "Sager," she rasped, "it was a dream. It was just a dream." She brushed his hair back behind his ears. Tell me what you saw," she whispered, her hands on his cheeks.

Bending his head to Rachel's chest, Sager squeezed his eyes shut against the moisture that had gathered there. He dug his hands beneath her body, arching her back, pressing her into his face. He wouldn't cry. He hadn't when it happened; he wouldn't now.

Gradually, Sager became aware of Rachel holding him. Her hands were in his hair, calming him, stroking him. She wasn't pushing him away. Wasn't struggling to be free. He lifted his head, venturing a look at her. She smiled at him. A soft smile. There was no fear in her eyes. No disgust. No condemnation.

"Sager, talk to me."

"Talk about what?" About how his father had had his mother killed? About how Rachel's father was selling her for peace in a plan that Sager himself had configured?

"About your dream. Sometimes it helps to talk."

"Not this time." He drew away slightly, easing his hold on her. "I think you'd better get back to your tent."

Rachel met his look. She saw the loneliness in his eyes. The desperation. She ran her hand along his arm, feeling the tension in his knotted muscles. "I think you could use some company for a minute."

"Go, Rachel."

"No."

He took her hand in his and brought her knuckles to his lips, then turned her hand over and kissed the inside of her wrist. Never before had he wanted company after one of his dreams. Holding her, feeling her in his arms, absorbing her warmth and her smell, helped chase his terror away. He bent to kiss the scratch he'd cut on Rachel's neck.

"I hurt you."

"It's nothing," she answered.

He sighed and looked into her eyes. "Your father shouldn't have sent me for you, Rachel." Why the hell had Old Jack been so easy to convince, anyway?

"He couldn't have sent a better man—I doubt another man would have helped me as much as you have."

"Another man wouldn't have cut your throat in his sleep."

Rachel smoothed a lock of jagged hair from his brow, smiling to ease the tension she still felt in his body. Another man would have done much, much worse, she knew.

Sager eased himself away from her warmth and went to crouch by the dead embers of the fire. He poured himself a cold cup of coffee and downed it in two sips.

"Sager—"

"Goodnight, Rachel," he said grimly as he came to his feet. Shoving his hands into his pockets, he walked into the dark prairie surrounding them.

The next morning, Rachel wasn't sure whether she heard bacon frying or smelled it first, but she woke to the wonderful reality of breakfast cooking. She dressed quickly, buttoning all the buttons on her coat before leaving her tent.

"Mornin'," Sager said, his gaze never leaving the sizzling strips of meat. His willingness to cook or clean their camp or do any of the work needed on this trek still unnerved her.

"Morning," He handed her a cup of coffee.

"I thought it best if I fed you a good meal now. We'll only be able to have a bit of jerky at lunchtime, before we cross the Laramie."

Rachel's mind snagged on that comment. She'd been afraid to cross large bodies of water all her life—and that was while in a wagon on a bridge. Sager wanted her to cross by herself, on her horse. *In* the water. Her grip tightened on her coffee cup.

He handed her a plate laden with beans and bacon. Her stomach rebelled against food; she couldn't eat when she was worried about surviving.

"What's the matter?" Sager asked.

Rachel stiffened. "Nothing."

"You're not eating."

Rachel set her coffee down and stirred the beans with her fork. He would be furious when she told him she couldn't cross the river. What would he do? Leave her? Take her back to the company? She couldn't go back.

"Rachel, I need you to eat. We got a tough day ahead of us."

Woodenly, Rachel lifted her fork to her mouth. One threat at a time. He was watching her. It was hard to breathe and eat. She carried another forkful to her mouth. She chewed and swallowed the mass, but her stomach rejected it.

She jumped to her feet and ran to the edge of the bushes where she fell to her knees and violently emptied her stomach. He came over to her and stood above her. She braced herself for his kick. He would yank her to her feet and make her eat, shouting at her for wasting food.

Rachel heaved again.

Sager knelt and lifted her braid over her shoulder, out of her way. She sucked in a breath, wishing he wasn't there, next to her, seeing her like this. He pushed his kerchief toward her. She took it with a trembling hand, covering her mouth, breathing in his scent. Breathing it again. She ventured a look at him.

"Are you sick?" he asked, concern in his eyes.

Rachel looked away. If she said she was, she could stall for more time, but then the river would just have to be faced tomorrow. And so would he. She shook her head.

"Then what's the matter?"

"I can't swim." The cotton fabric muffled her words.

"Oh." He sat back on his haunches, regarding her for a moment. "Wait here." He fetched fresh water from the stream and gave her a cupful to rinse her mouth out with. He took his kerchief from her and dipped it in the water, then handed it back to her. She pressed it to her hot face, beginning to feel a little calmer.

"You're scared." She nodded. "I've been scared like that before."

"You?" Rachel lowered the cloth and stared at him. "When?"

"When I saw my mother and sister killed, then had to live with their killer."

Rachel was shocked. He drew her to her feet, then pulled her into his arms. "If I promise you no harm will come to you at the river, will you trust me?"

Rachel leaned into his embrace, felt his heart beat against her face. No one but Sager had ever held her this way. Ever. First after the buffalo stampede, and now here. Was he always this calm?

Late that afternoon, Rachel stood on the river-bank, staring in horror at the wide, churning mass in front of them. She couldn't do this. She couldn't ride her horse across that death trap.

"Rachel, take your stockings and boots off." Sager had stuffed his socks into his boots and was tying his boots together with a strip of rawhide. He draped them around his neck. Next, he untied his guns, removed his gun belt and draped it over his boots.

Numb with fear, Rachel did as he bid. The morning was a cool one; a chill swept up her spine from the hard ground. She tied the laces together and draped them over her neck. His grim expression worried her.

"Are you afraid, Sager?"

"Of the river?"

She nodded.

"No. But I respect your fear. 'We are not given fear without purpose.'" *We are not given anger without reason. We are not given love without hope.* Blue Thunder's words, from a lifetime ago, sifted through his mind.

Sager lifted her boots from her neck and draped them around his. "I'll take your animals across, then come back for you." He touched her chin, then leaned forward and kissed her forehead. "Close your eyes if it helps."

She did not close her eyes.

She watched him ride his mount down the incline to the water's edge, leading her horse and mule. She watched the water level rise on his horse's long legs, watched it hit his horse's belly, moving higher still until it covered Sager's lower legs. She watched it rise above his knees, then gradually recede as he left the river on the other side. He dismounted and tethered her animals to a nearby bush. He set their boots and his gun belt down, then remounted and rode back into the river.

Sager pulled out of the water and came to a stop next to her. He took his coat off and folded it several times, settling it between his crotch and the saddle horn, giving her a comfortable place to sit. He wanted her in front of him as they crossed in case she panicked midway.

"Turn around," he directed. "I'm going to lift you to sit in front of me."

She turned with her back to his thigh. He bent down and hooked an arm around her ribs, beneath her breasts, and lifted her up. "I think it would be a good idea if we folded your skirt back. You saw the water came to my knees. I don't want you to have to change on the other side."

She looked at him warily. He tried to keep his expression benign, but excitement ravaged his gut as he watched her pull her skirt and petticoats up, baring her legs to midthigh.

Good Christ, she had perfect legs. Long and lean.

"Put your arm around my neck." She did. Unfortunately, it also meant her breasts pushed against his torso. "Let's go," he grumbled as he took up the reins and urged his mount back into the cold water one more time.

She looked anxiously about, watching the rising water, her eyes wide with fear. Her arms tightened about his neck. She drew her legs up, folding them against his chest. She buried her head in the bend between his shoulder and neck as she clung to him.

And then they were across. Sager rode up onto the bank. Rachel didn't move. Her shallow puffs of breath teased his neck. He looked down at the tight ball she'd folded herself into on his lap. Her bare knees were near his face, the soft linen of her drawers exposed. He had an inconvenient urge to run his hand down her leg to her flank to discover if her bottom was as well formed as the rest of her.

Instead he stroked her back, in no hurry to stop this moment. He liked having her in his arms. She made him feel worthier than he had a right to feel.

"We're across. You're safe." She straightened, looking around them with disbelief. He grinned at her. "You had no faith in me."

She touched his cheek. The look she gave him blew fire through his veins. He dismounted, then lifted her down, quickly setting her on her own feet—away from him.

"It's late," he said tersely, leading his horse toward the others. "We won't get much farther today. I'm going to set up camp. Do you think you could rustle up something for us to eat?" He walked away not waiting for her answer, not trusting himself to continue being so near her when she looked at him as if he were a hero.

That night, Rachel changed into her nightgown inside the privacy of her tent. She stretched out on the meager padding of her bedroll, exhausted but unable to sleep. For the first time in her life, she was aware of her loneliness. Sager's kindness showed her there was another whole aspect to life, one she'd never known about before. And having felt it, she desperately did not want to go back to her lonely way of being.

Quietly, she drew aside a tiny bit of her tent flap,

peeking out at Sager. He lay on his back, his booted feet crossed, his arms crossed on his chest, his hat on his face.

She drew her coat on, then went outside and knelt beside him. He didn't move. "Sager?"

"Mmm-hmm?" he answered from beneath his hat.

"Will you stay with me in the tent tonight?"

He yanked his hat off his face and looked at her as if she'd lost her mind. "No."

"I'm cold."

"Take one of the horse blankets."

"I don't want to be alone."

He lay back down and settled his hat on his face. "Rachel, men and women don't sleep together."

"Who will know?" she asked. He jerked his hat off his head again and glared at her. She quickly continued. "I've never had anything, Sager. I never had parents to gently guide me. I never had a mother to kiss my skinned knees. I never had a friend to share a laugh with, to be close to, to feel less alone with. Until you. Please don't make me sleep alone tonight."

Sager's amber glare was unrelenting. "Rachel, we're not friends. I'm a man and you're a woman. If I go in that tent with you, I'm gonna do what a man does with a woman when they're alone. I'm gonna make love to you."

Rachel didn't even blink. "If that's the price you want me to pay to have you near me, I'll pay it."

He stared at her, looking as if she'd just struck him. Then he rolled to his side, away from her, and put his hat on his face. "Go back to your tent and go to sleep. You've had a hard day."

She gave no further argument. In her tent, she sat with her arms around her folded knees, rocking herself. After a while, she heard a muffled string of curse words from Sager, then the crunch of gravel as he came toward her tent. He ducked inside, carrying his bedroll.

"Move over," he growled.

She scrambled to make room for his bedroll, then quickly slipped beneath her blanket. He took his boots off, then spread his blanket over hers and draped his coat over the top. In the dim light cast by the dying fire, Sager could see hope and fear tangled in her eyes.

He sighed. "Come here." He offered his shoulder to her. Without hesitation, she nestled against him. Like a friend.

Sager tried to shut his mind to the feel of her against his side, but it was impossible. Even worse, her scent whispered around him, tantalizing and womanly. "I'm sorry for saying what I did out there." He released a long breath. "It was rude. I didn't mean to offend you. I won't touch you."

Her only response was to snuggle closer to him. She pressed her face into his shoulder. He thought she might have kissed him, but it was impossible to be sure. "Go to sleep, Rachel. I've got you, and I won't let any harm come to you."

Sager silently cursed that vow. The cost was steep. She would not be his revenge. He would have to find another way to destroy the Taggerts.

He was beginning to be very, very afraid of this one, small woman.

Chapter Nine

Cassandra stood in the shelter of the cottonwoods lining the creek, waiting as the rider who just pulled up dismounted. She hadn't been sure he would come. This was their old rendezvous spot, but they hadn't been lovers for many months now. She never did feel much of an affection for the rustler. Her satisfaction in their affair came in knowing she was cavorting with her husband's enemy. Any enemy of Sid's was a friend of hers. Until now.

Tom's nefarious activities were hurting her son's holdings. Sid had told her that breed son of his would inherit the Circle Bar, but she meant to see that he would never live that long. And it was just possible that she could get rid of Tom in the process, ending the rustling. She knew he was greedy enough to take the job; his greed would be his downfall. No one would miss Sager, but the murder of a rancher's daughter would draw the law down on Tom.

"Tom," she greeted him.

"Cassie," Tom Beall tipped his hat.

"I have a job for you. Sid and Old Jack have

arranged a marriage between Old Jack's daughter and Logan. Sager's escorting her to the Crippled Horse. I want you to kill them."

Tom crossed his arms and smiled down at her, a sly look on his face. "I got almost enough Crippled Horse and Circle Bar cattle to fund my own spread on better land than I have now. Why would I want to spoil it for myself? If I kill them, the marshal and his deputies will be all over this place."

Cassandra tossed him a package containing a thousand dollars. "That's half of what you'll get when you do the job. You owe me, Tom. I've turned a blind eye to your little rustling operation, until now. But I'll do it no more. If you don't handle this, I'll confess everything to my husband. Have I made myself clear?"

Tom walked over to her, stopping so close that his face nearly touched hers. "Everything? Even how you initiated his boy into manhood? How old was he? Thirteen? Fourteen?" His laugh was scornful. "Was he as insatiable as you?" He picked up the package. "I'll take care of them, all right," he said in a low voice. "And if you say anything, your husband will learn everything. Then I'll take care of you, too."

Chapter Ten

"Rachel."

She heard Sager's voice, but it came from a distance. The sun felt delicious on her as she sat on the ground, leaning against the warm, sloping wall of a rock.

"We've got to leave." He crouched down in front of her. A shadow slipped across her face as he nudged her awake. She opened her eyes slowly. His head shaded her from the afternoon sun, but his eyes reflected the light from the rock behind her. Still in a dreamlike state, she lifted her hand to run her fingertips across his cheek, feeling the rough bristles of his unshaved beard. She was achingly aware of the volatile way he looked at her, aware of the knot she had in her stomach. His gaze dropped to her lips, and she imagined the feel of his lips against hers.

He drew her fingers away from his face, but he didn't release her hand. "We have to leave, Rachel," he repeated.

"I know." Her gaze traveled leisurely across his face, his hair.

"We've got about an hour's ride before we reach

Defiance." He stood and pulled her to her feet. Snatching up his saddlebag, he glanced back at her. "You can sleep in a hotel room tonight. Defiance ain't much of a town, but it's got a lumber mill and a general store, besides the hotel. From there it's a day's ride to your pa's house."

Rachel mounted her horse, feeling the distance of an invisible rift that now cut her from Sager. They'd spent the last three nights in each other's arms. Three nights of blissfully pure sleep. But tonight, they would be in separate beds. She'd have a place to sleep that didn't make her back ache.

And a room with walls separating her from him.

Sager hadn't exaggerated, she realized as they rode into town. Defiance was tiny. There were only a couple dozen buildings—at least three of which appeared to be saloons. One of the buildings had recently been whitewashed, making the others look old and dingy. As they pulled up outside the general store, a man who was sitting on a bench outside the nearest saloon stood up to get a better look at them. His eyes widened as he stared at the two of them, then he sidled into the saloon behind him, not daring to turn his back on them. Rachel glanced at Sager to see if he'd noticed the man's strange behavior. She couldn't tell from his expression whether he had or if it bothered him; his face was curiously blank.

Tying her horse and mule next to Sager's, Rachel followed him up the steps onto the boardwalk that led to the hotel and the handful of shops on this side of the road. A tall man came out of the saloon and other patrons spilled out of the doorway behind him—the man she'd seen earlier among them. The entire group stared at her and Sager.

Rachel sent a quick glance over herself, trying to determine why they'd attracted so much attention. Though she was filthy from the trail, she was still cleaner than some of them. If they weren't staring at her, it must be Sager. But why? What had he done to warrant this strange reaction from the townsfolk?

The rumble of the tall man's booted stride interrupted her thoughts. The whispers stopped. Even the breeze grew still. The only sound was the chink-chink of his spurs hitting the wooden planks. Rachel felt a chill slip down her spine. He was the man the others had followed out of the saloon—a leader of some sort. She wanted to step back, but Sager wasn't shrinking away, so she settled for slipping her hand in his. She felt his fingers close over hers, his grip warm, reassuring.

"Hank," Sager's deep voice broke into the tension. It wasn't so much a greeting as an acknowledgement of an enemy.

"Sager." The man did nothing as they passed, just watched them go.

Sager directed Rachel past a couple of doors and into the hotel. He secured lodging for the both of them, then went with her up the stairs to their adjoining rooms.

"That was strange," Rachel commented once they were inside her room.

"Yep."

"Do you think we should stay here tonight? Maybe we should keep on moving."

Sager lifted the curtain at her window and surveyed the street below. "Wouldn't matter now. Looks as if they were waitin' for us. If we left, they'd just come after us."

"Why?"

Sager looked at Rachel. "I'm guessing the rustlers who've been working your father's ranch were watching for me to come back to town. I don't exactly have a reputation for peacemaking, if you know what I mean. Their holiday is about to end." Sager studied her face. Nothing back East could have prepared her for the trouble ahead, trouble he'd laid at her feet by convincing her father to bring her out here. She was raw, fragile. "If you want, I can bring you up some supper. You don't have to leave this room."

Rachel told herself she was strong enough to face this. She'd been strong enough to survive in her aunt's household, strong enough to travel alone from Virginia to Missouri. Strong enough to survive her desperate hunger for Sager.

Bloodthirsty rustlers were nothing. "No. I'm not going to cower up here, afraid of what might happen. Besides, they're rustlers, not murderers."

Sager gave a dry laugh. "Right. Tell that to the two men your pa's lost and the three his neighbor lost. I'll get your stuff and order a bath for you. If your mind's set on coming downstairs, then c'mon down when you're ready—we'll eat in the dining room."

A short while later, Sager watched Rachel move down the last couple of steps. Her braided hair encircled her head like a golden crown. Her beautiful, prairie-sky eyes almost matched the color in her blue gingham dress—a dress that hung loosely over her slim shoulders and was too short around her ankles.

Sager frowned. Now that he thought about it, none of her clothes fit very well. A trip like this took a lot of preparation. Seems as though her aunt and uncle would have helped her accumulate the things she would need for the journey, like clothes and supplies. And a proper chaperone.

Nonetheless, baggy clothes and all, she took his breath away. "Rachel."

"Sager," she returned his terse greeting.

He should have offered her his arm, but he didn't feel like having her touch him, so he stepped back and waved her on to the dining room.

Once seated, Rachel opened her napkin and laid it across her lap, forcing herself to look away from Sager. Her diversion worked only a moment before her eyes returned to him. He had made a startling transformation. His hard jaw was clean shaven. He wore a fresh pair of tan trousers and a white linen shirt with a black bolo tie and his black vest. Cleaned up, he looked even more hard-edged, she thought with a strange catch in her breath. He arched a brow at her extensive perusal. She had the grace to blush, but couldn't quite swallow her smile.

"Something wrong, Rachel?"

She shook her head and looked away, reminding herself how misplaced her feelings for him were. The waiter came by, and Rachel absently gave her order. Forcing her mind to a different topic, Rachel thought about her father and his ranch. A familiar blend of fear and anticipation swirled within her. What if what Aunt Eunice had said about him was true? What if he really hated her, just as her mother's family said they did?

"What's my father like, Sager?"

A muscle bunched in Sager's jaw. The waiter brought the whiskey he'd ordered, and he took a deep sip. He looked down into his glass and shrugged. Old Jack was an ornery old bastard. Quick to bite off your head and the first to defend a man he thought wronged. "He's good at running the ranch," he answered vaguely.

"I wish I'd grown up at the Crippled Horse," she admitted quietly. "I used to make up stories about living on the Crippled Horse from events he wrote in his letters to me."

"Letters, huh?" Sager wondered just who had written to Rachel all those years. Probably Fletcher. Old Jack had depended on him not just as his range boss, but as his business manager, too. There was talk, some years back, about Fletcher and Old Jack forming a partnership, but the land Old Jack needed to widen his operations was bought up by his neighbor, Sid Taggert. Eventually, the talk of a partnership fizzled out.

"Rachel, your pa can't read or write. He didn't write them. Any of them."

She gave him a wan smile. "My aunt used to make me read his letters aloud in front of my uncle and cousins so that they could laugh at his poor English and ignorant ways." Ways she worked so hard—late into the night, with Master Tidwell to eradicate. To hear that her father hadn't written them, that they weren't even ridiculing the right person, was a bitter truth to absorb. She remembered how desperately she looked forward to those letters, remembered how her uncle would follow her back to her room and give her a tongue lashing about how useless and unwanted she was.

"Once in a while, they let me write back to him. I don't know if they ever posted my letters."

He frowned at her. "I don't believe I like your aunt and uncle."

The waiter brought their food, sparing her from commenting. This was her first normal meal since leaving Fort Laramie, weeks ago. The sight of carrots, green beans, mashed potatoes and a great big steak made Rachel's mouth water. She slathered butter on the fresh yeast rolls, surrendering herself to the delicious tastes.

They ate in silence, and after dinner Sager escorted her to her room. Inside, she lit a lamp while he checked the room, making sure she would be safe without him for a short while. The balcony doors were locked. The door between their rooms was locked.

He turned and looked at her. The way she stood in front of the single lamp lit a halo around her head. Without a doubt, she was the finest woman he had ever known. There was no fear in her prairie-sky eyes as she calmly regarded him. When her gaze lowered to his lips, Sager's chest locked up on him. He took a step nearer her. He wanted to touch her, wanted to feel the silken skin of her cheek, wanted to pull the pins out of her hair and wrap it around his fist.

He made the mistake of looking at the bed, letting his mind torture him with a vision of Rachel lying beneath him, naked, writhing, loving him. God, he wanted her. They'd spent three nights together. Three nights of sheer, sleepless torture, his unsated hunger for her growing each night. He looked at her, saw a blush heat her face. She must be a god-damned mind reader. *Don't touch her*, he warned himself.

"Rachel—" he rasped. It was hard to speak with his groin stiffening up. She looked up at him, soft and open. "Rach, lock the door after me. Don't let anyone in, not even me." He pivoted and walked to the door, exhibiting a force of will that shocked himself.

"Where are you going?"

"I want to go find that fellow we ran into earlier and see what all that excitement was about this afternoon. I won't be late." He left her room and took a couple of steps into the hallway, waiting until he heard her lock the door. When she did, he released the breath that he'd been holding and started toward his room to change out of his fancy clothes. It was good they would get to the Crippled Horse tomorrow.

Rachel looked forward to sleeping in the comfort of a real mattress, not a bed of prickly weeds on the rock-hard ground. It was a small compensation for not getting to sleep with Sager. She washed her face, brushed her teeth, braided her hair into its long nighttime braid, and donned her white cotton nightgown—the same one she wore the night she met Sager.

She turned out the lamp and slipped between the covers, her entire body melting into the mattress. Every way she turned was softness and more softness. In no time at all, she was fast asleep.

So deep was her sleep that she never knew men had entered her room until a meaty hand closed over her mouth. She screamed against the barrier across her mouth as her blanket was torn off her, but her cry had the volume of a whimper. *Uncle Henry! No!* How had he found her? Someone was holding her down. How many men were there? She kicked and struggled, banging the headboard against the wall to get Sager's attention, though she didn't know if he was back yet.

Two men flipped her over and shoved her face down into her pillow. They pulled her arms behind her, binding her hands. She couldn't breathe. Her head was burning. Air. She needed air. The fight began to go out of her just as she was turned back over.

"Get the blanket. We'll roll her up in that."

One man ran his finger over her breasts. "Too bad the boss wants her."

"Wouldn't mind seein' to my needs along the way. What he don't know won't get us killed," another gruff voice said. They rolled Rachel side over side until the blanket was wrapped completely about her. Then one of the men hoisted her over his shoulder and started for the balcony doors. Rachel realized they hadn't thought to gag her. She opened her mouth, trying to shout, to scream, anything, but to no avail. Her throat was dry with terror. She tried again.

Sam's Saloon was a large room, raw in its appointments except for the elaborately carved oak bar and a matching back bar with a long, elegantly framed mirror. The large front windows had panels of a green material covering the lower half and large, arching letters that read SAM'S SALOON AND RESTAURANT in the upper half. A few lanterns cast a dim yellowish light about the room. Several square and round tables were scattered haphazardly around the gritty floor, some occupied by cowboys.

Sager had just ordered a beer when a strange itch

took root between his shoulder blades. Looking in the mirror, he could see no one stood behind him. He turned around cautiously, seeking the cause of his nervous tension. A man sat in a dark corner, leaning his chair against the wall, braced on its two back legs. Even in the dim light, Sager could see he grinned at him.

For a minute, time peeled away. Sager was thrown back to the last days of war and the final counter-raids against the various groups of bushwhackers his small unit fought along the Missouri border with Kansas.

"Julian McCaid!" Sager laughed, going over to greet his old friend. He hadn't changed much in the two years since they had last seen each other. His straight brown hair was still short. His dark eyes had the same haunted look, too aged for a man not yet thirty. His clothes were stylish and well pressed. Only McCaid could look like he had a valet out here in the frontier.

Hell, he probably did.

"What brings you out here?" Sager asked as he vigorously shook hands with his former lieutenant.

"You convinced me during the war that this was the place to run livestock. I bought Hell's Gulch." The barkeep brought Sager's beer over and both men sat down. Sager was shocked. Hell's Gulch was a prime strip of land, five thousand acres of rolling grassland fed by several year-round creeks. If that land had been on the northern side of Defiance, Sager knew Sid and Old Jack would be fighting over it.

"What are you running? Angus? Herefords?"

"Sheep."

Sager cursed. "You like living dangerously, don't

you, McCaid? Anyone tell you raising sheep in cow country's a dangerous prospect?"

McCaid grinned. Sager knew that look. His friend rarely met a challenge he couldn't overcome, and he had a golden touch when it came to business investments.

"American wool suppliers have a wide-open market," McCaid explained. "Importers can't compete with domestic prices or quality. It looks to be a profitable investment. Besides, I'm keeping the critters on my land. I'm putting up fencing."

Sager shook his head, fast becoming convinced he was looking at a dead man. "Hell's Gulch is surrounded by open range. Some folks won't be happy about you fencing off those creeks," Sager warned.

"If they wanted to use the land, they should have bought it." McCaid leaned forward, looking at Sager intently. "I could use a foreman. You interested in working for me?"

Sager considered the offer, briefly. It would let him be near Rachel, close enough to make sure she was doing okay. Close enough to run into her and Logan, often, as they built their life together. Close enough to see her pregnant with Logan's children.

Close enough to die slowly.

"No thanks, McCaid. I have a rustler problem I'm dealing with for the Taggerts and Douglases, then I guess it's back to California for me."

McCaid looked at him curiously. "You work things out with Sid?"

"Not yet." *Not goddamned likely either*, he thought.

They both took sips of their beers. In the middle of the war, living hour to hour, Sager would never have thought he'd be sitting with McCaid at Sam's Saloon, catching up on the past years.

"You ever hear from Gage?" McCaid asked.

"Ran into him a couple of times." Sager grinned. "He's turned vigilante—'Avenger' they call him. He helps the good people of frontier towns remove their criminal elements. He's making a decent living at it. I told him to put me in his will, 'cause it ain't a job he's gonna retire from." He exchanged a look with McCaid. "He never did get married again."

McCaid shook his head. "It was a shame about his wife. Some of us never can put our guns down, and I can't say I blame him." He looked at Sager. "How about you? You planning on settling down?"

Sager looked at his beer. He hadn't thought of his future, not beyond what he was doing this summer, anyway. And now he needed to come up with another way of hitting the Taggerts. Hell, he would never be free of them. He should just let it go. Move on with his life. "I guess, when I find the right woman and a spit of land."

"Looked like you had the right woman this afternoon."

"That's Old Jack's daughter. I'm taking her out to the Crippled Horse. She's gonna marry Logan."

"Ah, that explains why you were holding hands with her."

Sager gave McCaid a hard look. "We ran into one of the rustlers working the Crippled Horse and the Circle Bar. Made her nervous."

"Too bad. Thought you looked happy. Can't say as I've ever seen you happy." McCaid leaned back in his chair. "So who's the rustler?"

"Tom Beall. I know it's him, but I can't prove it

yet." Sager sipped his beer. "What about you? You ever get married?"

He shook his head. "Marriage is not for me. I can't seem to pick just one woman. Some things don't change, I guess. I'm still lifting skirts, you're still angry, and Gage is still trying to make the world right."

Sager let that comment go. McCaid could be like a dog with a bone sometimes. He didn't want to talk about Rachel. "How long are you in town for?" he asked McCaid.

"I'll be at the ranch for the summer—should head home around the end of August. If you need help with your rustlers, let me know. I've got two dozen boys building a bunkhouse and a cookhouse. I'm not running sheep until the fences are finished. If you need us, we could make a quick run up north."

"I hope it won't come to that, but you may be hearing from me. You should come by anyway. I'm staying at the Crippled Horse."

"So what are you doing prowling through saloons when you've got a sweet young thing waiting for you back at the hotel?"

"That sweet young thing isn't waiting for me. I came out to find one of Beall's men, see what I can learn about what his boss is up to."

"Is he in here?" McCaid asked.

Sager had been monitoring the patrons, but hadn't yet seen Hank. "No."

McCaid flashed a hard-edged smile that Sager knew meant he was looking forward to rounding up trouble. "Let's go find him." He tossed a few coins on the table, then came to his feet and settled his hat on his head. "There's a couple more watering holes in this town. He's bound to be in one of them."

Sager followed him out to the street. "Finding people was never your strong point."

"True enough, but dealing with them once you found them was." McCaid grinned at Sager, but then looked thoughtful. "Too bad we don't have Gage with us. We could use a sharpshooter."

"I don't want to kill him, McCaid. I just want to talk to him. Beall may not be the only one benefiting from the rustling. I want them all." This was the least he could do for Rachel's father, who had taken him in all those years ago. He intended to settle Old Jack's rustler problem before he moved on.

A commotion further down the boardwalk drew their attention. Several men were standing around a wagon. A couple men were mounted, their horses making agitated half steps. As they watched, someone tossed a heavy bundle down to two men in the wagon.

"Sagerrr!!!"

Sager distinctly heard Rachel's muffled bellow. The hairs lifted on his neck as he realized the heavy bundle was Rachel. He ran toward the men, yanking the nearest one off his horse and decking him with a solid punch to his face. Several more men joined the fray, and Sager was glad he'd run into McCaid, who was laying out men with the pent-up fury of a baited bear. McCaid enjoyed a fistfight like no other man Sager knew.

Sager swung up into the saddle, intending to go after the wagon, which was already leaving town, when he caught sight of a man on the balcony shooting wildly into the melee. Sager drew his Colt and shot him, but didn't stay long enough to see him hit the ground. Seconds later, he heard a rider coming

fast behind him and was relieved to find it was
McCaid closing the distance between them.

The moon, though waning, gave off plenty of
light—an advantage and disadvantage; it made their
quarry good targets, but made him and McCaid
good targets as well. Sager could see three men in
the wagon, one in the back, two on the front bench,
all with guns. He picked off the one in the back, but
he missed his next shot as a searing pain cut through
his side. McCaid's two shots found their marks,
however, and Sager raced forward to stop the now
driverless wagon, leaping from his horse to the front
of the wagon.

He took the reins from the limp hand of the dead
driver and drew the horses to a stop, then set the
break. Blood pounding in his ears, he leapt over the
seat into the back where a blanket-wrapped bundle
lay silent and unmoving, half covered by another
dead kidnapper. Sager lifted the body by the neck of
his coat and the seat of his pants and threw him off
the wagon.

"Rach, I'm here. It's gonna be okay." He mumbled
words of reassurance, words of nonsense, aware only
of his need to have her hear him. He pulled the
blanket away from her face, wanting to assure himself that she was fine. Alive. Breathing. Her eyes were
open and staring. He palmed her cheek, turning
her to face him, cold fingers of dread gripping his
chest. When she blinked, he drew a ragged breath.

"Let's get you out of this blanket. I need to roll
you over," he said, as he did just that, twice. He cut
the bindings around her wrists.

"Are you hurt?" he asked, running his hands down
her arms, her legs. He saw no blood, no visible

wounds. Once she was free of the blanket, he helped her to a sitting position.

"Rach, honey, talk to me. Are you hurt?" He studied her pale face in the dim light as he brushed her hair back behind an ear. He didn't like how silent she was. Afraid she was in shock or perhaps had suffered a blow to her head, he drew her up to her knees, pulling her against himself as he wrapped his arms around her. He cupped the back of her head, his fingers gently kneading her skull, checking for an injury. Rachel's arms slowly moved up to close about his neck. She held him tight, then tighter. Their bodies were so close that Sager felt her gasp as her tension finally broke free.

"Hold me," she ordered in a fierce whisper.

"I've got you."

"Don't ever let me go."

Sager squeezed his eyes shut. "You'll be home tomorrow. You'll be safe there. Your father has plenty of ranch hands at his spread; not a one of them will let any harm come your way." He pulled back to study her face and saw the wet path of her tears. He wiped them off one of her cheeks.

"Rach, are you hurt?" She shook her head. He'd phrased the question badly. "Did they touch you?" She nodded. Sager swallowed an oath. "Did they— did they do more than touch you?"

"Yes," she whispered, burying her face in his neck. "They wrapped me up in that blanket and threw me off the balcony. Why, Sager? Why would they do that? Who were they?"

Sager sighed, relieved that was the extent of her injuries. "Enemies of your father." Just then Rachel noticed McCaid as he tied the horses he and Sager had ridden to the back of the wagon. She gasped and tensed in Sager's arms.

"It's okay, honey. That's my friend, Julian McCaid. He helped us tonight." Sager exchanged looks with McCaid over Rachel's head as he arranged the kidnappers' blanket loosely around her shoulders. McCaid climbed into the front of the wagon and threw the body of the driver to the ground, then took up the reins and gently turned the horses around. Sager settled Rachel next to him, his arm around her shoulders, his hand holding one of hers.

Rachel watched as they rolled away from the bodies of the three criminals. "Are we just going to leave them here? They need to be buried." she asked.

"If they were worried about their souls, they would have taken up another line of business a long time ago."

"Sager, it's not Christian!"

He arched a black brow at her. "I'll have someone from town come out for them. I don't want the bastards anywhere near you." A chill rattled through her, but Rachel didn't argue further.

The gunfire must have awakened half of the little town, for at least a dozen people stood gathered about, talking anxiously as the wagon pulled up in front of the hotel. Sheriff Kemp was there, with a couple of his ramrods. Sager climbed out, then he lifted Rachel down.

"What are you boys doing, raising a shit-storm like this? Thanks to you, I got dead men all the hell over town," the sheriff bellowed.

"There's a few more outside of town, too, you better add to the count," Sager answered, wrapping a protective arm around Rachel's shoulders. "This is Old Jack Douglas's daughter. Someone tried to kidnap her tonight." That announcement took the air out of the sheriff's lungs. A wave of chatter washed through the crowd.

"Sager, get her inside," Julian suggested. "I'll deal with this." He watched Sager lead Rachel into the hotel. "What kind of town are you running here," he turned on the sheriff, "where a gang of thugs can steal a decent woman from her bed? Makes me think I should reconsider buying Hell's Gulch."

The sheriff leaned toward him, eyes narrowed. "Maybe you should. It ain't right that a redskin breed like you own land around here. I wouldn't cry to see you go."

Julian grinned. It wasn't a friendly grin. "Maybe you should do your job and find the bastard who ordered this kidnapping. You wouldn't like her father to call in the marshals now, would you?"

Sheriff Kemp turned away with a muttered curse. He ordered several men to collect the bodies and directed the onlookers to go about their business. Julian rolled his shoulders, working out a knot that had settled there. He stepped into the hotel and slowly climbed the stairs to his room, thinking about how Sager looked as he checked Rachel over in the back of the wagon. Julian had had to turn away.

Perhaps she was intended for Logan, but Sager had already lost his heart to her.

Chapter Eleven

Sager paused outside the door to Rachel's room. "Maybe you'd rather sleep in my room tonight," he offered. "I'll use your room." Rachel greedily accepted. He opened the door and crossed the room to light a lamp on the bedside table. Heading toward her old room, he paused briefly to pick up his saddlebags. Rachel was standing in the middle of the room, arms crossed about herself, her face bloodless.

He stopped in front of her and couldn't help but smooth a lock of hair from her face. "Are you all right?"

She nodded.

"Want me to leave the door between our rooms ajar? If you need me, just call."

Again, she nodded. He leaned forward and kissed her forehead, confused by the feelings she stirred up in him.

Rachel drew a ragged breath. Her mind raced through everything that had happened since she first went to sleep—the men waking her, covering her mouth, touching her body, wrapping her tightly in that blanket. It made her feel filthy. Her night-gown was torn and soiled and stank of the dead men and the filthy wagon. She poured fresh water from the pitcher into its bowl, then ripped off her night-gown and scrubbed at her face and hands and body. She dried herself off with a towel, then realized she had nothing else to wear—all her things were still in her old room.

She turned toward the bed and caught sight of Sager's dress shirt looped over the back of a chair. She held it up to her nose, drawing in the scent of him she'd learned so well on this trip—sunshine and horses and man. It was a smell she would never forget. She pulled his shirt on over her head, reveling in the indecency of wearing something of his, of feeling his shirt against her bare skin. She had to roll up the sleeves, but otherwise it was a good fit, falling almost to her knees. It was made of cotton, and the fabric was soft with age. Without its stiff collar, it was wonderfully comfortable.

She climbed into Sager's bed and pulled the covers up to her chin. She felt his essence all about her in the room. He'd left his saddlebags on the table against the wall. His coat lay across the foot of his bed. She rolled onto her side, then rolled back. She tried to sleep, but couldn't relax. She wished Sager was with her, lying on his bedroll, an arm's reach away. She sat up with a sigh. How had she grown so dependent upon him in these few short weeks?

A quiet knock sounded on the door between their rooms.

Rachel's heart lurched, but her mind quickly reassured her that kidnappers wouldn't knock. "Sager?" she asked to make sure.

"Yes."

She pulled the covers up over her folded legs and called, "Come in."

Sager pushed the door open. She looked at him and he at her. His lamp was on, too; he must be as restless as she was, she thought. He leaned against the doorjamb. He still had his trousers on, and he had put a shirt on, but hadn't buttoned it.

"Can't sleep?" he asked. She shook her head. He looked at the floor and pushed a bare toe against a warped floorboard. It creaked beneath the pressure. "Want some company?"

Rachel smiled. That was exactly what she wanted. Desperately. "Yes."

Dousing his lamp, he then snatched up a bottle of whiskey and sat cross-legged on the foot of the bed, facing Rachel. He saw her pull her blanket higher about her folded legs, putting a barrier between them on the small bed. She was too pale for his liking, the stress of the night's events still heavy on her mind.

He held up the whiskey bottle, offering it to her. "I don't have any glasses, but I'm thinkin' a sip or two might do you some good." She looked at the bottle, and he thought for a second she was going to accept, but she shook her head.

He tilted the bottle back and took a generous swallow, watching her as the whiskey warmed his throat. A frown wrinkled her brow, and her teeth pulled nervously at her bottom lip as she stared at the blanket covering her legs.

"Take a sip. Doctor's orders."

"I'd best not," she said, absently adjusting the blanket over her knees. She wrapped her arms about her shins and held on with a white-knuckled grip.

"It isn't evil, you know."

She met his gaze. "I didn't say it was."

He took another swallow. "You didn't need to. It was in your look."

"That's nonsense."

"Is it? Prove it. Take a sip." He arched a brow at her, his look victorious.

"Oh, very well." She reached for the bottle. The lip of the bottle was wet where his lips had been. She tilted it back and filled her mouth with the fiery liquid. It was bitter and disgusting, but she forced it down her throat, then handed the bottle to Sager with an ill-concealed grimace.

"Good, isn't it?" He looked at the amber liquid fondly. "I bet it was aged a whole seven days before it was bottled."

She smiled at that. "They must have known no amount of aging could cure that gutrot."

Sager watched her. A grin tilted one side of his mouth before he took another swallow. "Rotgut, you mean." He handed the bottle back to her.

"No, thank you. I've had my fill."

"With one sip? I thought you easterners were made of sterner stuff."

"We are. That's why I've the strength to forgo the pleasure." That lopsided grin lit his face again and stole her breath away. He saluted her with the bottle, then tilted it back. Rachel watched his throat work as he took a couple of swallows. As he lowered the bottle she dropped her eyes and began fidgeting with the blanket over her legs again. She suddenly felt alone. Terribly, achingly, alone. Were it not for Sager, her father's hired desperado, she would be completely at the mercy of men like those who had tried to kidnap her tonight. Men like Hector Ramon.

What was she doing here, in the wilds of this god-forsaken Territory? She wished this trip was already over. She had defended herself against a rabid wolf and stood by herself against the wagon train women and fought off salivating lumbermen. And now she was alone in a run-down hotel with a whiskey-guzzling gunman whose arms she knew, whose kiss she craved. The knot in her stomach was proving useless against the tide of tears that threatened to flood her eyes. Sager leaned forward and set the bottle at her feet. She eyed it a moment. It was cheap whiskey, to be sure. But if she had enough of it, it might have a calming effect. She lifted the bottle and took a gentle sip.

A silence fell between them. It should have been awkward but it was nice, rather like a benevolent presence. Rachel studied Sager as he lay across the foot of the bed. He was a handsome man, she decided, but not in the parlor-room fashion of her uncle or his friends. She eyed the generous expanse of male flesh that his unbuttoned shirt exposed. He was rugged. Primal.

She sipped the whiskey again—twice—then handed him the bottle. She felt awkward suddenly, gawky like an adolescent. She wanted him to hold her, warm her. Make her feel safe. Yet nothing in his demeanor showed he was even interested in her. Had their time together meant nothing to him?

"So tell me, Sager—exactly what kind of woman is your kind?"

Sager choked on the whiskey he was swallowing. He looked her over, seeing her tousled blond hair falling about her shoulders. Her lips were full and seemed to ache for a kiss. His kiss. Her eyes, in the dim light of the single lamp, looked like the morning sky before the sun brightened it. He realized, with an unsettling shock, she was very much the kind of woman he liked.

"Women with long legs," he answered tersely, avoiding a direct response. He should get the hell out of here.

She turned and lifted her legs free of the blankets. His shirt was hiked up to her upper thighs. She pointed her toes as she straightened her knees. "I have long legs."

Sager couldn't tear his eyes away from her. How much whiskey had she taken? Her legs were indeed long and shapely. Months of walking and riding had hardened and toned them into instruments for a man's delight. He could almost feel them locked around his hips, could feel what it would be like to pump into her.

Jesu, this was torture. He didn't want her, he reminded himself. He didn't want any woman like her. He'd shied away from the genteel sort ever since his time at his father's house, under Cassandra's sweet, mothering care.

"Not bad," he admitted. "But I like a woman who knows what to do with a man and isn't afraid of doing it."

"Oh," Rachel said, deflated. She folded her legs in front of her, ignoring the blanket she'd hidden under before. There was no need to hide. Sager had no interest in her, whatsoever. Too bad, she thought. He really did have wonderful lips.

She leaned forward to take the bottle away from him. Maybe he didn't want her in the way a man wants a woman, but he had wanted to keep her company tonight. And he had come after her. She was safe with him. She didn't have to perform for him as she did for her aunt and uncle. She had to be sweet and docile and demure for them.

Her fingers were about to close around the cool glass of the bottle, when a strange urge overcame her. She reached past the bottle and touched his stomach. His muscles contracted reflexively, and she smiled at his reaction as she drew her fingers up his chest, along his neck, over his Adam's apple, over his chin, to his lips.

"I like your lips," she said, tracing them with a single finger. "I like the way they look. I like the way they feel." She leaned forward and pressed her lips to his ever so gently. "I like the way they taste," she said, her voice deep and whiskey-modulated as she tasted his lips with her tongue.

Sager felt his body tremble with the resistance he imposed on it. Rachel was on all fours before him. The top buttons of his shirt were undone, and he gazed hungrily at the heavy silhouette of her breasts her open collar revealed. He groaned. He was only a man. God help him, she was offering herself to him. He could feel her heat, her need.

His arm came up around her shoulder, and he buried his hand in her hair, cupping the back of her head as he crushed her lips to his. He thrust his tongue into her mouth, trying to satiate his infinite need to possess her. He felt no resistance from her, no hesitation. He broke the kiss to taste her lips, one and then the other.

"Do you like my lips?" she asked, foolishly seeking a compliment.

"Yes." His voice was hoarse with need.

She frowned down at him. "You like my legs, and you like my lips. Why don't you like me?"

Sager swallowed hard as his passion-drugged brain grabbed the first explanation he could think of. "It's bad form to become attached to the boss's daughter."

She looked so crestfallen that he could have kicked himself. Her lips were still damp from his kisses. He couldn't breathe, for wanting her. He sat up and put the whiskey bottle on the floor.

"Sager?" Slowly he turned to look at her. "Hold me."

He groaned, unable to resist her seduction. His arms came around her waist, and he pushed her back against the mattress. He laid half next to her, half on her, his leg twined with hers. He kissed her neck, the vee at the base of her throat, her collarbone. He felt her hands on his chest, felt her palms against his nipples. She pushed the shirt off his shoulders. He moved his hand over her waist, over her ribs, up to her breast. God, she was perfect. Soft and womanly, and so damned hot. He went to unbutton her shirt and felt her stiffen beneath him.

"Oh, good heavens," she gasped, staring over his shoulder at her hand. "I'm bleeding!"

Sager looked at her hand, then cursed and sat up, moving his shirt to look at his side. "It's not you—it's me," he growled.

Rachel lifted aside his shirt to get a better look at the source of the blood on her hand. She found the fallen wad of cloth he'd packed against his side. "What happened?"

"One of the bastards' bullets tonight. My bandage didn't hold."

The blood drained from Rachel's face as she had a good look at the gaping wound just above Sager's hip. It was at least four inches long, and narrow but deep. "You need stitches for this!"

He took hold of her wrist, stopping her examination. "Leave it," he ordered.

She met his eyes. "No. I'm going to find a doctor."

"The only doctor in Defiance is the damned barber. Just leave it. I'll be fine in a few days."

"You'll be dead in a few days."

"Then stitch it yourself."

Rachel blanched again. "Sager! I can't even skin the rabbits you bring me."

"Then leave it, Rachel."

"I can't." She frowned at him, her eyes filled with foggy determination. She turned the lamp up and left the bed to wash her hands. She fetched the sewing kit she kept with her toiletries from the saddlebag in her room and gathered up extra linens, the bowl and pitcher, and the bottle of whiskey. She laid her tools within easy reach and faced him again as she sat on the edge of the bed.

"All right. I'm ready." She met his look. Thank God she'd had the whiskey to fortify herself; she surely couldn't do this sober. "You'll have to take off your shirt." She busied herself with disinfecting the needle and thread with the whiskey while he shrugged out of his shirt. Then she held a cloth against his side to blot the whiskey she sprinkled over his wound. "I'm sorry. I know this hurts." He said nothing, his look stoic. He seemed prepared for what would come. His stoicism gave her strength. She took a deep breath, then began stitching.

She moved through the task in a blur. Her fingers felt numb—she was terrified that her sluggish movements hurt him worse. Though it took only moments, each second felt like an hour. When she finished, she sat back and drew a ragged breath. She wiped the hair from her face with the back of her bloodied hand.

"There. It's done," she said as she dampened a folded square of linen with whiskey and held it against his side. She secured it with another band that she wrapped about his waist, then went to wash her hands and put her tools away.

She was back a short moment later and stood facing him, hesitant and pale. Sager smiled at her. He lifted the covers on her side of the bed, wanting to tuck her away, safe from his touch.

"C'mon. Turn out the light." She doused the light, then climbed beneath the covers. Moonlight poured in through the window, washing the bed with a crystalline light. Sager laid on his good side atop the covers and looked over at her. Her eyes were enormous in the darkened room, her face whiter than white. He felt compelled to soothe her, to calm her frayed nerves. He leaned over and kissed her forehead.

"Thanks for the needlework, Rach. But next time I get hurt," he said with a grin, "remind me to stay in my own room."

"That's not funny, Sager. You needed the stitches."

"I wasn't joking." He laughed grimly, but then frowned down at her. "Are you crying?" Her answer was a quick nod. "Why?"

"Because—" A breathy gasp cut through her words. "Because I was sleeping and they came in and I thought Uncle Henry had found me but it wasn't him and they threw me off the balcony and—and I thought I was going to die and then a dead man was lying against me and—" A sob broke her litany. "And you got hurt and then I hurt you worse and—"

A quiet dread sliced through Sager as he unraveled her words. He shifted his hold on her so that he could look at her face. "What do you mean you thought Uncle Henry had found you?"

Her eyes widened and she buried her face in his shoulder. *No.* She couldn't tell him.

"What did that bastard do to you?" Sager held her even tighter. He pressed his lips to her temple, felt her shallow breathing. "Aw, honey, what happened?"

"My father had written that he wanted me to come out here. He said he'd made arrangements with Captain Norbeck. My uncle was furious. He came to my room that night. He said he'd waited long enough. He said no one was going to take me from him."

Sager felt rage burn through him. Helpless, impotent fury.

"He told me he was taking the family for a week to a party at someone's country estate, that when he returned he would make sure I paid my debt to him. He left me home because he feared I would run away or seek help from his friend's staff.

"While they were gone, another letter came from my father. This one had a bank draft in it for the trip. I made his man of business cash it for me. And I left. I bought tickets on various stages to get to Missouri, then rented a room until Captain Norbeck came to St. Louis."

"You went alone to St. Louis?"

"I had to. I couldn't chance being home when my uncle returned. I wore my uniform from my aunt's house. I said I was a widow, that my husband died of complications from wounds he suffered during the war. People were surprisingly helpful."

"Your aunt made you wear a uniform?"

"I wasn't raised as a lady, Sager. I was raised as a servant. They weren't happy they had to take on my mother's leavings. They made me work for my room and board."

Sager touched her cheek. "I think you may be the bravest person I have ever met."

She shook her head. "I'm afraid of everything."

He smiled. "And being afraid, you still forged ahead. If that ain't courage, well, I guess I don't know what is."

Rachel drew a shaky breath. She was beginning to feel she was on the brink of a new life. It might just be possible that she had stepped out of the shadow of her old life. For good.

A minute passed, thick with electricity as Sager gazed down at her. "Let's try to get some sleep, Rachel," he suggested, his voice strained.

"Good night, Sager." Rachel liked the way his arms felt about her. She was warm and safe, and very glad they had this one last night together. He continued to slowly stroke her back though his eyes were closed, and he looked as if he were trying to sleep. Her knee was between his. He hadn't buttoned his shirt, and she ran her hand up his smooth chest, against his heated skin. Her eyes lifted to his.

"Sager?" she asked, her hand coming to a stop on the corded column of his neck. "Is the pain terrible?"

"Yes," he rasped. "I'm on fire."

She winced. "What can I do to help?"

"Lie very, very still."

Rachel folded her arms between their bodies. She shut her eyes and ordered herself to sleep, but his heart was hammering against her hand. She breathed in his scent—tonight, a mixture of leather, whiskey and gunpowder. He moved forward slightly, and she lifted her face closer to his. His lips brushed across her eyebrow, the bridge of her nose, her closed eyes. She tilted her head, bringing her mouth in contact with his. His lips were gentle against hers, a pressure that contradicted the relentless pounding of his heart against her hand.

"This can't be helping," she whispered against his lips.

"Shhh. It's exactly what I need," he said, his mouth opening against hers.

Rachel's hand started a slow migration upward, across his chest, pausing over his nipple. It was hardened and teased her palm. She caressed the ridge of his collarbone and curved her arm about his neck. His kiss deepened, his tongue possessing her. He leaned over her, pressing her beneath his weight as his hand lowered across her rib cage, made the curve of her waist, and cupped her hips, molding her to himself.

Sager drew air into his lungs through clenched teeth as he struggled to calm blood pounding through his body, heating his groin. This was not going to happen tonight. It was not going to happen ever with her.

"Rach," Sager spoke stiffly, "my side's killing me," he said, blaming the pain that flamed his body on the wrong part of his anatomy. "Just lie here—lie still." He pulled her up against his chest, cradling her head on his arm as they lay on their sides. "Tomorrow starts in a few short hours. We'd best get some sleep." He closed his eyes and concentrated on making his breathing sound regular and deep. He waited for Rachel to doze off so that he could relax—it was the best he could hope for. He'd get no sleep this night.

God knew he'd had precious little since he met her. His stupid plan had backfired. He was the one who would be hurting knowing she was in another's arms when she married Logan.

They'd goddamn won again.

Chapter Twelve

Sager slammed through the double doors of the saloon and strode boldly toward the stairs to the second level. It was barely five o'clock in the morning. Rachel still slept back at their hotel room. An elderly man was behind the bar, cleaning up after last night's patrons.

"Hey, you! We ain't open yet!" he growled at Sager.

"That's good," Sager called over his shoulder as he took the stairs two at a time, "'cause I don't want any witnesses!" The man hurried after him. Sager reached the upper balcony and looked at the ancient barkeep. "I wouldn't, old man," he warned. "This could get messy."

The barkeep paused halfway up the steps and glared at Sager, before a look of resignation came to his eyes. He shook his head and went back down to his waiting chores.

Sager opened three doors before finding the room that housed Hank Ketchum, the man they had seen yesterday on the boardwalk. He was in bed with his purchased woman. Sager walked inside and looked at the two people asleep on the bed for a long moment before kicking the door shut. They woke abruptly. The woman gasped and drew the sheet up to her chin. Hank lunged across her for the pistol resting on the night table, but the sound of Sager's gun being cocked stopped him midreach.

"Go ahead and try," Sager suggested cheerfully. "I've come to give Tom Beall a message. I reckon he'll take my meaning whether you give it to him or you *are* the message."

Hank leaned back against the headboard. He looked at the woman in bed with him. "Get out," he barked at her. She rose naked from the bed and slipped into her wrap, then hurried through the door, eyeing Sager all the while. Hank stifled a loud yawn. "All right, breed. I've had my rude awakening. Now what the hell do you want?"

"I want you to give Beall my condolences." Sager smiled grimly.

The man cocked his head, his eyes showing the first signs of worry. "What are you talking about?"

"Your boss lost four men last night. Lucky you weren't with them. Tell him if he wants to take Rachel, he'll have to send a fucking army. And they'll still have to get through me."

"I don't know what you're talking about, boy."

"That's good, for your sake. But Beall sure as hell will."

Hank's eyes narrowed, and he looked at Sager venomously. "Why did you even come back? Your old man can't stand you and Douglas just uses you."

"I came back to see to business. My business. But I'm going to put you and Beall out of work while I'm here."

"This ain't your fight."

"The Crippled Horse silver in my pocket says otherwise."

"You're making a mistake. Beall's been working the Crippled Horse and the Circle Bar so long now, you can't touch him. He's got a senator and a couple of circuit judges on his payroll. He's so clean, you couldn't pin any dirt on him."

Sager laughed caustically. "Guess that explains why the talk of peace between the two ranches has him all knotted up. If Old Jack and Sid ain't at each other's throats so much, they might have a chance to see what's going on all around them." He smiled neatly at the rapidly paling man and continued, "Nope. I figure Beall's days in this Territory are numbered. If he's smart, he'll start packing up."

"Good morning!" Sager's voice boomed cheerily into Rachel's room. A tray of food clanged as he set it on the nightstand by her bed. Rachel pulled the sheet up over her head to block out the noise and the smell of food.

"Go away," she growled.

"I can't. It's time to hit the trail."

"I'm dead, Sager. I'm not moving. And please quit shouting!"

He pulled the sheet down from her face. "You'll feel better after you eat."

She caught a whiff of the eggs on the tray he'd brought and felt the bile rise in her throat. "Impossible. I'm never eating again."

Sager sat on the edge of her bed. "Well, then you

won't mind if I do, will you? No sense wasting perfectly good food."

She sat up and pulled herself to the far corner of the bed. She was surprisingly dizzy this morning and wasn't ready to jump out of bed and dress just yet. Nor did she want to be too near the breakfast tray Sager held on his lap. "Now I know why they call it gutrot."

"Rotgut," he corrected her.

"Yes. Who was that man with you last night?"

"Julian McCaid. We were in the war together. He's bought a spread on the other side of town."

This was an aspect of Sager that Rachel hadn't thought about—his friends. It made him more human. She tucked it away, saving it for a time when her mind was better able to focus. "Do we have to travel today?" she asked.

"We'd better. Could be there's more men comin' after you. The longer we stay, the more danger we put ourselves in."

The room had quit swimming a little. Perhaps what she needed was something to sop up the alcohol in her system. She reached over and took a roll from his tray, hoping it would ease her nausea.

"Are you looking forward to seeing your pa tonight?"

Rachel found it easier to look at the roll than at the shadows in Sager's eyes. She nodded, but couldn't find the words to pair with the motion. She'd waited eighteen years for this homecoming, but at this moment, she wished it was days away, not hours.

Sager took a sip of his coffee, then set the cup down and fidgeted with its handle. "Yesterday, you said you weren't raised a lady." He lifted his head, the look in his eyes shoving all rational thought from her mind. "Whatever your family may have told you, you are more a lady than anyone I know, Rachel Douglas."

At their midday stop, Rachel was still a bundle of nerves. The hotel had packed a feast for their trip today. The roast beef sandwich she held, under normal circumstances, would have tasted delicious to her. But now it was cold and chewy and did not sit well with the emotions stirring in her stomach. This was their last afternoon on the trail. They were already on Crippled Horse land.

Would she ever see Sager again once they reached the house?

She looked where he stood several feet away, his back to her as he studied the prairie. He had a sandwich in one hand and a tin cup in the other. She was glad he wasn't watching her—she didn't want him to see how nervous she was. The day that she had waited for all her life, the day she was to meet her father, had finally come. Yet all she could think about was how she wished she could stop time and keep them here, together.

"I guess we'll be home before sunset," he commented, turning to face her.

Home. She forced herself to swallow her mouthful of food. Soon she would meet her father, the man who had sent her to live with her aunt and uncle without ever coming to see her. Her invisible parent.

"Sager, where will you be after we reach the Crippled Horse?"

"I'm stayin' at the bunkhouse. For a little while."

"So I will see you, then, once we get there."

"Not much. It ain't my place to socialize with the boss's daughter."

Rachel stared at him. "I thought we were friends."

He gave her a warning look. "Don't put me in a corner."

She studied the hard lines of his face. His beard had started to grow back. The muscle in his jaw tensed as he returned her stare.

"I'd like to know I have a friend where I'm headed."

He frowned. "Rachel, men and women don't make good friends."

"You're wrong."

Friends. It would hurt less if she put a knife in him and twisted it this way and that. "I'm not wrong. I can't do it." He emptied his cup and tossed it down near the basket from the hotel. "Friends ain't gonna work, Rachel," he called over his shoulder as he went to gather up their horses from where they were ground-tethered.

She cleared their picnic site; then Sager brought her horse over. She shut her eyes briefly, trying to compose her emotions before looking at him. When she took her mount's reins from him, her hand brushed his. The touch seared her like a fireball. Her eyes flew to his face. He released the reins and captured her face in both hands as his mouth took hers. The kiss was hard and bruising, his tongue instantly in her mouth, filling her, adding his hunger to her own. She wrapped her free hand around his neck, tightening their embrace. Still, it wasn't enough. She broke the kiss and started it again.

Sager cupped the back of her head with one hand and pulled her against himself with his other. He kissed her chin, her neck, her cheek, before taking her lips again in a long, last kiss.

When it ended, he lifted his head and looked at her, storing away everything about her. Her lips were still moist from his. He touched them with the pad of his thumb as he searched her eyes to see whether she was as shaken as he. His groin hurt; he thought his erection might rip through his pants. His body wanted to finish what they had begun last night. Right now. He forced himself to drag cool air into his lungs as he looked at her passion-dilated eyes.

"You see, Rach, friends ain't gonna work," he said again, this time in a rasping whisper.

Six hours later, they were within sight of the corrals in front of the ranch house. A trellis over the front gate labeled her father's spread the CRIPPLED HORSE.

Rachel pulled even with Sager and broke the silence she'd kept since their lunch stop. "Why did he name his ranch the Crippled Horse?"

"Your pa's favorite horse was the first victim in the fight between him and Taggert." Sager looked at her. "Your ma was the second. Old Jack thinks the stress of the situation killed her. She didn't have what it takes to make it out here. He renamed his spread the Crippled Horse as a memorial. Sort of his vow to never forget."

They drew up near the ranch house. The front door opened and banged shut. Rachel's eyes flew to the porch, to the man who stood there. He stared at her a moment, then looked at Sager.

"You're early. I didn't expect you for another month or two."

"Your daughter was already on her way here." Sager grinned. "Caught up with her outside of Fort Laramie."

Old Jack's brows lifted as his gaze shifted to Rachel. She met his look, then dismounted. Summoning all of her courage, she moved toward her father, studying his face as she climbed the steps. She was shaking. He was as unfamiliar to her as he was familiar. He was smaller than she expected. And older, too. But they shared the same blue eyes, the same small nose.

"Hello, Papa."

He held out his hand. "You can call me 'Jack.'"

She looked at her father's hand. *Jack*. He didn't want to be her papa. She swallowed hard. Rachel took his hand.

"Meet with any trouble on the way in?" Old Jack asked Sager as he pulled her saddlebags from her horse and set them on the porch.

Sager nodded his head. "Hit a patch of it in Defiance. I'll come see you after I get the animals settled."

"Good. Supper's almost on the table, so get one of the boys to help you, then come on in. I'll have Mrs. Biddle put a couple more plates out."

Sager nodded. "I'll just wash up." He led their mounts and the mule away, leaving Rachel alone with her father.

"Well, let me get a look at you, girl." He took a step back. "Damn if you aren't the spittin' image of your mother." His brows lowered. "Did Sager mind himself while he was bringing you in?"

Rachel felt her cheeks color. Her father left her

with his wicked brother-in-law, but worried about
Sager? "I would have been lost without him. He was
every bit the gentleman."

"'Course he was." Old Jack scooped up Rachel's
saddlebags and ushered her inside the house.

Rachel looked around at the dark interior of the
house. Evening was quickly settling into night,
making the light from the kerosene lamps a welcome
gift. Two small windows flanked a massive stone fireplace on one wall. The room's sparse furnishings
were masculine—wooden chairs circling a gaming
table, several benches and other odd seats. The two
padded leather armchairs sitting before the fire
were her father's only vanity in the parlor.

"Mrs. Biddle!" he called to the housekeeper. "Mrs.
Biddle! Where in God's name are you?" he growled
impatiently.

"Yes, Mr. Douglas?" answered a generously propor-
tioned, middle-aged woman. She had a British
accent that was as startling as a river in a desert. Her
salt and pepper hair was pulled loosely into a bun at
the nape of her neck. Time had etched many wrinkles on her face, but her cheeks were still a pretty
pink and her eyes were a sparkling hazel.

"This is my daughter, Rachel."

Rachel watched Mrs. Biddle's haughty expression
warm as her gaze moved from Old Jack. The housekeeper straightened her apron, then came forward
with a smile, arms extended. She stopped in front of
Rachel as though deciding not to hug and went to
shake her hand, but decided that wasn't appropriate
either. In the end, she just grasped Rachel's arms

and smiled at her as though she were the answer to an ancient riddle.

"Welcome, dear! Welcome, indeed!"

Rachel smiled back at the woman, grateful for the warm greeting. "It's very nice to meet you, Mrs. Biddle."

"Look at you now. You must be fatigued near to death. Come with me. I'll help you wash up. Your father's supper can wait another minute."

"I—well—" Rachel hesitated. This was not the welcome she'd expected from the household of a man who had no regard for his daughter. That gave her a bit of hope. Perhaps he didn't know how awful her mother's family was. Rachel sent her father an apologetic half smile as she allowed herself to be sped away toward a long hallway that led through the family's sleeping quarters.

A short while later, washed and dressed in a fresh calico dress, Rachel braved the kitchen. She was pleased with the room's modern conveniences; two stoves stood side by side and were flanked by floor-to-ceiling cupboards. An indoor pump sat right on the counter next to the sink. Her gaze traveled to the long kitchen table around which sat at least two dozen cowhands. One by one, their conversations rolled to a stop, and they looked over at her.

Mrs. Biddle had warned her that her father kept an informal house, that he usually had his cowhands dine with him for meals in the kitchen—when their work permitted. Nonetheless, the sight of so many dusty, hungry, boisterous men seated around the long kitchen table was overwhelming to her. Rachel felt her cheeks begin to burn. In Aunt Eunice's house, she'd striven to be as invisible as possible. It took every ounce of courage she had to not turn and run from the room.

No. She was done running. She squared her shoulders and walked into the room. Her father looked up. He smiled, but it looked more like a grimace.

"Boys," he came to his feet, "this is my daughter, Rachel."

"Hello," she said, offering the men a tentative smile. They lurched to their feet with such speed that those on the far side of the table knocked over their bench. Her father introduced each man, but their names soon ran together.

Rachel moved near the end where her father sat, noticing that the only open spots around it were on either of the two benches, nestled between a couple of men. In order for her to sit down, she would have to lift her skirts to climb over the bench. Her dilemma grew more difficult as they waited for her to settle herself.

The range boss, Fletcher Harrison, was the first to understand the situation. He gave her an irritated look, then slapped the sleeve of the man sitting at the end of the table, next to her father, and motioned for him to move over. The cowboy, named Digger Mathis, turned red all the way to the tips of his wind-burned ears. He grabbed his plate and shoved his way down the table.

"Thank you so much, Mr. Mathis," Rachel said, taking the vacated seat next to him.

"Digger, ma'am. Just Digger."

Mrs. Biddle set the platters of food on the table, the momentary awkwardness forgotten as the ranch hands helped themselves to supper.

The back door opened. Rachel looked up. Sager stood in the doorway. His amber eyes sought and found her first. He was clean-shaven, though his ragged bangs framed his temple. He wore a blue cotton shirt and a worn leather vest that hung just to the tops of his pants. He'd shed his gun belt and looked surprisingly at ease with the men and this new environment.

She couldn't tear her eyes away from him until a lull in the conversation forced her to look away. He strode into the room, his boots echoing against the wooden floorboards. He chose a spot at the opposite side of the table from Rachel and made the others move down the bench.

Rachel smiled at Mr. Harrison and Digger, hoping to cover her reaction to Sager's arrival. Digger was the youngest of the men at supper as far as she could determine. His hair had to be newly trimmed, for a strip of white skin circled the back of his neck, from ear to ear.

"Tell me, Digger, how you came to have such an unusual nickname?" she asked, trying to make conversation.

Mr. Harrison snickered. "He was always rootin' around in the dirt." Rachel looked at her father's range boss, recognizing the derision in his voice, disliking him instantly.

"Were you a gardener before you came to the Crippled Horse?" Rachel asked the boy next to her, hoping to sooth the sting of Mr. Harrison's rudeness.

Digger's embarrassment deepened the color on his windburned face. "No, ma'am. I collect arrowheads."

"Arrowheads! How unusual! Would you show me your collection sometime?"

Digger looked at her, apparently surprised to have caught her attention. "Well, yeah. I guess I could—when it ain't so crazy with calves and branding an' all."

Sager stared down at the boiled dinner he'd placed on his plate, and sighed. He was trying not to listen to the sound of Rachel's voice across the table, trying to ignore the boys' obvious interest in her. He had no claim to her, no right to be possessive. He picked up his fork. Boiled potatoes. Boiled parsnips. Boiled pot roast. This was not the meal he'd looked forward to coming home to. What the hell had happened to the regular cook?

"Where's Ross?" he asked Old Jack once Mrs. Biddle had turned back to the stove.

"Needed him out with the others. Mrs. Biddle's takin' up the slack in the kitchen. Sure am glad you're back. Can use another pair of hands," Jack answered as he took a bite of meat.

Rachel listened as her father discussed ranch news; how many calves were born so far in the season, how many had died, the health of the herd, the quality of the range grass. She hadn't quite finished eating when the range boss jumped to his feet, swallowed the last sip of his coffee, and began calling off names for different watches through the night. The others all gulped their coffee, too, and hurried out the door. The room rapidly emptied, leaving only Sager, Rachel, and her father at the table, and Mrs. Biddle, who was already starting on the dishes.

Rachel folded her napkin and set it by her place. She began gathering plates and dishes from the table. There were no leftovers to deal with—the men were good at not wasting food.

"Rachel, dear, you look dead on your feet. I'll do this. You go get some rest," Mrs. Biddle said as she carried a load over to the counter.

Rachel was shocked. She sent a frightened look toward her father, wondering how he would react to having such a lazy daughter. He wasn't paying any attention at all. "I couldn't do that. This is too much for you."

"Nonsense. I'm used to it—it's been my sad lot in life for longer than I care to remember."

"Well, then, good night, Mrs. Biddle. Papa. Sager." Rachel had decided not to call her father "Jack." He'd been "Papa" to her too long to think of him by another name. Besides, it served to remind him that she was his daughter, like it or not.

The men bid her good night, holding their silence as she left. "I don't know, Sager," Old Jack grumbled. "I think I left her with her old prune-faced aunt too long. I'll probably kick myself for not bringin' her out here earlier."

"At least she's here now." Sager debated telling her father about the truth of her childhood, but decided against it. That was news Rachel would tell him when—if ever—she was ready. "Just go easy on her, Old Jack. She's easily spooked."

"She's my daughter. I think I know how to handle her."

"I don't think you know a goddamned thing about her." Old Jack's crafty eyes narrowed. Sager didn't flinch beneath his scrutiny. "Besides, she'll have you chasing your tail before long."

A smile cracked through Old Jack's customary frown. "Wouldn't that be a sight? Only other person who could ever do that to me was her ma."

Sager sipped his coffee. "So how are those talks with the Circle Bar going? Are they willing to exchange peace for a courtship?"

Old Jack rose and refilled his coffee cup from the pot on the stove. "Taggert's interested. We're talkin'. I don't know about Logan. The boy wants to meet her first. I appreciate your efforts, son. I'll admit, though, to havin' a good bit of curiosity about why you're suggestin' peace with the Circle Bar, given the bad blood between you and Taggert."

"Jack, you hired me to stop the rustling. To do that, you gotta catch the bastards. Regardless of what's between me and Sid, I know he ain't your man."

Jack considered his words a moment. "It sounded like you hit a spot of trouble coming in. What happened?"

Sager grinned. "It appears that word's gotten out about the peace you're negotiating. Seems some folks aren't too encouraged by that news."

"I'll be damned. You might be right after all."

"We ran into one of Beall's men in Defiance. He took it into his mind that the quickest way to put an end to your plans would be to make off with your trump card."

A look of foreboding entered Old Jack's eyes as a frown darkened his face. "If he touched my daughter, I'll string him up by his balls—"

"He didn't. But things with Beall are definitely gonna get mighty interesting."

Rachel looked about her room in the soft predawn light the next morning. It was a large space and, though it held only the bare minimum furnishings needed for utility or comfort, she loved it. It was her own. She was home at last. Before she could become too content, skepticism stepped on her burgeoning happiness. She knew nothing about her father, or his people, or why he finally brought her out here. She'd best not warm up to her new circumstances until she knew what to expect.

Surely her father didn't go to considerable expense to bring her out here just so that he could send her back. It didn't make sense. No, she was here to stay.

Dressing quickly, she straightened her room, then went to help Mrs. Biddle start work in the kitchen. She found clean aprons hanging on a peg inside the pantry and donned one. By the time Mrs. Biddle entered the kitchen, Rachel had coffee brewing and biscuits mixed.

Mrs. Biddle joined her and happily set about putting out dishes, delighted to have assistance. Rachel was busily mixing scrambled eggs when her father wandered in.

"Well, daughter," he said, taking his seat at the head of the table and watching her with that strained expression of his, "it's a busy time you've come to me at. Mrs. Biddle's the only other woman about, but I doubt she will be much company for you, busy as she is. When the roundup is done, we'll have a barbeque to introduce you to the folks in the area. We can get to work on your future then. I'm sorry there's not much for you to do, but I wanted to get to know you a little bit before you go gettin' hitched."

Rachel felt a tremor of shock. Hitched? As in married? Her hand tightened on the wooden spoon she held. *No. Please no.* She looked at him, but didn't answer him. She couldn't answer him.

Her father cleared his throat and slumped a bit in his chair, sending her a dark look. "Logan's the neighbors' son. A good boy. Seems it might be fittin' if you were to let him court you."

Her father didn't want her here. He hadn't summoned her so that they could finally meet. He'd summoned her to give her to a different master.

"Having the Taggert boy court you seems like a good way to end the troubles between us." His expression brooked no argument. "It's a daughter's job to do what her pa tells her. And I'm telling you to let Logan court you."

She heard her father's words as if from a great distance, her soul rejecting them. Sager said she was brave, that she was courageous, because even afraid, she didn't back down. "No." Her dissent was barely whispered. She turned from him to pour the eggs into the hot skillet.

"You got someone else in mind?"

"I'm not ready to get married yet." She glanced quickly at her glowering father. This was a test of sorts; she tensed for his reaction. "And I won't marry a man I don't love."

"Well, I ain't forcing the issue on you, daughter. It's just that it would be fine to have you out here permanent-like."

Their discussion came to an end as the back door opened, admitting a stream of hungry cowboys. Rachel looked up to see Mrs. Biddle smiling at her. She drew a ragged breath, filling her lungs, shocked that she had just confronted her father and was still standing. And he did want her out here.

The hungry cowboys kept Rachel busy cooking eggs and bacon for the better part of the next hour. When things finally slowed down, the boys and her father were gone.

Sager had never come in.

It was much later that morning before Rachel had a chance to get outside and look for Sager. She had to talk to him about her father's marriage plans for her. The Crippled Horse ranch, Rachel discovered, had at its heart a compound consisting of her father's home, a long, low building that housed the cowboys' sleeping quarters, an enormous barn, various other small buildings and several corrals.

Sager was nowhere to be found. When he didn't show up for the next couple of meals, Rachel asked her father about him.

Old Jack sipped his coffee and sat back in his desk chair. Rachel maintained her composure as he regarded her curiously. "He's hunting rustlers."

"Alone?" she asked, alarmed.

"That boy's lived alone longer than he ever lived with anyone. He likes it that way."

"When do you expect him back?"

"Can't say for sure, daughter. He comes and goes as he pleases."

Except for Sager's absence, the days following Rachel's arrival were pleasant for her. Her father's ranch hands treated her with respect and deference. They were loud and boisterous, often making her blush furiously, but no one was belligerent. Her father ran a tight operation, and she realized his men reflected his hardworking temperament.

Mrs. Biddle, glad for Rachel's offer to help, gratefully handed over the most onerous of her duties—the cooking. Rachel found it satisfying to be so desperately needed, and her culinary skills delighted the men.

She lifted the curtain in one of the living room windows. The clouds were breaking up at last, ending two days of cold late spring rains. She rushed from the room, eager to saddle her horse and go for a ride. She threw on her coat and grabbed her hat— an old plainsman one of the cowboys gave her—and hurried outside. The ground was a quagmire from the rain, the mud deeper than she thought. She groaned as she felt it slip over the rim of her ankle-deep boots.

When she looked up, she saw Sager leaning against a corral. She abruptly stopped, paralyzed by the hope that flooded her soul. He smiled at her. She smiled back.

"Rachel! Where are you, daughter?" Hearing her father's voice, she looked back at the house.

"I'm here, Papa! What is it?" She saw him leaning over the porch railing and waved to him.

"I need to speak to you! Come on inside!" He didn't wait for her, but hurried back indoors.

Rachel tried to lift her feet, but succeeded only in working herself into the mud a little deeper. She glanced down at the liquid earth about her and tried again to free her feet. She should never have stopped moving—if she'd just kept walking, the mud wouldn't have cemented her in place.

"Want some help?" Sager called from his safe vantage point.

She gave him a chagrined smile and nodded. His eyes held hers as he strode purposefully over to her.

Barely pausing, he lifted her into his arms and carried her out of the hungry muck. Rachel wrapped her arms around his shoulders.

"Miss me?" he asked, looking down at her.

"More than you would believe."

He smiled down at her, the fine wrinkles at the corners of his eyes spreading his humor across his face. As they shared a look, the humor slowly left his eyes, to be replaced by something dark and desperate. Rachel felt her heartbeat speed up.

"You'll be having some visitors soon," he said.

"Who?"

"The Taggerts."

Rachel sighed. So, he did know about her father's plans. "I can't do it, Sager."

He stopped several feet from the house, Rachel still in his arms. "Your pa has had to look over his shoulder for too many long years. It tends to wear on a man." He paused, studying her eyes. "You're his only means of starting peace talks with his neighbor. You don't have to marry Logan. But Old Jack's about as diplomatic as a polecat. He wouldn't know where to begin rebuildin' the bridges he needs to. He needs you because *you* do."

Listening to Sager, Rachel couldn't help smiling. His reproof showed he wasn't the cold desperado he made himself out to be. And it made meeting Logan a whole lot easier. "You care about my father," she announced, a little stunned.

"Not a hell of a lot."

"Yes, you do."

"No, I don't."

"Well, I'll help him the best way I can, but I'm not marrying Logan."

"That'll have to do, I guess." He deposited her on the steps to the ranch house. Her boots squished beneath her as she made contact with the wooden steps. She stared down in dismay at the mess she was making on the large porch, feeling the cold liquid inside her boots.

"I can't go inside like this! Mrs. Biddle doesn't have time enough to keep up with the house as it is, let alone my dragging half a field in with me." She sat on the highest step, intending to take off her stockings and boots. Unfortunately, the mud went everywhere her skirts did.

"Oh, yuck!" she groaned.

Sager grinned. "Need a hand?" She nodded. "Don't move. I'll be right back." When he returned a moment later, he set a bucket and a rag beside her. He unlaced her boots and pulled them off, dropping them to the ground.

"Lift your skirts for me."

Her gaze met—and locked—with his hard amber eyes.

Chapter Thirteen

Immediately she wished she hadn't looked at him, for the heat in his eyes leapt into her blood. She lifted her skirts away from her calves, complying woodenly with his order. He ran the rag over the hem of her skirt, removing the excess mud. Then he reached up just past her knees and rolled her thick stockings down, baring first one leg, then the other, his touch none too gentle. "I had hoped once I got you home I could quit being your nursemaid," he growled.

She smiled, glad for his banter, relieved to focus on something other than the disturbing undercurrent licking at her nerves. Why couldn't he be the one courting her? Her father seemed to have a high regard for him; surely Old Jack wouldn't stand in their way. "You do have some commendable qualities in that department."

A muscle knotted in Sager's jaw as he dipped the rag into the water and squeezed the excess liquid back into the bucket. "How do you figure?" he asked, though he thought better of it instantly.

"You're not afraid of snakes."

Sager lifted her foot, cradling her heel in his palm while he rinsed the dirt away with the cool water. It should have tickled her and might have been an incredible torture, but his strokes were sure, gentle. Thorough. "And, you've a light touch," she added, her voice dropping to a whisper as she watched his hands. "Not all nursemaids are gifted with that." He looked up at last. She tried to smile at him, but the bleak look that came into his eyes stopped her.

He switched feet, pulling the cloth slowly between each of her toes, from smallest to largest. He propped her foot on his muscled thigh and began washing in small circles about the inside of her ankle. His movements weren't those of a nursemaid. And they weren't simple, cleansing strokes.

Rachel's breath caught in her throat as she realized the tenor of his touch had changed. She shouldn't let herself be absorbed by the feel of his hands against her skin. She heard a sound in the distance—a carriage or a wagon approached.

"Sager—" she started to object, but stopped when he lifted her other foot and placed it against his other thigh, spreading her legs before him.

"Sager," she tried again, tearing her eyes away from the concentric patterns he made against her skin to look at his face. His brows were furrowed. His jaw knotted.

She dipped her fingers in the now-murky water and flicked the drops on his face. "Sager!"

"What?" He frowned at her.

"I think they're here."

He looked over his shoulder briefly, before muttering a curse.

Good grief. She shut her eyes, mortified at the compromising position they were about to find her in. The buggy was still a fair distance down the drive. Surely only the outrider could see them, but hopefully not too clearly. Her life was cursed! She couldn't move without spreading mud over everything, which was why she was in this position to begin with—she had to wait for Sager to finish. She leaned to one side of Sager, venturing another look at the approaching Taggerts, feeling like the street urchin her aunt always called her with her dirty feet naked and exposed for all to see.

She sat back and frowned up at Sager. "Oh, bother!" she growled, wondering how she could extricate herself without losing the rest of her shredded dignity. Sager arched a brow at her. "This is appallingly awkward," she commented. She started to scoot away, careful not to move too suddenly and so make herself appear guilty of a crime. But Sager took hold of her ankles and would not release them.

"Be still. If you put your feet down here, you'll ruin all that I've just done. I'll lift you away from the mud on these boards." He leaned forward and, setting his hands about her waist, lifted her to her feet onto the top step. "I could, of course, carry you inside and really reduce the risk of messing up Mrs. Biddle's cleaning. . . ." he offered with a crooked grin.

Rachel felt the muddy hem of her skirt settle about her ankles and cringed inwardly. "That won't be necessary," she said between clenched teeth, trying to keep her voice from carrying to the approaching Taggerts, whose buggy had stopped at the far end of the porch. She frowned down at her feet,

wishing the gown—soiled as it was—covered them.
She hoped they hadn't seen her sitting with her bare
feet on Sager's thighs.

The Taggerts were near enough now for her to get
a better look at them. There was a slim middle-aged
woman and two tall men, one of whom was her
father's age, the other her age. She studied the
younger of the two men—Logan, she assumed. The
buggy's outrider. Though a shadow from his hat
made it impossible to be certain, he appeared quite
handsome. His stride was lithe, as purposeful as his
father's. She couldn't quite tell what color his hair
was. Though tanned, his face didn't have the weathered look of the elder Taggert. His eyes, she could
tell even from this distance, were a hard, pale color.

The woman with them was dressed in a pink morning gown whose color exactly suited her. Her dark
blond hair was elegantly coifed and only slightly gray-
ing at her temples. Rachel became acutely conscious
of her own bare feet and soiled skirt.

The door behind her opened and snapped shut
as Old Jack joined them on the porch. "Ma'am." He
nodded toward Mrs. Taggert, then faced the men.
"Sid. Logan. Well, I expected you sooner or later. I
want you to meet my daughter. This is—" He looked
over at Rachel and happened to glance down at her
muddy skirt and bare feet. He frowned, the sight
distracting him from his introduction. "Where are
your shoes, girl?"

Rachel was certain she turned four shades of red.
"They had mud on them, and I didn't want to soil
the house, Papa." She turned from him, wanting to
take the attention away from her feet. "I'm Rachel,"
she said, leaning forward to shake hands with the

visitors. Her heart beat nervously. Papa certainly hadn't given them much of a welcome. This feud of his would never end with his open animosity toward them. Rachel smiled politely at the Taggerts. "Won't you come in? I'll have Mrs. Biddle put some coffee on, and we can visit in the parlor."

They looked at her as though she'd just spoken to them in some foreign tongue. Even her papa stared at her with his mouth agape. And Sager just shook his head, his arms folded across his chest. Surely social courtesy was not so alien to these folks that it shocked the wits out of them, Rachel told herself as she started for the front door. She lifted her skirts away from her legs and Mrs. Biddle's clean floor. "If you'll excuse me," she called over her shoulder, "I need to change, then I'll join you. Papa, please show them the way." Sid came up the steps to hold the door for her. "Sager, won't you come, too?" she asked at the threshold. She wasn't sure what had possessed her to invite him, other than the fact that he was her only friend. If ever a situation called for the support of a friend, this one certainly did.

He exchanged a look with Sid and then Logan that chilled her flesh. He completely ignored Mrs. Taggert. "No, thank you. You're on your own, sweetheart."

Once in her room, Rachel stripped out of her soiled clothes, rinsed the rest of the dirt from her legs and hands, then jumped into a fresh outfit in record time, terrified the whole while that her father and the Taggerts were about to draw guns on each other. Perhaps Mrs. Taggert would have a calming affect on them. But then again, Rachel thought, remembering the woman's regal deportment, her haughtiness would

hardly lessen the group's tension. She thought of
Sager's words as she tried to formulate a plan. How
was she going to help her father find the peace he
sought? Perhaps something as simple as a little kindness and hospitality would show the Taggerts her
father's goodwill toward them.

She, of all people, knew kindness would go a great
distance toward building bridges.

Straightening her hair, Rachel gave herself a quick
once over in the mirror. Her skirt was a blue calico
and her blouse white cotton with a high collar. Her
reflection wasn't quite the image of sophistication,
but it was nonetheless serviceable. She hurried
down the hallway, slowing to a more appropriate
pace outside the living room. She saw at once that
things weren't going well, but at least no one was
dead—yet.

In the middle of the room there was a coffee table
around which sat four ladder-back chairs, two on
each side. Backing up to that were the two leather
chairs that faced the fireplace. The furniture arrangement was itself inhospitable, she thought with a
frown. Had she realized how tense this first meeting
would be, she would have rearranged things days
ago. As it was, Sid stood off the side, looking out one
of the windows flanking the fireplace. His wife sat
next to Papa in one of the stiff-backed chairs, eyeing
her clenched hands. Papa stared across the coffee
table at a stony faced Logan.

Logan. Rachel couldn't help taking a prolonged
look at him, wanting to appease her curiosity. He
was a little older than herself, she thought, but not as
old as Sager. He'd removed his hat, and she saw now
that his hair was blond. Sun-bleached and straight.

And he was regarding her father with a steady, cold gaze from his pale gray eyes.

Rachel swallowed a groan at the room's palpable tension. Logan and her father came to their feet; Sid, who was already standing, simply turned and looked at her. Mrs. Taggert merely raised her head and frowned at the far wall.

Mrs. Biddle had left a coffee tray inside the door, and Rachel carried it to the table between her father and the youngest Taggert. She set it down and took her seat, bidding the men to make themselves comfortable. Never before in her life had she actually served anyone coffee in a social setting such as this. She and Master Tidwell had practiced this, however. He'd be pleased to know her lessons were not wasted.

"Mrs. Taggert," she asked, "how do you like your coffee?"

"With just a little cream and a touch of sugar, thank you."

Rachel prepared her cup, then asked Mr. Taggert the same question. He seemed about to decline her hospitality, but he looked at Old Jack's forbidding face and apparently reconsidered. "I'll take mine black, ma'am. And you can call me 'Sid.' We don't stand on formalities out here."

She smiled and brought his cup to him. "Logan, how do you like yours?" she asked.

"Just a little sugar." He looked at Old Jack. "A little goes a long way."

Rachel bit her lip as she fixed Logan's coffee, careful to keep her face a blank as she moved the plate of her oatmeal cookies closer to his reach. "Papa? How about your coffee?"

"Don't care for any. Need something stronger." He crossed the room and poured himself a stiff measure of whiskey without offering any to his guests. His rudeness mortified Rachel, but she covered her reaction by preparing her own cup of coffee. Her father returned to his seat next to her and resumed his malevolent glare at Logan. A painful silence descended upon the room and threatened to stretch into several minutes. The coffee had proven woefully inadequate as a conversation starter.

"It's nice to meet all of you, though this situation was a bit of a surprise. Sager never mentioned you on our trip," Rachel said to the room at large. At her comment, Sid turned from the window to watch her speculatively.

Logan grinned, though his humor didn't warm his eyes. "Now why is that not surprising?"

Again there was silence. Looking at the hard expressions on the faces of the men in the room, Rachel saw the obstacle to peace that existed between their two ranches.

"So tell me," Mrs. Taggert interrupted the quiet, "did you enjoy the trip here?"

Rachel sipped her coffee, wondering how to answer that question. She looked directly at Mrs. Taggert and told the truth. "It was the best thing that ever happened to me." She looked at her father. "And it was a great relief to meet up with Sager. I never went to sleep hungry once he joined the company." Rachel took another sip of coffee.

Glancing at Mrs. Taggert over the rim of her cup, she noticed an odd whitening about her mouth. Rachel wondered, with a sudden sinking feeling, if Logan's mother was as scandalized by her traveling alone with Sager as the women of the wagon train had been. Perhaps it would be best to face the issue head-on rather than letting it fester, along with everything else that stood in the way of her father's peace.

"I assure you that Sager was quite a gentleman. In fact, he saved my life more than once."

Logan's mother turned her ice gray eyes on Rachel. "Indeed? Surely you weren't ever in real danger?"

Rachel looked at the pool of dark liquid in her coffee cup, unnerved by Mrs. Taggert's interest. "No, I'm sure I only exaggerated the danger to myself. But several times I quite feared for my life." Rachel looked up with a smile, though her gaze did not return to Mrs. Taggert. She looked at Logan instead. He had the same eyes as his mother, but his expression was tempered with some indefinable quality, something akin to rationality. Rachel set her cup down, deciding it was time she got to business before she lost her resolve.

"May I speak plainly?" she asked, watching Logan.

"Please do," Logan answered her.

"I understand you and I may be the means of achieving peace between our families."

The younger Taggert held his silence. Rachel stood and walked away from the small arrangement of chairs, moving to a position from which she could see Sid, too. "The tension in this room tells me peace won't come easily. I wonder what makes any of you think marriage would bring a truce at all?"

Sid eyed her, then looked at his son before he answered. "If there is to be peace, Rachel, it will come with patience, forbearance, and a good deal of luck.

Your question is a hell of a good one. A marriage alone won't do it."

Rachel caught the glance Mrs. Taggert flashed her husband, and wondered whether she, too, was against the match. Perhaps she'd found an ally in the forbidding person of Mrs. Taggert.

Old Jack downed his whiskey. "You're my only child, Rachel. You and your husband will inherit the Crippled Horse. It stands to reason that once you're married to Logan, he won't have a mind toward rustlin' my cattle anymore."

Logan's eyes narrowed as his gaze rotated to Old Jack. "I've never rustled from you," he said quietly. "I've been too busy protecting our herds from you to spare time for forays of my own!"

Rachel cleared her throat and moved to stand near her father. Why was he behaving this way? He was only making things worse. "Well, I would welcome the opportunity to get to know you, Logan," she hedged. Sager's admonishment came to mind. Her father needed this small thing from her. While she would not mislead Logan into thinking they might form a permanent attachment, she did not need to say at the outset that it was impossible either; the ground they walked on was too tenuous to support any barriers.

Besides, what could the harm be in agreeing to befriend him? Especially if their friendship became a friendship between their families and led to the peace their fathers needed? She held her hand out to the younger Taggert.

Logan turned his angry eyes on her, and Rachel bore the heat of them without flinching. He glanced at her outstretched hand a minute before rising to take it in his own.

"You sure you want to do that?" he asked.

"Of course. Peace is an important prospect."

"True." He smiled at her. "May I call on you this weekend?"

"Why don't you come by for dinner Sunday?" she offered. "And your parents—please."

"We'd enjoy that, Rachel," Sid said, accepting her invitation as he left the window and came to stand next to his son.

"No!" Mrs. Taggert shot to her feet. She looked at the three of them standing there, and began to straighten the folds of her gown. "That is, it wouldn't be polite to impose on their hospitality, what with Rachel having just arrived. It's only right that we give you time to settle in, dear. I think it would be best if you dined with us this Sunday, Rachel. And— Jack," she added belatedly.

A little bemused, Rachel accepted. "Very well, Sunday it is."

Sid set his large hand on her shoulder. "It's been a true pleasure meeting you." He sent Jack a mean-ingful look, then looked back at Rachel. "You're a breath of fresh air around here, believe me."

Her father came to his feet. "Amen to that. A breath of fresh air and a taste of honesty."

Sid met Old Jack's look. "'Bout time there were some of both in these parts."

Rachel looked from her father to Sid. Trying to distract them, she took hold of Logan's arm and moved him toward the front door, hoping the men and Mrs. Taggert would follow. On the porch, she faced Logan, watching him as he set his hat on his head and sent a glare back at her father. He was tall. Almost as tall as Sager. His face, though extraordinarily handsome, lacked Sager's hardness. Rachel fidgeted with her sleeve cuff as she wondered whether that was good or bad.

Old Jack stood next to her as the Taggerts took their leave. Rachel waved to them, ignoring the ugly glare her father sent their way. She watched their coach disappear down the road, inordinately glad this first interview was at an end.

"What did you want to see me about, Papa?"

"Mmm-hmm. Wanted to tell you the Taggerts was coming over this morning. Forgot to say anything at breakfast."

Rachel tried not to smile. "Thanks for the warning." Her father shook his head, as if putting the whole nasty visit out of his mind as he went back inside. Rachel turned to follow him and caught sight of Sager sitting on the edge of the bunkhouse porch, sewing a tear in the leather of his saddle. She headed toward him, careful to skirt the dense quagmire that snagged her earlier. Next to him sat her boots, cleaned and shined.

"Hello," she greeted him as she leaned against one of the porch roof supports.

Sager looked her over briefly, not bothering to stand. "Looks like you survived." He turned back to his saddle.

"They're nice people. I don't understand my father. He seems to want to mend things between the Crippled Horse and the Circle Bar, yet he was impossibly rude to them just now."

Sager gave a harsh laugh. "He's been fighting

them a long while, Rach. It goes against the grain to be nice to someone you've hated for so long."

A moment of silence fell between them, a gentle quiet like the ones she had gotten used to during the long trek to the Crippled Horse. She glanced back toward the main house, her gaze settling on the living room window Sid had occupied through most of the awkward meeting.

"Well, it's official now, Sager," she announced in a voice more solemn than she'd intended.

He looked up at her. "What is?"

"Logan and I have agreed to get to know each other."

Chapter Fourteen

Sager blinked, then looked away, letting his eyes rest on the horizon behind her. *Jesu!* What a tomfool plan this had been—using Rachel in a trade for peace. It seemed so easy when he'd proposed it to Old Jack. And now that he knew her, it was too late. Her words felt like a brace of razors twisting in his chest.

"That's great, Rach." He stood and hoisted the saddle to his shoulder. "That's just great." He walked around her to the corral. He needed air. And lots of it.

"Why can't it be you?" she asked, her words so faint, he almost ignored her whisper. He stopped, but didn't turn around.

"I got no say in your future, Rachel. I'm not the staying kind." *He'd come back to this Territory for only one reason—to destroy the Taggerts. He wasn't the man she thought him to be. She would hate him when he'd done what he had to do.*

* * *

Three days later, Sager sat astride his pony, eyeing the Crippled Horse cattle in the south pasture. He had ridden the entire circumference of the rangeland Old Jack used to graze his herds, but was no closer to learning how Tom Beall was getting the cattle off Crippled Horse land. He frowned as he looked at the herd. Beall wasn't carrying them off into the thin air; there had to be a trail that Sager hadn't found yet.

He lifted his face and let the bright sun beat down on him. His eyes were dry and bleary from wind and grit and lack of sleep. Closing them briefly to rub the dust from them, he saw Rachel.

Rachel.

He saw her as she was during their journey here—her sun-streaked blond hair. Freckled cheeks. Turquoise eyes, stormy and changeable—eyes a man could lose his soul in. Her tiny waist and full breasts. Breasts he touched. . . .

He opened his eyes abruptly, thrusting the vision of her aside. Gazing at the endless range before him, he realized, these past few weeks, he felt as if he had come home. But this wasn't his. And she wasn't his.

He dismounted and led his pony a few paces. Leaning against the naked dirt side of a narrow ledge, he sighed and turned his attention back to the work at hand. He had missed something in his circuit of the rangeland. Beall's trail was here somewhere, and he was determined to find it. And the sooner, the better, for then he could end this business with his family and get the hell out of the Territory.

And this time when he left, he would never return.

* * *

Rachel's father drew the team to a halt in front of a lovely, sprawling ranch house. Tall windows greeted visitors from within a porch that circled the entire dwelling. Pristine white pillars were set at regular intervals and dainty cutouts decorated the many eaves like wooden spider webs.

"I guess this is the place," Old Jack said as he came around to help Rachel out of the wagon.

She smiled at him as he set her down. Straightening his string tie, she sent him a quelling look. "Of course it is, Papa, and well you know it. The Taggerts have been your neighbors for—how many decades has it been now?"

He grumbled something inarticulate about squatters taking a man's best land, and turned toward the house. Rachel followed him. She was as nervous as he was. The well-being of their two families rested on her shoulders.

A movement caught her attention from the corner of her eye. She turned to see Sid hurrying toward them. He was still in his work clothes—homespun pants and a flannel shirt loosely tucked into the waist of his pants. Rachel felt a tightening in the pit of her stomach. She wanted to ask her father what time it was, fearing they had come too early, but Sid was now close enough to hear. If only there wasn't so much riding on this meeting—everything they said and did had to be excruciatingly correct.

Sid jogged the last few steps to them, holding his hand out to her father. "Glad you could come. I told Cassandra I'd work this field this afternoon, that way I could see when you drove up." He turned to Rachel. "Sorry we're not cleaned up yet." He nodded back toward Logan, who was washing his hands and face at the water pump. "Seems there's never enough time to get all the work in."

"Please—don't worry about it," Rachel answered. "And I'm sure we're early. Did you say you're planting already?"

He set his hands on his waist and nodded, making a frown. "Could be too early—it being only mid-May, but I think we'll be all right. Want to see?"

"Yes! Thank you." The family garden was a subject Rachel had broached a few times with her father. He'd always grumbled that it was too early, that another hard frost was headed their way. She sent Old Jack a glance, warning him to behave as she took hold of his arm and pulled him forward.

They passed the corner of the house, and Rachel got a better glimpse of Logan. He'd hung his shirt over the fence post and was dousing himself with cool spring water. His chest was broad and tanned, a curious contrast to his pale hair. He straightened as they moved past and waved to her and Jack. She smiled and waved back. Water glistened in the dark blond hairs of his chest, sparkling in the sunlight. She stared at him surreptitiously, waiting for the sense of breathlessness to overtake her as it always had when she saw Sager—with or without his shirt. But that feeling never came, and she turned away before her curiosity could be noted. Perhaps it was just that she had an artificial sense of security with her father and Sid here.

Closing her mind to both Logan and Sager, Rachel focused on the things Sid was pointing out about his vegetable garden, the neat rows that would soon be green beans, peas, corn, squash and other vegetables. The tour was brief, and when Sid had finished detailing his plans for the season's household crops, he walked the two of them up to the house.

"Rachel, Jack," Mrs. Taggert said, crossing the parlor to greet them. She sent Sid a baleful glare as he passed her to go change. "Please come in. I've had some lemonade prepared. Would you care for a glass?"

"Yes, thank you. That sounds delicious. Papa, will you have some as well?" Rachel asked. His grumpy face looked even more irritated than usual, but he nodded. When Mrs. Taggert turned away to call for the maid, Rachel made a face at him.

"What?" he asked.

"Stop it, Papa," she admonished in a hushed voice. "We're guests here."

"Yeah," he scoffed, "dinner in a wolf's den."

Mrs. Taggert followed a maid over to the small side table and poured three glasses of lemonade. "Here we are. Please have a seat. Logan and my husband will be along shortly. I tried to get them to do that field tomorrow, but sometimes they get something in their heads and just won't let it go."

"Mmm-hmm," Jack replied. "I've firsthand experience with that."

Rachel took a determined swallow from her glass. "Papa, isn't this delicious lemonade?"

"Rachel, tell me about yourself," Mrs. Taggert asked as she leaned back more comfortably in the settee. "I understand you're from Virginia."

Rachel stiffened. Instinctively, she knew if Mrs. Taggert comprehended the truth of her upbringing, this whole farce would be for naught. "I lived with my aunt and uncle. They have a town house in Alexandria."

"I see. And what is your uncle's profession?"

"He is a lawyer."

"How interesting." Rachel watched Mrs. Taggert's mouth curl into what was either a very predatory or very practiced smile. "Logan has political aspirations, Rachel—it's only fair to let you know. It wouldn't surprise me at all if he were to head up this Territorial government of ours one day."

Mrs. Taggert seemed pleased to talk about Logan, and Rachel's relief was palpable that she didn't need to go into detail about her life.

"Of course, the Territorial government will only be the start for him. I expect he will eventually be situated in our nation's capital." Rachel's attention lagged as Logan's mother intoned her son's many virtues. Mrs. Taggert certainly was a changeable creature, Rachel thought. At their first meeting, she seemed set against the match, but today, Rachel felt she was blatantly being sold on the position of Logan's wife. Lord, she felt deceitful. She meant to be Logan's friend, no more. She wanted to shout that there would be no marriage. Not now. Not ever!

"Have you taken a chill, dear?" Mrs. Taggert interrupted her own diatribe to ask Rachel.

Rachel's gaze swiveled from the room's heavy furnishings to Logan's mother. "No," she answered just a little too quickly. "Well, perhaps I did from the ride over here."

"I understand," Mrs. Taggert commiserated with her. "It's been terribly cool this spring. I imagine you'll be glad to return to the Washington area and escape the harsh weather we have here."

A streak of desolation shot through Rachel. "No!" Both her father and Mrs. Taggert gave her shocked looks.

"Of course—what was I thinking? The trip out was terribly arduous, and here I have you turning around and heading right back."

Mrs. Taggert's comment gave Rachel a chance to compose herself. "Not at all. Sager made the journey quite tolerable. But I came out here to get to know my father better."

The sound of men's voices distracted Mrs. Taggert, much to Rachel's relief. She knew she'd committed another faux pas in mentioning Sager—judging from Mrs. Taggert's drawn expression. Of course it was bad form to mention one's hired gun when one was trying to end a feud.

"Ah, Logan!" Mrs. Taggert's face lit up like the sparkling water of a fast-moving brook when she greeted her son. Sid preceded Logan into the room, but Rachel noticed that Mrs. Taggert didn't glance at her husband as she walked passed him to loop her arm around her son's. Her theatrics were obvious and embarrassing to both the Taggert men. Rachel sent a quick glance her father's way. His brows were lowered in such a deep glower that he appeared oblivious to everything, which was probably for the best, Rachel thought. Had he noticed, doubtless he would have said something uncouth about it.

Sid greeted Rachel with a warm handshake. He looked at her father and smiled. "How about some whiskey, Old Jack?"

Her father lifted his brows long enough to look at Sid and accept. Whiskey in hand, he seemed more himself.

"Rachel and I were just getting better acquainted, Logan," Mrs. Taggert said. "She grew up just south of Washington."

"Ah," Logan said, again with his smile that wasn't a smile, "my mother no doubt informed you of my political aspirations?"

Rachel studied his expression, trying to determine whether they were his aspirations or his mother's for him. "Yes, quite thoroughly."

A servant announced that dinner was served. Logan disentangled his arm from his mother and offered it to Rachel. Though he made the proper motions, there was nothing welcoming in his stance. She set her hand on his arm and made the mistake of looking back to be sure her father was properly escorting Mrs. Taggert. To her horror, she saw the three remaining adults standing about in some disorder until Sid offered his arm to his wife. She wondered if her father intentionally shunned Mrs. Taggert, or if he was poorly versed in the proper etiquette for such things. She was doubly grateful for her lessons with Master Tidwell; at least she knew what to expect in this situation.

They walked from the parlor across the hall to the dining room, and paused while a servant drew open the beautiful pocket doors, revealing an exquisite cherry dining room table laden with linen and china and silver.

Logan helped Rachel to her place at the long dining room table, then took his seat next to her. Across from her sat Mrs. Taggert. Old Jack sat next to Mrs. Taggert, frowning at the table. Rachel didn't know whether he was reacting to the room's formality or the amount of silverware set by each place. If he didn't understand the practice of walking in to dinner, she had little hope he would cope with the complicated place settings.

She was relieved, however, that he instinctively mimicked her, watching which utensil she used before touching his own. By the time dessert was served, Rachel had relaxed her vigilance. She stirred her coffee and set the spoon down. She was about to respond to something Sid said, when she happened to look over at her father and noticed he was eating his chocolate torte with his coffee spoon—a small error, yet a grievous one.

Rachel knew this ridiculously elaborate Sunday dinner was a test to see if she had the sophistication to be a senator's wife. Peace between the Crippled Horse and the Circle Bar depended upon Mrs. Taggert's acceptance of her—and Papa. She sent her hostess a quick glance to see if she noticed Papa's transgression. She had, and her lips were pressed thin with disapproval. Rachel felt her shoulders sag. Peace was too important an issue to let this shallow woman's arrogance destroy what little progress had been made, yet gaining her approbation was proving to be a significant hurdle to cross.

Logan cleared his voice, and Rachel ventured a look in his direction. Disregarding the dictates of proper etiquette, he picked up his coffee spoon and cut into the torte, drawing his mother's attention from Old Jack. This was his first friendly overture. Rachel smiled at him and was surprised to see his eyes warm slightly as he returned her regard.

"You've been quiet, Old Jack." Sid looked at her father. "Was everything to your liking?"

Old Jack swallowed his mouthful. "Mmm-hmm. I've just been concentrating. Never seen so damned many forks and spoons and whatnot for a single person."

Though Sid's laughter filled the sudden silence,

Rachel's mouthful of torte became dry as dust. She chewed and chewed but couldn't seem to swallow.

"It is a little overkill, I guess," Sid admitted, "but Cassandra was determined about it. Something about a princess and a pea." He wiped his mouth, then folded his napkin and set it by his plate. Leaning his elbows on the table, his humor evaporated as he studied Old Jack.

"Tell me, how is Sager?"

Rachel kept her expression carefully bland, pretending indifference to Sid's question as she listened hungrily for her father's answer. She hoped no one could hear the sharp hammering of her heart. Why was Sid interested in the well-being of her father's hired gunman?

Curious about how the others at the table perceived this question, Rachel looked at Mrs. Taggert. Her face had become drawn. Apparently Sager, as a discussion topic, was worse than her father's breaches of etiquette. And Logan looked furious. A muscle ticked in his jaw.

"Well enough, I guess. Keeps to himself, he does." Old Jack pinned Sid with a look. "Why'd he come back, Taggert?"

Sid shook his head. "I was hoping he might have told you."

"Nope. He just rides in one day this winter and says he's come to settle an old debt. What debt would he be meaning, do you suppose?"

Sid's dark eyes took on a bleak look. "I can only imagine."

Logan slapped his napkin down on the table and came to his feet. "If you'll excuse us, I think I'd like to take Rachel for a short walk."

Mrs. Taggert inclined her head. Old Jack looked as sour as curdled milk. Only Sid seemed pleased with Logan's request. Rachel forced herself to breathe normally as Logan led her from the house.

They walked down the lane in front of the Taggerts' home. Evening had come, changing the sunlight to a warm orange that poured over the green prairie. Crickets chirped and robins sang their warbling evening song. Rachel looked at Logan, and he at her. He shoved his hands into his pockets and faced forward.

"I have to admit that when my father told me about his and Old Jack's plan for the two of us, I wasn't happy. I don't like the thought of someone else planning my future."

Rachel smiled as she looked down at the gravel and low weeds in the dirt lane as they walked. She was disenchanted with the whole engagement idea; it was a tremendous relief to hear Logan admit he was, too.

"But then I saw you, Rachel, and the idea suddenly wasn't as repulsive as I first thought."

"My goodness, Logan," Rachel laughed. "Was that a compliment?" she teased.

Logan did chuckle at that. His humor seemed real this time. "What I am rather awkwardly trying to say is that I don't know what to do about this situation."

"I don't either. Why can't our families be friends without sacrificing us?"

He shrugged. "I never understood the feud between the Circle Bar and the Crippled Horse. When my father came here, his spread was just a fraction of the size of Old Jack's. I think your father thought of him as a nester. For years he tried to get rid of him. But Sid's nothing if not stubborn. He added to his holdings and turned it into a respectable ranch."

Rachel smiled. "I can see my father doing that. He's rather tenacious. So there's no rustling going on?"

Logan frowned. "I think our fathers might have rustled from each other in the early days. But not anymore. It's not the way either of them runs his operation." He looked at her, the humor gone from his face. "Someone is rustling from the Circle Bar though, and from your father as well. Whoever it is, he's making it look real bad for the Crippled Horse and us, implicating one or the other according to whose cattle he's rustling. Old Jack hired Sager to stop it."

"Do you know Sager?"

Logan stopped walking and turned to her, studying her face. "Sager's my stepbrother. He's Sid's true son."

Rachel's mouth dropped. No wonder Sid was interested in him. "I don't understand. Why does he go by the name *Sager*? Why is he living at the Crippled Horse rather than here?"

"It's not my story to tell, Rachel. You would have to ask him those questions."

Rachel felt a chill of foreboding. The Taggert family was terribly broken, and now she stood between two brothers. She crossed her arms in front of herself and looked away from Logan's pale gray eyes.

"I don't know what to say. I don't think I am ready to get married, Logan."

"Perhaps, Rachel, you would let me call on you next Saturday? We could make a picnic and see if we can work through this."

"I'd like that."

* * *

Rachel watched her father across the breakfast table. He had been moody since they returned from the Taggerts earlier that week. She'd tried a few times to start a conversation with him, but he'd met all of her attempts with monosyllabic answers.

"Papa, I'd like to get our vegetable garden planted today," she said after breakfast, as men filed out the door. This was a topic she had been round and round with her father, but today she meant to stand her ground. She'd hoped having seen the Taggerts' garden would make her father more reasonable, but nothing pleased him.

"You don't know anything about gardening, daughter," he said dismissively as he turned to speak to one of the hands.

"That's not true," Rachel contradicted him. One of her many responsibilities at her aunt's house had been maintaining the cook's herb garden. "I'm an accomplished gardener, Papa."

"For flower gardens back East, maybe, but not here. Things is different here. Different soil, different vegetation, different weather."

"Nevertheless, it's time it was planted."

"No," he answered.

"No?"

"I can't spare a man, and you can't do it yourself."

"When do you think someone will be available to help me?"

"Not for a few weeks."

"It can't wait that long, Papa. The growing season is short here; the garden needs to get planted now if I'm to get enough vegetables canned to hold the ranch through this time next year."

"No sense planting it now, girl. I told you, most

likely we'll have another frost in the next couple of weeks." He wiped his mouth and threw his napkin beside his plate, marking an end to the discussion as he scrapped his chair back and came to his feet.

Rachel, too, came to her feet. "The garden needs to go in now, Papa. If you cannot spare a man, then I will do it myself."

Old Jack's blue eyes flashed with anger. "Forget the damned garden, girl!" he roared. "You ain't goin' to be here long enough to tend it, much less get to the canning of it."

Rachel felt as if the wind had been knocked from her. "Where am I going to be?"

"Married to Logan or back with your aunt and uncle." He waved his hand with extreme agitation. "You're going to leave us and go on about your life."

This argument wasn't about the garden. It was about her. She looked at her father, wondering if he'd missed her as much as she missed him.

"I'm not leaving here, Papa. I am never going back to Aunt Eunice's. I'm not marrying Logan. I will be here to see to the canning."

They glared at each other a long, tense minute. Then Jack waved his hand again, finished with the whole issue. "Never mind. Ask Sager to help."

"Is he back?"

Jack nodded. "Got in last night. He'll be staying near the house the next few days. Might as well put him to work." Old Jack stormed out the back door.

Rachel sighed as she watched the kitchen empty. Her father's vehemence still echoed in her brain. She thought suddenly of all the lost time, all the years she'd never had with him.

She helped Mrs. Biddle clear the table. "Well, dear, that was one argument I didn't expect you to win."

Rachel smiled at the housekeeper. "I'm finding he's not the only Douglas with a stubborn streak a mile wide."

"Why don't you go on over and speak to Sager—before your father changes his mind."

"Good idea!" She hung her apron by the back door and went outside. Her stride was purposeful as she crossed the distance between the house and the bunkhouse. She stepped onto the rough porch with her shoulders squared and her heart hammering with determination. She'd get that field planted today if she had to dig it with her bare hands!

The barracks door was open, and she heard some of the men teasing Sager about becoming a farmer. One mentioned something about it being something new for Sager to plow, and Rachel gritted her teeth against the earthly guffaws that met that comment.

She stepped forward and knocked on the wooden door frame. "Excuse me—" she spoke to the men nearest the door.

They spun around to look at her. One of the hands at the back of the room started to add to his friend's farming joke. "Close yer trap, Jess. Miz Rachel's here," Ross barked to the cowhand and the room at large.

"I don't mean to intrude," Rachel spoke into the sudden silence, "I just need to see Sager."

"Yes, ma'am. He's right there." Digger pointed to a bunk midway through the room.

Rachel stepped inside the long building. She felt uncomfortable invading the men's space, yet her curiosity got the better of her. The room was long and narrow, with small windows placed at intervals of about a half-dozen paces. Each man's bunk looked as though it were his own private area. Clothes hung on the bedposts and on pegs in the wall above the beds. Boots sat next to some of the mattresses. One sleeping area even boasted a furry pair of chaps hanging on hooks on the wall.

But it was Sager's area that most drew her attention, and she let her eyes absorb every detail about his sleeping area, from his boldly patterned blanket to the clothes neatly hung on hooks at the head of his bed.

"What can I do for you, Rachel?" Sager asked, cutting into her curious perusal as he slowly came to his feet.

Rachel drew her hands behind her back and tried to look nonchalant—a difficult task being the center of so much male attention. "I wondered if you'd mind helping me plow the field at the side of the house?"

Someone at the back of the room snickered. Sager sent him a look that silenced him. Rachel felt the heat of her blush rise in her cheeks. What were they laughing about?

Sager sat back down and drew on his boots without giving her an answer, leaving her to fidget and wonder whether he was going to help her. He straightened and faced her in the low-ceilinged room. Rachel watched him warily. She wished she'd waited for him outside, wished he wouldn't decline her request in front of everyone.

"Let's go."

"You'll help me?"

He arched a brow at her. "You did want me to, didn't you?"

She flashed him a quick smile before hurrying out into the bright sunlight. She walked ahead of him away from the bunkhouse, yet his long strides soon overtook hers. He reached the edge of the field before her, giving her a moment—a delicious, private moment—to let her eyes feast on the sight of him.

He wore tan-colored homespun trousers and a faded blue shirt. Creases ran horizontally at the back of his knees, but the muscles of his calves and thighs stretched the fabric taut. He'd left his gun belt at the bunkhouse. The suspenders he wore accentuated the inverted triangle of his chest and broad shoulders. A strip of rawhide tied his black hair—hair that poured down his neck like liquid tar.

Perhaps he felt the weight of her perusal, for he turned. She should have looked away, but her gaze shifted to his face. Their eyes met and held. He'd caught her inspection, she knew, but he didn't tease her. That simple fact sent waves of tension through her. What was it that she felt for him? Rachel wondered. Why couldn't she forget their kisses?

She drew even with him. He turned to look out at the field before them. The warmth of the past few days had sprayed the ground with grasses and wildflowers and prickly weeds.

"Do you want me to keep with the lines of the old field? Or shall I widen the borders?" he asked.

"I'm not sure Papa has enough supplies to plant what's already there."

He looked at her. "Take it as far as you can go. You might surprise yourself."

She held his look. "You're right."

The boys were being raucous as they left the bunkhouse. Sager glanced over at them. "I'll hook up the plow," he said, moving toward the barn.

Rachel refused her natural inclination to follow him with her gaze. Instead, she went back to the ranch house and her waiting chores. Sager wouldn't have her field ready for sowing for a little while yet, and there was too much to do for her to stay there mooning over him.

A breeze tossed the curtains aside and blew across Rachel's face a short while later. She turned the bread dough out on the table to knead, looking out the window now and then to watch Sager guide the plow through the dirt of her garden. He leaned his back against the leather traces, calling encouraging words to her father's workhorse. Row by row, he drew deep, straight furrows in the field. She turned the dough and leaned into it a little harder, forcing herself to stay focused on the task at hand.

When that was done, she cleaned the work table and washed her dishes, leaving them stacked to dry as she hurried to change. She decided to borrow a pair of trousers and a shirt from her father—it would be easier to work in the garden in pants than in a skirt. She smiled at herself as she pictured Aunt Eunice's face, how scandalized she'd be at the thought of Rachel wearing anything but a skirt—a black maid's uniform, in fact.

Chapter Fifteen

The furnishings in her father's room were as spare as everywhere else in the house—a narrow rope bed, a wash stand, two trunks, a chair, and an armoire. The armoire housed only a single suit and three shirts—no work clothes there. Rachel headed toward the first of the trunks. She frowned as she saw that it was stuffed with women's clothes. Farm clothes of serviceable fabrics. They'd been rolled up and looked as though they'd been carelessly tossed in there.

She pulled out a blouse and held it up to herself. It wasn't much larger than she was. It might be a nice fit. Whose clothes were they? Not Mrs. Biddle's—unless, of course, they had belonged to her before her girth had widened. Had they been her mother's? Rachel folded the blouse and returned it to the trunk with hands that shook slightly. Why had her father kept them? She closed the first trunk and looked at it a second, considering the aspect of her father's personality that it revealed. His room, indeed his entire household, had been pared down to a

Spartan existence; everything had a use and place. Yet, despite his natural inclinations, he had preserved a trunk of his wife's possessions.

Opening the lid of the second trunk, Rachel found exactly what she'd been looking for. This one was only half full, but it, too, held clothes that had been rolled up rather than folded. She found several pairs of denim pants and plenty of cotton shirts. Deeper inside, the clothes were folded. Perhaps Papa didn't wear these as often, she mused, lifting out a pair of the heavy cotton trousers. They were too long, and too large in the waist, but once she'd cinched the waist with a belt and rolled up the pant legs, they would be just fine.

She took the trousers and one of Papa's shirts back to her room. The shirt was definitely oversized. She tucked it into the pants and rolled up her sleeves, deciding the fit was genuinely comfortable. She tied a handkerchief about her neck, pulled on her boots, grabbed her wide-brimmed plainsman's hat, and hurried out to join Sager.

Standing at the edge of the field, she watched him a minute, admiring the control he maintained over the plow horse and the earth beneath him. He had already turned over two-thirds of the field. A strong breeze blew past, and Rachel lifted her face to the fresh air. It was cool, but the sun was strong. Perspiration dampened Sager's shirt, matting it to the rippling muscles of his chest and arms, and when he changed directions, she saw that a dark column shadowed his back.

She set her satchel of seeds and her work gloves down at the edge of the field and returned with a bucket of cool water drawn from the well. Sager stopped and wiped his brow with his forearm. She saw him scrutinize her odd apparel, but she ignored the obvious amusement in his eyes.

"Thirsty?" she asked, thrusting the dipper toward him.

He took it from her. Cupping the bowl of the dipper in his hand, he raised it to his lips and guzzled the water. He gave it back to her empty and waited for her to refill it. Twice more he drank from the dipper. When at last he'd quenched his thirst, he arched his back and stretched his arms, easing his cramped muscles. "So"—he nodded toward the plowed portion of the field—"this what you wanted?"

"It's perfect," Rachel answered, aware that he was watching her again. He seemed about to say something, and she stood there, waiting for him to speak. Her feet were rooted in place. She couldn't turn away from his amber gaze, close her mind to the sensuous curves of his lips, forget the way his arms felt about her. . . .

A corner of Sager's mouth tilted in a lopsided grin. "Your garden ain't gonna plant itself."

She smiled slowly. "It won't, will it?" Reluctantly, she started away, then stopped. "Sager—" He looked at her. "Thanks for helping me today."

He shrugged. "Sure."

Rachel donned her work gloves and began planting seeds for green beans within Sager's neatly dug furrows. The work went quickly. It wasn't until she straightened to stretch her aching back that she noticed how far she had gotten. She looked at the expanse of the newly turned earth. This was a good garden, she decided. Its vegetables would carry the Crippled Horse through to the next spring. Midway down the next row, a dark stone caught her attention. She picked it up and looked it over in the palm of her hand. It was an arrowhead, she realized with absurd delight.

"Sager!" She ran across the field toward him.

He ducked out of the plow's harness, freeing himself to face the danger that made her run to him as he scanned the horizon.

"Look what I found!" she called breathlessly. Stopping almost on top of his feet, she held out her hand to him.

He cupped his hand beneath hers. His thumb and forefinger spread open the fold of her hand. Rachel watched him frown down at what he saw. Perhaps he didn't realize what it was. "It's an arrowhead!" she supplied impatiently.

"So I see. But that's not what's so fascinating."

Rachel looked at her small treasure, trying to see it from his perspective. "What do you mean?"

"It's your gloves"—his eyes grazed her father's clothes—"your getup."

Rachel jerked her hand away and put the small stone into her front pants pocket, pulling the material straight as she slipped her hand inside. "What's wrong with what I'm wearing?"

"Not a thing." Sager smiled. "Not a damned thing."

"Don't tell Digger I found this. I want to surprise him." Sager studied her face, his expression bemused. No doubt he thought her impossibly simple to be pleased by something so common. Needing a show of dignity to weather his intense regard, she put her chin up defiantly.

"I wouldn't tell him just yet, if I were you," he drawled. "There's a reason he's called Digger. You don't want all your hard work here dug up while he looks for more, do you?"

Rachel smiled. "Perhaps I should wait until winter to show him," she said over her shoulder as she walked back to her seeds.

Sager finished the plowing a short while later and took the horse and plow back to the barn. By the time he'd tended the horse and cleaned the plow, Rachel was nearly at the end of her planting.

"Rach, give me the satchel. I'll finish for you," he offered.

"You don't mind?"

"Why would I?"

She pulled the strap over her head and looped it over his. She would have stepped back, but he caught her wrists and held them against his chest.

"How have you been?"

She searched his eyes. "I'm not sleeping as well as I did those last few nights we were on the trail." Rachel almost laughed at the shocked expression on his face. He released her hands as if singed by them.

She spun around and left the field. At the steps to the house, she hesitated. She didn't want to return to her chores indoors. Not when Sager was so near. She fetched a watering can and filled it at the well. It wasn't until she reached the edge of the field that she realized how impossible it would be to water the entire area with her little watering can. Fortunately Sager hadn't seen her yet; he would tease her about her unrelenting naiveté. He looked uncomfortably hot, she thought, standing there as he was, putting out the last of her seeds. Rachel smiled to herself as she walked up behind Sager.

Before he could look around and see what she was

doing, she lifted the can and poured cool water
down his back. He turned on her, a look of savage
fury in his eyes. She cried out, expecting any reaction from him but that. She dropped the can and
ran toward the edge of a copse of trees that bordered the field.

He caught up with her a few steps into the
wooded area and pulled her back against his chest.
One of his arms held her immobile, pinning both of
her arms within his embrace. "I don't think I'm the
only one needing to cool down," he said, his lips
near her ear. She felt his voice shiver through her
like the rumble of a drum. He pushed her leg forward with his thigh as he lifted the watering can and
poured water down her leg, from her knee to her
boot. Slowly, he raised the can's nozzle, showering
her thigh, her hip. He poured the water over his
arm where he held her, letting it pool against her
waist before it spilled over to run down the front of
her trousers.

Rachel reached behind her, arching her back and
gripping his pants as she braced herself against the
shockingly cool water. She leaned against his chest
as he raised the can still higher. Water spilled off her
breasts, molding the cotton fabric to her hardened
nipples.

"Open your mouth," he commanded. She did as
he bid, tasting the streams of water. He kissed her
wet cheek, lifting the small rivulets of water from her
skin with his tongue. Her back still to him, she ran
her hands up his arms to clasp his shoulders.
"Rachel," he rasped, kissing the soft skin behind her
ear. He dropped the watering can, freeing his hands
to move up her ribcage, to cover her breasts. One

hand continued up to her throat, catching her jaw, turning her for his kiss.

She moved in the circle of his arms to face him. His lips were against hers before she completed the turn. He dug his hands into her hair. Rachel pressed against him, but couldn't get close enough. She opened her mouth, welcoming the thrusts of his tongue as her arms circled his neck. His hand moved from her hair, down her spine, to the small of her back. He flattened her body against his. A shiver coursed through her.

"Rachel," Sager rasped as he leaned back to look at her. He cleared a smudge from her face with the pad of his thumb. "Rachel, I—" A sound interrupted him. His head came up, and she saw him frown.

"Taggert!" He swore, his arms falling away from Rachel. He took a step toward the house.

"Sager! Please!" She pulled him back. It was hard to move, hard to think—she was still dazed from his kiss. "I don't know what's between you and your father, but it doesn't serve the peace my father is so desperately trying to build."

Sager frowned at her. "Who told you he was my father?"

"Logan." She saw the tension in Sager's eyes, saw his jaw knot. "Stay here. Please. I'll go see what he wants."

Rachel straightened her shirt, grimacing at the dark wet stain down the front of her body. There was nothing she could do about it now, not if she wanted to keep Sid and Sager separated.

"Hello, Sid!" Rachel waved a greeting as she hurried over to him.

"Rachel!" he said, shaking her hand.

She plucked self-consciously at her wet shirt, thinking she ought to explain why she was soaking. "I look a sight." She held up the watering can. "Had a fight with the water pump."

"You look lovely, as always. Is your pa available?"

She shook her head. "He's out with the boys. We're shorthanded this year. He's running ragged trying to get all the work done."

"It has been a tough year, ma'am," he commiserated with her. "But it won't be the last difficult one we see, I reckon." He nodded toward the field behind her. "That Sager over there?"

Rachel felt her cheeks warm. She followed his glance a little anxiously, but was relieved to see that Sager had left the woods and was planting the last few feet of her garden. She looked at the copse where she and Sager had just been, trying to gauge how much Sid might have seen. Fortunately there was enough undergrowth in and among the cottonwoods that he couldn't have seen much.

"Yes. He's helping me get the garden in."

Sid started toward the field. "Maybe I'll just go say hello."

Rachel stepped in front of him. "That's not such a good idea, Sid."

Sid glanced at her a moment before sighing. He looked back at Sager. "He's a good man, Rachel."

"I know he is."

Sid smiled at her, a smile that came from his heart. "Good."

What was between these two? Rachel wondered. Sid's expression just now was filled with a longing, a great, vast emptiness. Why did Sager hate him so?

"Won't you stay for supper?" she asked Sid.

"No, ma'am. I'm just back from Defiance. Had to pick up some lumber. I took a short detour to see if I could catch your pa. Tell him I came by, will you? I'll be back. There's something I've got to say to him." He swung up on his pony. "Take care, Rachel. Thanks for the invite."

"Sure, Sid," she answered, trying to keep the worry out of her voice. "When you come back, come at supper time. I'm helping Mrs. Biddle with the kitchen duties." She'd learned a good cook in these parts was more renowned than the most popular outlaw— and certainly more loved. No doubt even at the Taggert ranch they'd heard about the dangers of Mrs. Biddle's efforts in the kitchen, and she didn't want Sid to have an excuse not to dine with them.

Sid couldn't help grinning. "I'll do that." He tipped his hat and was off.

Rachel watched him ride away, then went to the steps. She'd best get inside and clean herself up; her bread would need tending soon. She looked back at the field, at Sager, her heart still hammering in her chest. As if sensing her thoughts, Sager looked over at her. Their eyes met. The weight of his gaze had the feel of an embrace. She wanted to go to him. She wanted to finish what they had begun. Lord, it was getting harder and harder to keep herself away from him, she thought as she turned toward the kitchen.

"Is the garden all planted?" Mrs. Biddle asked a little while later as Rachel was peeling carrots.

Rachel watched the housekeeper move about the room, gathering kitchen linens for the wash. "Yes.

Sager was a big help." She braced herself for the lecture she was sure would follow. Had Mrs. Biddle seen them in the woods?

"I'm glad to know that you're making friends with him."

Rachel's head shot up, and she stared at the housekeeper. Mrs. Biddle's acceptance of Sager was shocking. And comforting. "He's not an easy man, Mrs. Biddle."

"I don't see how he could be, dear."

"What do you mean?"

The housekeeper set her basket down on the table and leaned against it as she considered her words. "His father took him from the Shoshone when he was just fourteen. He was never accepted here. That boy could always run faster and hit harder than the local lads. He got into scuffles all the time—not that he started them, mind you. He just never walked away from them." She shook her head. "Never once. His father traveled frequently, seeing to business. If you asked my opinion, I think his father couldn't stand to be around Mrs. Taggert. May the Devil keep her, she treated Sager like an ill-favored servant.

"Oh, goodness!" Mrs. Biddle straightened. "Look at me! Standing here gossiping as if I had the time to do it! Just let me get these dirty cloths in to soak, and I'll come give you a hand with those vegetables."

Rachel picked up her half-peeled carrot and continued where she left off. She moved through the rest of the afternoon mechanically, her mind dwelling on Sager. She looked forward to seeing him at supper. Perhaps after the meal was finished, they could talk.

That evening, as the table filled with hungry men,

Rachel loaded baskets with her fresh bread. She didn't notice that Sager had come in and taken a seat until she turned with a basket and their eyes met. His face was unreadable. A mask. His expression held no feeling for her at all.

His reticence should have made it easier for her to maintain her composure, but it didn't. Her heart sped up, and her breathing became shallow and fast. It was impossible for her to act casually around him—yet it was crucial. She knew that her father watched her. She turned her attention to her father.

"Papa, don't eat yet." She smiled at him. "We should say grace," she directed, taking a seat across from Sager at the end of the table.

Old Jack's fork stopped inches from his mouth. He set it down with a glare at her foolishness, not yet comfortable with this new behavior she'd introduced into their routine. The others at the table hastily swallowed and set their forks down as well. Bowing her head, she took hold of the roughened hands of the cowpunchers on either side of her and began, "Dear Father, we thank you for the blessings before us and pray that you will help our garden be fruitful again this year. Amen." She opened her napkin and spread it in her lap, ignoring her father's baleful stare.

"The garden's in then—you're finished with it?"

"For the time being, Papa." Why was he such a hardened man? How long would it take her to break through to him? She smiled at him. "You were right to have me ask Sager for help. I couldn't have done it without him."

Her father grunted an answer and focused on his plate. The conversation lapsed into the usual accounting for the day's work. Sager was silent, preoccupied.

Now and then she would catch his eye and, though every time they looked at each other a hot flush colored her cheeks, his face betrayed no emotion. She wondered if he was really as oblivious of her as he seemed. Watching him, she reached her foot across the distance separating them beneath the table. His fork stopped halfway to his mouth, and his eyes widened slightly. Rachel studied her plate, fearing she would laugh out loud as she moved her foot up the outside of his calf.

Suddenly, he moved, stretching his long legs across to the space in front of her seat. Her foot retreated quickly, but not to safety. Sager lifted his water glass to his lips, watching her over the rim as his legs insinuated themselves between hers. He took a sip of water, the liquid slowly filling his mouth as his legs gently spread hers wider apart.

Rachel watched the heated look in his eyes and tried not to stare too openly, though her soul fed off the passion in his amber gaze. She licked her lips nervously and felt the weight of his gaze trace the moisture her tongue left behind. She had barely touched her meal and couldn't possibly take another bite. The room was suddenly too hot, too small, and far too crowded for her liking. Sager, darn his hide, was both aware and totally uncaring of the effect he had upon her. She watched his powerful hands as he cut into a piece of the steak on his plate. Did his blood run as hot as he made hers run?

Rachel tried to make a pretense of eating her dinner, but all she managed to do was move her food from one side of the plate to the other, praying all the while that no one would notice her discomfiture. When she tried to ignore Sager, he widened her legs a fraction more. Her eyes flew to his face, but his gaze was on her chest, measuring her shallow breathing. She tried to squeeze Sager's legs closed so that she might retrieve her modesty, but his legs were far stronger than hers.

"Rachel! I asked what you planted in your garden?" her father interrupted her thoughts, repeating a question she hadn't heard him ask.

"Ah—" Rachel stared at her plate, trying to focus on an answer that would make sense. What had they planted today? She looked at Sager for help, only to see him watching her with an arched brow as if he, too, awaited her answer. His legs moved between hers, opening them as wide as the material of her skirt would permit. God, she couldn't think about that now. She relaxed her legs, giving up the fight. Submitting to Sager.

"Beans," she answered her father, "and corn, peas, peppers, carrots and squash."

"Hmm. Well, check with Mrs. Biddle to see whether we need any canning supplies."

With that, the men started to rise from the table. Sager pulled his legs away from her. Rachel couldn't meet his eyes, couldn't even breathe until he'd left the room.

Rachel helped Mrs. Biddle clear the table and wash up, anxious to give her hands something to do and her mind something to focus on other than the look in Sager's eyes.

"Why don't you take a cup of coffee to your father, dear? He and Fletcher are in his den working on the accounts. The coffee should be ready now."

Rachel lifted down a tray and began filling it with the coffee, cups, cream and sugar. "Mrs. Biddle, how

do you know Sager so well?" Rachel asked, voicing
a question that had stayed with her since their talk
earlier.

"Oh, I've been here a long time. Longer than I
ever meant to. Sager worked here as a lad before
he left."

"Is that when he went to California?"

"I don't know. There were rumors, of course.
Word was he hired out as a gunfighter right away. It
was a terrible thing. He was only sixteen, just a boy
still. Sid looked for him once again. He tried long
and hard to get his son to come home. Then, of
course, the war started, and we got word he'd volun-
teered with the Union, that he was fighting along
the Kansas and Missouri border."

"How long had he been gone?"

"A good ten years, I'd say. Maybe it's been eleven
already." She paused, counting the years. "Yes, it
must be. He is five years older than Logan, and
Logan came back just this spring. Sager was only
back a few months before he went to get you." She
cocked her head, giving Rachel a searching look.
"You're mighty curious about him, miss."

Rachel smiled at the older woman. "I am, aren't
I?" she answered, offering no apology. "Why is he
here at the Crippled Horse and not working for his
father?"

Mrs. Biddle poured the coffee into the serving
pot. "There's bad blood between him and his father.
Don't know why, but it's just always been that way.
I don't think that stepmother of his was any help,
either. Here you are, dear. Fix your father some
coffee, and see if you can cheer the old grump up
a bit."

Rachel balanced the tray on her knee as she opened the door to the den. Her father looked up from his desk. Fletcher, too, looked up from where he was standing behind the desk. A frown darkened his face. He stopped talking and watched her set the tray down, waiting for her to leave.

"I've brought some coffee. How do you like it fixed, Papa?" she asked, in no hurry to be gone from the room.

"Black with whiskey in it. Bring over the whole bottle, girl. It's on the table by the window."

Rachel did as he bid, watching as he poured a healthy measure into the cup. She fixed coffee for Fletcher and herself, then took a seat in front of her father's desk, ignoring the range boss's consternation.

"I'm glad you're here," Old Jack said, eyeing her. "I want to talk to you." He took a sip of the steaming brew. But no sooner had he set the cup back in its saucer than a coughing fit overtook him. Rachel rushed to get him a cup of water. He held a handkerchief to his lips, and when he took the water from her, she saw spots of red on the white cloth.

"Papa! You're not well!" Why hadn't she noticed this before? She'd heard him coughing, but just thought it was because of the dry, dusty air.

"Old Jack, you can't keep pushing yourself," Fletcher added grimly.

He downed the water and glared at the two of them. "I'm fine." His voice was raspy. "There's not a hell of a lot I can do about slowing down until we catch those confounded rustlers. It sure ain't ending by itself." He looked at his range boss. "Sager was right. It ain't the Taggerts doing it. If it were them, they would have stopped by now."

Fletcher shrugged. "I don't know anymore. Maybe it is. Maybe it ain't. Maybe Sid's just real smart and knows you'll clear him, what with your kids getting together and all."

"It's not the Taggerts, Papa. I'd know," Rachel interjected.

"I heard Taggert stopped by this afternoon," Fletcher said. "What did he want?"

Rachel didn't like the tone of his question. "He said he'd come back in a few days, said there was something he wanted to talk to Papa about."

Old Jack grunted. "I've been thinking about that barbeque I promised you. I don't want to wait to have it."

Rachel sat on the edge of a chair near her father's desk. Not the barbeque. Not now. She was just getting settled in here. And Papa was too sick to be working as hard as he was, much less entertaining the Territory at a barbeque. She wondered if he was feverish.

"It can't be done right now, Father. Mrs. Biddle and I haven't a spare minute to plan a large party. Let's wait just a little longer. The men are too busy to be able to come anyhow."

"The calving will be done in a week or two. Already the births are beginning to slow down. We'll take a break before gettin' to the brandin' and have us a barbeque. Plan for three weeks from now. I'll give you a list of names. Invite them all. I want it to be known who you are, and that I give you willingly to Taggert's son."

Yes, but which son, Papa? Rachel added silently,

then shook herself. "I haven't decided to marry Logan yet."

A commotion at the front of the house drew Rachel's attention and kept her father from answering. Just as she got to the door of the den, it was opened abruptly. A drawn Mrs. Biddle entered.

"Logan sent word that his mother is ill. He thinks she's dying."

"What happened?" Rachel asked. "Is there anything we can do?"

"No, he's sent for the doctor." Mrs. Biddle stood at the door a moment longer, twisting her hands in her apron, before picking up the coffee tray and disappearing into the hallway.

"Fletcher, go get Sager. He oughtta know about his stepmother."

Rachel and Old Jack sat in worried silence while they awaited Sager. He entered the den alone moments later, answering Old Jack's summons.

"Give Sager a drink, daughter," Old Jack commanded, pointing to the whiskey bottle. Rachel poured a small measure into a glass and handed it to him. His fingers brushed hers as he took it from her. He rotated the glass in his hand, but didn't sip its contents as he eyed Old Jack.

"What's the occasion, Old Jack?"

"I'm afraid I've some bad news."

"I'm listening."

"Your ma's taken sick. Real sick." Jack watched Sager's stony expression. "She might be dying, Sager."

"My ma's already dead. And you know it." He jammed his glass down on the table near the door. "Thanks for the whiskey."

Rachel listened to the echo of his boots against

the hallway floor and jumped as the front door slammed shut. For a moment, she sat unmoving in the stunned silence of the room. The night held the weight of so many conflicting pressures that she didn't know which to deal with first. She wanted to go after Sager, but her father had another coughing attack.

"Papa, I think you should get in bed. I'll bring you some hot tea—the coffee's too strong for a cough."

Old Jack lurched up from behind his desk. "The hell I will get into bed! I'm going to talk to the men." He stalked across the room toward her, leveling his blackest glower on her. "What I don't need is you pampering me."

Rachel stepped in front of the doorway, blocking his exit. This close to her father, she saw that his face was chalky, his features drawn. "And what *I* don't need, Papa, is a dead father! Either you get yourself to bed, or I'll have a few of the men tie you up and drag you there!"

Jack's eyes narrowed. "That's mutiny." She returned his look stare for stare. "Oh, hell!" he cursed. "I wasn't going to be long anyway. I'll talk to the boys in the morning, but I sure as hell don't need any help gettin' to bed."

Rachel stepped back, allowing him access to the hallway. "Mrs. Biddle put fresh water in your room this afternoon. Wash up and get into bed, and I'll bring you that tea."

She returned moments later, tea in hand. His door was ajar. She knocked quietly, then walked in. He was lying down with the sheet drawn up to his chest. He wore his nightshirt, but he hadn't washed any of the grime from his face. His eyes were tightly closed—so tight that she knew he wasn't asleep.

The air outside had a decided chill to it, and his window was open. She set his tea on his nightstand and crossed the room to close the window.

"I sleep with it open, girl." He was looking at her through one eye; the other was still shut tightly.

Rachel lowered the window, leaving it only cracked, and turned to him. "Then you'll sleep with a blanket."

"Humph." He mumbled something under his breath and shut both eyes again as she pulled a quilt up over him.

"Good night, Papa," she said. And then, just to underscore the fact that she had the last word, she kissed his forehead.

Too restless and too pensive to sleep, Rachel left the house and strolled toward her garden, drawing her shawl tighter about herself. She needed to find a little tranquillity in the chaos of the evening.

She stared at the straight rows Sager had plowed, liking their orderliness. Her eyes followed the moonlight's grayish trail across the field to the edge of the copse where she and Sager had embraced. The memory of that interlude filled her with sinful warmth. Her mind conjured up the image of Sager leaning against the trunk of a sapling. She wished he were here now. She wanted him to hold her and tell her Papa would be fine. She wanted to apologize for her father's rudeness. She wanted to hear the story about his mother. She knew so little about him, though thoughts of him filled every moment of the day.

She stared at the image awhile before she blinked. It wasn't her imagination; he was truly there, watching her. Calling to her wordlessly.

She looked at him, resisting the tide that pulled her toward him. He was so much a part of this land. She could picture him living comfortably with his Indian family. She could see him happily surrounded by miles and miles of empty rangeland. But could she see him in a home?

In her home?

Chapter Sixteen

As Rachel watched Sager, a stiff breeze kicked up, blowing away the last of her will to resist him. She slowly closed the distance between them. He watched her until she stopped directly before him. He held her gaze, his pale eyes enigmatic, hurt.

The breeze tossed wisps of her hair across her face. He reached out and tucked them behind her ear. The rightness of his touch made Rachel tremble. He circled his arm about her shoulder, pulling her against himself. She pressed her face into the rigid strength of his chest and breathed deeply of his fine masculine scent.

"I'm sorry about your mother, Sager." She looked up at him, half expecting him to turn from her, to shut her out. He held her gaze a moment, then looked out at the field before them. "I know about the aching emptiness her passing must have left with you," Rachel continued. *I've lived with that pain all my life.*

He shut his eyes and clenched his jaw.

"But you must release the anger."

When his eyes opened, pools of moisture caught

the moonlight. "My mother liked butterflies— 'summerbirds,' she called them. Summerbirds and half-breed children. There was nothing she had that she wouldn't gladly give to someone in need."

Rachel stayed in the circle of his arms and watched the breeze rustling the leaves of a nearby branch, listening to his voice rumble through his chest.

"When my father's men came for me, they came with guns. I know now that they must have been watching us for days, waiting for a time when I would be separate from the men. The women were gathering berries; I was supposed to protect them. I had only a knife, but still I wounded two and killed one. Against their guns, I had no chance. Ma faced those men like a she-bear. They laughed at her. They laughed as they blew a hole in her chest big enough for me to crawl through.

"My older sister gathered the other kids and sent them running for the camp. When she tried to grab me, they shot her hand off—she died from that wound, I found out later. And then they came for me, dragged me home to the butcher who sent them." He looked at Rachel, seeing not her but his memories of that day so long ago. He was silent a moment. "That is the anger you'd have me forget. I can't, Rachel, not until I understand all that happened that day."

Rachel felt his pain so keenly, that for a moment, she couldn't speak. This was the fear he'd said made him sick. Until she met Sager, she had no memory of a life free of the domination, bullying, and beatings that she'd endured at her aunt and uncle's home. Sager, on the other hand, had had a good life among people he loved ripped from him in one brutal day.

She wondered which hell was worse.

And he believed his father killed his mother? No wonder he behaved as he had toward him. She looked up at Sager, her eyes pleading with him. "I don't understand. I know that I haven't known Sid long, but that doesn't seem like something he would have done." He watched her steadily. The wind tousled his bangs, shading his face with jagged streaks of black.

"Sometimes, Sager, when we're children, we don't see things the way adults do," she said as his amber eyes held hers. "Were there other men around your family that day? Did your father just face your mother and kill her? Or was he threatened by men from your village?"

"My father wasn't there. His hired men took me."

"Does he know what they did?"

"I don't know. I never talked to him. Never." Sager thought of Cassandra, who was, at this very moment, dying. She'd always been at her worst when Sid was away, and Sid had been gone a lot, trying to find markets for his cattle. She'd come to him the first night he was there. Shucking her robe in front of him, he remembered the sight of her breasts showing through the transparent fabric of her negligee. Naked white breasts. He'd never been with a woman, but he was no stranger to what happened between men and women. And in any culture, it was an insult to fuck another man's wife.

Sid either didn't know about Cassandra's nocturnal visits, or didn't care. He was more upset by Sager's refusal to speak to him. After a short while, Sager had lost interest in Cassandra and began locking his doors against her. When he did, she had a couple of the ranch hands beat him up. He moved to the Circle Bar bunkhouse, but she was still able to corner him. He left and came to work for Old Jack, Sid's longtime enemy, before leaving the Territory altogether.

"I couldn't talk to my father," he said aloud to Rachel. "I couldn't look at him. It was hard enough for me to be in the same room with him. I didn't know how much my silence bothered him until he confronted me about it. At fourteen, I was already as tall as he was. He shook me, but I acted as if he wasn't there. He cussed and told me that he'd been looking for me all my life. Said I was his son and that I sure as hell better acknowledge him. He even hit me a few times, but it did no good. To me, he was already dead. He was invisible. After that, he didn't care."

Rachel frowned. "Sager, the Shoshone aren't a migrating people, are they?"

"Not over great distances. Why?"

"If you'd been born among the Shoshone, and lived there your entire life, then why did it take him so long to find you?"

Sager shrugged. "I don't care, Rachel."

She sighed. Giving his shirt a quick tug, she said urgently, "Talk to him. For me."

Sager said nothing in answer to her request, but the expression in his eyes changed, darkened as he looked down into her eyes. She became intensely aware of being alone in a sheltering copse of trees with a man who made her blood boil. She should leave—she knew she should go; to stay was to invite trouble.

"When's your barbeque?" Sager asked, changing the subject.

Rachel focused on his question, delaying her decision to go inside—for another moment at least. "I don't know. Papa wants to have it in three weeks. But he's got a fever, and he's coughing blood. And now with Logan's mother sick, I think we should wait a few weeks. I've sent Papa to bed. Tomorrow I'll head over to the Circle Bar and ask Sid to send the doctor this way when they can."

Sager caught a strand of her hair and trapped it behind her ear again. He gazed down into her eyes for a long moment. "C'mon." He gave her a smile. "I'll walk you back to the house. Morning comes early around here." He took a step, then looked back to her and held out his hand.

Rachel melded her fingers with his and let him draw her toward her father's ranch house. At the steps to the porch, he paused, facing her. The light in the house lit his features. "G'night, Rachel." He smiled again, but it didn't ease the desolation in his eyes as he bent forward and kissed her cheek.

Sid Taggert waited in his office for Logan to send the doctor down to him. He didn't want to see Cassandra until he knew what he was dealing with. This wasn't the first time she'd taken to her bed with an incurable illness. Usually she did it when the stress of her sins grew too weighty. He sighed, massaging the bridge of his nose. Perhaps he'd been a bad husband.

God knew she'd been a bad wife.

"Sid?"

"Come in, Doctor. Come in."

Dr. Felder set his leather medical satchel down in a chair and walked slowly toward him. The doctor's lips were pressed thin, and Sid knew without being told that this was the last incurable illness his wife would suffer.

"I'm afraid she's not doing very well. She's lost a lot of blood."

Sid's brows lowered. "What happened?"

"She's been shot."

"Shot?" Sid bellowed. "Where was she hit?"

"The lower abdomen. Looks like it was done at close range, too. This happened yesterday?"

Sid was too stunned to think clearly. He shoved his hand through his hair as he tried to recall the day's events—hell, it was halfway to morning already. "I don't know. I returned from Defiance yesterday, and Logan told me she was ill. I don't know what she did—where she might have gone. She usually goes for a ride in the afternoon." Sid stopped his pacing and pressed both hands to his face, trying to focus on what might have happened. He hadn't loved Cassandra for a long, long time—maybe not ever. But to have her gut-shot in cold blood racked him with guilt. Who could have done this? And who would be their next target?

He took another turn about the room. Despite her faults, Cassandra had trusted him to provide a safe life for her. And he'd let her down. She wasn't the wife he'd wanted. She wasn't Isabel. Perhaps, if he'd been more tolerant—if he'd just humored her—they could have been happy. But he'd wanted a true life-mate, a full partner in the ranch's operations. And she had just wanted to be the grand lady.

"Doc, will she live?"

He shook his head. "I don't know. She's lost too much blood. I've given her something for the pain. It'll make her sleep soon. You'd best go see her."

Sid had the doctor shown to a guest room, then slowly walked up the steps to the second floor. He paused inside the doorway to Cassandra's room. Lamps were lit on either side of her bed. For a moment, he just stood there, staring at her. Comparing— as he always did—his ambivalence toward her with his love for Isabel.

Cassandra's lips were white. Her eyes looked sunken. She had been shot less than twenty-four hours ago, yet already she'd traveled such a distance between life and death.

"Dad, come here," Logan said in a hushed voice, his gray eyes beckoning Sid with the earnestness of a six-year-old child. "Her hands are growing weak."

Sid moved his leaden feet toward his wife. He sat down on the opposite side of the bed from Logan and looked at Cassandra. She probably didn't even know he was there, he thought. But her hand lifted and slipped into his as though that were a familiar action. Sid stiffened but didn't pull his hand away. Her fingers were already cold. He watched her face, waiting for that moment when her muscles would release their hold on her features. A smile lifted the corners of her mouth. He'd kissed that mouth once. Found warmth there, warmth that nearly chased away his aching loneliness for Isabel.

Suddenly the fingers he held dug their nails into his hand painfully. He watched her gentle smile twist into a hellish frown as her eyes flew open and she fixed him in her stare. "You dare to come here! You are not fit to clean my shoes!"

"Mother!" Logan said, suddenly alarmed for her, for Sid. He tried to restrain her, but she summoned Herculean strength and fought him as she continued to shriek.

"I never loved you! Never! Thank God there is nothing of you in Logan."

"That's enough, Mother," Logan choked.

Cassandra relaxed in her son's embrace without releasing Sid's hand. She lifted her free hand and brushed her cold fingers across Logan's face. "Do not call this man 'father' ever again, for he has no claim to that title. He can't be your father while that breed he calls his son is still alive. He should have died, Logan. The others he was with were hit—all of them! I saw to it. My one regret is that the breed lived, for in letting him live, I failed you." She drew an anguished breath. Her voice lowered to a whisper, which both men had to lean forward to hear. "Tom was supposed to kill him, not me."

"No, Mother. No—"

Cassandra settled back against her pillows, pain crumpling her face. Sid watched the life fall from her body even as he felt the nails retract from the furrows they'd dug in his hand. He stood and backed away from the bed, wondering, for the first time in all the years they'd been married, what kind of poison she'd filled his boys' heads with. What did she mean about the others being hit? Was that why Sager hated him? And had Cassandra been dealing with Tom Beall? God, she was a crazy bitch.

He left the room. He couldn't stand to see the sorrow in Logan's face as he pressed his cheek to

Cassandra's. He stumbled into the hallway and, leaning heavily on the banister, made his way downstairs and into his office to his waiting decanter of brandy.

Rachel knocked at the bunkhouse door first thing in the morning. It was early yet—just after dawn—but she wanted to catch Fletcher before she headed out for the morning. Someone was awake, for a thin stream of smoke rose from the chimney at one end of the building, filling the morning air with the smell of wood smoke.

"Hi, Digger," Rachel said in a hushed voice when he opened the door. "I need to talk to Fletcher."

"He ain't here. Would Ross do?" he asked.

"Yes, I guess so."

"Hey, Ross!" Digger shouted into the room. "Miz Rachel's here to see you."

Rachel listened to the hurried rustling of blankets and clothes. She moved away, discreetly turning her back on the door as she awaited Ross. She was glad, actually, that Fletcher wasn't available. He'd been less than welcoming yesterday evening.

"Ma'am." Ross tipped his hat at her as he came out onto the porch and closed the door behind him. He had donned a pair of pants over his red flannel underwear, but wore no shirt and his feet were still bare.

"Ross, my father is not feeling well—he's coughing blood. I don't want him to go out with the boys today. Perhaps you could stop by his room after breakfast and get any instructions he might have for the men and pass it on to Fletcher?"

Ross pushed his hat back on his head and scratched his forehead. He looked at Rachel as though she were loco. "He's never not gone out before, ma'am."

"He's very sick. I'm going to ride over to the Taggerts' ranch and see if I can get their doctor to stop this way before he leaves the area."

Ross grinned. "How'd you get your pa to take himself off to bed—and agree to stay there today?" he asked, still chewing on that bit of news.

"It wasn't easy. He certainly is stubborn. He doesn't know I won't let him up yet."

"You're a lot like your ma, Miz Rachel. She didn't take no nonsense from him either."

"You knew my mother?"

"Indeed I did. She was Old Jack's life. 'Bout killed him when he had to send you to live with your aunt and uncle. Been mean ever since."

Rachel sucked in a sharp breath. "Why did he send me away?"

"Couldn't raise you himself out here. Not with your mother gone and only a bunch of old cowpunchers for company. And it just weren't in him to remarry. Yer pa didn't want you to be a cowboy. Wanted you to be a lady. And that you are." He smiled at her. "You even look like her, Rachel. I bet it just cuts through Old Jack sometimes, what with you bossin' him around and such like she did."

How different her life would have been had her father decided to brave it out and raise her here instead of sending her away. "Ross—was my mother nice?" Or was she like her sister, Aunt Eunice, whose black soul had twisted her into a cruel shadow of a woman.

"Yer ma was a true lady, miss. She took care of us all. Not a mean bone in her body."

Rachel nodded, oddly saddened by that news. "Thanks, Ross. I wish I had known my mother." Rachel smiled. "Look in on him in a while, okay?"

"Will do."

Rachel left the bunkhouse and went straight to the corral to fetch her horse. She saddled him and turned him about toward the gate, but her way was blocked.

"Mornin'."

"Sager!" Rachel answered, unable to keep the smile from her face.

"You headed over to the Circle Bar already?" he asked. Rachel nodded. "You goin' alone?"

"Mrs. Biddle gave me directions." Though she had ridden there once with her father, she hadn't paid enough attention to the route. "She said I'm to ride west for twenty minutes until I come to a streambed, then cross the creek and ride northwest for another twenty minutes or so."

Sager looked at her intently. "She tell you about the patch of cottonwoods you'll cross through?"

"No."

"She tell you about Deadman's Hill?"

"No."

"How much food are you bringing?"

"Just what I've packed for the Taggerts. Sager, their ranch is less than an hour's ride from here! I'll be back before noon."

"Not with Mrs. Biddle's directions, you won't." He pushed off the fence and came toward her. "You'll be so damned lost, we won't see you for a fortnight.

Guess I'll come with you." He smiled up at her. "I'd hate for you to spend a day entertaining wolves."

He caught his pony and saddled him quickly. They rode single file through the early-morning countryside. The sun hadn't warmed the air yet, but Rachel enjoyed the chilly temperature. They crossed the creek and passed through the cottonwoods. They even passed a few hills, but none that seemed deserving of the name *Deadman's Hill*.

Rachel drew even with Sager. "So where's Deadman's Hill?"

"In Texas."

"Texas? Why did you tell me to watch for it?"

"I didn't. I asked if Mrs. Biddle had told you about it."

Rachel pulled her horse to a stop. "Her directions were fine."

Sager nodded and his lips curved into a boyish grin as he looked back at her. "In fact, you could have simply stayed on this path, and you would have reached the Taggerts' directly."

"If you wanted to ride with me, why didn't you say so?"

His smile faded. "Asking for what I want isn't easy, Rachel. Especially when it comes to you." He held her gaze a moment. She couldn't breathe. She didn't want to breathe.

She wanted him.

He turned and continued down the path.

They rode into the front yard of the Circle Bar a short while later. Sager's features had grown tense and his back was ramrod straight. Rachel dismounted and handed her reins over to him. "We won't be here long. You don't have to come in." For

an answer, he merely looked at her, great dark
secrets crowding behind his amber eyes. She gave
him an encouraging half-smile, then pulled out the
loaves of bread and the crock of stew she brought for
Sid and Logan, and walked toward the house.

At the top of the porch steps, she looked back to
find that Sager had dismounted and was leaning
against the corral fence. He crossed his arms over his
chest and watched her. She continued on, shifting
the food to her other arm so that she could knock.
Just as she lifted her hand to knock, the door was
jerked open and Logan lurched out onto the porch.

He looked exhausted. Fatigue had bruised his
eyes, and his hair was mussed as though he'd raked
it with his fingers. He paused a moment, surprised
to see her standing there.

"Rachel," he greeted her. His cheeks were wet
and fresh tears trailed down his cheeks. He wasn't
sobbing, just quietly mourning.

"Oh, Logan, I'm so sorry," Rachel whispered, assuming the worst. She touched his arm, wondering
how she could make it hurt less. "What can I do to
help?"

Logan shut his eyes, but the tears kept rolling
down his face. When he opened his eyes again, he
looked away from her, out across the prairie that
rolled in front of the Taggert home. Rachel knew
when he spotted Sager, for his expression changed,
hardened. He left the porch and walked down to the
corrals where Sager stood.

Rachel set the bread and stew down on a nearby
table and turned to watch Sager and Logan at the
corral fence. Such a contrast, Logan's white-blond
hair to Sager's inky black locks. They were almost of

a height, which surprised her, for Logan seemed much younger and slighter than Sager.

The door opened behind her, and Sid joined her on the porch. His face was drawn, his eyes troubled. He, too, watched his sons.

"She's at peace now," he announced.

"I'm sorry, Sid. What happened? We only got word that she was ill."

He turned his haunted gaze on her. "She was shot, Rachel. I had no idea until the doctor told me this morning. I thought she just had another of her many illnesses."

"Shot!" Rachel gasped. "Sid, who would have done that?"

"I don't know, but I sure as hell mean to find out. This damned trouble has to end. It's good Sager came with you today. You shouldn't be riding out alone until we've ended this range war."

She nodded. "How are you holding up?"

He sighed. "Truthfully, I'm glad she's gone. She was never happy here, never happy with me." He put his arm around Rachel and pulled her gruffly to his side. A minute of silence passed. "I love my boys, Rachel. Both of them," he added fiercely. "It's just that so much water's gone by—"

"Yes, but the river still flows, Sid. They need you."

He sniffled and stepped away. Rachel looked at his hard profile. Perhaps she'd said too much. She was still a stranger here, an outsider to the Taggerts' problems. "My father is not feeling well. He's coughing blood. I was hoping to catch the doctor before he left."

"He's already gone, but I'll send Logan after him. He should be over to your place by this afternoon."

"Thank you. Can I give you a hand here? Have you anyone to help prepare Cassandra?"

"We're fine. I guess her maid will see to most of it."

"I brought you a few things." She pointed to the table where she'd set them. "I didn't know what you might need."

"Ah, Rachel, you're as kind and beautiful as your mother was, God rest her soul."

Logan stood stiffly at the fence, staring unseeingly across the field. "She's dead," he announced in a flat voice.

Sager dug around in his mind, searching for something to say, some comfort he could give his brother. He and Logan had known each other for thirteen years, yet they were still strangers. "You were the only one, only thing she truly cared about," he said at last.

Logan turned his ice gray eyes on Sager. "For a time, she loved you, didn't she?"

Sager's laugh was coarse. "That wasn't love. She wanted to fuck a savage." He saw his brother's fist coming and didn't dodge it. When he took a blow to his stomach, instinct kicked in. He wrestled Logan to the ground, trying ineffectually to stop him. It wasn't until Sager had a knee in Logan's diaphragm and his hands around Logan's neck that his brother stilled.

"She sent those men that day. She confessed it all. She wanted to kill you. She did it for me. She wanted you dead."

Vaguely, Sager heard Rachel and Sid running toward them. "Sager! Stop it!" Rachel's voice barely penetrated his mind. It was Cassandra. All these years. She, and not Sid, had hired the men who destroyed his family. He released Logan and sat in the dirt next to him, his mind replaying that bloody day, lashing him with the knowledge that he'd become a lover to his family's killer.

"Logan—are you hurt?" he heard Rachel ask as she knelt beside his brother.

"I'm fine."

"Sager! What were you thinking?" Rachel admonished him.

What indeed? He looked at her, unable to answer her. Slowly, he forced himself to his feet, feeling heavy, as though he was tied to the ground. His father was there, standing before him. The worry in his eyes was too raw to look at. Sager moved woodenly to his horse and mounted, waiting silently for Rachel.

"I'm sorry," Rachel said, standing awkwardly by Logan and Sid. "I don't know what came over him."

Sid squeezed her shoulder. "Never mind. It will pass. I'll send Logan after the doctor. And we'll be over once your pa's had a little time to feel better."

Sager was already riding away when Logan helped Rachel mount her horse. She waved farewell to them, then pushed her horse into a lope to catch up with him. They rode in silence a few miles. Sager's face was like carved stone. She wanted to comfort him, to say something, but what? Just when she could stand the silence no longer, he pulled up. A narrow path led off to the right. He waited for her to come even with him, his eyes staring into the barren hills ahead of them.

"Sager? What is it?"

"Follow the path we're on. It'll take you back to the Crippled Horse."

"What about you? Where are you going?"

"There's something I need to do," he said, adjusting the reins in his hands. He didn't meet her eyes. "I'll see you back at your father's spread." He turned his mount down the narrow path and rode away from her.

Rachel watched him disappear as a pain tore a hole in her chest. His pain. She nudged her horse to a slow trot, leaving Sager, giving him the room he needed. But the further she moved away from him, the heavier he was on her mind. He was alone now, as he'd been his whole life. He'd pushed everyone away. His father. His brother. He kept her at arm's length. She drew to a stop. Maybe, just maybe, he'd finally met in her the one person he couldn't push away.

She turned around and headed back in the direction he'd taken. About a mile down the path, the barren hills gave way to a ridge of cottonwoods and some underbrush. She found Sager's vest discarded along the side of the path.

Then his shirt.

Then one boot and then the other.

Chapter Seventeen

Rachel peered into the towering old cottonwoods sheltering a large, spring-fed pool of hot water that drained into a wide, fast-moving creek. Sager's horse was tethered to a bush. She dismounted and tied her horse near his. Bending down to retrieve his clothes where they lay, haphazardly discarded, she set them in a neat stack. She stepped deeper into the hidden grove and found him sitting on an old log, wearing only his denims. His elbows were braced on his knees. His head was bowed, his forehead on his folded arms.

Rachel knelt before him, putting her hands on his arms, and waited for him to look up. He lifted his head, his eyes bleak.

"Go home, Rachel."

"No."

"I don't want you here," he growled.

"But I am here, Sager, and I'm not leaving."

"I told you before not to seek me out." He spoke between clenched teeth.

Rachel gave him a little smile. "That warning only had value when I was afraid of you."

"You should still be afraid of me." *My soul is black.*

Rachel's hands moved up the tense muscles of his arms to cup his face. "Sager, don't shut me out."

He winced and dragged her into his arms, burying his face in her neck. Rachel gripped him as fiercely as he held her. He drew her up on his lap, spreading her legs on either side of him. She could feel his thighs beneath hers. She threaded her fingers in his hair, cupping the back of his head as she leaned forward to kiss his jaw, his cheekbone. She brushed her lips against his, inviting him to kiss her.

His mouth twisted against hers. His tongue thrust into her mouth. Searching. Plundering. Drinking of her as she drank of him. She met his thrusts, sliding her tongue along his. His thumbs pressed into the flesh below her breasts. Fire took flight along her spine, and she arched against him. He held her unresisting body with one arm as his mouth tasted her lips, her chin, her neck.

His free hand moved over her face, her chin, touching her as if he'd lost his vision, lost his way. She felt his hand move down her chest to grip her breast. She arched into his hand, her cotton garments transmitting the heat of his skin like a hot breath.

He started to pull her shirt from the waist of her skirt, and she drew apart from the kiss to watch as he ran his hand up between the material of her shirt and the fabric of her camisole to palm her breasts. She wore no corset—she'd been in too much of a hurry to catch the doctor this morning to take the time to dress properly. The sensation was exquisite.

She moved against him, unconsciously bucking her hips against his.

He pushed her shirt and camisole up, baring her breasts to the cool air. He dragged his gaze away from her body, his eyes catching hers as his hands moved up her ribs to close on her naked flesh. A little huff of air escaped her lips as she saw his dark hands on her pale skin.

He bent his head to her chest. Rachel shoved her hands into his black hair as his lips touched her skin. Never had she experienced anything that felt like this. He kissed the entire circumference of her breast before his mouth closed on her nipple. Liquid heat boiled within her, settling in her stomach, then lower. She tried to move closer to him, but his hold was remorseless as he kissed and tasted and suckled her flesh.

"Sager," she breathed, saying incoherent words.

He lifted his raven head, his pale eyes black as he looked at her. His nostrils flared. "Take your shirt off," he whispered, his voice raspy with desire. Rachel removed her jacket and began unbuttoning her blouse, vaguely aware of his hand on her leg, beneath her skirts. He moved over her knee, slowly rising to her thigh, stopping where her legs joined. He gently touched a part of her so exquisitely sensitive that she cried out and took hold of his shoulders.

"You still have your shirt on," he coached.

Breaking her focus on what he was doing under her skirts, she opened the last few buttons, unfastened her cuffs, and drew her shirt off her shoulders. His thumb rotated against her. She bucked against his hand.

"Take your camisole off."

She drew the thin garment over her head, naked now, from the waist up. Sager's eyes feasted on her skin. For the first time in her life, seeing herself from his eyes, Rachel felt beautiful. His hand moved up her ribs. Open palmed, he brushed against her tightening nipple. Her body throbbed, anticipating something more.

He shoved his hand in her hair, lowering her mouth to his. He nibbled her upper lip, her lower lip. His mouth twisted against hers, opening her for his possession as his finger found the opening in her drawers and eased along her inner folds. Her body rocked against his hand. This was shocking. And delicious.

She was dimly aware of his mouth leaving hers, the feel of his unshaven cheek as his chin moved down her neck. His hand cupped her breast, lifting it to his mouth as his thumb worked its magic below. Fire shot along her bones, searing her from the inside out. She cried out, gripped his shoulders. His hand left her sensitive flesh, and she felt him unfasten his pants.

He adjusted her position on his lap, and she suddenly felt something thick and blunt at her opening. She tensed, fearing what would happen next.

"Easy, sweetheart. Easy. We'll go slow." His hands held her hips as he eased into her. She felt herself stretching to accommodate his size. He drew out, then pushed in again, slowly, further. He ran his hands up her back, massaging her tension away, holding her body against his face so that he could nuzzle her breasts. His tongue laved her nipples, and when he moved from one to the other, the cool air continued his gentle torture.

Rachel gave herself over to the pleasure of being in his arms. She ran her hands over his shoulders, feeling his muscles bunch beneath her hands. Everywhere she touched he was taut strength. She could feel him throbbing within her, holding himself still.

When he reached beneath her skirts and touched that sensitive part he'd worked earlier, Rachel felt separated from her body. Numbed. On fire. The world narrowed to just the two of them. She moved against him, taking him deeper. He pulled out and pushed in again. The sensation teased. Suddenly, feeling exploded within her. She felt him surge into her, felt a sting, and all rational thought left her in a rush. She bucked against him, felt him take hold of her hips as he thrust against her. Her legs curled around his back, her body taking him deeper. Rachel cried out, carried on wave after wave of mindless joy. She felt him tense, holding her tight to his body as he spent himself inside her.

As the feelings ebbed away, Rachel collapsed against his body. They both struggled to breathe. Too soon, he leaned back to look into her eyes. Shadows crowded his amber eyes.

"That was extraordinary." Her heart was still hammering.

He smiled, but it didn't warm his eyes. He lifted her off his lap and came to his feet, bringing her with him. "I come here every time I've been to the Circle Bar."

Rachel looked at the dark pool of water behind her. Steam rose in wispy curls. Here and there heat percolated to the surface. Sager removed his pants. He drew her into his arms for a kiss. She felt his hands work the fastenings of her skirt, then her petticoats and drawers, dropping them to pool about her ankles. She was as naked as he was. It felt decadent, standing so with him in the dappled sunshine of this hidden grove.

She ran her hands over the soft skin of his bare chest. Her fingers smoothed across the rippling muscles of his belly. He lifted her hand and kissed her knuckles. "Will you come into the water with me?"

She looked at the dark pool again. She swallowed. "No. I'll wait here. You go."

He shook his head. "Come in with me. Please."

She felt a knot of emotion as she looked into his golden eyes. She'd followed him here to give him ease. How could she deny him? But how could she do what he asked?

His fingers caressed the tense skin of her face. He leaned his forehead toward hers, his other hand twined with hers. "Rachel, do you trust me?"

She drew a shaky breath. "I trust you. I don't trust the water." She looked at the steaming pool. "It's deep. And it's dark. I don't know what's in there."

Sager smiled, a slow, easy smile that lifted the shadows from his face. "But I do. Nothing's in there other than warm tingly water and smooth river pebbles. It's too hot for anything scary." He stepped backward into the water, drawing her in with him.

Warm water closed over her feet. Steam caressed her calves. Another step. The rocks were smooth beneath her feet. He paused to let her become accustomed to the water. She closed her eyes, drawn back inexorably to her first experience with water, when she became aware she lived in hell. Her hands tightened on Sager's. She fought the need to spin around and find safety on the bank.

Her eyes opened. He filled her vision. "Sager, what is your first memory?"

He gazed at her, considering her, considering her question. His eyes became unfocused as he looked into the past. "I was three summers. My father was teaching me to ride. I sat before him on his pony." He lifted his hand, looking at his palm. "I clutched a fistful of the pony's white and brown mane. 'Feel the pony's stride,' my father said. 'Close your eyes and feel him with your body, in your legs. Catch his rhythm. A warrior must know his horse as he knows himself.'"

Sager paused, looking at her. "I still remember what it felt like to know when that pony was going to step, when he was going to hit the ground, the feel of the wind, the feel of my father behind me. 'Let go, my son,' he said. 'Lift your arms and look at the sky.'

"I closed my eyes until I felt the horse beneath me. I pulled my hand out of the mane, and I lifted my arms. My father did, too. My arms barely reached beyond his chest. His looked like long columns into the sky. I thought one day I would be big like him and have long arms, too. When we returned home, he tied a feather in my hair, then let me snuggle with my mother." *She'd been so proud of him, she whom Cassandra had slaughtered.*

Thinking of Cassandra in the same breath as his mother soiled that memory. He wouldn't do it. He wouldn't let her steal the good times, too. He focused on Rachel. "What about you? What was your first memory?"

Rachel swallowed and forced herself to look at Sager, not the water. "I don't know how old I was. I didn't celebrate birthdays. But my youngest cousin was six, and I'm two years younger than him, so I must have been four. We were on a picnic—my aunt, uncle, my cousins and I. I don't know why they brought me with them. They never did again. We were playing with a ball. It was fun. It was the first toy I remember. My cousin kicked it into the river. I watched it float downstream. I didn't want to lose it, so I rushed in after it.

"The shore didn't have a gentle incline. Only a few steps in, and the bottom gave way. I went under. My clothes were heavy. I fought to the surface, but couldn't find footing. I heard my cousins' governess screaming. I bobbed out of the water, once, calling for my aunt and then my uncle. I saw them standing at the shore, looking at each other. I don't think they heard me. I went under again. And the next thing I knew, a stranger was yanking me out of the water."

She remembered what happened afterward, too. They'd locked her in her room for a week. "Somehow, they found out how scared I was of the river. When I was really bad, they would take me back to the river and make me stand there, next to it. Sometimes they would let my cousin take me." She looked at Sager. "I guess I was bad a lot."

Fury was evident in the rigid lines of his face. He took hold of her arms and walked her out of the water, his gentle touch at odds with the rage in his eyes. "We don't have to be here, Rachel. I'll take you to the desert. You won't ever have to be afraid again."

"That's just it. I don't want to be afraid anymore. As long as I am, they still own me." She watched the corners of his jaw knot and unknot reflexively. "Help me, Sager. Help me to not be afraid."

He drew in a long breath and released it slowly. He

lifted his head and gazed at the trees surrounding them. She waited in silence. He looked at her again, taking her measure. "You will have to relearn the water."

"How?"

He frowned. "I don't know. Maybe throw away all that you know about it. Pretend you've never seen it before, never known it. The water's not cruel, Rachel. People are. The water just does what it does. Meet it now, for the first time, with someone who will never hurt you.

"We'll go back in, slowly. If you want to stop, we'll stop." Rachel nodded. He took hold of her hands and eased her back into the water. They walked in until it reached above her knees. "Let your mind dwell only on what your body senses. Tell me what you see."

She looked straight ahead, seeing the wall of his chest. "I see you." He smiled and lifted her chin. The sky was a brilliant turquoise blue, the sun still low enough to shine through the flat leaves of the cottonwoods, lighting them like stained glass. "I see sunlight through the trees."

Sager turned her around. He wrapped his arms over hers and held her against his chest. "What do you see now?"

She looked at the bank, half expecting Uncle Henry or Cousin Jeremy to appear. There was only some low shrubs, a couple of fallen logs, the hard-packed dirt of the bank. "Nothing."

"I see more than nothing. Tell me what you are looking at."

"Shrubs and dirt. Our horses and clothes."

He turned her back around and led her a couple

of more steps in. "Now close your eyes. Empty your mind of all thoughts. What do you feel?"

She considered her answer. There were no teeth to tear at her flesh, no hands to yank her in deeper. What did she feel? "The water is hot—not burning, but a pleasing temperature. I feel small, smooth stones. And bubbles against my leg." She kept her eyes shut, her mind still, knowing life only through her skin. "The breeze is cool. When the trees shift, I feel sunshine. And I feel your hands, strong and steady under mine."

"What do you hear?"

You're a stupid, inconsiderate, little girl. It's no wonder you're an orphan—who would want you? Stand here and think about your behavior. Her hands tightened on Sager's. She opened her eyes and looked at him as she fought to tell her mind her senses weren't lying.

"Memories can only hurt if you let them, Rach. I'm not asking what you remember. Tell me what you hear."

Her aunt and uncle and cousins weren't real anymore. She was here, alone with Sager. He was real.

"I hear a robin. Other birds—finches and a dove. There are crickets, too. And some throaty sound, I think—a frog? I can hear the creek beyond us." She listened more intently and smiled. "I hear bubbles from this spring. It pops and sighs."

He smiled at her and pulled her into his arms. She welcomed his hug. So many times he'd held her like this, as if she were special, worth sheltering.

"Honey, does any of what you see, hear or feel scare you?" She shook her head. He stroked her cheek. "You survived them, Rach. That makes you braver than any warrior I know." He bent and lifted her into his arms. She wrapped her arms about his neck, intensely aware of the feel of her body against his, her water-heated skin against his. She was unable to pull her eyes from his. The look he gave her caught her soul.

He walked until the water was just above his waist. "I'm going to set you down. We're just going to stand here." He eased his hand from beneath her knees, but kept his arm around her back. The dark, hot water swallowed her legs. She stepped closer to him, standing on his feet, her knees against his legs. She wrapped her arms around his waist and laid her face against his chest.

The water bubbled and sighed in one ear, and his heart beat in the other. This was heaven. Contentment filled her with warmth like a state of grace. She looked up at Sager, wondering if he felt what she did. Steam dampened his shaggy black hair, plastering it to his face. He looked into her eyes and smiled.

"This is why I always come here after being to Sid's." He lifted handfuls of water and poured them over her shoulders. Thin rivulets drained from her slim body, and his eyes followed their movement over her skin. He ran his hands up her arms, over her shoulders. He cupped her face and bent toward her. His lips took hers. His tongue entered her mouth. She didn't know where she ended and he began. She was as hot inside as she was outside in the steaming water.

"There's more," he whispered against her mouth.

"More?"

"Put your arms around my neck." She did as he ordered, glad for the excuse to be close to him. He touched a kiss to her lips and smiled down at her. "Hold on." He leaned backward in the water. Holding her with an arm around her waist, he kicked the water and navigated his way out into the middle of the pool.

"How deep is it here?" she asked apprehensively.

"Six feet, I suppose. Deep enough for a good swim. Hold on to my back, and I'll take you for a ride." He turned onto his stomach, and she looped her arms about his shoulders so that her body lay along the length of his as he swam through the water. He swam from side to side, dipping her under the water every now and then for the barest of seconds. His powerful body cut through the water as though born to the task. Holding his shoulders, she felt his muscles flex and stretch beneath her hands. She felt small on his back. Water pooled between his shoulder blades. She dipped her face into it, tasting the mineral rich water. Tasting Sager. When at last he swam toward the bank and released her in shallower water, she was breathless.

"You make it look so easy."

He laughed at the wonder on her face. "It is. I could show you how," he offered.

"All right."

"First thing you have to learn is how to breathe while you swim. Put your face in the water and blow air out of your mouth. Like this." He bent forward and ducked his face in the water.

Rachel watched bubbles rise past his ears and burst toward the surface. She bent down next to him and did as he did. She heard the roar of the bubbles as they boiled past her ears. She lifted her head and smiled at Sager, heedless of the water still dripping off her face. She licked reflexively at a drop of water as it rolled down her cheek and into her mouth, unprepared for the heat that shot through his eyes.

"You've got that down," he announced suddenly. "Now let's try another thing." He moved further out until he was waist-deep in the water. She followed him. "Let me show you how to float." He leaned back until he was lying flat upon the water. His arms were spread wide, and his eyes were closed. He looked entirely at peace—no small feat, Rachel thought, considering he was resting atop the water.

Her gaze flowed along the length of him, trying to understand what it was that held him up. Her eyes traveled from the tips of his fingers, up his arms to his shoulders and chest, down the hard surface of his stomach to his manhood. And there her eyes stopped.

Indeed, her breathing stopped as well.

Water pooled in his lap, nestling his engorged member as it lay against his abdomen. She could see the dark, curly hair about its base, the dark vein that nearly ran the enormous length of it. A warmth began to spiral within her that was hotter than the water. Her eyes continued on down the length of his thighs and knees and calves to the tips of his toes. But it was pointless. She forgot what was she was trying to learn. Her gaze flew to his face to see if he'd noticed her perusal, but his eyes were still closed. She was light-headed, and now—more than ever—feared drowning.

"Your turn," his deep voice broke into her musings.

"What?"

He smiled. "To float."

"Oh." She tried to return his smile, but it was a

weak attempt. She was supremely conscious of her own nudity. She opened her arms and leaned back in the water as he'd done, but all she managed to do was sink beneath the surface. Again she tried and again she sank. She gave him a helpless look. "I told you I was a lead weight."

"You need to lift your legs. Like this."

He started to show her by floating again. "I remember! I've got it." She refused to be treated to another look at his male parts—her concentration was weak enough as it was. "Like this?" She leaned back and lifted her legs, but only succeeded in sinking a little faster this time.

"No. Like this," he said, supporting her with an arm beneath her legs and one beneath her shoulders.

Rachel felt his gaze cloak her skin as her nipples tightened beneath his perusal. "Close your eyes," she ordered, unable to concentrate on the floating exercise.

"Why?" he countered. "You didn't." She gasped and started to pull away from him. "Sorry, Rach—" He caught her again. "Just close your eyes and concentrate. Spread your arms as I did. I've got you—you won't fall. Feel the movement of the water. Find the line between water and air."

She tried to concentrate, but she could feel his gaze as surely as she felt the water swirling over her. Her stomach tightened. What was happening to her? All of her senses were overstimulated. She listened to the birds singing overhead, the buzz of summer insects, the water that roared in her ears. But loudest of all was the thundering of her heart.

"Please, Sager, you must close your eyes! I fear the weight of your gaze will drown me."

"Concentrate, Rach. Feel how light you are in the water. Listen to the sound of your breathing. There is nothing, Rachel, but you and the water. Know that, and you will have beat your fear."

His voice was hypnotic. She no longer cared whether he perused her as she had him. Stress seeped away from her as she gave herself over to the weightlessness of floating. She relaxed into the gentle swaying of the water. If she could do this, she could swim. If she could swim, water would just be water, not some lurking monster waiting to grab her.

That realization woke her from her reverie. Her body folded into the water as she came to her feet. Her face was alight with excitement at her success. He smiled back at her. The moment lengthened. Their smiles faded, chased away by a desperate intensity. He moved back a step, but she followed him. She knew from his rigid stance that he was making an effort not to touch her—how many times had she seen this same, hungry posture in him? And she thought he hadn't wanted her, hadn't found her attractive!

Her hands crossed the distance between them, flattening themselves against his stomach. Her eyes lifted to his, searching their darkened, stoic depths for a hint of emotion, encouragement. Her fingers glided northward on his chest, over his ribs, over his nipples. She moved her palms in a circular motion over his raised flesh and heard the sharp intake of his breath seconds before his arms encircled her.

He crushed her naked body against his. His eyes, no longer hooded, seared her with his hunger even as his erection throbbed against her tender belly.

"Rachel," he rasped as his lips took hers, "let me love you again. Now." He broke the kiss to test her

upper lip, then her lower lip, then the hollow of her
cheek. Her arms looped around his back, over his
shoulders. She felt him run his hand down her side,
over her hip to her thigh. His strong fingers massaged her muscles, wringing a moan from her.

Sager's amber eyes blackened with hunger. He
cupped the back of her head and crushed her lips to
his. She opened herself to him completely, welcoming his tongue into her mouth. His arm around her
back pressed her breasts against his chest. Each
breath they took intensified the sensation against
her aroused nipples.

Holding her, he knelt down, bringing her with him
in the shallow water. He pressed kisses to her cheek,
her jaw, her throat. She arched her back, giving
him access to all that he desired. She wanted to
touch him everywhere, to have him touch her everywhere. When he sat back and stretched his legs out
beneath her, he lifted her onto his lap. Straddling
him, she was impossibly aware of his hard member,
aware of the indentation it made beneath her.

She brought her mouth to his, needing to taste
him again. Their tongues dueled, each gaining and
giving ground. His hands at her back moved her
back and forth in the water, creating a rhythm that
kept time with the waves of desire washing through
her. She held him with her arms and legs, wanting
to feel more of him.

He arched her back against his hand so that he
could mouth her nipples. Rachel cried out when his
hot mouth fastened over the hot wet silk of her skin.
Molten tension ignited in the pit of her stomach.
Her fingers dug into his shoulders. He teased her
flesh with his lips and with his teeth.

"Rachel, oh God, Rachel," he growled as his lips came back to hers. "This can't happen again. Why did you follow me here?"

Rachel took his face in her hands and kissed him fully on the mouth. "You needed me," she spoke against his lips.

"Rachel, I am nothing. You were meant for a man like Logan."

She gave a harsh laugh. "So you and my father and the Taggerts say."

"It's the only way."

"It's never the only way, Sager."

"I'm not staying here, Rachel. I'm a wanderer. I have nothing to give you, no patch of dirt with my name on it. Just a helluva a past that'll probably catch up with me one day."

She didn't answer him with words, for she didn't know what to say. Her mind had closed down, but her body knew what to do. She touched him with her hands and her mouth. She touched his lips. His eyes. The hard curves of his shoulders. The wide veins in his arms where his heartbeat lived.

His hand slipped between their bodies. He touched the indentation of her waist. His fingers melded to the outline of her hips and moved inward to the most sensitive place of her body, the core of her femininity. He massaged her gently, finding her rhythm instantly. Her toes curled and uncurled, digging into the smooth pebbles and rocks. Her breathing was shallow, erratic. A need within her grew and grew as she pressed against his hand. When he pushed his finger inside her, her control broke. Her body convulsed with hot, liquid fire. She cried out, again and again, until he filled her with his own body.

Her legs locked about his waist, and she gasped as he surged into her. She knew nothing but the pleasure bursting—exploding—within her. Minutes and forever passed, then just as it began to slowly subside, Sager pressed her hips into his, locking their bodies together, sending her back into flight with him. He groaned and clenched his teeth against his release.

When it was over, he collapsed back against the bank of the pool, bringing her with him. The air cooled her feverish skin as she lay atop his chest, her legs still open over his. They stayed entwined a long minute afterward, each struggling for breath.

At last, Rachel propped herself up to smile down at him. His eyes were shadowed again, and he didn't smile back at her.

"I don't ever want to hurt you," he said, shoving his fingers through his hair. Reality returned in the wake of his calming passions, and it was far colder than the air. "Rach, this is a complication you don't need right now. I—"

She lifted herself away from him. "You didn't bring a towel with you, did you?" she asked, interrupting him.

He looked at her a long minute, but left his thought unfinished. "Yes." She watched as he left the water and went to his satchel. He withdrew a white linen and held it up with an apologetic look. "There's only the one. I didn't expect company. Come out—I'll dry you off."

Rachel took the towel from him, certain her body couldn't withstand another round of his gentle ministrations. "I think I'd better do it myself."

"Maybe so." He grinned at her before leaving to gather his discarded clothes.

Rachel dried herself as best she could, then slipped into her pantalets. "Sager, I—" She stopped and gaped at him. He'd pulled his pants on over his wet skin, but hadn't yet donned his shirt. She couldn't drag her eyes away from him. His chest was smooth and tanned. Water droplets on his skin sparkled in the sunshine.

His eyes darkened as he watched her watch him. Rachel pulled the towel over her head, shutting him from her view as she rubbed furiously at her hair. She'd thought she couldn't withstand his touch, yet her own imagination was just as effective!

"I don't think I'll ever get dry!" she said, trying to cover her lapse. She couldn't even remember what she had started to say a moment ago.

Sager placed his hands over hers. "Here, let me." He startled her; she hadn't heard him move behind her. "We'll raise a lot of suspicions if I bring you home bald."

She surrendered the towel and steeled herself to his touch. He moved the linen gently over her head, drawing the water into the towel. His motions were measured, calming. She remembered how she had felt in the water, in his arms. And when he lifted the towel aside and bent to kiss her neck, she leaned into him. He wrapped his arms about hers, pulling her against himself.

"We'll take the long way back to the Crippled Horse. You'll be dry by the time we get there."

She turned in his arms, her hands against his bare chest. She wanted this interlude to never end. She wanted to stay in his arms forever. The look at the back of his eyes worried her. She didn't want him to build a wall between the two of them as he had with everyone else he'd ever cared for.

"Will I have another swimming lesson soon?"

He caressed her cheek with the back of his hand. "I'm not the right teacher for you, Rach."

"Your eyes tell me differently."

They looked at each other a long moment before he pulled away to let them both finish dressing.

Sager adjusted the cinches on both horses. "Let's get back. You need to check on your father." He helped her to mount, his haunting eyes following her. "By the way, what did Cassandra die of?"

"Oh, Sager—she was shot!" Rachel answered, surprised she'd forgotten this bit of news.

His brows lowered. "You knew she'd been shot and would have gone to the Circle Bar alone this morning anyway?" He cursed. "Why didn't you tell me?"

"I didn't know, Sager. No one did. Sid didn't even know until the doctor told him."

Sager shoved his fingers through his hair, then swung up on his pony. "Let's go. I want to see what's happening at the Crippled Horse. Sid didn't have any ideas about who did it, did he?"

"No. But he said he meant to find out."

They rode out of the grove and into the blinding sunlight. Sager actively watched the passing landscape, which made Rachel edgy. She found herself scanning the hills, searching for stealthy men moving about.

"Sager," she said, looking at his hard profile, "I am sorry about what happened to Mrs. Taggert."

He adjusted his hat on his head. "She deserved it. If anything, it was too kind an ending for her."

"You can't mean that!" Rachel gasped. The look he gave her left little doubt he did in fact mean that very thing. Rachel frowned, wondering at his reaction.

They took the long way home, riding in silence. Rachel's hair was dry enough that she could finger-comb and braid it, returning it to some semblance of order as she tucked it under her hat.

Fletcher came running over to them as they rode into the yard. "Where the devil have you two been?"

Sager's brows lowered. "What's wrong?"

"Digger's been shot, too. A couple of the boys found him in the north pasture. He ain't bad off. The shot just nicked him. But the damned thing scared him so bad he fell off his horse and hit his head on a rock."

"Who else was shot?" Rachel gasped as she swung off her horse.

"Mrs. Taggert, of course," Fletcher said, looking at her strangely.

"Goodness—" Rachel started to comment on how fast news traveled, but Sager interrupted her.

"Who did it?" he asked. Still astride, he looked down at Fletcher.

The range boss shrugged. "Said it looked like Indians, but he couldn't be sure. He didn't get a good look at them."

"Them? How many were there?"

"Digger said he thought he heard two shots fired from different guns, so either one man with two guns, or two men."

Rachel gasped. Sager swung down. "Fletcher, put Rachel's horse up. I'm going to gather some supplies and head out there. C'mon, Rach." He drew her away from the range boss before she could question him further.

"Sager, who would do such a thing?"

"I don't know, but it sure wasn't Indians," he said under his breath. "Why shoot a woman and leave her scalp intact? Why only kill one white-eyes if you've come for killing? It doesn't make sense. Shooting Cassandra and leaving her alive is something only a white man would do."

He propelled her up the steps at the back of the house and into the kitchen. Inside, he closed the door, then stood looking down at her. A jumble of words crowded into his mouth, too tangled to speak.

"Rachel, you are not safe here. I don't trust Fletcher. How could he have known about Sid's wife when Sid himself only found out this morning?" He took hold of her arms, rubbing them as if to help his warning penetrate her skin.

"Please stay aware of what's happening around you, Rach. Don't go riding until I get back. If these two men were dressed up like Indians, this wasn't a random shooting; they were targeting your father's men. Except for Ross, keep the boys away from your father. I don't know who's trustworthy and who isn't yet."

Rachel rested her hands on his arms. "I'm scared for you, Sager."

"I'll try to get back as soon as I can, but don't worry if I'm not back for a few days. May take a while to find what I'm looking for." He kissed the cool skin of her forehead. "Stay close to the house till I know what we're dealing with."

* * *

Tom Beall rode east across the property line from the Circle Bar onto his spread. The division between his land and Taggerts' neatly lined up with the boundary between sweetgrass and dry scrub. He cast a jaundiced glance over the desert comprising his meager ranch. He had as many acres as Taggert, but almost no grass and damn little water. He couldn't even run a tenth of the cattle that Taggert ran on his spread.

He'd gotten the land dirt cheap, but he hadn't worried at the time about its limitations. He had planned to set windmills at intervals to draw water at key points for his herd, which he had done, but every damned one of them had run dry. There was no water to be had for hundreds of feet below his land, it seemed.

He wanted the Crippled Horse and Circle Bar ranches. It was as simple as that. He'd offered to buy Old Jack and Taggert out, at a fair price, but neither took the offer. Then he'd come up with a partnership plan, with him taking the burden of marketing their cattle. That also had failed. But he had found an ally in the Crippled Horse boss, Fletcher.

Fletcher twice had a partnership opportunity fall through. He was bitter. And stupid, Tom thought with a grimace as he considered how Fletcher botched his latest task—Cassandra's murder. The fool gut-shot her, leaving her alive long enough to tell everyone the truth about what was going on. Hopefully, she never regained consciousness. If that wasn't bad enough, Fletcher had shot one of the Crippled Horse ranch hands, too, in a weak attempt to make it appear Indians had done the killing. It would have been so simple to just make it look like suicide. Cassandra was unstable. No one would have questioned her passing in that manner.

Fletcher had put everything they were working toward at risk. Tom cursed. If Old Jack or Taggert got wise to what was going on, they'd bring the marshal in. Fletcher had better keep his eyes peeled and watch for an opportunity to get rid of Sager. Tom meant to make it clear that this chance was the last to come Fletcher's way.

Tom kneed his horse into a slow trot. If he played his cards right, he could still get what he wanted. Fletcher said Old Jack was planning a barbeque to introduce his daughter to neighboring families in the region. Maybe it was time to make use of the girl, he thought with a grin.

Chapter Eighteen

"Papa," Rachel announced herself cheerily as she entered his room later that afternoon. He was paler, appearing thinner even than when she had seen him just hours earlier. "Logan has brought the doctor to see you."

"I don't want no barber pokin' at me, Rachel. Don't you bring him in here."

"He's a real doctor, not a barber, Papa." Rachel cast a glance over her shoulder, hoping the doctor hadn't heard, hoping he was still in the hallway where she had asked him to wait. The poor man was near dead on his feet after his night at the Taggerts'; he didn't deserve to be subjected to her father's temper.

"Damned sawbones ain't any better, girl." He pushed himself to a sitting position, the effort forcing a cough from him, coloring his lips with pink spittle.

"Oh, Papa! Let me help you sit up. And quit grousing. I insist you let him examine you." Dr. Felder cleared his voice at the door to her father's room, announcing himself as he entered.

"Well, Old Jack," he said, smiling, "I didn't think I'd ever be summoned to tend you!" He set his satchel down on a chair that flanked the door and removed his jacket. After pouring fresh water from Jack's pitcher into its matching bowl, he rinsed his hands. "In all my years doctoring the folks in these parts, I've never been called to see your father," he told Rachel. "He has the constitution of an ox."

Dr. Felder took his satchel to Old Jack's bedside and removed his stethoscope. Rachel watched helplessly as her father crossed his arms over his chest and glowered at the doctor.

"I'll tell you like I told my daughter—I don't want no sawbones poking at me. I jest got a little cold, that's all."

The doctor lowered his head to look at Old Jack over the rim of his spectacles. He sighed, then put his stethoscope back into his medical bag. "Well, Old Jack, suit yourself. I'm sure I'm the last one who would force you to take care of yourself. Your daughter already paid me, though, and I don't intend to refund my fee, seeing as you wasted my time coming over here and all."

Rachel met her father's baleful glare, delighted with Dr. Felder's quick thinking. She hadn't paid him yet, but she'd gladly give him twice his fee if he'd make her father accept his ministrations.

Old Jack mouthed an oath that Rachel politely ignored, and uncrossed his arms. "Since you've cheated the girl out of my money, you might as well have a look at me. I ain't got anything serious though."

Rachel stood anxiously at the foot of the bed while

Dr. Felder examined her father. When he was finished, he packed his utensils, rinsed his hands, pulled his sleeves down and picked up his jacket without saying a word. Old Jack's angry flush was slowly replaced by a sickening pallor as his eyes followed the doctor to the door.

"Told you I wasn't sick, Doc."

"Actually, you've an advanced case of pneumonia. I'm going to give your daughter an elixir for that cough and directions for a strict diet to help you rebuild your strength. I want you to stay in bed for the next couple of weeks. I'll check on you every few days." He turned to Rachel. "May I speak with you outside?"

"Of course, Doctor." Rachel pulled the covers up higher over her father. "Rest, Papa. I'll be right back."

"Go on with you. Quit fussing over me," he growled, but didn't push her hands away as she tucked his quilt about his chest.

Rachel followed Dr. Felder to the kitchen, where Logan still waited. The doctor wrote instructions down for her father's care.

"Old Jack must have complete bed rest if he's going to shake this. Here's the elixir for his cough. Its primary ingredient is laudanum to help him sleep." He handed her the corked bottle and the instructions he'd written, but hesitated before releasing them to her. "You are able to read?"

Taken aback, Rachel frowned. "Yes, of course."

"Good. That's good. I was going to suggest that you have Mrs. Biddle or Fletcher help you otherwise."

He pulled his coat on and started for the door, where Ross was waiting to take him to the bunkhouse to look at Digger. Logan came over to her as the doctor left. His eyes were shadowed with fatigue and sorrow over his own loss. He took her hand and stared down at her fingers as his thumb moved over her knuckles.

"I'm sorry your father's so sick, Rachel. I hope he's better soon."

"He's one stubborn man, Logan. I'm worried about him."

Logan's gray eyes lifted to hers. "You know, we never went for that drive I promised you. Maybe we should do that in a few days, after my mother's funeral. I'll bet we could both use a break by then."

Rachel smiled, grateful for the offer of companionship. Sager told her not to venture from the ranch, but surely with Logan she'd be safe. "I'd enjoy that, Logan."

"How about next Wednesday?"

"That would be great—if my father's well enough for me to be away. I'll pack a basket."

Logan set his hat on his head. "Send word if it's not convenient. Otherwise I'll be by around eleven in the morning." He gave her a ghost of a smile, then was gone.

Rachel watched him walk to his horse and mount up as the first niggling of guilt began to plague her. She'd accepted his invitation as a friend, though she knew he'd extended it as part of his courtship. Perhaps, had she not met Sager, she might have fallen for Logan.

She stopped dead still and listened to herself, a cold sweat slowly chilling her skin. She was in love with Sager. And Logan was caught in the middle of this snarl, ignorant of her feelings for his brother.

She wrapped her arms about herself as she thought

back to the events of this morning. So much had happened. So much had changed. How was it she was still the same person? What would she tell Logan on Wednesday? She had to say something. It would be too cruel to leave him hanging, a victim of the peace effort between their families.

The morning of the picnic dawned bright and cool. A breeze blew through the kitchen, carrying with it the sweet smell of snow melting in the Rockies. Rachel let the cool air blow over her, knowing that too soon the sun would heat the day. Looking forward to an afternoon out, she moved through her chores with more enthusiasm than she had any day since Sager left. Though her father was not significantly better, Mrs. Biddle had insisted she take a break and keep her date with Logan.

Logan collected her promptly at eleven. The housekeeper greeted him at the kitchen door. "Good morning to you."

"Mrs. Biddle," Logan returned the greeting. His eyes swept the room as he looked for Rachel.

"She's just gone to fetch her bonnet. Why don't you take the basket to the wagon? I put a quilt with it, so you should be all set."

"You're a treasure, ma'am. When you get tired of Old Jack's grouchiness, you'd best come work for us!"

"I may just do that one day," she answered, a girlish titter breaking from her lips. Rachel came into the kitchen, tying her bonnet. "Logan's got the basket and the quilt. Now you just go on and enjoy yourself. Don't worry about your father. I'll pester him all day long. If he takes a bad turn, which I

don't expect him to do, I'll fetch you back. Where
do you think you'll be?"

"I'm taking her to the bride lands."

"Oh, it's lovely there! Off you two go, now!"

"Thanks, Mrs. Biddle. I'll be home in time to help
with supper." Logan helped her up to the buck-
board bench. Rachel settled back, determined to
relax and enjoy the afternoon—her first free one
in countless months. The sun beat down on her
shoulders, negating the late morning's cool air.
Rachel lifted her face to catch the breeze. She listened to the sound of the wagon as it rolled over the
grassy plain. Except for the creaking of the wood
and leather, and an occasional wicker from the
horse, the prairie was quiet. Now and then they
would scare up a lark, and its sweet call would sing
out. Nearly an hour away from the ranch house,
Logan pulled up at the flat crest of a high hill that
was flanked on one side by the vast prairie and on
the other by the steep mountains of the Medicine
Bow range.

Rachel walked to the edge of the plateau, awed
by the vista that spread for hundreds of miles before
her. She felt as if she stood at the top of the world.
Her father's house and barns and bunkhouse
looked tiny in the distance. She looked at the im-
mense land before her for a long moment, but
couldn't get her fill. The wet spring colored the grass
of the treeless, rolling prairie a deep, verdant green.
The sky was a bright, impossibly blue color. Puffy
white clouds rolled past, casting shadows over the
hills below. Rachel thought of her trek across these
prairies, thought of how frightened she'd been the
night she met Sager, thought of how well he fit these

barren hills and rugged mountains. She hugged
her arms about herself. Where was he now? When
would she see him next?

She smiled at Logan as he joined her at the edge
of the plateau. He was handsome and thoughtful; he
would make some woman a wonderful husband.
Now would be a good time to tell him about her
feelings for Sager.

"It's beautiful here, Logan."

"Very beautiful. It's your land, Rachel—your
dowry. Do you see the line of the creek about half a
mile to your left?" Rachel looked where he pointed.
"That's Stoney Creek. It's fed by a lake behind this
plateau and borders the Circle Bar. Your dowry
lands run from this side of Stoney Creek, halfway
to your father's house, over to this side of the mountain. About five hundred acres in all."

He smiled down at her. "Let's eat something, then
I'll show you the lake behind us."

Rachel was silent as Logan turned from her to
unload the basket and quilt from the wagon. This
was what she was asking him to give up because she
cared for his brother. How would he respond? She
liked Logan and wanted—needed—his friendship.
She watched him spread the quilt, deciding to wait
to tell him, just a few moments more.

Logan set the basket on the quilt at the foot of a
single, ancient cottonwood. The lone tree was the
only resident on the high plateau. Its shade gave
needed relief from the unrelenting sunshine and
beckoned to her. She joined him, kneeling next to
the basket to unpack the meat pies, bread and cheese,
and tarts Mrs. Biddle had sent. Logan poured cool

water from an earthenware jug and handed her a white, enameled cup.

He leaned back against the trunk of the cottonwood. "Do you like it here, Rachel? Are you comfortable at the Crippled Horse?"

The question surprised her. Or perhaps it was her answer that surprised her. "Yes, very much."

"My mother was never at home here. It was too rough, too uncivilized. My father took her back East as often as he could, but I think it only made her more discontented." He took a bite of his bread, chewing in thoughtful silence a moment. "With the railroad coming, it will be an easy thing for you to go back to Virginia, should you want to visit family and civilization."

"I have no wish to ever go back to Virginia, Logan." Her stomach tightened at the thought. Now was the time to tell him. He was so kind. How would she say it? She looked at the plate in her hand, her food untouched.

"Logan, you know that peace between our families is very important to me?" He nodded, encouraging her to continue though she sensed an odd stillness about him, as someone tensed for bad news. "I've given some thought to our situation." She watched Logan, saw his eyes harden.

He set his plate down, the food forgotten. "Some things, Rachel, should just be said outright."

"I'm in love with Sager."

Logan's lips thinned and a muscle worked in the corners of his jaw. He got to his feet and walked to the edge of the plateau. Rachel watched the rigid set of his back until her own tension made her walk over to stand next to him.

"How long?" he asked without taking his eyes off the bride lands. "You've only known him for a short time. How long have you felt this way?" He looked at her, reading her expression. "We trusted him to be a gentleman, to bring you in untouched. I trusted him with you." A derisive laugh broke from his lips. "I should have known better."

Anger seeped into Rachel's veins, like hot, liquid metal. She gripped her hands to keep them from shaking. Much was at stake here—hopes and dreams and lives. "I don't like what you are implying, Logan."

"Does he share your infatuation?"

Rachel lowered her eyes. "We haven't spoken of our feelings."

"Why is that?"

"Logan—"

"I'll tell you why." Logan turned toward her, moving marginally closer. A dull thundering began in Rachel's head. "It's because he takes and takes and gives nothing in return."

"That's not true, Logan."

"You haven't told him because you know he'll bolt. You don't need a man like that, Rachel. You need one who will stand beside you, who will be a constant source of strength for you. Not someone who can't wait to leave, someone who can't stand the confinement of civilized life. You need someone to lean on."

"Like you?" she spit out.

"Yes, like me." He took hold of her arms and brought her against himself, his lips taking hers in a searing touch as his hand moved to cup the back of her head. The thundering in Rachel's head grew louder, louder still until the ground seemed to shake. She shoved against Logan, hating that he knew her fear. Hating that he was probably right about Sager.

In the next instant, Logan was ripped away from her. Sager had a hold on Logan's shirt and pounded him in the stomach. He managed to land another solid blow, before things became well matched as Sager and Logan punched each other relentlessly.

Rachel watched in shocked silence for the space of a heartbeat, then hurried toward them. "Stop it! Stop it, you two! You're brothers, for God's sake." She pushed her way between them, affecting an immediate cessation to their violence. She held a hand toward each of them, making sure they weren't going to resume their fight. Sager looked as if he'd ridden hard for a long distance. His trousers and coat were covered with dust, as was the kerchief at his neck. His black hair looked gray with the residue from the trail.

"What the hell were you thinking, kissing Rachel?" he growled over Rachel's head.

"Kissing Rachel?" Logan thumped his chest. "Kissing the woman our families intended to be my wife? What the hell do you think I was thinking?"

"She's not your fiancé."

"No? Is she yours?" Logan countered. Sager didn't answer. He was breathing hard. He wiped the back of his hand against his torn lip.

"Jesus, Sager. You take. You don't think. Everything's about you, about what you want, what you can grab and ruin because you're angry, because your life started in a bad way." Logan looked away, drawing a long breath and releasing it slowly.

"You left, you just took off, leaving me to deal with a crazy mother and a broken father. I tried. But nothing I did made Mother happy. And nothing I did caught Sid's attention. He was always wishing I were you. I got a college degree to please Mother, and came back to this godforsaken wilderness trying to make your father glad I was his son, yet he never sees me.

"And now he and Old Jack arrange a courtship for me. Me! And you take the girl. You take it all, Sager. You take it and break it." He looked at Rachel. She wasn't entirely sure that he saw her until she noticed a hint of regret enter his eyes. "I'm not going to do it again," he said, turning back to Sager. "I'm not going to stay here and pick up the pieces and keep this goddamned family together." He pointed to Sager. "You are no brother to me. Not anymore." He pivoted on his heel and began cleaning their picnic site, tossing things into the basket. He grabbed the blanket and started toward the wagon.

"Logan." Sager's one word stopped him in his tracks. Rachel folded her arms about her waist, her heart breaking for these two men as she looked from one to the other.

"I can't argue about being a rotten brother." Sager's tanned face was flushed, his eyes bleak. "Hell, I've been no kind of brother to you at all. But Sid needs you now. The Douglases need you. For them, I'm asking you to stay. I've found out where the cattle are being moved. I need you to see this through, then you can leave, go where ever the hell it is you're all fired up to get to."

Logan exchanged a long look with Sager. "And what about Rachel?"

"What about her?"

"You took her. You used her so that you could send her to me soiled. You used her like you used my mother."

Rachel gasped. Her gaze flew to Sager, but she could read nothing in his shuttered expression. He did not deny Logan's accusations, but she knew better. She knew him. *You will not survive me,* he'd warned her. Perhaps defiling her had been his original intention; he hadn't seen it through. When they did come together, it had been her choice, and even then he'd tried to send her away.

Rachel searched for some means of cutting through this tense moment. "I belong to neither of you," she spoke softly, eyes glued to her clenched hands, "nor to my father, nor to my uncle. I am my own person, and the choices I make are my own."

She ventured a look, first to Sager, who watched her with a curious stillness in his face, then to Logan, whose anger had not dissipated. She retrieved the picnic blanket and basket from Logan.

"Now, I would like to resume this picnic," she said as she spread the blanket, then began laying out the picnic contents again. "Sager, there is plenty. I hope you will join us."

In no mood for polite company, Sager was about to decline when he realized he would be leaving Rachel to his brother's clutches. He took a step toward his brother, invading his personal space as he shoved his face into Logan's. "If you ever say or do anything to imply Rachel is less than a lady again, I will kick the shit out of you."

Logan did not blink and did not back away. "If you

don't fix this situation, I will. Think on that, big brother."

Rachel cleared her throat. "Mrs. Biddle packed some sweet tea. Would either of you care for a cup?" she asked, determined to ignore the thrill that rippled through her at the realization that these two men circled each other like angry dogs because of her. No one had ever fought over her before. In a baffling way, it made her feel powerful. Yet it was as dangerous as a double-edged knife, capable of cutting both ways. And Sager's family had enough wounds without the two of them fighting over her.

"Where've you been, girl? You're late tonight," Old Jack growled from his bed later that night as Rachel carried a tray of coffee fixings into his room. She set it down on his bedside table and brought out the chessboard. Their evening coffee had become a nightly ritual that they both looked forward to, though her father would never admit it.

"I'm no later than usual, Papa. The boys were hungry tonight. They kept asking for more helpings at supper." All except Sager, who never showed up for the meal.

"What did you make?" He sniffed the air but, judging from his frustrated expression, had no luck yet distinguishing scents.

"I made a roast, with gravy and mashed potatoes and the last of the canned green beans," Rachel said as she handed her father his whiskey-laced coffee.

Old Jack's lips thinned as a pensive look entered his eyes. He shook his head. "You're a better cook than Ross. The boys won't let him come back to the house, Sager told me. You spoil them, what with all your baking and such."

"Thank you, Papa." Rachel smiled, inordinately pleased that Sager had said that of her.

Her father eyed her as she set the board up. "It's your pretty face."

Rachel looked at him, not certain she'd heard correctly. "What is, Papa?"

"It's what's going to get you in trouble."

"What do you mean?" she asked, hoping he wasn't well enough to notice that his observation made her blush.

"There aren't many women hereabouts, girl. It ain't fittin' that a fine young female such as yourself stays unattached. It just makes for problems among the men."

Rachel frowned at him, wishing that this night, of all nights, they might have their coffee and play their game of chess and not talk about her getting married.

"Have you sent out invitations for that barbeque? Time to get this thing moving," he urged.

"Yes. I sent two of your men out to deliver them. I do wish we could have held off until you were back on your feet."

"I'll be fine by the time two more weeks rolls around. You'll see."

She smiled at him. "I guess you're too mean to stay sick for long."

"Hrmph," he grumbled, focusing on the chessboard. They played a few minutes in silence. Rachel graciously let him slaughter her pawns. When the front door opened and closed, she looked at her father, wondering if he was expecting someone. She was just about to ask him when Sager called out a greeting. Her eyes lit up. Her heart began to hammer, and her breathing stalled. Oh, God. *Sager.* She caught herself seconds before she called him back to her father's room, realizing her father might prefer his privacy.

Rachel stood up. "I'll just go speak with him."

"No, call him in here," her father ordered. He sat up a little straighter in bed and leaned a little less heavily against his pillows as Rachel called Sager back.

She stood by the door as Sager entered. He must have noticed her intense perusal, for the corners of his mouth tightened into thin lines, but he said nothing to her. Rachel looked away to hide her reaction.

"Hello, Old Jack," Sager greeted her father. "Rachel," he said stiffly.

"Sager," Jack returned the greeting, interested in what he was seeing pass between the two young people. "You find anything out there?"

Sager smiled grimly. "Beall's been using the Coyote Trail. He's been taking your cattle up the mountain and bringin' them down well outside your rangeland."

Jack eyed Sager. "That's some news, son! We might finally catch the bastard! Yes, siree!" He looked at his daughter and then at the half-played game of chess. He couldn't concentrate on it now, not while his mind was buzzing with other thoughts.

"Let's finish this game tomorrow, girl. I've won three straight nights now; I guess it won't kill me to put it aside tonight. 'Sides, your mind wasn't in it anyhow."

"You haven't won anything yet, Papa." Rachel put the board away, careful not to disturb the pieces. "I'm still teaching you the game."

Old Jack lifted his cheek for Rachel's kiss. "Go on with you—I gotta to talk to Sager."

Rachel carried the coffee tray, and Sager held the door for her. She was acutely aware of him. He could have stayed across the room and let her deal with the door herself, but he didn't, and her heart thrummed painfully with that knowledge. She ventured a glance up at him, wondering if he had so thoroughly built a wall about himself that she was now invisible to him as Sid was.

One look at his eyes and she knew; his gaze held no emotion, like an empty glass. She might have been a breeze going through the door for all the interest he showed in her. She couldn't hide the hurt that flashed across her face, little though it bothered him.

"Well, boy? Tell me again what you found. Quit dawdling over there and come talk to me," Old Jack ordered impatiently from his bed, dragging Sager's attention back to him.

Sager shut the door as quietly as he could, the pain in Rachel's eyes slicing him like a brace of razors. It had to be, he reminded himself. He was no good. God knew she deserved better. He couldn't chance another encounter like the one at the spring. He moved his feet away from the door, walking away from what he wanted as he'd done every day for the past thirteen years.

He turned a chair around and straddled it, sitting near Old Jack so that their voices wouldn't be overheard. "Beall's been taking your cattle straight up the mountain, just a few at a time," he said. "Looks as if he's used other trails near there, too, but the Coyote Trail's the most worn. I can't believe we missed it before."

Old Jack made a face as if he wanted to spit, then remembered Rachel had taken away his spittoon. "Who'd have thought he'd take 'em over the damned mountain?"

"I think your range boss is a party to it."

"Fletcher? Hell no! He's been my right-hand man for ten years. He does all my accounting. I trust him completely."

"Who better to avoid your suspicions? He hid what he and Beall were doing until it couldn't be hidden, then he blamed the Taggerts. Your marrying Rachel off is a big threat to him. And it makes her a threat, Old Jack."

Old Jack's shoulders slowly slumped and the ravages of his sickened body showed in the hollows about his eyes. "I just got Rachel here, Sager. Jesu, I don't want her hurt."

"We know who and where, Old Jack. Let's close in."

"You got a plan?"

Sager eyed the gnarled old rancher before him. "Tell Fletcher that in honor of Rachel's engagement to Logan and the peace between the Crippled Horse and the Circle Bar, that you and Sid are both bringing in a hundred head of cattle—yearlings ready for the brand—for the new couple to set up their own operation."

Old Jack stared at Sager a long moment, his eyes slowly bugging. He began to cough violently and reached for the glass of water on his bedside table. "You want me to do *what*?"

"Beall's greedy, Jack, but he ain't stupid. He knows we're watching for him—ready for him. The draw has to be big enough to get him to herd-ride his caution. If he thinks he can get his arms around that many unbranded yearlings, he'll try for them. And then we'll have him."

"Well, I got a problem with that. I ain't so certain I want Rachel to marry Logan when it's you she makes calf eyes at."

Had Old Jack punched Sager in the stomach, he couldn't have knocked the wind out of him any better. Sager sat still, waiting for Old Jack to clarify his statement.

"You think I woulda let you anywheres near my daughter if I didn't have a secret preference for you as a son-in-law?" Old Jack held up a hand, forestalling any argument from Sager. "Now don't get me wrong. It ain't that I don't like your brother. He's a good man, and in a pinch, he'll do. But I'm thinking he's more likely to take her on outta here to go live in some fancy city. You, on the other hand, I think you could put some roots down here."

"I'm not a good choice, Old Jack. I've got no money, no land, and a helluva bad reputation." *Not to mention I've destroyed what was left of my family.* The best thing for everyone would be for him to get the hell out of here.

"You got a reputation as a straight shooter, son, and that ain't something to shake a stick at. I don't care about the money or the land. You think my girl can run this spread by herself? Hell no. She needs a man to help her. I ain't gonna be here forever. I'd like her to pick a man equal to the task."

Sager's eyes narrowed. "Did she talk to you? Did she tell you to say this to me?"

"The only thing she said to me on the subject was that she ain't partnerin' up with someone she don't love. I reckon, if you put your mind to it, you might get her to love you. Maybe you should smile at her now and then, quit being so mean looking."

Sager's heart started beating in his chest again as he considered the possibilities. He had no idea Old Jack was so fond of him.

"And just so we're clear," Old Jack continued. "I don't want my daughter starting her own ranch. There's room enough for you here. I ain't planning on living forever, and I didn't start the Crippled Horse for my own entertainment. The dowry land's just for show. It ain't big enough to run cattle. And I ain't leanin' toward Logan, so I won't be announcing any such thing."

Sager swallowed the grin that shined up from inside him. He shrugged to pretend indifference and came to his feet.

"Well, give what I said some thought. I'll be gone for a few days—I'm going to see Blue Thunder. I need him to watch the Coyote Trail for us. If you run into trouble while I'm gone, send down to Hell's Gulch for some help. My friend Julian McCaid just bought it. And whatever you do, watch yourself around Fletcher. He's in this up to his neck."

Chapter Nineteen

The kitchen door opened on an endless stream of hungry men the next morning. The lure of coffee and the promise of a good breakfast—their last, perhaps, for several days—drew them to the kitchen. The morning sun hadn't sufficiently brightened the world, and so several kerosene lamps were lit, adding their astringent scent to that of freshly brewed coffee, bacon frying on the stove, and biscuits hot from the oven.

Rachel turned the bacon in the pan one more time. Worry had kept her awake well into the night. She felt sluggish and irritable and couldn't seem to keep the hot grease from spattering her hand.

"I'll do that, dear." Mrs. Biddle came over to her side. "You go ahead and sit down."

Rachel lifted a platter of scrambled eggs. "Thanks. I'll just set these out." As she started toward the table, the back door opened, admitting a final cowboy. Rachel looked up, a generic smile of greeting on her lips. For the breadth of a second, her smile froze as she met amber eyes, the same as those that haunted her through the night.

Sager.

His hair was loose about his shoulders. His guns were slung low over his hips, a holster tied to each thigh. He hung his long overcoat on a hook by the door and came to the table. As Fate would have it, he sat opposite her. She tried to listen to the morning's conversations. Yesterday, or two days ago, or anytime before the picnic, she would have listened avidly. The boys were heading out to work the southwest pasture—some of them would be gone several days. They joked about having to withstand Ross's cooking and wondered if they'd survive. Rachel smiled at all the appropriate moments, but their voices faded before her preoccupation with Sager.

He was leaving, she knew, for otherwise he wouldn't have strapped on his guns.

He would be back, she told herself. He wouldn't be this casual if he were leaving for good. Rachel swallowed a bite of scrambled eggs, her throat suddenly dry as sawdust. She sipped her coffee. It burned her lips, but she welcomed the pain—it explained the moisture in her eyes.

"Rachel?"

Digger's voice broke through her musings. She leaned forward and peered down the table at the shy cowpuncher.

"Mrs. Biddle said you might have some of your baking left over from yesterday. Is there enough for us to take with us? Especially them cookies?"

Rachel smiled. "I'm sure there is. I'll get it for you after breakfast."

Fletcher drew the cowhands' attention then,

giving out orders for the morning's work. Rachel left the table to wrap up the muffins, cookies, and extra bread she'd made the day before. The men gobbled the last bite from their plates, swallowed the last sip of their coffee, and hurried out the door. Digger grinned at her when she handed him the basket.

"You be careful of that leg now, Digger," Rachel advised.

"Yes, ma'am. But you know the bullet only skinned me. It's lookin' better every day." He put his hat on and headed outside after the others.

Sager, the last to come in, was the last to leave. He carried his empty plate over to where Mrs. Biddle was washing dishes. Rachel couldn't tolerate his indifference any longer. It stung like salt rubbed into her aching heart. She left the kitchen, hurrying down the hallway and out onto the front porch. Leaning against the far banister, she took in several gulps of the cool morning air. She folded her arms about her waist and squeezed her eyes shut to stave off the tears that threatened to start, knowing that if she gave in now, she'd never quit crying. A minute passed. Then another. Gradually her breathing evened.

The front door banged shut, and Rachel knew without looking that Sager had joined her. He crossed the porch to sit on the banister and leaned back against the support beam nearest her.

She didn't acknowledge him at first, but then her gaze pivoted to him. "You're leaving," she said.

He nodded, watching her. A gust of wind blew onto the porch, curled against the corner and blew back out again. It pulled on a lock of Rachel's ivory hair, drawing it across her cheek and lips as it passed by her face. He longed to touch her, to blow over her as the wind did.

"I'm sorry about yesterday, Sager," Rachel apologized, unable to bear leaving it unsaid.

"No, Rachel. It was my fault. I intruded."

Rachel searched his eyes but saw nothing past his shuttered expression. She stared at him, memorizing everything about him as he half-sat, half-leaned on the banister. His boots were old and scuffed at the toes. The denim pants he wore were sun-bleached and slightly thinned at the knees. The holster thongs about his thighs emphasized the strength of his legs, his body. His long black hair lay over one shoulder, blending into the color of his dark leather coat. His pale eyes were the same color as his buff vest, an eerie contrast to his dark coloring.

She crossed the distance separating them, meaning to keep on moving until she was back in the house, out of sight of him. Instead, she stopped next to him. He watched her warily, like a chained dog watches a stranger. That Sager's chains were invisible and of his own weaving made them all the harder to break. Rachel wondered whether it would be best to give him time or to force the issue, because she damned sure wasn't giving up on him.

She lifted his hand, melding her fingers with his as she brought them to her lips. "Come back to me, Sager." His nostrils flared, and the muscles of his jaw tensed. She saw him blink, and wondered what words he shut away from her, from himself. He pulled her into the circle of his arms, burying his face in her neck. She held him tightly, absorbing his strength, strength he denied himself. She kissed the top of his head, drawing in the windswept scent that was his essence. Her hands dug into the rich, silken length of his hair. She drew back slightly to look down into his eyes. "Swear to me, Sager, swear that you will come back."

He met her look with a frankness that speared her soul. "I can't do that, Rach."

Sager looked down into the ravine below. The breeze blew against his skin, gently, like the breath of a soul. Blue Thunder sat astride his pony and was silent at Sager's side. Sager hadn't only come in search of his brother to have him watch the trail; he came to ask the questions he had long avoided knowing the answers to.

Blue Thunder was older; he would know more of the childhood they shared. Sager remembered only bits of what Sid had told him when he'd first come to the Circle Bar; his English hadn't been very good at the time. He had tried so hard to ignore his father, he'd turned a deaf ear to his words. Still, Sager remembered being told that Sid and his wife were traveling alone through the Territory, looking for a place to settle. He remembered Sid saying his wife had been abducted in an Indian raid on their campsite, that supposedly she'd been pregnant with Sager at the time. When he was fourteen and first heard this, Sager hadn't believed it.

He wondered, now, if Blue Thunder's memories would corroborate Sid's story. "Tell me about my mother," he asked Blue Thunder as they sat astride their ponies on the bluff. "Who was she?" Sager felt his brother's scrutiny.

"You have never asked me this before."

"I should never have survived that day, Blue Thunder. For all these years, I wished I hadn't. I didn't want to live at the cost of our mother's and sister's lives. And I didn't want to be the son of a murderer. But Sid didn't send those men that day. Cassandra did. And now I need to know how I came to be among the People." Sager had spent thirteen years hating Sid and Cassandra, Logan and himself. For thirteen wasted years, he'd been chasing death; he wasn't sure he knew how to chase life.

"My heart does not know a time before you lived with the People," Blue Thunder began. "You have always been, and will always be, one of us." He paused, carefully beginning his story. "I only knew our mother. I did not meet yours."

Sager looked away. Far below, a ribbon of water wound its way around and among ancient boulders. Sager watched the slow, steady path of the water, and listened to his brother.

"You came to us from the Sioux. Your mother's name was Is-a-bell. It is said she had the eyes of a wolf, as you have. Her hair was as black as a blind man's night. The Sioux warrior who took her from the white-eyes loved her. But she was already growing a white-eye's child. This warrior didn't mind, for it meant she would bear fine strong sons for him. But Is-a-bell did not like the warrior. After her son was born, and her strength returned, she tried to escape with her baby many times—one time too many. For a punishment, the warrior took her white-eye's son away."

Blue Thunder fell silent. Sager lifted his face to the breeze. He thought of the years Sid spent looking for his wife and son. He had been a greenhorn at the start of it all—the Sioux would have sent him on one wild goose chase after another, playing with him, tormenting him.

Sager wondered how he would feel if Rachel was stolen from him? How had Sid survived without his Is-a-bell? How could Sager walk away from Rachel?

"The warrior traded the white-eye's infant to our people for six blankets. Our mother's heart hurt for the white-eye's orphan who was lost to both his father and his mother. She sent Father to ask the council to allow him to adopt the infant. That is how we came to be brothers. That is the story of your beginning."

"What happened to Is-a-bell?"

"It was learned many years later that Is-a-bell died the winter she lost you."

Sager nodded, his heart dark. So, he thought with a sigh, Sid hadn't lied all those years ago. Blue Thunder's words brought another unexpected—and unwanted—revelation to Sager; he and Blue Thunder weren't of the same blood. He had become a son as fully as if he'd been born to his parents. No one ever spoke of the adoption. He'd assumed he was a half-brother or cousin to Blue Thunder. "We're not brothers, then," he commented, needing to face the whole, ugly reality.

Blue Thunder looked at him impassively. "Not brothers of the flesh, that is true. But you are no less of a brother to me."

Sager looked away, struggling for the stoicism he learned as a child. A gust of wind blew against the crest of the bluff. He stared at the huge expanse of prairie that lay in front of the mountains. His future, in his brother's few words, was now as open as that

vista. He thought about what he'd almost done to
Sid and Logan. Guilt slammed into him.

"Your wife has given you life," Blue Thunder said
triumphantly. "I knew she would."

Rachel. Sager shut his eyes against the pain that
clawed into his chest. He had to set her free. He
could not chain her to a man like himself.

"You must follow your heart in this. And in your
heart, she is already yours."

"Perhaps," Sager admitted, grasping his brother's
forearm. It was time to leave. "I'd best get back. I'm
expecting trouble."

Blue Thunder nodded, his grip firm on Sager's
arm. "I will watch the Coyote Trail, as we agreed."

Sager unfastened the brace of quail—his hunting
take for the day—and handed them to his brother.
"Here, keep these," he said, before moving his pony
down the steep hill.

Rachel lifted a hand white with flour from the
bread she was kneading, and waved to Sid Taggert
through the window as he walked up the back stairs.
It was a reflexive action. Mechanical. It required no
thought. No rationalization.

It was about all she could manage this morning,
two weeks after Sager left. Her barbeque was coming
up in two nights. She wondered if Sager would
come, then cursed herself for continually dwelling
on him.

"Your pa still laid up, Rachel?" Sid asked after
exchanging greetings with her.

"He is, Sid, but he's feeling much better now. I'm
making him rest until the barbeque, though, for

he's still not himself. I don't suppose I'll be able to keep him quiet long after that."

"He's lucky you were here, Rachel. I reckon the old cuss would have been too stubborn to admit he was sick. He might have been dead and buried if you hadn't gotten here when you did."

Rachel was unable to suppress a shudder at that gruesome thought.

"Sid Taggert!" Mrs. Biddle remonstrated from across the room. "Go along now and visit with the 'old cuss' and leave Rachel in peace."

He winked at Rachel before crossing the room. "Yes, ma'am, Mrs. Biddle. Maybe you can find an extra piece of that apple pie that no one will be wantin'? Looks mighty tasty." He grinned at the housekeeper before stepping into the hall.

"That man!" Mrs. Biddle grumbled, staring into the hallway after him. "He could charm the skin off a snake. No wonder his boys are so charismatic." She caught Rachel's tight-lipped smile and wished she hadn't spoken. "Oh, goodness. I didn't mean—I didn't think." She knew something of what ailed Rachel; she'd seen the eyes she and Sager made at each other—it was plain for any who cared to look that Rachel wore her heart on her sleeve.

"It's all right, Mrs. Biddle. He does have sons worthy of his pride. Why don't you take Sid and Papa a couple of slices of pie? See if they're killing each other back there. Their silence makes me nervous."

Mrs. Biddle agreed and quickly filled a tray. The door to Old Jack's room was ajar, and she entered as she called a greeting to the men.

Jack watched his housekeeper make a fuss over

Sid, and he glared at her until she left. "You Taggerts have turned the women in my household into mush."

Sid laughed as he studied his old enemy. "I wanted to talk to you about that."

Jack stopped chewing, a mouthful of pie spreading his cheeks like a prairie dog's at mealtime. "You thinkin' of backin' out of our deal?"

"No." Sid shook his head for emphasis. "Nope. I wanted to broaden our arrangement."

Jack eyed him suspiciously.

"Our deal was that in exchange for your Rachel and my Logan getting married, we'd make a peace pact. Well, that's not changing. Just that I figure I've got two sons. I want you to accept which ever one Rachel chooses."

Jack thought of the tension he'd been feeling between Rachel and Sager. Hell, he didn't care about the peace pact anymore. He just wanted to see Rachel happy. Spooky how like her mother she was. Sager better come home with his thinkin' straight where Rachel was concerned or he'd have to straighten it for him.

"I'm way ahead of you, Sid," he said gleefully. "Why do you reckon I sent Sager after Rachel, anyway? I figured their trip back would give them a good introduction to each other. And if they didn't suit each other, well then she still had your Logan to get to know once she got here."

Sid stared at the grizzled man in front of him, his eyes narrowed before he burst out in a hearty guffaw. "You are a wily old bastard."

Old Jack grinned. "By the way, I was sorry to hear about Cassandra."

Sid shrugged. "I guess it's best she's moved on. She wasn't happy here, with me."

"Some aren't, you know. This land ain't a kind place." Jack sipped his coffee, eyeing Sid over the rim of his cup. He nearly laughed at the picture he and Sid made, two old men—old enemies—sitting and visiting. Sure was a turnaround. "Life's kinda strange, ain't it?"

Sid smiled. Strange yes, but all in all, it wasn't half bad. The pie was good. Hell, he might take an interest in the widow Biddle, if Rachel could teach her to cook like this. "I'd guess it doesn't get much better." He leaned back in his chair and propped his booted feet up on Jack's bed. "So you'll take either of my sons?"

"I'd be honored by either, Taggert. Your Sager's come up with a plan for catching Tom Beall."

Sid smiled as he looked at Jack. "What is it?"

"He wants us to gather up a hundred yearlings each so the new couple can put their own brand on 'em. Thinks that'll pull Beall in like a bee to sugar."

"Bet he's right." Sid eyed Jack. "I'll do it if you will."

Jack shrugged. "I don't exactly want the young 'uns to go off by themselves. Kinda thought they'd take up here with me. Or with you. Hell, even help us both."

"Yeah, I guess so, Old Jack. Maybe we should let them decide for themselves. I reckon if the cattle will stop Beall, I'm for it, though." Sid looked about Jack's room, his gaze falling on the chessboard. "Didn't know you played chess."

Jack's eyes sparkled. "Sure shootin'! I've been playing for years. Care to try me?"

"That I would. Yep, I sure would."

* * *

Rachel sat on the front porch, a blanket about her shoulders. It was late. She should go in. Sager had been gone a full fifteen days. She adjusted the blanket over her robe. The days were warming up nicely now that summer was coming, but the nights were still cool. She stared off toward a hill in front of the house behind which rose the near-full moon. As she watched, a rider appeared. He came to the top of the hill, a black shadow in the wash of moonlight. Rachel's heart slammed into motion.

It was Sager. She knew it, though easily a hundred yards separated them. Could he see her on the porch? Had he come home or did he intend to keep his distance as he had while they traveled with the wagon train? Dropping her blanket, she crossed to the railing and waved to him. For a moment, he didn't respond. She thought he would head back the way he'd come. Instead, he turned his pony toward the house and came down the hill toward her, pulling up beside the porch. Her face was illuminated by the moon, but his was still shadowed. Her mind raced, trying to think of something to say—something light or something suitably somber, she couldn't decide. He'd come back. And he'd come to her.

"Are you hungry?" she asked, eager to fill the silence.

"Yes," he said, the simple response resonating with his deep voice.

"I could make a sandwich for you—I cooked a roast tonight."

"Do you have any of that fresh bread of yours?"

She nodded. "Why don't you put your pony up, then come inside?"

He swung off his paint. He stood for a moment before her, as if there was something he wanted to say. Her eyes searched his face, but in the dark light, she could read nothing from his expression. He led his pony away, and she headed toward the kitchen, wondering what he'd wanted to say.

In the kitchen, she pulled an apron on over her bathrobe. She sliced several thin pieces of meat, then cut enough bread for two sandwiches. She spread fresh butter she'd made herself over the bread, assembled the sandwiches, and set them on a plate. She turned, intending to take them to the table, but he stood directly behind her. She hadn't heard him enter the kitchen, expecting him to be longer with his pony.

He seemed as surprised by her sudden movement as she was at finding him so near. His thigh was pressed between hers. The holster of his gun pushed against her hip. Her eyes were wide with shock and need and hunger. She handed him the plate, ignoring his nearness. "Can I pour a glass of water for you?"

He took the plate and put it back on the sideboard behind her, pinning her between his arms. "That would be nice. The colder the better," he drawled. He bent forward, brushing his lips against hers. "Rachel," he rasped.

A tremble shivered through her at the light caress of his lips, the breath of his whisper. She touched his wrists and edged her hands up his arms, over his shoulders and locked them around his neck. He smelled like sunshine and wind, trail dust and horses. He hadn't shaved in the time he'd been away. She touched her lips to the space just above his lip, turning her head this way and that to feel his shadowy mustache. Her lips whispered across his, then she pressed her chin against his, feeling his beard with her own soft skin.

"I missed you," she whispered.

He gave a wry laugh, a sound that was almost a groan. "I nearly killed my pony getting back to you." He cupped the back of her head with one hand and leaned forward to kiss her. His touch this time was anything but gentle—it was a touch meant to feed his passions, to feed hers. But their need was insatiable; the deeper they kissed, the more they hungered.

Rachel felt everything about him, storing each impression so that she could savor this embrace when she was alone. She felt the leather of his vest beneath the palms of her hands. His hard thighs were braced against her body. The edges of his gun belt dug into her ribs. The skin about her mouth tingled from the friction of his beard. His tongue swept inside her mouth, its rhythm desperate with need. She coaxed his tongue deeper into her mouth, suckling what he offered and glorying in his response. Her legs could barely sustain her weight by the time the kiss ended.

Sager held her in the circle of his arms, his forehead pressed to hers. His breathing was labored. She felt his withdrawal and tightened her arms about him.

"I can't—" he growled, pulling back to look at her. He hadn't meant for this to happen again. "Rach, I'm hungry and filthy and tired to the bone. I'm sorry."

"Don't be." She smiled at him. "Sit and eat. I'll heat some bath water." She fetched a glass of cold water for him, then filled two huge pots and put them on the stove to heat.

Sager watched her move about the room. Being here with her felt right. Why it did, he couldn't say. This wasn't his house or his ranch. She wasn't his; Logan needed a woman like her. But so, God forgive him, did he. He had no right to do what he'd already done with her, and even less right to spend the evening with her. Yet here he sat, in her kitchen, eating her food, watching her.

Rachel pulled the tub in front of the warm stove. When she started to lift one of the heavy, boiling pots of water, Sager was instantly at her side.

"Let me help you, Rach. It's too heavy."

She handed him the quilted potholder and stepped aside. Steam filled the air as he emptied both pots of hot water into the tub. He tempered the bath water with a couple of buckets of cold water. Rachel fetched a bar of soap from the pantry. When she returned, Sager had doffed his gun belt and vest. He had pulled his shirt from his pants and was nearly finished unbuttoning it. She stopped in her tracks, her eyes locking with his. She would not look further down his body, she told herself. But his bare skin called to her, beckoned her touch. His fingers lowered to another button, and she inhaled sharply at the movement. They stood several paces apart, yet the friction between them made it feel as though their bodies were next to each other, touching. She saw his eyes darken and knew he'd noticed her reaction. His long fingers lowered again. She tore her eyes away.

"Rachel—" His ragged whisper was filled with the same torment that haunted her.

She stubbornly refused to look at him. He walked

over to her. She should leave. She should hand him the soap and go. They'd been lucky no lasting effects remained from their last encounter. To tempt Fate again was simply foolhardy. She had no hold over him, could never keep him forever. He'd made it perfectly clear that he didn't mean to stay here. Tonight, the old grimness was back in his eyes.

"It isn't right that I be here with you," his voice broke into her thoughts. Her eyes shot up to his. "But then I've spent more than a decade redefining 'right.' Maybe I've just gotten too good at it." He unfastened his last shirt button. His shirt hung from his shoulders, exposing a dark column of bare skin from his throat to the top of his pants.

"Rachel, please stay. I could use the company." He was begging for company, he thought wryly—he who had shunned human contact since his time with Cassandra. "I won't touch you."

Rachel handed him the soap, conscious of the fact that his fingers did not brush hers as he took it from her. She ventured a look at the bare expanse of his chest as he doffed his shirt. His skin was slightly discolored where the bullet had skinned him during their stay in Defiance weeks ago. She lifted her hand, wanting to brush her fingers along his new scar. Sager leaned infinitesimally toward her at her gesture, but she pulled back before she made contact. She wanted to touch him, wanted to feel his arms about her. She knew from the kiss they had just shared that he wanted those things, too. She looked at his face as she dropped her hand, deciding to give him time, to let him come to her. She saw his mouth return to a hardened line as he visibly struggled to maintain his own resolution. He pivoted and sat on a bench to remove his boots and woolen socks. His flat stomach made barely a ripple as he leaned forward. With an inward groan, Rachel tore her eyes from him and busied herself washing up a few odd dishes left over from the evening. She heard a small splash as Sager stepped into the tub.

"Rachel, is there some coffee left in that pot?" Sager asked.

"Yes. I'll bring you some," she answered without turning around. She poured him a cup and started toward the tub, but stopped short. His long body was folded up in the bathtub that had always seemed so large to her. She couldn't restrain a laugh at the image he made.

Sager looked up at the lyrical sound that slipped past her lips. He arched a brow at her, trying unsuccessfully to keep his face expressionless.

"I'm sorry!" she blurted.

"Don't be. You have a beautiful laugh." He reached out for the coffee.

She handed him his cup. "I'll get you a towel." She was too edgy to keep him company, too fearful of her weakening resolve where he was concerned.

"Rachel—" He stopped her retreat. "I hate to ask this of you, but would you mind helping me with my hair? Your tub's a sight too small for me to dunk down."

"I—I—" she hesitated.

"Please?"

Well, the tub *was* too small, she reasoned. She longed to perform that service for him, to sink her fingers into his beautiful black mane. "I shouldn't," she spoke her thought aloud, then instantly wished she could call it back.

"Then don't." He shrugged, unaware how painful his nonchalance was to her. "But I did promise not to touch you."

Rachel caught a hint of a challenge in his voice; if he was man enough to invite her to his side without breaking his vow, then she could show him she was woman enough to meet him halfway. Taking a towel from a pile of folded linens that Mrs. Biddle had left out, she walked to the tub and knelt at Sager's back. She loosened the leather thong holding his black hair. The steam had dampened the edges of his hair, making it cling to the rippling muscles of his back. She lifted her hand, intending only to finger-comb his hair, but her willpower floundered. She touched her palm to the silky, dark skin of his back. A tremor rippled through him at the contact, shooting liquid heat through her.

She drew her hands upward, over his shoulder blades, directing the pads of her fingers through the drops of water that sparkled with lamplight. She lifted a bucket.

"Hold your breath," she warned before pouring a thick stream of water over his head. The water was cold in comparison to that in the tub; the muscles in his back contracted in response to the shock of it. He said nothing though, keeping his silence about him as an invisible, protective mantle.

Rachel lathered the soap and applied it to his hair. She breathed a ragged sigh as her fingers gathered his raven locks into the soapy foam. This was surely sinful, she thought, working her fingers back and forward and around.

"Close your eyes," she warned again as she rinsed

his hair. She combed her fingers through his hair, making certain she'd rinsed all the soap away.

"Sager?" She stepped in front of him, careful not to glance into the center of the tub. He held the edge of the tub in a white-knuckled grip. Had she hurt him? Did she get soap in his face? Kneeling, she offered him a towel.

He opened his eyes and gazed at her with a look that was at once white lightning and black hunger. He took the towel and mopped his face.

"I'm done," she told him.

"No, you're not."

"Sager—"

"Wash me," he bade her.

"I cannot." It was barely a whisper.

"Take up the cloth and bar." His eyes were compelling, hypnotic. Beneath his blazing amber gaze, she was defenseless. Her hand trembled as she retrieved the wet bar of soap. She dampened the small washcloth, averting her eyes from his lap as she lathered the cloth, then touched it to his chest. She caressed his muscular torso, rubbing the cloth in sweet, tantalizing circles from his diaphragm to his collarbone, and then back down over his nipple. She lathered the cloth again, then made a path across his other nipple to his collarbone.

Sager's gaze was upon her. She could feel its weight, its heat. Lifting his heavy arm, she washed his shoulder, lathered the dark hair of his underarm. His hand rested in hers, palm to palm. He didn't hold her hand—the touch was hers not his. Her washcloth traveled down to his hand and fingers. She made a circle of her thumb and forefinger and lined it with the soapy cloth, then spread his fingers and inserted them, one by one, into the cloth. He drew a sharp, almost pained breath, and her eyes flashed to his face only to be impaled by his silent, raging need.

Supporting herself with a hand on his chest, she leaned across him and washed his other arm. She felt his irregular breathing beneath the pressure of her hand. She moved around to his back and knelt again behind the tub.

Her nails glided across his back as she brushed his hair off to one shoulder. Again she lathered up her cloth. The muscles of his back bunched in anticipation of her touch. She rubbed the cloth across his back, letting her bare hand move in time with the circles she made with the cloth.

Sager gritted his teeth. It was torture. Unmitigated, nerve-racking torture. He'd sworn he wouldn't touch her, so why did he seek to torment himself—and her—with this contact? *Had he decided to fight for her?* he asked himself for the hundredth time since he left Blue Thunder.

She was at his side again, cupping water in her hands, lifting them to rinse his torso. His head throbbed. Blood thundered through his groin, as it had since he'd seen her on the porch. He grabbed her wrists and lurched to his feet, drawing her with him.

"Stop!" he growled. "You must stop! I should not have asked you to do this."

His wet skin dampened a mirror image of itself on her white apron as he held her wrists and kept her against his body. His eyes burned into hers with a fierce anger. His nostrils were flared. His grip was cutting off circulation to her hands, but Rachel didn't care. Indeed, she could think of little except the feel of his body pressed against hers.

"Stop what, Sager?" She searched his eyes. "Stop needing to touch you? To run my hands over your skin? To breathe your scent? To hear your voice? I cannot stop." She drew a ragged gulp of air. "I don't know how."

"You were not meant for me. I'm a bad choice, Rach."

"Then why do I feel whole near you, and only you? Why do my days drag by until I catch a glimpse of you? When I'm near you, I cannot breathe— I cannot hear for the blood pounding in my ears. I cannot think when I'm around you. I only know that I must touch you, hold you."

He released her wrists and set his hands on either side of her waist. His fingers dug into her sides as he fought the burning desire within himself.

Her arms slowly encircled his neck. "Hold me." The words slipped past her lips as a whispered plea. "Touch me, please, Sager."

His arms wrapped about her in a crushing hold. He bent to graze her neck, to let his tongue feel the beat that pulsed there. He growled against her skin as he stepped from the water. He set a muscled thigh between her legs as his hands massaged her back, her ribs, her shoulders. He touched her everywhere he could, pressing her warm, pliant body to his. He wanted more. Much, much more. She was a fever in his blood, a hunger in his loins. He would devour her tonight and rid himself for once and for all of this unending lust.

Sager untied her apron and lifted it from her head, then tossed it aside. He pulled back from her, watching her through eyes of amber flames as his hands fanned out along her ribs, as they moved up over her breasts. He untied her bathrobe and let it fall to the ground. His trembling hands set to work on the buttons fastening the neck of her nightgown, then lifted the material over her head and dropped it to the floor. Except for her pantalets, she was naked. Vaguely he heard her moan, felt her fingers dig into his arms—pulling him closer—as his lips fed off her silken white skin.

He pulled her into his arms, and his hands cupped her buttocks. His cock throbbed as he lifted her and rubbed her against his hardened ridge. Her legs circled his hips. He felt her lips move in a line along his collarbone, felt her warm mouth open on his shoulder, felt her teeth gently graze his skin. In a haze of burning desire, he carried her over to the cupboard and set her down. Instantly, he was inside her, taking her through the slit in her pantalets.

She tightened her legs about him, drawing him even deeper into her. He withdrew, slowly, slowly, feeling her small inner muscles tighten around him. When just the blunt head of his cock was against her, he slowly pushed his way back into her sheath. He buried his head in her breasts, holding their heavy weight, sucking her contracted nipples. She groaned and tightened her arms around him. He lost his control. He pounded into her hot wetness.

The cupboard shook with the power of his thrusts, rattling dishes and plates and cutting into Rachel's passion-fogged mind. They were making too much noise. Her father had succumbed to a drug-induced slumber, but they might awaken Mrs. Biddle.

"Sager," she kissed his neck. Unable to help herself, she ran her tongue against the bristly line of his jaw. "Sager—stop!" she said against his lips.

His arms tightened about her as if fearing to lose her. "No," he said, though his body slowed. Why had she stopped him? He was so near to reaching his climax, so near to bringing her to ecstasy. "Please, Rachel. God, don't make me stop. . . ."

"Let's go to my room. We're making too much noise here. Mrs. Biddle will come to see what's going on."

He lifted her from the cupboard, holding her with his hands braced under her buttocks, her legs locked about his hips. He was still deeply embedded within her body. He took a step toward the door and felt the impact of his stride resonate up the length of his cock, into her.

"Where is your room?" he asked through clenched teeth, not certain he could hold off his climax.

"The last room on the left," she answered, arching her body against his.

He groaned and kissed her lips, allowing his tongue the free release he sought for his body. But this, too, weakened his restraint, for she drew his tongue into her mouth, suckling it as he had her breasts. He walked the tortuous distance to her room, and managed to close her door before losing his control.

He lifted her hips, moving her body up and down over his cock as he crossed the room to the bed. Her breasts brushed his chest with each pass her body made. He lowered her across the mattress without breaking contact. He wanted her to come now, to come with him. His fingers gently stroked the center of her need. He arched over her to kiss her breasts, to let his tongue circle her nipple, all the while still moving within her. He felt her fingers dig into his back, felt her push her hips up with a rhythm that complimented his.

And then he was lost. He drove deeply into her, pounding against her body, pouring his seed into her. She bucked beneath him, matching his thrusts with her own until slowly, ever so slowly, they settled back down to earth.

He looked down at her, his face framed by his raven-black hair. Rachel smiled into his golden eyes, and wondered at the dark shadows she saw there. His gaze lowered to her lips briefly before returning to her eyes. The emotions housed in his eyes were hard and fierce. They thrilled and terrified her. He pulled away from her body and from the narrow single bed. He looked at her a long moment, then without a word, he opened the door and walked into the hallway.

Rachel trailed after him. By the time she reached the kitchen, he had pulled his pants back on and was emptying the wash water. She retrieved her clothes and hastily donned her nightgown and robe. He set the room to rights, then pulled on his boots and shrugged into his shirt. He stopped silently before her, then touched her neck, his thumb caressing her cheek. He leaned forward, his eyelids closing over the haunting sorrow in his gaze. He kissed the silky skin of her cheek. He'd been wrong. So damned wrong. One more night with her hadn't been enough. A lifetime of nights wouldn't be enough.

"Rachel," he said, "what do you wear to sleep at night?"

She felt the warm breath of his words on her skin. "A nightgown," she answered with a shrug. "Why?"

His lips curved into a lopsided smile. "Don't wear it tonight."

"Sager, that would be indecent!"

He pulled his coat on over his unbuttoned shirt, then picked up his vest and gun belt. "Who would know?" he asked as he bent to kiss her cheek. "Good night, Rachel."

Chapter Twenty

Rachel folded down the coverlet from her bed. Her mind was reeling with the knowledge that Sager had come back to her—they had made love again! She turned down the lamp on her nightstand and removed her robe. For a moment, in the dark, she stood immobile, looking down at her bed. She heard Sager's question again. *What do you sleep in at night?* Her heart pounded ruthlessly, as though she was frightened of something. The house was quiet. Her drapes were drawn. Her door was closed. Who would know? she asked herself.

The long cotton nightgown she always wore seemed suddenly stifling. She unfastened a button or two to let the cool night air touch her skin, but that did little to soothe the heat within her. She remembered watching Sager as he'd unbuttoned his shirt in the kitchen, remembered how slow his movements had been beneath her perusal. She unbuttoned her nightgown all the way, her wrists moving over her breasts, which still tingled from Sager's mouth.

Who will know? Sager's deep voice answered her

unspoken thoughts. Well? *Who would know?* she repeated to herself. She drew her nightgown up over her head and laid it at the foot of her bed, atop her robe. She slipped between the sheets and reveled in the delicious decadence of her nudity. The answer to her question came to her, just as sleep claimed her tired body.

Sager would know.

Rachel was up early the next morning, eager to see Sager at breakfast. She collected the day's eggs and milked the cow while the barnyard was still dark. After lighting the kerosene lamps in the kitchen, she set a pot of coffee on the stove.

"My goodness, you've been hard at work already!" Mrs. Biddle commented as she poured herself a cup of coffee. "Your Sager must be back now, I'm guessing."

Rachel smiled. "What makes you think that?"

Mrs. Biddle stirred her coffee. "Might be that smile on your face and not the worried frown you've been sporting the last few weeks."

Rachel's smile grew wider. "I'm about to put the sausage on to fry. And I just finished the pancake batter. Why don't you sit down and have an easy morning for a change?"

"Well, I don't mind if I do," Mrs. Biddle said, seating herself at one end of the long table. Soon the room was filled with cowboys, and Rachel was kept busy cooking batch after batch of pancakes. It wasn't until Mrs. Biddle took the spatula from her that she realized Sager had taken a seat at the table. "Go sit down, dear. I'll take it from here," she said with a wink.

Rachel looked at Sager. He was watching her, his

expression shuttered, reserved. Her knees felt weak suddenly. She took a seat across from him, in the place Mrs. Biddle had just vacated, and busied herself with pouring a cup of coffee. He set his mug by hers for her to fill both cups at once. Mrs. Biddle piled two plates with pancakes and sausages and started toward the table. She was chattering about how Sager was always the last to come in, when her boot crunched on something in her path.

"Oh, goodness! What was that?" she muttered, kicking the tiny item out of the way. Rachel heard what sounded like a button skitter across the floor until it hit the far wall. Had she lost it last night? Her eyes flew to Sager's as heat suffused her face. Mrs. Biddle set their plates down, then hurried back to the stove to pour more batter onto the griddle. Rachel tore her eyes away from Sager. How had she ever thought him stoic? She made a couple of slices in the stacked pancakes before her, but she was too tense suddenly to eat.

Fletcher soon gave out the orders for the day, most of which involved preparations for the barbeque. Sager and her father had decided to let Fletcher continue in his current role, to not give him any idea they were watching him. It wasn't an approach Rachel was comfortable with, but she did her best to interact with him normally. The men finished off their meal and hurried outside. Sager left to see Old Jack as Rachel helped Mrs. Biddle clear the table and wash the dishes. Rachel began to dry the dishes, but Mrs. Biddle stopped her.

"Don't worry with that. Your father needs some company. I can finish up here myself."

Rachel didn't argue—she hoped to catch Sager.

She left the kitchen, her ears tuned for the sound of Sager's and her father's voices. The hallway was silent, though, and she knew a moment of wicked disappointment at having missed him. Rachel stopped at an armoire that held the household linens and withdrew fresh sheets for her father's bed. She closed the paneled door and started down the hall just as Sager left her father's room. She stopped short at the sight of him, the cool linens pressed against her chest to still the violent hammering of her heart as his gaze consumed her. She walked toward him, but he stood immobile, watching her approach, neither welcoming her with a smile nor abandoning her in the hallway. Her arms tightened on the linens as she forced herself to pass him.

"Rachel," he said, stopping her with a soft whisper as his arm curled around her waist and he brought her against his body. "Tell me, what did you sleep in last night?"

She drew a ragged breath, her senses screaming as she resisted the magnetism between them. They were only a few feet from her father's doorway. Anyone could come upon them in the hall. Still, his lips brushed her earlobe as he spoke, and she could not resist leaning into him a little. "My bed," she answered evasively.

A low growl of satisfaction broke from his lips to ripple against her throat. "At least you slept. My dreams were tormented with knowing what you weren't wearing."

Rachel's hand moved up his shoulder. "Sager, will you be at the barbeque tomorrow?"

He didn't answer immediately. "Do you want me to be there?"

"Yes."

He pulled free, and she looked up into his stark, handsome face. "Then I will be."

Rachel walked across the yard to greet Sid and Logan. Many more people had come for the barbeque than she had ever expected. Some she knew had traveled for days, for few lived near the Crippled Horse or the Circle Bar. Wagons were parked in a line in an empty field near the main house. A temporary corral had been set up for the horses and mules of visiting families. Friends of her father's or Sid's had been rolling in since the morning.

The Crippled Horse was more alive than Rachel had ever seen it. Children ran and played and laughed, delighted to find others their own ages whom they rarely got to see. The visiting women had gotten to work right away, helping Rachel and Mrs. Biddle set up areas for food and liquid refreshment. A line of tables stood covered in multicolored, mismatched patterns of tableclothes. Each was laden with pies and cakes and breads. Several cook fires were smoking near the tables, heating communal dishes. Lanterns and torches had been placed about the area for use once the sun set. Groups of men walked here and there, catching up on news of each other's ranch. Many were assisting with the last minute work on the raised dance floor.

"Rachel!" Sid called out as he came over to her.

"Hello, Sid. Logan." She smiled, offering her cheek to Sid. He gave her a quick hug and a fatherly peck. Someone shouted a greeting to him, and he waved back. "Looks like one heck of a shindig. You should be proud of yourself."

Rachel smiled. "I can't take all the credit. Mrs. Biddle did most of the planning. But where did all these people come from?"

"Folks hereabouts would come a long way to see some fireworks," Sid answered. "I think they don't believe the truce we've struck. They'll be disappointed."

She laughed. Sid flashed her a smile, then excused himself to greet a family standing nearby. Rachel turned to Logan. He was dressed handsomely in a black suit with a white, round-collared shirt and a black string tie. He was tall and lean. She considered the fine bone structure of his face, thought how clearly his intelligence shone from his pale gray eyes. This was the first time they had talked since that miserable picnic in the bride lands. Rachel stood before him, more nervous than she would like to admit.

He studied her in silence for a long moment, then lifted his head and looked beyond her briefly, before his eyes returned to hers.

"Rachel," he sighed, "I owe you an apology. My behavior toward you has not been something I am proud of."

"You've done nothing to apologize for." Rachel smiled. "This was an awkward situation for all of us."

"It is my greatest regret that Sager saw you first." He took hold of one of her hands. "I've also learned something." A lopsided grin eased his face. "When I finally do settle down, I hope the woman I find will be as perfect for me as you are for Sager."

Rachel felt a catch in her throat. "I'm not sure Sager would agree with you about me."

"I think he would." Logan pulled her hand through his arm as he turned toward a refreshment table. Seeing a couple of women he knew from town, he gave them a hearty wave and drew Rachel over to introduce her.

"Leah? Audrey? Can that be you?" Logan's surprise was not feigned. He had not seen either woman since before he left for college. He had left them as young teenagers, and now two beautiful women stood before him.

"Logan!" the women both cried out. They ran to him for a fierce hug. Logan lifted and twirled them. He kissed the cheek of each one, then set them back on their feet, keeping an arm around them.

"I cannot believe my eyes. Look how you've . . . grown."

"How *we've* grown? You are finally taller than us," Audrey said.

"And a dress, Leah!" Logan teased. "Have you left your men's clothes behind?" he asked the girl on his right side. She was a fetching creature with violet eyes and dark auburn hair.

He and Audrey had helped her rig up a set of his old clothes to hide her growing curves when she was just thirteen and already attracting too much male attention. They had hoped to make her too disgusting to catch the attention of the itinerant males who drifted through Defiance. Seeing her in a dress tonight, her violet eyes flashing, her feminine curves proudly though conservatively displayed, Logan had to admit being shocked at the woman she had become.

"Leah, you are truly stunning." He shook his head in true bemusement. "And, Audrey, I would never have believed you could be any more beautiful than you were when I last saw you, but you take my breath away!" She had indeed grown into a lovely woman, with her sage green eyes, dimples in both cheeks, and her silky, light brown hair. Dragging his eyes away, he looked at Rachel, at last remembering his manners.

"Rachel, I'd like you to meet two of my very good friends, Audrey Sheridan and Leah Morgan. And this is Rachel Douglas, Old Jack's daughter." As Rachel came forward to greet the women, a shadow moved behind Leah, a hairy darkness that resolved itself into the menacing shape of a wolf. Rachel gasped and drew back, her mind flashing back to the night she met Sager and the rabid wolf she had confronted.

"Oh! I'm so sorry! Wolf, down," Leah ordered the beast. It complied instantly, lying at her feet.

"That monster is Leah's steadfast companion, Wolf," Logan announced.

"I rescued him after a nasty run-in he'd had with a porcupine. It left him too scarred to live in the wild. He lost one eye in the attack. When I fed him, I think he thought I was his new pack leader. He followed me home and has been with me ever since."

Audrey looped her arm through Rachel's, distracting her from the fierce-looking wolf as she drew their small group over to some nearby chairs. "So it is in your honor that we come for this wonderful gathering! It was very kind of you to invite us out here."

"I'm glad you could come." Rachel smiled. Despite the wolf, she was truly relieved to finally have some feminine company. "I hope we'll see more of each other. There are so few women out here."

"Of course!" Audrey answered. "We don't get out of town much, but Jim at the general store can tell you how to find us the next time you come to Defiance."

"Logan, Audrey and I grew up together," Leah explained to Rachel. "Mr. Taggert would bring Logan into town in the summer for days at a time. I think he felt bad that Logan had no other children to play with out here. We had great fun fishing and swimming and climbing through the hills."

"Leah taught me to hunt," Logan said with a grin. "And to fish, and throw a knife and clean a gun."

Rachel looked at the beautiful woman next to her, shocked at the revelation. "My mother and I live alone," Leah said. "I often provide fish and game for the restaurants in town as a way of supplementing our income."

"I would like to learn those things," Rachel announced. If she learned independence and self-reliance, then Sager might not find her such a burden.

"There's no way Sager would allow that," Logan scoffed.

"Sager!" Audrey gasped. "We heard he was back, but why would he care—" Her eyes flew to Rachel's face.

Rachel felt her skin heat and lowered her gaze to look at the folds of her skirt.

Logan grinned. "I tried, rather ineptly, to gain Rachel's heart, but she had already given it to my brother."

Both Audrey and Leah took hold of Rachel's hands. "He is so angry!"

"He is a drifter!" they exclaimed at once.

Logan looked at Rachel and shook his head. "I don't know. I think Rachel has changed him." A toddler came over to Audrey and struggled up into her lap just then as Mrs. Biddle and Leah's mother,

Mary Morgan, joined their group. Logan greeted both women and introduced Rachel to Mrs. Morgan.

"This is a surprise, Audrey." Logan smiled at the tiny, blond girl in Audrey's lap. "You didn't mention you had settled down."

Audrey winced. "I haven't. This is my foster daughter, Amy Lynn. You knew Dulcie and Marty before you left. Since then, we've grown to include Kurt, Joey, Colleen, and little Amy Lynn here."

Logan couldn't keep the shock from his face. Audrey and her brother had a lean existence as it was. Her parents had passed away while he was at school. Audrey had taken over her mother's laundry business, he knew, but even that work, at its best, could not support so many children.

"How do you do it? Does the town help you?" he asked.

Leah gave a derisive laugh. "Defiance help its orphans?" She looked at Logan. "No, she gets no help from the town. I help with my hunting. And we keep a vegetable garden together."

"And your mother sends us bread every day." Audrey smiled at Mrs. Morgan, who was the town baker. "We get along well enough."

Logan gave her a hard look. "Next week, I will come to Defiance and open an account for you at the bank."

"Logan, no! I couldn't accept that. It isn't proper."

"There's nothing proper about letting a friend struggle. This isn't an indecent proposal. I've made this offer in front of our friends. Please, Audrey, let me do what I can."

Mrs. Morgan squeezed Audrey's shoulder. "Accept

his help, honey. The children need clothes and school books and so much else."

Rachel watched this exchange with unmitigated interest. These four women were not dependent on men. They supported themselves in this rough territory. Amy Lynn wiggled out of Audrey's lap and came over to look up at Rachel. She lifted her arms to be picked up, and Rachel did just that. She looked at the orphaned cherub, whose eyes held not a hint of sorrow, and knew, with a stunning certainty, that she had come home.

Sager leaned against a fence post and watched as Logan greeted Rachel. The evening light had stretched into dusk. The torches were being lit. The band was warming up, each instrument issuing musical sounds independently of the others, filling the evening with discordant notes of banjos, fiddles and flutes. Sager had set guards at several strategic spots around the gathering. He doubted Beall would make a showing at so public an event, but he didn't want to be unprepared for trouble either. All was as safe as he could make it. It was time to join Rachel now.

"Still watching her from afar, are we?" Julian McCaid said as he came over to stand with Sager.

"I think I could spend the rest of my life looking at her." Sager grinned. "In fact, I think I will."

McCaid made a disgusted sound. "I thought you were more man than that. I thought you would be more resolute in acquiring what you wanted."

Sager's smile widened. "I'm going to marry her."

"Is that so? Then why is she on your brother's arm, not yours?"

"I asked him to stay with her while I set up patrols."
As they watched, Logan and Rachel joined two other
women. They saw Logan sweep the two women into
his arms and spin them around.

McCaid straightened. "Who are they?"

"Not sure. Logan mentioned he was having a few
of his friends from town come out." The music
started up in earnest and dancers were called to the
floor. "Why don't we head over there and see if
Logan feels like sharing?"

Rachel watched the small group as Logan introduced Sager and his friend. This was her first opportunity to get a good look at Julian McCaid since that
terrible night in Defiance. He was, indeed, a handsome man. A bit taller than Sager with a heavier
build, he had straight, coffee brown hair and dark
brown eyes. Audrey and Leah seemed suddenly shy;
for all their effusive chatter with Logan earlier, they
grew silent around Sager and Julian.

Logan asked Leah to the dance floor. Julian offered his hand to Audrey, who sent a look to Mrs.
Morgan and Mrs. Biddle.

"You go on, dear," Mrs. Biddle answered. "We'll
keep an eye on Amy Lynn for you."

Rachel smiled at Sager, pleased her two new
friends were being accompanied to the dance floor
and hoping he would ask her. She was nonplussed to
see him looking intently at the little girl she still held.
He glanced from the toddler to her, his eyes filled
with dark emotion. Rachel came to her feet and
handed the child to Mrs. Morgan, then faced Sager
again. He stood immobile, like a man poleaxed.

Vaguely she was aware of Mrs. Biddle and Mrs. Morgan taking Amy Lynn away. "Sager, what is it?"

He lifted his hand and gently touched her cheek. She smiled at him, unnerved by his intensity. "I want to see our children in your arms." He moved a step closer. "I want to fill this ranch with our children." He cupped her face in his hands. "I love you, Rachel Douglas. I want to spend my life with you. I've been a damned fool and I know it. Please tell me you will marry me."

Rachel laughed and threw her arms about his neck. "Yes, Sager, I will!" She kissed his chin, his cheek, his mouth. "I will! I will! I love you so much!"

Sager wrapped his arms around her and held her tightly. "I'm not much of a catch. But I'll work hard. I'll work with Old Jack to make the Crippled Horse all that it can be. I'll make it the home you want it to be."

"Sager, right here, in your arms, is all the home I need." He kissed her then, his mouth slanting hungrily across hers. Rachel laughed and cried as he kissed her until she could barely stand.

After a moment, he pulled back to look at her. "I'd meant to wait until we'd dealt with the rustlers to declare myself, but something snapped when I saw you holding that baby. I love you, Rachel Douglas." He was about to kiss her again when he heard someone announce himself with an authoritative clearing of his throat. He turned to find Old Jack glaring at him.

"You care to explain to me, Sager, why it is that you're manhandling my daughter?"

Sager grinned down at Rachel, then smiled at Old Jack. "She's just agreed to become my wife, Old Jack."

Old Jack's brows lowered even further. "That how it is, Rachel? You gonna marry Sager?"

"Oh, Papa." Rachel moved away from Sager and took hold of her father's hands. "I love him so much. Please don't be angry—please wish us well!"

Old Jack's lips thinned. He pulled free of Rachel, setting one hand on his hip, and wiped the back of his other hand against his eyes. "You aren't foolin' an old man, now are you?"

Rachel laughed and hugged her father. "No, Papa. Do we have your blessing?"

"Hell, yes, you got my blessing!" He gave Rachel a brief hug, then shook hands with Sager, leveling a dark look on him. "You better make my daughter happy, boy. It won't go well with you if you don't."

Sager grinned as he looked at Rachel. "I'll gladly spend the rest of my life making her happy."

Fletcher and Tom Beall sat astride their horses on a high ridge, a couple of miles away from the festivities going on at the Crippled Horse. They were too far away to hear the music, but they could see the fires and lanterns that sparkled in the distance.

"You give the boys the whiskey?" Tom asked Fletcher.

"I did. They were sure pleased to get a few free bottles of the stuff."

"Good. That laudanum should put them out of commission when we burn the bunkhouse down around them. We'll have that many fewer men to deal with when we ride in later in the week." *The Crippled Horse will yet be mine*, Tom thought gleefully as he watched the little fires glitter in the distance.

Chapter Twenty-One

Rachel slept fitfully that night. She dreamt she was traveling with the wagon company once again. Her body felt the exhaustion bred of walking for hours on end as she had when her horse had needed a rest. And when she rode, her bones felt each of her horse's jarring steps until her teeth ached. She remembered the thirst that never eased up. The hunger. The loneliness.

Captain Norbeck's voice cut into her dream, capturing her attention. He was cautioning the company about prairie fires started by the careless management of campfires. Rachel smiled. The company was lucky to have been able to hire Mr. Norbeck, in spite of the man's foibles. His knowledge and experience were reassuring. The dream shifted. Mr. Norbeck's voice changed. Perhaps she had misunderstood before; he wasn't lecturing—he was shouting! Rachel looked where he pointed. A fire!

She stumbled back from the heat surrounding her. Everywhere she looked, the waist-high grass was on fire. The horses and livestock were screaming. Men were shouting. A wagon was on fire. She tripped, falling to her knees as the fire's hot breath singed her cheek. No matter how she tried, she couldn't get to her feet. The hideous roar of the flames beat against her mind. She looked up suddenly as if someone called her name. Amber eyes flashed like tawny flames. Sager! Where was Sager?

Her fear gave her the freedom at last to move her frozen body, and she jolted upright in her bed. The haze of her nightmare faded. She breathed a calming sigh, recognizing her bed, her room, the orange glow from the window.

Dread shot to the bottom of her stomach as her eyes flew back to the window. She threw off her covers and ran across the room. It wasn't a dream! Dear God! The bunkhouse was on fire! She hurriedly pulled the door open and rushed into the hallway.

"Where are you headed, missy?" a stranger leered at her from her doorway. Two more men stood behind him in the hallway. Rachel swallowed convulsively as she backed into her room. She knew instinctively that the house must be empty—everyone was helping with the fire. *Don't ever let anyone back you into a corner.* Rachel heard Sager's warning from their time with the company. She quit backing up. The men entered her room and surrounded her.

"We ain't gonna hurt you, little gal," the man before her said. "Yer jest gonna take a little ride with us." He took hold of her arm.

Rachel dug her heels in, about to resist as a movement in the hallway caught her attention. A shadowy form passed the doorway. Was it another intruder? She doubted it—he would have made his presence known. She walked toward the door, a man holding each arm. At the doorway, she tore free, shoving one of the men through the portal.

The room exploded with activity. She barely noticed the man collapse in the hallway as she took on the two still in the room. One of them grabbed her arms. Using him as leverage, she kicked the one in front of her, knocking him out into the hallway. He uttered a loud groan seconds before the shadow in the hall laid him out, stacking his body on top of that of his inert comrade.

The man still holding Rachel locked an arm around her waist. She felt something prick the skin beneath her chin—he'd drawn a knife on her! She grasped his wrist with both of her hands, trying to steady the pressure of his knife.

Logan entered her room, standing just inside the door, his legs braced apart, his hands wrapped about the butt of a pistol. "Let her go, and I'll let you walk out of here," he ordered, his voice low and calm.

"Like hell you will. I ain't lettin' go of her—she's my ticket out of here. Back away from the door."

Rachel met Logan's eyes. In that fraction of a second, their minds connected. She heard him count—*one, two, three!* She slammed her foot down on her captor's, spinning free of his hold, her hands still locked about his wrist. Gunfire exploded in that instant, tearing the man from her as his blood splattered over her white nightgown and she fell backward onto the floor.

Logan reached down and helped her to her feet. "Are you hurt, Rachel?" She shook her head, absently straightening the fabric of her nightgown.

"Logan, what's happening? The bunkhouse—"

"I don't know. I was coming to get you when I saw

you had some company." He looked her over critically. Blood from the dead man stained her gown. Her sleeve was torn, and her cheek had a scrape on it. "You sure you're okay, Rachel?"

"I'm fine. We've got to find Sager."

"Go ahead. I want to tie these two up. I'll be right behind you."

Outside, Rachel drew a fortifying breath as she tried to calm her terror. Several cowpunchers were at work throwing water on the burning building. Rachel searched the gathering for Sager or her father, but saw neither in the busy crowd. She ran toward the burning bunkhouse, calling for them. No one heard her cries above the screams of the ponies in the corral nearest the fire.

Rachel was desperate to find Sager. She asked one and then another cowboy about Sager, but none knew where he was. She hurried through the crowd, calling for Sager. Someone grabbed her, arresting her progress. "No! Let me go! I must find him!" she shouted, turning to see who held her. "Logan!"

"Rachel!" He gripped her arms. The empty look in his face shot fear through her stomach.

"Oh, God, Logan. What is it?"

"No one has seen him. He may not have made it out of the bunkhouse."

She took hold of his shirt as fear weakened her legs. Her fists bunched the fabric as tears wet a path down her cheeks. Rachel's lips parted on the breath of a new sob.

Logan studied her, wanting to reassure her. "It's possible he wasn't in the bunkhouse when the fire started. You know how he wanders about at night."

Rachel straightened her shoulders and drew a

ragged breath, her mind clinging to that slim hope as she marshaled her strength. "I will find him, Logan," she vowed as they hurried toward the crowd gathering outside the bunkhouse.

The first thing Sager felt was the heat. The second was the throbbing pain inside his temple. He propped himself up on his elbows, trying to remember what the hell had happened. Why was he sleeping on the floor and not his bunk? Why couldn't he remember anything? He had had a couple of glasses of whiskey that some of the boys were passing around, but a few glasses wasn't usually enough to lay him low like this. He shook his head, trying to clear his mind. Gray smoke filled his lungs, and his involuntary cough finally jarred him awake.

The strange taste in his mouth had nothing to do with the bitter air he was breathing. His nostrils caught the acrid scent of burning wood. Jesu! The bunkhouse was burning. He was lying in the middle of a fire! He tried to stand, but his legs crumpled beneath him. What the hell was wrong with him? He felt drugged. Or poisoned . . .

Moving across the floor on hands and knees, he tried the door. The damned thing was locked. He stood to kick the door, but the heat and smoke engulfed him. He buried his face in his arm and managed to land a solid kick against the door. Flames had already eaten at the hinges, weakening the portal. Under the force of his second kick, the door flew open and fire poured freely around the opening.

Sager stumbled out, coughing and gagging as his lungs struggled for air. He fell to his knees on the porch. Someone shouted and ran over to help him get away just as the roof began collapsing.

"Holy shit, Sager!" McCaid barked. "I thought Old Jack and I got everyone out of there," he said as he helped Sager move a safe distance from the disintegrating bunkhouse. Sager dropped to his knees, gulping the fresh air as he braced his hands on the ground and tried to focus on what McCaid was saying.

"Looked like the fire was set in two places. Whoever did this made certain it was a thorough job. They wanted you and all the other hands dead."

Sager looked into the gathering crowd, his eyes searching for just one person. His head throbbed, and he was having a hard time focusing. McCaid helped him to his feet. Old Jack was there. And Sid and the boys, too. But where was Rachel?

Sager straightened as a bolt of fear ripped through him. What if Jack had left her alone at the house? What if this fire was just a diversion? He left McCaid and started running, praying for her safety—praying for the first time in his life.

Chapter Twenty-Two

Sager's head felt ready to rip open with each jolting step he took. If Rachel was hurt, so help him God, he would shred the man who dared touch her.

And then he saw her.

Firelight danced on her skin where the neckline of her nightgown hung open. Smudge marks soiled the white cotton fabric. One of her sleeves was ripped, and an enormous red stain colored the bottom third of her nightgown.

She saw him then. Their eyes locked. He saw her hand flutter to her mouth, relief and anguish visible in her blue eyes. Tears were streaming down her face. She didn't stop walking until her knees touched his legs.

"Rachel—what did they do to you?" he asked in a hoarse voice, staring at the blood on her nightgown as he reached for her shoulders.

She wrapped her fingers about his wrists. "Nothing. Oh, God, Sager, I couldn't find you."

"Honey, you're bleeding." His words came out slowly—fear for her and searing anger for the bastard who had harmed her made speaking difficult. He bent and scooped her up into his arms. He had to get her inside, had to get her off her feet. God, he had to stop the bleeding. She wrapped her arms about his neck, flattening her body against his.

"I will kill them, Rachel. They will die slow and painful deaths," he vowed as he moved toward the main house with her in his arms.

"Sager, I'm fine. Truly. This isn't my blood. It's from the man Logan shot."

He pulled back and looked down at her with dark and furious eyes. "What man? What happened, Rachel?"

"I woke and saw the fire. I was hurrying out of my room when they came in—"

"Who?" he interrupted her.

"I don't know. They weren't at the barbeque. But Logan was there and between us we overpowered them. He had to shoot one of them, and it's his blood on me. I'm fine, Sager. Truly."

A jagged sigh broke from his lips. He squeezed his eyes closed as he pressed a kiss to Rachel's forehead. He should have been there for her. He should have stayed at the house. "I almost lost you tonight." They were still several feet from the porch, but Sager's legs slowly buckled beneath him. He went down, still cradling Rachel in his arms as he hit his knees. "I'm sorry. I'm so damned sorry."

Rachel tightened her arms about his neck. "It's okay, Sager. We're not hurt. Logan said no one had seen you. And I couldn't find you. I love you, Sager. I love you so much."

Sager smoothed the hair from her face. "I love you, Rachel Douglas." Cupping her jaw, he crushed his lips to hers, claiming her. Devouring her. A long, long moment passed as she sat on his lap, the two locked in each other's embrace. Reality gradually sifted through the warm haze surrounding them. Sager lifted his head to gaze down at her with troubled eyes.

"Let's get you cleaned up. Ross may need help tending some of the boys. Can you walk?" he asked, helping her to her feet.

"I'm fine. Just dirty." She smiled up at him. He led her toward the dark house.

"What did Logan do with those men he caught?"

"He tied them up and left them on the porch . . ." Her voice dropped off as they topped the steps and stared down at the length of cut rope that had recently restrained two men. Sager lifted one of the severed ends. "You sure your man inside was dead?" he asked, sending Rachel a look.

She shivered involuntarily as she remembered the gruesome sight of the man Logan had shot. "Quite."

Sager looked at the house. "Great. Could be we're about to find who cut them free. Stay behind me, and go as quietly as you can," he whispered.

Rachel moved closer to him. She took hold of the waistband of his pants as he went through the front door. They moved like shadows through the living room, dining room, and kitchen, but found no one waiting for them. Sager sent a glance back to Rachel, silently checking her state of mind before they moved down the hallway to the family bedrooms and her father's office. They looked in the den, Old Jack's room, the guest rooms, and Mrs. Biddle's bedroom—saving Rachel's room for last. Rachel stayed at the threshold of her room as Sager lit a lamp. The man Logan shot was gone. The only indication he'd ever been there was the blood smeared across the floorboards on one side of her bed.

Sager cursed. The absence of the bastards was like a signed promissory note. They'd be back, he knew. "Why don't you change while I clean this mess up?" he suggested.

Rachel nodded, but held her silence as she skirted the stained floor to slip behind her dressing screen. By the time she had stripped, washed, and donned fresh clothes, Sager had removed all physical traces of the violence that had invaded her room. He stood just inside her door, leaning against the wall when she emerged from behind her screen.

"You okay?" he asked as she stopped before him.

She nodded, then shook her head. "I'm frightened, Sager."

He took her into his arms. "I know. But I'm here, and I'm not leaving you ever again. You won't be alone." She gave him a tremulous smile, forcing herself to be strong.

Nevertheless, she was grateful for the lamps Sager had lit all along the hallway, in the living room, and throughout the kitchen, for no darkness remained in the house to cast frightening shadows.

Sager made a pot of coffee while Rachel laid out medical supplies on the table and set more water to heating. Minutes later, Ross came into the kitchen, followed by Mrs. Biddle, Mrs. Morgan, Leah, Audrey, and a stream of Crippled Horse cowpunchers and visiting friends. Rachel helped Mrs. Biddle and Ross clean and bandage countless light burns and abrasions while Mrs. Biddle handed out coffee and Leah and Audrey fed everyone sandwiches.

Sometime later, Rachel looked up to see that her

father and the Taggerts had come into the kitchen. Her father's hands were black with soot. She gently turned them over, checking them for burns. He made a face at her ministrations, but didn't stop her. Though she could see no blisters, Rachel couldn't quell the terror that had come back to life in her stomach. She looked up into his eyes, seeing him through the haze of her tears.

"Papa—" she began, but he stopped her as he gruffly pulled her into his arms.

"Hush, girl. No need for caterwaulin'. We'll rebuild it. You'll see."

"How can you, Papa? It's been a lean year."

"We'll find a way, daughter. You think I'm gonna live with these rough types in my house any longer than I have to?" he asked, a twinkle in his eyes as he nodded toward the men around the table.

Rachel felt someone squeeze her shoulder. "He's not without resources, Rachel," Sid said, smiling down at her. "Your pa will have his barracks again as soon as we can get some lumber in here."

Rachel smiled through a fresh wash of tears. "Thank you, Sid."

Old Jack cleared his throat. "I shouldn't have brought you out here, Rachel. I had no idea how dangerous the situation would be. I don't like you in the middle of it. I've decided I'll be sendin' you home to Virginia in the mornin', girl. Sager can fetch you back when this mess is all done."

Panic ripped into her. "No, Papa. I'm staying here."

Old Jack shook his head. "This ain't no place for a woman. Hell, Rachel, it ain't no place for my daughter. That's why I never brought you out before. Nothing's changed. I should've known better."

Sager moved to stand behind Rachel. He slipped an arm about her waist and pulled her back against him. A silence blanketed the room. "Things have changed, Old Jack, since Rachel's agreed to marry me. I'll be here to look after her. She won't be going anywhere. There's a thousand miles of empty range-land between here and anywhere even remotely safe enough for her. And getting her there is a huge expo-sure. This is the safest place for her to be right now."

Old Jack's crafty eyes narrowed as he looked at Sager. Rachel could feel the tension in Sager's body as he braced himself for her father's reaction.

Old Jack muttered a curse that burned Rachel's ears. "Then you're moving in here." He pointed at Sager. "And you don't let Rachel out of your sight until this mess is done, you hear me?"

"I hear you, Old Jack."

Suddenly everyone started talking at once. Logan came forward, and Sager watched him warily, re-membering the events up in the bride lands. "I was hoping you'd come to your senses, Sager."

Sager held out his hand to his brother and was relieved when he clasped it.

Rachel gave Logan a heartfelt hug; then he moved away to let his father in. Rachel's gaze shifted to Sid. He stood off to the side, making no move to come nearer. She couldn't blame him—Sager had refused to acknowledge him for so very long. The expres-sion in Sid's eyes was haunting, like an orphan staring after prospective parents. She sent Sager a look, silently imploring him to start mending fences. Sager's gaze was already locked with Sid's. After a moment when neither spoke, Sid lowered his eyes.

His shoulders slumped as the air left his lungs, his body slowly deflating.

"Well, good night all," Sid said, not looking at anyone in particular. "It's been a hell of a day, and I've had about all I can stand. Think I'll go on to bed now." He left the kitchen through the hallway door, heading to the guest room that Mrs. Biddle had set up for him.

Sager felt the muscles in his back knot up. The small group stood still and silent, waiting for his reaction. It was here—the moment he'd feared and awaited his whole adult life, the moment when his past and present slammed into one another. He bent toward Rachel. "I'll be back," he whispered against her temple.

He walked into the hallway and watched his father's retreating back. He tried to call out to him, but didn't quite know how to force words through the barrier he had kept about himself for so damned long. Sid stopped in the hallway as if he'd heard Sager leave the kitchen. He turned slowly around. Sager stared at him, cursing the words dammed in his throat.

"Sid . . ." he said at last, not wholly certain his voice carried.

"Yes, son?"

Sager swallowed hard. "I'm sorry."

Sid said nothing for a long moment. Sager half expected him to turn his back and walk away, as Sager himself had done so many times. But he didn't—he walked toward Sager.

"The fault was mine, son. Mine alone." He met Sager's wary eyes. The energy of an old and wrongful hatred stood between them, a thick, impenetrable wall. Sager didn't know how to respond to his father. It felt unnatural to talk with him.

Sid smiled, easing the awkwardness of the moment. "Welcome home, son. I've been waiting for you." He held out his hand.

Sager looked at his father's large, callused hand. He took it in a firm grip.

"You've made me proud, all these years," Sid said.

Sager laughed caustically. "I don't know how—" He buried his gaze in the shadows at the end of the hall, leaving his thought unfinished.

"You've been on your own since Cassandra took you from the Shoshone. You've been alone, boy, but you've come up square. What's not to be proud of?"

"I came back to ruin this family," he said, his eyes pivoting back to Sid. "I blamed you for the butchery that day. I blamed Logan for taking my place. And Cassandra—"

"God, I wish I'd found you first."

"Would you have taken me away?" Sager asked, perversely interested in his father's answer.

"Don't know. Not the way Cassandra did, I suppose. I probably would have gotten to know you. I would have talked to your parents. Between them and me, I guess, we would have figured out what was best for you." He paused to wipe the back of his hand against his eyes. He cleared his throat, then sighed into the silence that fell between them. "I sure as hell never wanted to outlive your mother, son."

"Is-a-bell." Sager said her name, beginning to feel a bond with the woman who had been his blood mother.

"So you know about her?"

"Yes."

"Is-a-bell," Sid said, repeating Sager's pronunciation of her name. "She'd just told me we were expecting you when the Sioux took her. Damned near went insane looking for her, for you." He paused. "Cassandra came along about the time I learned that your mother had died many years earlier. I held on to Cassandra like a light in the dark. With her and Logan, I thought I had a chance for a family again." He looked at Sager. "I needed that. But, God, I'm sorry I did it."

Sager shrugged. "It was good that you brought Logan to us. He needed you."

Sid nodded. "I got to see him grow. I helped make him a man." Sid's gaze moved over Sager's tall frame.

Sager lowered his eyes, waiting for the inevitable criticism as he stood before his father bare-chested, bare-footed, a true savage. He was filthy and ragged and, thanks to the fire, didn't have a shirt or a pair of boots to his name. His hair was long and smelled like burnt tar. He was nothing like Logan. Clean-cut and white, the kind of man a father could be proud of. Sid lifted his arms to Sager's shoulders. Sager couldn't suppress the shiver that rippled through him at the contact. He met his father's eyes, observing him through his wall of indifference.

"Look at you now. Look how strong you are. You're as tall as I once was. Taller, maybe." He ran his hands down Sager's arms and back to his shoulders, learning his son through touch like a blind man, seeing in his muscle, sinew, and bone the infant he'd never held, the boy he'd never known, the man he'd rarely seen. "Isabel must be smiling down at you right now. She had your same beautiful eyes." Sid smiled into Sager's cautious eyes. "I'm glad you came back, son. And I don't care why you did." He pulled Sager into a fierce hug. It took a second for Sager to respond, but then he wrapped his arms about Sid's shoulders, returning the hug just as fiercely.

"What are your plans now?" Sid asked when they parted.

"I don't know. I didn't really expect any of this," he said with a rueful grin. "I never thought Rachel would have me. Perhaps I'll build her a house in the bride lands."

Sid nodded. "That would be nice. You know, of course, that the Circle Bar is yours. You are welcome to live there, with me."

"It's mine? What about Logan? He's been more of a son to you than I ever have."

"Logan inherited land back East from Cassandra. She always wanted him to return to the States. I've provided a financial settlement for him in my will—he isn't without resources. If he chooses to stay out here, he'll have what he needs to start his own spread. But you're my eldest—the Circle Bar belongs to you, as it always has. Logan knows that. So did Cassandra. I think that's why she wanted you dead."

Sager looked at his father—truly studied him for the first time in a long time. Without the filter of hatred, without the bloodlust that usually colored his vision, he realized Sid was just a man. The arrangement with Logan wasn't fair, to Sager's way of thinking, but that was something he would address with his father when things were more settled.

"I know you're tired, but we should meet with Old Jack tonight," Sager said. "Logan killed a man who tried to take off with Rachel while everyone was distracted with the fire. The men who did this aren't finished yet. We can't afford to not be ready for them."

Sid nodded. "You're right. Let's get to it. Son." He clapped Sager on the shoulder as they moved toward the kitchen.

Chapter Twenty-Three

Rachel crossed her arms in front of her as she leaned against the jamb of the open front door. "Is that smile for me?" Sager asked, his deep voice interrupting her thoughts.

Her smile widened as she focused on him again. "Yes," she answered. They looked at each other for a long moment. He was indeed a sight for sore eyes. Though he'd been sleeping in the guest room just down the hall from her, she'd seen little of him these past five days. He'd risen early and retired late, working tirelessly to fortify the Crippled Horse. Julian had also stayed with them since the barbeque, adding the force of his men to those from the Circle Bar and Crippled Horse. With so many men, her father's ranch had become a fortress. Surely this would work out fine, she tried to reassure herself.

Rachel focused on Sager, letting her gaze dip over his body. The clothes he wore were all new, thanks to the supplies sent in from the Circle Bar. Blue cotton shirt, indigo jeans, and black cowboy boots. Everything he wore heightened his predatory looks.

His feet were propped up on the porch banister, his legs crossed at the ankles. His head rested against the back of the chair. The sun spilled over his face and hands, warming his hard body. Sitting there on the porch, his chair tilted on its back legs, he looked supremely relaxed, like a sleeping wolf.

Rachel's gaze strayed toward the arsenal scattered about his feet—a rifle, two shotguns, two pistols, and what looked to her like a week's worth of ammunition were laid strategically before him. He was waiting, and he was ready, and that reality sent a cold wrinkle of fear down her back.

"Come here," he said, reaching a hand out to her. She put her hand in his and let him draw her onto his lap.

"I've missed you," she said. "Is everything done?"

He nodded. "There's just the waiting now."

Her eyes narrowed as she looked out at the open vista spreading before them. The sun's glare was painful. Summer had finally arrived and with a vengeance. Were it not for the constant wind, the dry, hot air would surely roast a person in just a few short minutes. "Do you really think Tom Beall will come back?" she asked, wishing it weren't so.

"He's tried twice to get you." Sager studied her face. "You're his ace in the hole. There's no way in hell that either Sid or Old Jack would hand Beall over to the marshal if he's got you, and he knows it."

"I'm glad Sid and Papa aren't here." Sager had sent their fathers to Defiance to telegraph Cheyenne and await the marshal and his deputies. The marshal couldn't ignore their summons since they were owners of two of the largest ranches in the area.

He grinned at her. "They should be well out of the way when Beall and his men ride in here."

Rachel leaned against him, watching the horizon warily, not sure what to expect. Would Beall's gang ride in like a pack of lunatics, shooting wildly? Or would Beall come in by himself and try to sneak her away? Would they come by day or by night? A knot settled in her stomach, and she was helpless to dislodge it. She closed her eyes, forcing herself to think of other things. No sense borrowing trouble. Beall would come when he would come.

Sager looked at her, quietly studying her. The wind blew her hair across her face, and he smoothed it back behind her ear. She met his gaze and posed a question that had bothered her for a while. "When we're married, will I be Mrs. Sager?"

Sager's lips thinned as his eyes lifted to the hills in front of the house. A long minute passed before he answered her.

"When I first came to the Circle Bar, I considered myself Shoshone. I wanted nothing to do with Sid or his family. I had a finely honed distrust of all white men. The attack on my family only made me hate them all the more. Sid told me over and over that I was his son, that my Christian name was Brent Taggert. Though I refused to accept him or my name, I think, in my gut, that I believed him. There were too many irregularities between me and my family in the village that being Sid's son explained. My eyes were too light. I was too tall. My tan faded in the winter. So I took the name of the only white man I'd trusted—a trader named Albert Sager who had come to my village many times. I did it to hurt Sid. And I did it to keep a link between me and my people. It was my only concession to being in a white man's world. Taking Sager's name was my acceptance and my defiance."

He looked at Rachel. "So I guess you'll be Mrs. Brent Taggert, if that's okay with you."

"It is. It's wonderful." Rachel smiled, silently trying out her new name. "Blue Thunder is your brother, isn't he?" she asked, curious about their relationship.

Sager studied her before answering. "He was ten when I came to live with the Shoshone. He took me under his wing for the next thirteen years. He can be a bit overbearing," he said with a reluctant grin. "He was twenty-four the summer our sister and mother were killed. Our father had been dead a year by then, so it was up to Blue Thunder to hunt down the men who had taken me and avenge our mother's death."

"Does Blue Thunder know it was Cassandra who ordered the attack?"

Sager nodded. "He knows now. Perhaps he knew even then. And I think Sid understands why I couldn't accept him all those years ago." He sighed and looked beyond her as a silent moment passed between them. "When Sid and I spoke the other night, he welcomed me home. *Home*, Rachel. I haven't had a home in thirteen years." He studied her face as his arms tightened around her. "I like this. I like sitting on this porch. I like holding you. I'd like this to be home, Rachel."

"It is your home, Sager."

He smiled ruefully. "Summer's half over. Normally I would be thinking about moving on. By autumn I would be miles away from wherever summer found me. And in winter, I'd be someplace else still. But I'm going to be here in the winter. And next summer, I'll sit out here again. With you." He kissed her cheek. "You gave this to me. It's a debt I'll never be able to repay, but I'll gladly spend the rest of my life trying."

Rachel tightened her arms about his neck and kissed the hard line of his jaw. "You owe me nothing, Sager, and I'll gladly spend the rest of my life proving that to you." He kissed her then, a hard, possessive kiss that sealed their understanding, cemented their future, and freed their love. She forgot they were on the porch, waiting for Beall's men to attack. She only cared that she was in Sager's arms, that his tongue was hot and probing, that she would soon be his wife.

"What names do you think we should consider for our first born?" she asked dreamily as the kiss ended.

Sager gave a dismissive shrug. "Honey, first things first. Let's get rid of these rustlers. Then get married, then settle on names."

"I think we should start with names." She looked at him, waiting for him to understand what she was telling him. He grew very still, studying her. He looked down at her still-flat stomach, spreading his hand across her abdomen.

"Just exactly what are you saying, Rachel?"

Rachel smiled into his frightened eyes. "You're going to be a dad sooner than we thought."

Sager squeezed his eyes shut and slowly exhaled a breath he had not been aware of holding. When he opened his eyes, he looked at Rachel through eyes that were strangely damp. "How do you feel? Are you well? Some women become very ill, especially with their first pregnancy. I don't think you're eating enough, and you look tired to me—"

Rachel laughed and put her hand to Sager's lips, stopping his hurried speech. "I'm fine. I just want this trouble to be over. I don't want to live in fear any longer."

"Your father was right. We should have sent you someplace safe."

"The only place I am truly safe is near you. No one could protect me the way you can." Sager enveloped her in an enormous hug. Seconds later, as gunfire peppered the house, her mind was sluggish to register her new circumstances. Sager, however, had no such handicap. He moved like lightning, rolling the both of them off the chair to get behind the wooden barricades he'd set about the front porch.

Rachel lay on her stomach on the floor of the porch, looking out at the field from the edge of the heavy oak chair they had just been sitting on. Standing on the crest of the hill, backlit by the bright sun, were at least a dozen riders. As she watched, other riders joined them, spreading out to form an ominous line a hundred yards from the house. Cold terror seeped from the pores of her skin. Sager shouldered his rifle and fired off a couple of shots. A scream let Rachel know he hit one of his targets.

Sager took advantage of the pause in gunfire to order her inside the house. "Lock yourself in your room," he added tersely.

Rachel couldn't tear her eyes away from the line of men in front of the house, but knew she couldn't leave him. "I can't go, Sager. They'll kill you." He'd fortified the Crippled Horse defenses, but Beall's men had come in so quickly, with no warning. Perhaps the men weren't in their places.

"Inside. Now. Keep an eye on Mrs. Biddle. Make sure she doesn't do anything foolish—like trying to run out the back door."

Rachel threw him a look of appeal, but he was unyielding as he reloaded his rifle. She scooted backward towards the door, leaving Sager alone to face Beall and his men. More than a dozen against one. They were going to kill him. She looked at Sager. Studying him. Terrified that she would never see him alive again.

Slowly, fiercely, a determination filled her veins; Sager wasn't going to go down alone. She reached up and opened the door and crawled inside, determined to find some weapon with which she could aid him. Her father had taken his rifle. What weapons remained were with Sager out front. But perhaps there was something they overlooked. A pistol maybe. There had to be something she could use to help defend her home. To defend Sager.

"Good Lord, what's happening out there?" Mrs. Biddle gasped as Rachel got to her feet inside the door.

"It's Beall and his men." Rachel wrapped an arm about the housekeeper's waist and led her away from the front door. "We've got to get some weapons." She left the housekeeper at the hallway to hurry on to her father's office. "Did Papa take everything?" she asked over her shoulder.

"I don't know, dear, but I've got some guns in my room. I'll bring them to you."

Old Jack's gun rack was bare. Rachel searched the desk drawers and found not so much as a bullet. She hurried toward the door of the office, intending to get a knife from the kitchen when Mrs. Biddle came into the office with a rifle in each hand. Rachel frowned down at them. They were smaller than the ones her father had housed in his gun rack. "Where did you get those?"

"They were Mr. Biddle's wedding present to me," she said dryly, her expression pained as she looked down at the matching pair of ladies' rifles. "He was a very . . . practical man," she explained. "I should have known then, perhaps. Ah, well. Here they are, anyway. I've kept them oiled and ready for just such an occasion." At Rachel's continued look of disbelief, she added, "I wasn't born in this godforsaken country, and I don't intend to die here, either." She smiled at Rachel. "At least not today. Come along, dear. I'll show you what you need to know. You had better do the shooting. My eyesight isn't what it was when Mr. Biddle gave these to me."

Rachel's hands shook as she repeated the exercises the housekeeper showed her. She practiced sighting a target, loading and unloading until it felt natural to her. She nodded at the housekeeper, who opened the window beneath which they squatted. Sager turned, hearing them behind him. His eyes locked with Rachel's. For a moment she expected him to order her away, but he didn't. His acceptance of her right to defend her home filled her with a warm sense of rightness. She smiled at him. "Just keep your heads down, both of you!" he ordered.

"Hey, breed!" Hank Ketchum's grating voice called across the field. "I brought a fucking army!"

Mrs. Biddle made a quiet "hmph" sound as she sat on a footstool behind Rachel. Rachel bit her lip, too distraught to chance giving in to a fit of giggles lest she sink into hysteria.

"That's good, Hank," they heard Sager call back. "'Cause you're gonna need them."

"Now listen, boy. We just want the girl," Tom Beall

shouted. "No need for you to get hurt in the process. Send her out, and we'll be on our way."

"Can't do it, Beall. Why don't you just go on your way? You can't be paying those boys enough to die today."

"They ain't gonna die, breed. You don't need to worry about Rachel; I give you my word that I'll take care of her."

"Like you took care of Cassandra?"

The wind carried the sound of Beall's grating laughter through the window where Rachel crouched. "Oh no, I was tired of Cassandra. I ain't tired of that little gal in there with you, boy. And you gotta know I need her, now, after all that's gone on. But enough of this palavering. You got to the count of ten. If you don't send her out, we're coming in."

Rachel counted the seconds with each beat of her heart. When the time had passed she peeked over the edge of her windowsill as Beall sent half his men to circle the house. Another tense minute passed while he waited for them to get into position. She ducked down and gave Mrs. Biddle a pained look.

"They're circling the house. What are we going to do if they come in the back way?"

"The doors and windows are locked, dear. If they come in that way, they'll have to break a window. They won't take us unawares," she answered, her voice supremely confident and businesslike. "Remember, though, that Logan and Mr. McCaid are also watching the house. We will be fine. This will all be over before you know it."

They heard Beall shout to his men, "You know what to do—shoot the breed and get the girl." Rachel squeezed her eyes shut and offered up a quick prayer for deliverance, then once again peeked out from the edge of her window. As soon as she did, she realized her mistake, for she'd lost track of Beall's men when she'd spoken to Mrs. Biddle. They'd overturned a wagon, and she suspected a few were hidden behind it. She could see the brim of one man's hat behind the corner of the stables. But where were the others?

"Rachel!" Sager's loud whisper caught her attention. He pointed to a heavy stand of bushes and held up two fingers; a barrel near a fence post—one finger; the wagon—three fingers; then the stables— three fingers. Nine men in all here in the front. "Don't fire until I stop to reload, and then only if you have a clear shot. Understand?"

She nodded, feeling focused again. She practiced sighting through the rifle. She targeted the hat brim of the man at the corner of the stable. Her finger tightened on the trigger, still practicing. Could she do this? Could she take a man's life? Suddenly, Sager's gun fired, and the man she'd sighted crumbled at the edge of the stables. Gunfire erupted then like fireworks, dozens of bullets showering down on the house, thudding, snapping, splintering wood. In short order, Sager took several more down before pausing to reload his rifle.

Aware of the break in gunfire from the porch, Beall's men moved in closer, scurrying like cockroaches for new shelter. Rachel watched in agony as one came closer and closer. She did not want to shoot. She wanted to warn Sager, but feared distracting him from his task. He hadn't finished reloading. He was not ready for the man. She was a coward. Her palms were sweating. The man stepped out into the open, boldly coming after Sager. Rachel's finger pinched the trigger. She missed and fired again. The man flew backward, his rifle flying from his hand.

Sager's head shot up. He exchanged a quick look with her, then turned back to the men. She handed her rifle to Mrs. Biddle and took up the second gun. Shots were exchanged for perhaps another ten minutes before a tense stalemate was achieved. Rachel became aware of gunfire coming from the rear of the house. She exchanged a victorious look with her housekeeper. They weren't alone—Logan and Julian had gotten into position after all. It wasn't just the three of them against all of Beall's men!

Gunfire was heard all round the house now. Rachel's worst fears were realized as she noticed that reinforcements had joined Beall's men out front—with Fletcher leading them! Bodies were scattered on the field in front of the house, and blood leached into the dry dirt. She sent off a couple of shots while Sager reloaded, but didn't manage to hit any of her targets. She'd just switched guns with Mrs. Biddle again when they heard the sound of breaking glass coming from the back of the house. Some of Beall's men must have gotten through Logan's and Julian's positions.

"You stay there, Mrs. Biddle. You'll have a clean shot toward the hallway." Rachel pushed one of the heavy oak armchairs toward the housekeeper for cover from gunfire, then took up a position at the corner of the hallway while Mrs. Biddle reloaded her rifle. Rachel's body screamed as she waited silently for the first man to come out of the hall. She forced all thoughts out of her head. *Just don't panic,* she told herself. *Stay calm. Stay calm.* She listened to the sounds of boots hitting the floor as a man came through the window. Seconds later there was a thunderous crash as the back door was kicked in. Doors were thrown open in the hallway as the men spread out to search the house for them. At last she heard a man approach the living room. Rachel's hands tightened on the cold barrel of her gun. She exchanged a look with Mrs. Biddle, communicating with a nod of her head that the housekeeper was to shoot the first man through.

Mrs. Biddle's gun exploded. A man crumpled to the floor at the edge of the hallway, mortally wounded. The next man was preoccupied climbing over the fallen man and watching for more gunfire; Rachel was able to shoot him, dropping him on top of the other man. And then Rachel lost control of the situation. The next two men through grabbed her and wrestled her gun away. She fought them as best she could, but against their combined strength, her struggles amounted to little. Rachel knew Mrs. Biddle couldn't get a clean shot at them, not with her in the way. The men who held her were dragging her toward the back of the house. She tripped them, and kicked and thrashed so that they finally resorted to one holding her arms and the other holding her feet. She was nearing the back door when she heard Sager start toward her at the front end of the hallway.

Sager plowed through Beall's men who had come into the house, fighting them one at a time in the narrow hallway. And when three came at him at once, he responded like a man driven by demons. He shouted a Shoshone battle cry that made Rachel's back stiffen in fear. Julian had come in the back door by then, and between him and Sager, they took on the remaining men, getting to Rachel before the others could get her out of the house.

"Run, Rach. Run!" Sager shouted at her as he and Julian exchanged punches with Beall's men.

"Sager—" She hesitated, wanting to aid him.

"Now! Dammit!" he answered, not looking at her as he took a hit in his stomach that doubled him over. One of the men started to come after her, and Rachel lifted her skirts and ran for all she was worth through the back door. She managed to get down the stairs before a man grabbed her from behind.

"Right into my arms, darlin'. I like that!" Hank's gravely voice spoke directly into her ear.

Sager came through the back door. He stared down at them. Blood ran from a corner of his mouth. His sides were heaving from his exertions. His shirt hung askew on his chest. "Let her go, Hank. You won't get away. Beall's dead. You got nowhere left to run."

"As long as I got her, I'm a free man, breed." He lifted his pistol, pointed it at Sager's broad chest, and pulled the trigger.

A queer whistling sound came to Rachel's ears even before she heard the report of Hank's gun. An arrow flew past her, embedding itself in Hank's wrist, pinning him to the side of the house like an ugly bug as his bullet flew wide of Sager and embedded itself in the wall of the house.

Rachel's stunned senses seemed to take note of several things at once. In the far distance, she saw her father and Sid riding toward them. Closer in, another half dozen of Beall's men were engaged with Logan and some of the Crippled Horse cowboys. Blue Thunder, whose arrow had saved Sager, and several other Indians were galloping closer every second. She heard Sager telling her to go with Blue Thunder and his braves.

She did as he bid, running for Sager's brother. Barely slowing his pace, Blue Thunder leaned over and gripped her arm as he swung her up behind him. He turned his mount at the last second before they would have collided with the house. Rachel clung to him, her face buried in his back. She felt him ready another arrow and watched as it took down one more of Beall's men. Instead of riding away, as she expected, Blue Thunder circled back toward the house as his braves streamed in to join him. They dispatched the remaining few men who had ridden in with Beall just as Old Jack, Sid, and Logan reached the house.

Blue Thunder pranced his horse in tight circles as he shouted at Sager. Rachel heard the triumph in his voice. Sager answered him, his grin wide and white in his battered face. Then, without warning, Blue Thunder took off, pushing his mount to a gallop that left Rachel breathless.

Sager watched them ride away, knowing that battle-blood was still hot in his brother's veins. Then Old Jack and Logan were running up the steps. They were angry and laughing and pounded him on the back. Sager looked for his father, and saw him a few feet away, sighting down his rifle toward Blue Thunder.

Time grew warped for Sager. It seemed a million miles separated him from Sid. He knew with a cold certainty that Sid's bullet would hit Rachel in the back, killing her and their baby. Sager had faced the whole group of Beall's men with less fear than he felt now as he leapt from the stairs and rushed his father. He grabbed the rifle, wrapping his hand around his father's as he shoved the gun up into the air. It discharged harmlessly above their heads. Sager took hold of his father's shoulder with his free hand, and stared into the unfocused terror in Sid's eyes.

"It's happening again. All over again, but to you this time," Sid said, his words half mumbled as they spilled from him. "They've taken her. It'll break you, Sager. To never see your son. To know what they're doing to your wife. Why did you stop me?" Tears streamed down Sid's weathered face. "It would have been better to kill her now, mercifully. Quickly. They took you away. She couldn't live without you. Without me. She died slowly, her heart broken."

Sager stared at his father, feeling the full impact of his life, the truth of his loss, the pain Sager himself had heaped on his father's shoulders. He eased the rifle out of Sid's grip and tossed it to Logan. He didn't know what to do, what to say to reach his father. Speaking to Sid was still foreign to Sager, and touching him was intensely alien, but he had to reach him. It became imperative to heal his father, to mend the past. To start over. He cupped his hand against the back of Sid's head, bowing his forehead to his father's.

"He won't harm her," he assured Sid. "He's my brother. I grew up with him." Sager felt a warm, salty liquid sting the cuts on his face and realized that he, too, wept. "He helped us today. You saw him and the others fight Beall's men. Rachel is safe with him." Sager swallowed hard. His father's shoulders were shaking. "I'm sorry for what happened to my mother. For what happened to you and to me. I'm sorry for what I did to you, Dad."

Sid drew a long breath, a cleansing, healing breath that seemed to scrape out all the old scars and wounds and corrosive thinking, leaving him lighter as he exhaled. He looked up. He straightened his shoulders. He wiped his face. A long moment passed as he looked at Sager.

"It's okay, son." He touched Sager's face, his hands stiff and old. "Jesus," he sighed, "I nearly killed Rachel."

Sager grinned. "'Nearly' is the important word there. Why don't you come with me? Let's go get her."

Sid smiled back at him. "Let's do it."

Sager started handing out orders. "McCaid, throw these bodies in a wagon and take them to Defiance. You'd best line them up and get a photograph taken, if you can. They won't be much to look at by the time the marshal gets there. There's probably a bounty on a few of them. If any of them are alive—I think Hank is—throw them in the jail and post a few men to stand guard. I wouldn't trust Kemp to keep them locked up.

"Logan, you'd best head back to the Circle Bar and make sure no mischief occurred there."

Logan nodded and shared a look with Sager, seeing him stand arm in arm with Sid. The war was over. Neither man spoke, but Sager had a strange feeling that a long time would pass before he would see his brother again.

It was dusk before Sager found Blue Thunder's campsite. He and his men were seated in a half circle around a large fire. Rachel sat next to Blue Thunder, her hands folded primly in her lap. Dismounting, Sager ground-tethered his and Sid's horses, then called a greeting to his brother as they approached the campfire. Blue Thunder rose, his expression somber in the fading evening light. His braves sat tensely, watching Sid. Sager knew some of them from his childhood and others from his adult interactions with the tribe, and a few he didn't recognize. Sid and Blue Thunder exchanged a charged look. Blue Thunder had killed the men who had taken Sager away that day long ago, all except Sid. Sager wondered again why Blue Thunder had let Sid live, whether he had known, even then, that it was Cassandra who sent those men.

As Sager introduced the two men, Sid sent Rachel a look, assuring himself of her well-being. Blue Thunder moved to block his view. "My sister is well," he announced curtly. "Do not concern yourself with her." He turned to Sager. "Why have you come?"

Sager had to work to keep the smile from his face. Marriage was a serious affair and needed an appropriate level of dignity, at least for the bride price negotiations. That Blue Thunder had taken this role upon himself was a measure of how much he respected Rachel. Sager felt a strange swelling in his rib cage.

"I have come to take my bride," Sager announced.

Blue Thunder gestured to the fire. "Let us sit and discuss this." When Sager and Sid had taken seats, Blue Thunder looked from Sager to his father. "There can be no talk of marriage between my sister and my enemies."

This, Sager had not expected. He gave Blue Thunder a warning look, but his brother ignored him as he focused entirely on Sid. A moment passed in charged silence. Sager wished he'd been able to prepare Sid for this meeting. At last, Sid broke the silence.

"My wife did your family grave harm. I deeply regret her actions. I would be honored if you would help me find a way to make amends, perhaps with a number of cows, though such would be a poor exchange—some cattle for human lives." Sager hadn't expected this discussion, but he was proud of his father's humility and generosity.

Blue Thunder was silent for an exceptionally long time. He stared over the fire into the horizon. Even Sager had a hard time guessing his thoughts. "I would accept fifty cows," Blue Thunder announced as he looked at Sid.

Sid met his look. "Thirty," he countered.

"Fifty. For each, my mother and my sister," Blue Thunder insisted. "It is two lives your wife took, in addition to stealing my brother from me. He could have joined many hunts and provided well for our people."

Sid and Blue Thunder stared at each other, until Sid accepted the offer. "One hundred head of cattle, then."

"Good. It is done. My mother and sister would be pleased. Now we can discuss the bride price." Blue Thunder looked at Sager.

"Why would I pay you a bride price for a woman who is already my own?" Sager asked.

"You have not yet taken her to wife, have you?" Blue Thunder responded.

"No."

"And I do not see a representative of her family here to negotiate for her, so the task falls to me, her brother."

Sager gave Blue Thunder a dark look. "You are not her brother."

"You are my brother, and as your wife, she becomes my sister. You cannot have her if you cannot respect her," Blue Thunder admonished.

Sager exchanged a look with his father. He had no possessions of his own, and it did not feel right to trade what belonged to his father. But Sid gave him an almost imperceptible nod. "I offer thirty-five additional cattle," Sager announced.

Blue Thunder looked outraged. He stood abruptly. "We have finished our discussion. You may leave. She stays with me."

Sager's eyes narrowed. "I will not leave without Rachel."

"Then make an offer that does not insult me. Do you think that I value my sister less than you value your sister or mother?"

Sager slowly came to his feet. He stared at his brother, wondering at his ability to talk inside out. He could twist an argument until his opponent fought against himself. Sager folded his arms before him. "Fifty head of cattle."

"My sister is a live woman, flesh and blood." He pounded his chest angrily. "She will give you many sons. You think to value her as a dead woman? Sixty cows and two bulls," Blue Thunder countered.

Sager exchanged a look with his father, who had a strange twinkle in his eyes. Sager nodded and extended his arm to his brother. "It is done." They clasped arms.

Sid rose as well. He smiled into Blue Thunder's eyes as they took each other's arms. "I thank you for taking care of my son so long ago. You've done me a great kindness. If you are ever in need, I hope you will let me help you."

Blue Thunder nodded. He turned to Rachel and held out his hand. "It is safe for you to go with my brother. He has shown deep affection for you. He will make a good husband."

Rachel took his hand and came to her feet. She smiled at him, thinking how frightened she'd been of him when they first met that cold spring evening. She squeezed his hand and thanked him, then turned to Sager. He smiled at her, but seemed reserved. She wanted to run into his arms, but he turned away. He mounted his horse, then emptied the stirrup and gave her an arm to swing up behind him. She wrapped her arms about his waist, smiled at Sid, then turned and waved to Blue Thunder, her new brother, as Sager set his horse in motion.

Epilogue

A knock sounded on Rachel's door. It was time. She held a hand against the excitement twisting in her stomach. She felt as tense now as she did a month ago, after Beall attacked the Crippled Horse, when she had waited with Blue Thunder for Sager to come.

"Come in," she bade when the knock sounded again.

Old Jack stepped inside and closed the door. He stood there a moment, a shadowy smile on his face. His gaze took in the slightly yellowed white silk gown she wore. The lace collar was high and modest. Her sleeves were three-quarter length, and more lace spilled from the cuffs. He remembered her mama in that dress. She'd worn little white flowers in her hair, too. "You look beautiful, daughter. You make an old man proud today, I reckon."

Rachel smiled and closed the distance between them. "Thank you, Papa." She leaned forward and kissed his cheek. "I'm ready."

"Rachel," he said, gripping her arms as he studied

her face, "the ring Sager's going to give you was your mother's. She would want you to have it."

Rachel bit her lip. "Papa, don't you dare make me cry before we get out there!"

Old Jack turned and opened the door for her. "You cry? Hell's bells, daughter. Weren't you the one who fought off Beall and his men just as cool as you please? And what about the rabid wolf that cornered you?"

"Who told you about the wolf?"

"That Blue Thunder character." Old Jack looked out the window and grumbled, "Half the damned world is here again, eating my food and drinking my whiskey. And what in tarnation was all that racket in the house earlier? Sounded like an Injun war party was movin' in for good."

"That was the cleansing ceremony, Papa. Blue Thunder felt it was bad for Sager and me to start our new life in a place where there was so much death. He wanted us to burn the house and move, but we wouldn't. So he performed a ritual to cleanse the house of bad spirits."

"Much more of that racket, and I would have moved on, too," he muttered as he led her through the house and out to the front yard.

Rachel heard the silence thicken as those gathered noticed her arrival. She glanced over the crowd, grinning helplessly. Julian stood as Sager's best man, and Leah was Rachel's maid of honor. She had hoped to also see Logan and Audrey, but Logan left a few days after the shoot-out, and Audrey was home nursing her foster children through an outbreak of chicken pox.

Rachel searched for Sager and found him standing

before the preacher. He wore a gray wool suit with a starched white shirt. The high collar was a stark contrast against his swarthy skin. The breeze tousled his loose, inky black hair. Blue eyes locked with amber, and Rachel's world narrowed to the space surrounding Sager as they exchanged vows and became husband and wife. A cheer went up among those gathered. Sager grinned down at her as he sealed their vows with a kiss. "I love you," he swore against her lips.

"I love you, too."

The crowd closed in about them and the next hours passed in a blur for Rachel. The sun had begun its descent when she headed toward the kitchen to fix another pot of coffee.

Sid came over to Sager, a smile on his face. He put a hand on Sager's shoulder. "You've made me a happy man, son."

Sager looked at his father's outstretched hand before he took it in a firm grip. "Those are words I never intended to hear from you." He grinned ruefully. "I'm sorry for chasing Logan away."

"You didn't. He's gone off to grow up. We all do that. He'll get his legs under him, and when he does, his feet know the way home." Sid smiled. "Yours did."

Mrs. Biddle and Mrs. Morgan were sitting on the porch, taking a much needed break from the day's work. Leah was leaning on the banister, her enormous pet wolf lying at her feet, panting in the late summer heat. Rachel smiled at them tiredly as Mrs. Biddle reached out and squeezed her hand.

"You were beautiful today, dear. Just beautiful."

"Thank you, Mrs. Biddle." Leaning against the banister, she looked at the guests and tables scattered over the newly mowed grass. "It was a fun day, wasn't it?"

"The best I can remember in a very long time. And now you and Sager can start your new life together," Mrs. Biddle sighed.

Rachel put her hand on her stomach and gave Mrs. Biddle a meaningful look. "We've already started on that."

Mrs. Morgan gasped. Mrs. Biddle squealed with delight. And Leah came forward to hug Rachel. "I can't wait to tell Audrey! When will the baby come?"

"Late spring, I suspect," Rachel answered, laughing as the two older women pulled her into fierce hugs as well.

"Sager a father . . . my, my," Mrs. Biddle commented with a sniffle. "The baby brings things full circle for that boy. You've helped a lot of folks do some healing, child. I'm so glad you came out to us."

Rachel straightened and stretched. Remembering her earlier intention of making more coffee, she excused herself and went into the kitchen. Hearing the door open and close behind her, Rachel turned. Sager was striding over to her, grinning, his eyes on fire. He'd discarded his suit coat and starched collar. His white cotton shirt lay open against his chest. He stopped just before her and set his hands on her waist, drawing her against his heated body.

"I've had to share you all day, Rachel Taggert. I can't stand it much longer. I want my wife all to myself. Now." He bent forward and kissed her with a passion that confirmed his words.

Rachel circled her arms about his neck and sighed against his mouth. "I don't think we can just sneak away."

Sager began backing her toward the main portion of the house. "I think we can. . . ."

"But what will our guests say when they don't see us?"

Sager's white teeth flashed in a lusty grin. "I know exactly what they'll say."

About the Author

ELAINE LEVINE lives with her husband in a small town on the Plains just east of the Rocky Mountains in Colorado. By day, she writes custom business software applications. And by night, she crafts emotional stories of love and redemption.

Elaine enjoys hearing from her readers. You can learn more about her upcoming stories at www.elainelevine.com.